THIS PROUD HEART

THIS
PROUD
HEART

by Pearl S. Buck

New York

P. F. COLLIER & SON
CORPORATION

To
R. J. W.

THIS PROUD HEART

I

"SUSAN GAYLORD is going to be married." She heard the words as clearly as though a voice had spoken them, as though everything was speaking them, the trees about, the bird in the elm tree not far from where she and Mark were standing together in Tramp's Woods. A small early spring cricket chirped it shrilly. And Mark's voice, plain and deep, was asking her humbly, "Susan, will you—could you marry me?"

She had known very well that this was the day and hour Mark had planned. There were no surprises in this man whom she had known from the time he came, a boy, trudging to school in the fifth grade, large and shy, from a nearby farm. They had accompanied each other through school, she always gay and he always large and shy on the edge of the crowd watching her. She had known his eyes were upon her from the first day.

"I want to be married," she said, throwing her head back, "and I want to marry you." He trembled. She could feel his big hands on her shoulders trembling. It was over. She was going to be married. She had decided out of all she wanted to do that most of all she wanted to marry—that first.

Now he was drawing her to him. She felt the unfamiliar pressure of his hard square body against her. She was not small, nor even as slight as most girls were. But against him she felt herself diminished and she enjoyed this strangeness, without being shaken by it, though now he was kissing her passionately and deeply.

"I've wanted to do this ever since that first day in fifth grade," he said.

"You wouldn't even choose me in a kissing game!" she cried, laughing.

"I hate kissing games," he said shortly. "I want kissing to be the real thing." He held her a moment, still and close.

"I know," she whispered.

They stood in long silence. She leaned against him, her restlessness gone. It had been difficult to know what she wanted to do. Long ago old Professor Kincaid had said to her in English class, "Susan, you can write if you want to." But then her father had taken her to New York to see a play and she had wanted to act. For years she felt herself acting upon a stage, making out of herself a character she was not. She could be anyone she chose. But then there were her hands. She wanted to make with her hands. She liked to feel materials in her hands with which to work—materials more tangible than music, though her father had taught her music. She was restless, not knowing quite what her hands must do because she liked everything. She wanted everything. That was when she decided to marry and have a great many children.

She paused a moment in her thoughts, remembering how her hands had felt last week when she was making that head of her sister Mary. They had felt swift and skilful, and in her joy she had cried to Mary, "I've got you, Mary! Look!"

Mary came and looked and Susan waited. And while she waited for Mary to speak, to say, surprised, "It's exactly like me, Susan! It's wonderful!" Mary put out her hands and crushed the wet clay into pulp.

"You've made me hideous!" she said passionately. "It's hateful of you!" And she broke into crying and ran out.

Susan, too shocked to speak, had picked up the clay and kneaded it back again into nothing. But all the time she knew by the feel in her hands that what she had made was Mary, whether Mary liked it or not. The palms of her hands burned, remembering, and her fingers opened and closed.

"Mark!" she said. She drew back to look at him. "When we're married shall you mind if I take up sculpture seriously? Of course I wouldn't let it interfere."

"I want you always to do what you want," he said. His clear mild blue eyes grew shy. "I'm not good enough for you, Sue," he said. "I know that. My folks aren't—so much. And I'm not. And you are the smartest girl in the town."

"Oh, nonsense!" she said blithely. "Who am I but a poor professor's daughter?" She wanted suddenly to begin everything at once. She kissed him again, quickly, sharply, and she laughed and seized his hand.

"Let's run!" she cried, and they ran homeward through the wood.

"I'm going to be married!" she thought, to the tune of the ecstasy of her flying feet, "I'm going to be married!"

"I wish, Susan," Mrs. Gaylord said, "that you weren't marrying so young. You're tied down once you marry."

"I want to marry," Susan said.

Her mother did not answer. They were working alone in the sewing room, cutting and basting her wedding gown. They had been alone ever since the breakfast dishes were washed, and all the time she knew that her mother had something to say to her. It would be something indirect and sidewise in meaning, because her mother was shy of talk about marriage. Once, years ago, when Mark had first come to see her, her mother had tried to say something to her. She had come upstairs at midnight, flushed with an exultation she did not understand, and her mother was waiting in her room for her, wrapped in her brown wool dressing gown, her hair in little braids to make tomorrow's waves.

3

"I feel I should say something to you, Susan," she said, her eyes miserable.

"What is it, Mother?" she asked, gazing at her mother straightly.

"At your age, I mean," her mother said. She could feel her mother's shyness, and she grew hot, and her heart beat hard once or twice.

"You mean about Mark?" she inquired stiffly.

"I mean about any young man," her mother said.

"You needn't mind, Mother," she said quickly. "Mark and I are all right. Besides, I can take care of myself."

"Well," her mother sighed, "as long as you know what I mean—"

She had kissed Susan confusedly, a blush spotting her cheeks. When she went, the belt to her dressing gown trailed so that it caught in the door as it shut.

"Oh, dear!" she called from outside.

"Here—I'll do it," Susan answered, and set her free.

Now, this morning, Susan smiled in half mischief. She had laughed a little to Mark last night. "Mother will feel she has to say something to me when I tell her we are truly engaged," she had told him.

"About me?" he had inquired, soberly. "I can see your dad shooting up his eyebrows and asking me, 'Why should you marry my daughter, young man?' I wouldn't know what to say. I flunked his poetry course, you know, Sue!"

"Mother wouldn't care if you did," she answered, laughing at him. "No, she'll just want to talk to me about life."

"Facts, and all that?" he had inquired solemnly again, and she had nodded, and then they had laughed together. . . .

"Shan't you have a few small tucks at the back of the neck?" her mother asked.

"I've basted them in already," Susan replied.

4

She whirred the sewing machine down the long seams of the train. Then she tried on the skirt.

"You have a real notion of style," her mother said reluctantly. "You did it so fast it ought not to be right, but it is. I don't see how you do it."

"I feel it, right or wrong, in my fingers," she said.

Yes, she knew that inexplicable feeling of passionate trueness to a line already conceived in her brain. She had it about many things, most of all when she modeled. But it could be there in sewing a seam, in stirring a cake, in arranging flowers in a bowl. There was always the knowledge of how everything should look and be, pictured in her brain, and her fingers were swift and nimble slaves, obedient to the vision. She smiled and added, "I ought to be able to get my own wedding gown right."

She could have bought the gown. Her father said, "Get what you want, Susan," and he gave her a hundred dollars. "It's the price of at least twenty poems. God, how cheap poetry sells! I'm glad your young man deals in real estate instead of verse!" Her father taught literature in the small Eastern college on whose campus they lived, though poetry, he said, was his real work, only he could not convince anybody that it was. But anything he earned from poetry was not to be spent on what he called bread and butter.

She had taken the hundred dollars gratefully and looked carefully at the wedding gowns in all the stores in town. The more she looked the more clearly she saw her own, and that it was none of these. She must make it. She bought, therefore, yards of heavy satin, just off white, but not on the dead side off. This satin, white though it was, was warm white. She paid ten dollars for a very little fine lace, and ten more for a mist of fine tulle.

"Don't you want a pattern?" the clerk had asked.

"No, thank you," she said.

5

Shaping the stuff to her own body, she forgot that it was her wedding gown in some deeper fulfilment. She even forgot Mark. She was making something. Whenever she made things she was swept along upon the making. A harmony filled her being. She smoothed the satin against her strong young flank.

"I must say it hangs beautifully," her mother said and sighed.

"Tired?" Susan asked quickly, hearing the sigh.

"No," her mother said, and shut her lips. It was growing hot under the low eaves of the sewing room, and her mother pushed up her glasses and wiped her round wrinkled face with her white apron.

Then in the silence of the room, across the harmony within her, Susan became conscious of discord. It was there like the buzzing of a wasp against a windowpane. She lifted her head. Her sister Mary was playing Mendelssohn's *Consolation* slowly and carefully, flatting each time the essential sharp in the melody. She hesitated a moment, listened, and the flat struck her ear with true pain. She put down the satin and went quickly to the door.

"What—" her mother began, but Susan did not stop. She must, she must reach Mary before she came again to that sharp. She was full of a dread that was physical. She opened the parlor door quickly.

"Mary," she said gently. She was always gentle with Mary, five years younger than she. At the piano Mary turned her dark little face toward her sister, inquiring. Her thin small lean hands were still clawed above the keys.

"Darling, you— Shall I just show you?" Gently she pushed Mary along the piano bench and began to play, fully and softly, the melody. "There—and there—do you hear? It's saying, 'Don't be sad, not any more—remember, oh, remember, all the joy you've had!'—so it's major, not minor. There!" She played it with relief, glad to assuage the pain of the false note.

6

She repeated it, to comfort herself, swelling the melody to its fullness, forgetting Mary, pressing relief into herself.

"I can't ever play it like that." Mary's voice sounded small and discouraged in her ear.

"Of course you can," she replied gaily. She got up from the piano bench. "Would you like to try it for me? I'll show you—"

But instantly she felt Mary's mood. After all, Mary's fifteen to her twenty— "No, of course you'd rather work it out yourself. You can, you know. You're doing beautifully with your music." She was eager to make Mary happy again. She wanted everybody about her happy.

"I don't think I'll practice any more now," Mary said. She closed the book. Her small red mouth was tight.

"All right, darling," Susan answered and smiled. "I'll fly back to my sewing. Would you like to come and see my dress?"

"After a while," said Mary. She did not look at Susan, nor smile. She pushed back her straight black hair with both hands and walked slowly away.

Susan picked up the satin pile.

"What was the matter?" her mother asked.

"Mary was striking a note flat," she said.

Her mother did not answer. Under the low roof the heat seemed suddenly to surge intensely upward.

"I know you don't mean it," her mother said, after a moment, "but Mary's very sensitive just now—it's her age. If I were you I believe I wouldn't correct her for anything."

"Oh no—I didn't correct her," Susan answered quickly. "I'd hate to do that. It's just that a note struck falsely is so hard to bear. It makes me shiver—it makes my mouth dry, and my palms wet. It's silly but I can't help it."

"It's better to go where you can't hear it," her mother said, and after a moment she added, "You're a little apt to be bossy, Susan. You want to take care."

She did not answer, feeling her mother's rebuke. She often felt this cloud rising between her and others, a small cloud, which she would not acknowledge. She had learned that if she did not answer, or try to explain herself at all, if she allowed the surface of events to move on again, the cloud would disappear. And she must have happiness. She could not breathe in cloud.

"Shall I go and make the gravy?" she said.

"Well, if you will," her mother replied, and added, "I don't know but what you make that stew gravy better than I do now, anyway."

She bent to kiss her mother. "What nonsense!" she said gaily. But her mother did not smile back. She wished often her mother could smile. Why not, when everything was good? But there was so easily that cloud between her mother and herself. When she and Mark were married, she thought in the kitchen, tying an apron about her waist, there would be no clouds. She loved this home, but the home she would make for Mark, that would be her own, a thing she had made.

"I want so to be married," she repeated to herself, passionately.

She lay in Mark's arms, in the moonlight, under the shadowy oak tree by the porch. They had spread down a rug and watched the moon come up at the end of the road. The house was full of light. Her mother was in the kitchen, her father in the living room correcting papers. They could hear him groaning over and over, "Oh, God—oh, good God!" She knew that he would lean back and close his eyes, motionless for a few seconds before he could go on, tortured by love of a perfection he never found. Now Mary was in the parlor practicing again. She sat up and listened for a quivering instant.

"Ah, thank God!" she cried and laughed.

"Amen, but why?" Mark asked.

"Mary played it right that time," she said. He wouldn't understand what she meant, but never mind. Mary was playing with stammering fingers, carefully right, and Susan lay back, full of a delicious ease which had nothing to do with Mark. Oh, rightness was so comforting and so comfortable! To see a thing in its proportion, whatever it was, to draw its outlines true and sure and simple—that was bottomless content, which lightened all the world. Mark did not answer. He was looking at her and now she could see he did not know what she meant. She could not tell him, because it had nothing to do with him, because it was an instinct she could not put into words at all, and so she was compelled to speak quickly of something else.

"I have my wedding gown half done!" she whispered.

"Sweetheart!" he whispered back. "There's nobody like you! I don't know another girl in this town who'd do it!"

"It's such fun to make things," she said.

"But you do everything so well," he said, half troubled. "You play and sing, you paint and cook and model." He waited, and then he said, humbly, "I'm not good enough for you."

She hated his humility. It made him faintly repulsive to her. She did not want to marry a man who felt himself small beside her. She must speak of something else again to drive it away from her. She said, "I want to do your head, Mark. You've a beautiful head. Let me see it!"

She sat up and turned his head against the moon. She passed her hands delicately, feelingly, over its outlines. She could see just how it must be begun, a firm strong pressure upon the clay to make this profound and plastic curve at the base of the brain, strong thumbs inward to make the wide hollows of the eye sockets. A familiar deep ache rose in her. Moonlight and oak tree slipped from her. Even he became dim. There was

9

only this grave rugged head in her hands. She thought with longing of the mass of wet clay under a damp cloth in the little alcove off her room. She stirred, then quieted herself again. How ridiculous to want to leave her lover on a moonlight night to make his head in clay! She drew his head forward against her breast. This was better, infinitely better, this warm real head against her breast. She must be sure that she did not miss the warm reality of anything, letting that escape her while she made its image.

One by one the lights went out in the house. The piano stopped and the kitchen grew dark. For a moment her father and mother came out on the porch.

"Ha, you two dew-drenched mortals!" her father called into the darkness of the shadow where they sat. In the moonlight his silvery hair shone softly and his beautiful face was clear. The discontent of his mouth and eyes was lost for the moonlit moment.

"Good night, good night!" she called softly.

"Good night, sir!" Mark's voice echoed hers.

"I'm being put to bed," her father complained. "It's the way of the young generation!"

They laughed, and her father lingered a moment.

"At that, I guess there's nothing else to do," he murmured, and yawned.

"You could find yourself another oak tree," Susan called.

"Susan, it's not too damp, is it?" her mother cried. "You can sit in the living room!"

"Oh, pshaw, come to bed, Jenny!" her father said and pulled her away.

So the house grew still and dark. She lay with her head on Mark's shoulder, dreaming.

"What are you thinking about?" he asked at last.

"Everything," she said. "No, not thinking—feeling and seeing."

10

"What do you see?"

She caught her brain still for a moment and looked at it to tell him what she saw. There were a hundred pictures—the little house they would live in, blue curtains, a table set with a perfect meal she had made, healthy little children with her eyes and Mark's mouth, Mark's head in clay, finished and exactly as she wanted it, herself giving a party, her friends gay with ease in her home, and beyond that, and beyond that, like bright piling clouds lit with sunshine, the years of the future.

She said, "I want to be the best wife in the world, the best mother. I want to make a lot of lovely things in stone and bronze, perpetual things. I want to see the world and people—there isn't anything I don't want to do."

He was silent a moment. "If it weren't you," he said, "I'd think you were crazy. But you're not like anybody else." He added after a moment: "You'll always do what you want. I wish I were half as sure I could."

She felt the slight shadow of a cloud over the moon. "What I want is you," she whispered quickly. In the darkness she moved her hand to his head and moved it slowly over his hair, his ears, his throat and chin, and forgot. . . . Tomorrow morning she'd get up early and begin Mark's head. . . .

"Darling!" he whispered, and turned his lips to meet her hand.

"Darling!" she answered, and touched his lips with fingers as sentient as the fingers of the blind. There, let her remember the curves of the lips for tomorrow morning. Thinking of it, she sat up restlessly.

"What's the matter?" Mark asked, surprised. Without knowing it she had been scrambling to her feet. She checked herself, shocked.

"I don't know—nothing!" she faltered, and sank back against him.

"You're a funny girl!" he said. "Just as I was making love to you, you start to go off somewhere!"

She remembered now that he had been talking to her. She was ashamed and a little frightened.

"Oh, I love you, I love you!" she whispered, forcing herself by her own voice.

But he was chilled. His arms about her were doubtful. "Sometimes you seem to be someone I don't know," he said.

"Oh no, Mark!" she protested. What was this cloud in the glorious night? "Love me forever!" she besought him, and pressed his head down until his lips were on hers.

"Of course I will," he promised stoutly.

"Love me, love me!" she insisted. "I belong to you—only to you!" She pressed herself upon him. She would be his above all else. No other need in her was so deep as this. "Let's be married soon!" she whispered. "Next month, instead of June!"

He seized her and held her, confused by her changefulness, stirred by wish.

"Why not?" he said. "I'll ask for a raise tomorrow!"

They clung together, alone in the night, the earth warm beneath them, the oak tree dark above them. It was he who sprang to his feet first.

"I'd better go," he muttered. "It's late."

"Yes," she said unsteadily. She lay a moment, looking at him.

"Susan, get up!" he whispered, and she rose and put back her hair. She had wanted to know, to be sure, she could forget everything but Mark. And now she was sure.

They walked to the gate. The moon was high and the light was so bright they kissed each other quickly, lest they be seen from other houses along the street, from windows and from late rockers on front porches. He leaped over the gate and smiled at her. "Tomorrow!" he said. "Tomorrow!" she answered. She stood in a sort of triumph, watching him go, watching his figure grow smaller. She wanted him more than anything.

. . . And then, as she watched, she felt a will tugging at her. She waited a moment more until at the bend of the road he turned and waved and was gone. Like a dart flung out she flew into the house and up the stairs to her own room. It was not so late, scarcely midnight. She shut the door softly and went at once to the mass of soft clay in the alcove and turned on a drop light and slipped into her work smock. She was trembling with happiness. Now, now, she could make it. She lifted a ball of the clay, and then a little more. That would be enough. She began to shape it exactly as she had seen it in her mind, roughly at first, in broad generous lines. She worked for hours, singing under her breath once or twice, "Oh, that will be—glory for me! Glory for me, glory for me!" But she did not know what she was singing. She was perfectly happy alone in this house, alone in the world. She was getting it right. It looked like him already. She set it firmly on the wooden block she used for a base, and stood back.

Now, so outlined, she could let it wait until morning. No, wait—she would do the lips finely now, while her fingers remembered them so vividly. She touched and shaped, absorbed in his lips. Now—now—this was how they were. Oh, the lovely content of making something right! She stepped back and held the light low. It was Mark's mouth—she had made his mouth! She sighed as one sighs after fulfilment. Mark had broken their moment together, but she had come straight into this deeper and lonely fulfilment. She could sleep now. She was released. She stumbled into the bathroom and washed, half asleep. In ten minutes she was sleeping, dreamlessly, in utter rest.

"But I don't see why you're hurrying the wedding so!" her mother was saying at the breakfast table, bewildered.

Susan was used to seeing that cloud of bewilderment on her mother's faded pretty face, but until she saw it she always forgot it in some ardor of her own. She had come dancing into the dining room to sing like a song, "Mark and I are going to be married next month!" And instantly the cloud was on her mother's face.

"Married life lasts long enough anyway," her mother said.

"Hear, hear!" her father murmured, digging at his grapefruit.

"Don't you agree with me, Father?" her mother went on.

"I do indeed, but this time it's none of my business," he replied.

"You're a young girl such a little, little while," her mother complained, "and then your freedom's gone!"

"Mark and I think we'll be more free after we're married than before," she said. "I'll get the eggs."

"Well, you'll do what you want," her mother sighed, "though, dear me, how we can finish everything!"

"I can do it," Susan said.

Mary, her large black eyes solemn, looked from one face to the other in her accustomed stillness. Alone with her mother she chattered freely of small personal things, but not before her father and Susan. She was to be Susan's only bridesmaid, and to Susan she seemed both reluctant and pleased. Catching the look in her eyes, Susan paused at the kitchen door. "Your dress next, Mabs!" she said gaily. "Oh, I can just see it, a fluff of peach ruffles under a big hat!" Mary smiled painfully, as though she could not at all see her own small dark face above peach-colored ruffles under a big hat. Left to herself she chose dolorously the straightest and stiffest of garments, feeling desperation at her own ugliness. Peach-colored ruffles, she had said, would make her look like a prune. "Silly!" Susan had cried, laughing. "With your eyes!" Mary said nothing now, but sniffled a little.

14

"Where's your handkerchief?" her father shot at her over his paper.

She jumped. He could be hearing nothing at all, and then suddenly leap out at you. Besides, she had no handkerchief. Susan, bringing in the eggs, tucked a fresh little handkerchief in her neck as she passed, and smiled.

"Use your handkerchief, dear," her mother said absently. She was looking out of the window. "There's Mark!" she said suddenly. "I wonder if something's wrong so early?"

But Susan had already seen him. She was at the front door.

"I've started your head!" she cried, breathlessly. "Want to see it?"

"I have to hurry," he answered. "Here—kiss me. Sue, I got thinking over getting married. Suppose I don't get a raise?"

"Oh, let's go on and do what we want," she said robustly. "I tell you what—don't ask for a raise! I've an idea. Mrs. Fontane wants a Cupid for her garden, and I told her I could make it for her. I'll ask her a hundred and fifty for it."

"A hundred and fifty!" he said. "That's a lot of money! I don't earn that in a month. It's more than a raise would bring me from now until June."

"So we'll be married!" she coaxed him.

He hesitated, gazing into her bright, dark eyes. "I don't like to take your money," he said.

"Oh, silly!" she cried scornfully. "We're sharing everything else, aren't we?"

"You're so darned pretty!" he whispered. He lifted her in a quick embrace. "There! I've got to run."

He was gone, and then she remembered he had forgotten to look at the head. But it did not matter. She could work on it a little more, and it would be better. She went dancing back to the dining room.

"It's all settled!" she said, helping herself largely to eggs.

"Poetry comes slow these days," her father said mournfully. He was reading the advertisements for positions. " 'Male help wanted. A man to tend stable, drive car, tend furnace, help with gardening.' Now—there's a job for a dried-up poet. 'Couple wanted. Wife to cook, mend, help in general housework.' Jenny, my dear?" He lifted heavy handsome black eyebrows at his wife.

But she paid no attention to him. Years ago she had been alarmed at his seriousness over advertisements, but now she knew his seriousness meant nothing, not any more than his jokes. She could not tell the difference between them, and she ignored both.

"You needn't work your poetry for me," Susan said calmly. "We're all arranged." After breakfast, as soon as she had washed the dishes, she would go over to Mrs. Fontane's and see if she still wanted the Cupid.

Her father leaped from his chair. "Then on with the wedding!" he cried, and pulled Susan to her feet.

They danced madly for a moment in the large solemnity of Mary's gaze as she bit into her toast. Mrs. Gaylord poured herself a third cup of coffee, her lips moving in abstraction. She began to whisper something. Susan stopped.

"What did you say, Mums?" she demanded.

Mrs. Gaylord looked up, startled.

"I was just saying over the spool silk we're out of," she said. "We ought to have two spools of the white."

"I'll get them after breakfast," said Susan.

"Well, got to go," said her father. "There are fifty young poets waiting for me in Lit. 6— Oh, Lord! Some of 'em are even worse than Mark was—though I've not forgotten him. It gave me real pleasure to flunk that young man."

"I know he tried," Susan said indignantly. "Mark always does his best."

"What's that got to do with it?" her father inquired. He

was feeling frantically in his pockets. "Where's my red pencil?" he demanded excitedly. "There's no use trying to teach that class if I've lost my red pencil!"

Susan rose and began searching his pockets.

"Mark can't help it if he's not good at poetry," she said fiercely. "You're not to hold it against him, Dad! Here's your pencil, in your vest pocket."

"Thank God!" her father said fervently. "Now I'm myself again! Of course I don't hold it against him. Probably he'll make you a better husband because he's no poet. All I say is, doing your best has no relation to poetry. It's a spring in you. It flows out if it's there, and it doesn't if it's not there. G'bye, Sue." He kissed her cheek and went off.

As soon as he was gone Mary rose slowly and reached for her bag of books and came and stood silently while her mother looked her over, straightening her narrow black hair ribbon. Susan, on her way with a heap of dishes, stopped and blew a kiss into her younger sister's neck.

"I'll have something for you to try on by tonight," she promised.

"All right," Mary said. Her voice was clear and toneless.

Over the kitchen sink, sousing the dishes in and out of hot foaming water at high speed, Susan thought tenderly of her little sister. Perhaps when Mary grew older, they could be friends. Girls of fifteen were always shy. She would make Mary's dress lovely, and she could wear it to parties—a fall of tiny ruffles over the shoulders to hide the little skinny arms, a ruffle of lace shirred about the neck to soften the color too warm against her sallow skin. She planned heartily that she was going to see that Mary had prettier clothes now that she was growing up. She would make a little satin evening wrap for her after the wedding, when she had time. There were so many lovely things ahead to do, and she had so much time to be her own, a whole long life. Nobody died young in her family. Her ancestors promised her life, long as theirs had been long. She could do everything, and do it all with completeness and perfection. There was peace in her. "Oh, that will be—glory for me!" she sang under her breath as she wiped her hands dry.

She darted upstairs a moment to see Mark's head. Putting aside the wet cloth, she stood before it, and she felt her hands go out to it. She modeled busily a few moments, half guiltily, and then covered it up again, and washed her hands and put on her hat and coat and went downstairs and put her head in at the sitting room where her mother was dusting.

"I'm going to buy the thread," she said.

"Mercy!" cried Mrs. Gaylord. "Are you finished the dishes already?"

"You think you can do it?" Mrs. Fontane said doubtfully. "I shouldn't like my garden spoiled."

"You needn't take it if you don't like it," Susan said, "but I know I can do it."

"A hundred and fifty dollars is a lot of money for a girl," Mrs. Fontane said, but she smiled.

"If you think it's too much—only I wasn't going to do a bare Cupid," Susan answered in haste. "I had a plan to make him kneeling over the pool, to look at himself, his little wings fluttering, you know, and his bow and arrows slipping down. He'd be kneeling on an old stump, and there'd be a butterfly on his shoulder."

"Well," said Mrs. Fontane, "if I like it, I don't really mind."

Mrs. Fontane was one of the summer crowd, the rich, bright crowd who bought old houses and farms and spent fortunes on them for a summer month or two.

"Go ahead, you handsome child!" Mrs. Fontane smiled. "I suppose I'm crazy when I'm one of the few people who could get David Barnes to do me something really good. But it would be amusing if you made something I liked."

"I wouldn't want you to have it if you didn't," Susan said stoutly. She made her voice calm and held her knees firm, though she was inwardly trembling. "Goodbye, Mrs. Fontane." She put out her hand. "Thank you very much."

"Goodbye, child," said Mrs. Fontane. "And you say a month?"

"In a month at most," said Susan. "Then it has to be cast, you know. I'll have to send it away."

"I'd like it there while the irises are in bloom," Mrs. Fontane said.

"It will be there," said Susan. Of course she could do it. She had always done everything she wanted to do.

When the white-haired butler had closed the door behind her she ran down the road, humming under her breath, "Oh, that will be—glory for me!" . . .

How did a little naked boy look? She would go around by Lucile Palmer's and look at Tommy. He'd be having his bath now, and she could just see again how a boy's body stood, sturdily, and how the knees—

She walked swiftly toward the small bungalow where Lucile lived. She and Lucile had been schoolmates in high school, but she had gone to college and instead Lucile had married Hal Palmer who had been in their high school class, and Tommy was born the next year. Hal had a job in Baker's shoe store. He was always very nice when she went in. "It's a pleasure to sell you a pair of shoes," he always said. "You take a good average last, and yet your foot has style. Most women have something wrong with their feet, anyway." He held her strong shapely foot in the palm of his hand admiringly. "Grand arches you got," he always murmured.

"Oh, Lucile!" she called at the open door of the little bungalow. The breakfast dishes were still on the table in the dining room.

"Ooo-hoo!" Lucile's voice answered. "Bathroom!"

She went toward the bathroom and found Lucile, dishevelled, her long blond hair falling down her back, fighting a wet and slippery Tommy.

"He's just determined to get back in the tub," she wailed. "And he's so strong you can't bend him!"

Tommy, in grim silence, escaped and began clambering back into the tub. Susan laughed and picked him up and held him high above her. He looked down at her gravely, like a flying cherub, and then smiled. A score of impressions were flowing into her brain from him—his head, his eyes, the flare of his yellow hair, his warm round firm body, his chubby shoulders and outspread starry hands, the flung outspread length of his strong little legs. She lowered him and set him on his feet. He had forgotten his tub and stood lamb-like, staring at her, while she dried and dressed him.

"Oh, Tommy beautiful!" she cried, laughing. "How do you do anything all day but play with him, Lucile? I want dozens of them."

"It's all very well when you see them only once in a while," Lucile complained. "But when you have them all the time, Susan, you'll find it's a chore. They don't mind you a bit."

She listened smiling, gazing into Tommy's wide blue eyes, not believing Lucile's impatient voice. She could manage. She wouldn't have any trouble with her children!

"Now I have to feed him," Lucile said. "Then I hope to goodness he'll sleep—but he probably won't."

"I just ran in," said Susan. "I wanted to see him."

"Coming to the bridge club this afternoon?" Lucile asked. "It's at Trina's today."

Susan shook her head brightly. "I'm busy," she said. "Mark and I are going to be married earlier."

They paused, looking at each other.

"Well," he said, "I guess Mark's waiting."

"Yes," she said. "I must go, Dad."

"Yes," he said, "of course. Well, goodbye."

She kissed him and ran on. Once she looked back and he was still standing there. She waved to him, but he did not move, and she dared not stay and went hurrying to Mark. He was already in the car, and the engine was beating.

"Nobody see you?" he asked.

She shook her head and laughed. "Nobody but Dad."

He bent his head and kissed her quickly and then the car started, jerking a little. She felt strange and excited. His kiss had still not brought him near. The car stalled.

"What's wrong with this thing?" he exclaimed, and jerked at the gears.

She glanced down.

"Here," she said, laughing, "the brake—"

He had forgotten the brake.

"You've married a stupid fellow, Sue," he said ruefully.

She shook her head, smiling. "Dad does the same thing," she said. "I'm used to it. He curses and swears because the car won't move."

"And you let the brakes go," he said.

They were roaring along now, through the windy spring day. And she held in her mind Mark's words. "You've married —you've married—a stupid fellow," he had said, but he was wrong. She had married *him*.

"I'm married," she thought, and wondering, she looked ahead, not upon hills and trees and green meadows, but into eight uncertain years.

And now, alone, there was still an inner wall of shyness between them to be pulled away—or perhaps it would fall. They would be alone for a week on the edge of this lake, the little cabin they had borrowed from her father. He had

"You are!" cried Lucile. "Since when?"

"Last night," Susan said.

"It's the full moon," Lucile cried with roguishness. "Goodness knows *I* know what the moon can do! Hal proposed to me on a moonlight night and I took him, though I hadn't any idea I would two hours before. That's how it happens, and you get caught."

"I'm not caught," Susan said. She laughed. "I want to be married."

"You'll get over it," Lucile said, twisting up her hair.

"No, I won't," Susan called. She was on her way through the tiny hall. "Goodbye, Lucile!"

But passing through the little dining room she paused and looked at the table. The old ache to make beauty and order stirred in her. She'd just help Lucile a bit—besides, dirty dishes were so ugly. Quickly she gathered up the dishes and tiptoed into the kitchen and then turned on the water and washed them and set them away. There were so few it was absurd of Lucile not to get them out of the way. Tiptoeing again through the dining room she wiped the table, and set a little bowl of artificial flowers on it. Artificial flowers! Lucile ought to be ashamed. There were wild flowers at the end of the street, if nothing else, there where the wood began. She tiptoed out into the street and went swinging home, smiling, the shape of Tommy warm in her hands. She'd just run upstairs and block it out roughly this morning, and sew this afternoon.

Her mother was dusting the dining room.

"Back already?" she called.

"Yes," Susan called. "Here's the thread."

Up in her room beside Mark's head, she shaped out in rough posture the figure of a small fat kneeling boy. It would be fun to work on curls and dimples and small star-like hands— Mark's head, too—she'd make this baby face look a bit like Mark—Mark's little son in bronze, looking at himself in a pool. She'd make a pool in her own garden some day for her own little son to kneel and look into. She began to hum softly, "Oh, that will be—glory for me—glory for me—" She was going to be married.

They were being married. Walls that had stood between her and Mark were rolled away by words chanted and sung, by her own firm quivering assent, by Mark's white-faced stern assent. She put out her hand for his ring, the air about them became music, and they turned and walked down the aisle. They were married.

"I was afraid you were going to faint," she whispered outside the church door, in the moment before the people sighed and smiled and turned to go away. Why was it people tempered their joy in weddings with sighs?

"I felt in a daze," he said. "It was as though I were someone else."

They had been used so long to the walls that now that they were gone, now that they had rolled away like mists at morning, leaving them visible to each other, they built their own walls of shyness. They had been in a dream of unreality while the walls were being pulled away by words, by cries and shouts of laughter, by banter and good wishes. People said again and again, "I hope you will be happy!" Their voices were gay, but their eyes were doubting. "I am sure we shall be happy," she said. Yes, as soon as she and Mark were alone, as soon as they could begin their life, they would be happy. She had her hand in Mark's arm, but it was not her hand, not his arm. They were two dolls, standing dressed beautifully, smiling, while people passed before them. But they would not be real until this was over, until she and Mark were alone. . . .

"Come and cut the cake," her mother whispered.

She pressed Mark's arm.

"We must cut the wedding cake," she whispered, and then

22

she turned and walked into the dining room and he stood beside her. There on the table was the great round white cake. She had made it herself, her mother hovering about, greasing the pans and testing the oven.

"Seems as if you shouldn't make your own cake," her mother had said.

"I like to make it," she had answered.

Now she pressed the silver knife into the rich dark stuff. People were crowding into the tiny room. She could hear Lucile's squealing voice, "Oh, how scrumptious, Susan!" and she smiled. But this moment was not so deep to live as had been the moment in the kitchen when she had put sugar into a bowl, and butter and the clear yellow of eggs. She had been aware every moment of that making, the stirring and sifting, the whipping of the frothy egg whites, the dark rich fruit—all of it had gone into the meticulous making of the brown and fragrant mound she drew at last out of the oven. She had been aware every instant, "I am making my own wedding cake—" Now cutting and dividing it, listening to jokes and ta[lk] of dreams, this cake was no more than any other. It had b[een] precious only in the making.

Everyone was eating, drinking, talking. She caught M[ark's] eyes. "Now?" his lips shaped. She nodded and slippe[d] They had planned days before how they would slip o[ff] going separately, would meet at a certain spot where [he] left his small rackety car.

She ran to her room, changed into a sweater and [ ] ran down again through the kitchen and the backy[ard.]

No one had seen her. Yes, someone—her father [com]ing out of the kitchen door, his coattails flying.

"Susan!" he called in a loud whisper. She st[opped and] came up panting. "I just wanted to—I had to [ ] to count on me, of course, just the same."

"I know," she whispered.

built it for them all when she was a child, but they had not come to it often then. Her mother had hated the stillness, the loneliness, the gnats, the owls in the night, the old rusty stove. So they had given it up, and her father had come alone for a day sometimes. But he never stayed long.

"Guess I'm not big enough to stay alone," he would say, joking.

"You're grown up, aren't you?" Susan had asked once, when she was a little girl.

"I'm not sure," he had replied gravely.

But he had kept the cabin.

"Might want to go there sometime," he said.

She and Mark had driven here two days ago to bring food and books, and to sweep and dust. She had thought, packing her books in her own room to bring them away, "Shall I take clay, or a paint box? What if I want to make something at the cabin?" No, she would not take these things on her honeymoon.

She did not know how much she would ever want to use them again. Perhaps she would not need them any more. She had packed them not for the honeymoon, but to be taken to the house where she and Mark had chosen to live. The alcove in her old room looked empty and forlorn when she had put everything away into a big box, to be taken to the small new house. The Cupid was finished and kneeling now among the budding irises in Mrs. Fontane's garden. Mark's head she had carried herself down the street and set up in the new attic. The head was not finished. Something was wrong with it. She had the mouth perfectly, but the eyes were wrong under the brows. Do what she would, they continued to look like empty sockets.

"It's not right—it doesn't speak," she had said to him one day. They were in the little new house, getting it ready for this day that was now over.

"Speak?" he had asked.

"When I have them right I seem to hear them speaking," she said.

"Gosh, it looks enough like me to make me feel queer," he said, staring at it.

They had stood looking at the clay face and then Mark said suddenly, "I'll look like that when I'm dead."

She did not answer, she could not bear to answer, because he was right. It was exactly Mark's face, dead. She wrapped it quickly in the damp cloth.

"It's not finished, that's all," she replied. "I'll bring it to life." It would be the first thing she would do when they came back, when they began their real life.

But now in the cabin without reason that silent perfect mask haunted her like the face of some dead memory. She kept thinking of it when she looked at him, while they talked, while they unpacked. They stood before each other, they kissed, and she saw not his face, but the mask she had made.

"Aren't we silly!" she laughed. "We've been longing for this moment. Here it is—and we feel odd with each other!"

He looked down at her without a smile. "I still feel as if it were not us," he said. In his eyes was emptiness. She—she must make the reality. His face must not be to her the clay mask she had not finished, the mask which, pathetically, humbly, was waiting until she finished it and brought it to life.

"Come," she said practically, "let's unpack our bags and get our supper—then a swim by moonlight, Mark?"

"Yes, let's!" he assented eagerly.

To do something together would make it all real again. They would feel they were the two who had planned these very hours, now come after so long. That was what was the matter. They had dreamed this moment so long that they could not draw it out of dreams. Though it was here, though they were

26

in it, it seemed still to come. He followed her while she hung up their garments on nails behind a cretonne curtain, while she set the pine table for the two of them, while she broiled the beefsteak and made coffee. He could not find much to do. She was so swift in every movement, so exact. She seemed to be doing everything at the same time. He stood helpless before her certain speed.

"You're wonderful!" he said. "I—you make me feel useless."

She was putting into a clear glass of water the red roses she had worn at her belt when they left her father's house. She was setting them on the table. But when he said, "You're wonderful!" she flew to him and buried her face against him.

"Oh, don't, don't!" she cried, strangled against his breast. "Don't call me that!"

He was astounded. "Why, I meant it!" he exclaimed. "Don't you like to be called wonderful?"

"No—no—no—" she cried, stifled.

"Well!" he gasped. "Well! I don't understand— Most people—"

She lifted her head suddenly and sniffed.

"The steak's burning!" she cried. "That's not very wonderful of me!" She ran to push it hissing upon the plate. He could not tell whether she was laughing or crying.

"I'm hungrier than I have ever been in my life," she cried gaily. They were busy over the food, almost at ease with each other now, in the candlelight.

"So am I, you darling," he said.

They were almost real again, but not quite. She thought, pondering upon his eyes, "It's just this flickering candlelight that makes them so shadowy that they seem empty. They aren't really empty. I love him so. He's my husband." Outside of her loving him, beyond this being of a woman, married to

27

Mark, that was she, her busy brain went on talking to itself. "That head looks exactly like him now. Perhaps I've done the best I can with it—perhaps it won't come to life. Perhaps I can't make life. I wonder if I can be a real sculptor?"

Ah, yes, but she would make life, she said resolutely. They rose and sat together on the little porch overlooking the lake while he smoked his pipe. They sat very closely in silence, realizing at last each other's presence.

"This is the beginning," she whispered.

"The beginning of our life," he answered.

In the moonlight and the silence they grew clearer to each other, closer. The individual color faded out of their faces, their eyes, their flesh, and some closer outline appeared. She felt his being, breathing, warm, expectant and shy.

"Now for the lake," he said suddenly. They undressed in the moonlight and there were their two bodies, white as marble. He was like a statue of marble. He would be cold as marble to touch. But she also was like marble, she thought, looking down at her own body, and she was not cold. He stood motionless, gazing at her, and she felt him, cold with shyness.

"Come!" she cried. "Let's run to the lake."

For she wanted life and movement in their two white carved bodies. They ran, hand in hand, and leaped and swam out into the lake together. They swam out and then in again to the beach. He was shivering.

"It's too cold," he said. "Let's build the fire."

They ran back to the cabin and barred the door against the night and the darkness of the woods, and he piled up the logs in the fireplace, and she knelt and lit the dry kindling, and the fire blazed. They knelt before it a moment, and then she felt herself drawn to her feet against him, her head pressed back to meet his kiss. And yet in that one instant before his kiss came down to still it, her brain drew aside from her and said

28

to itself quickly, "There—that's the look I need for the mask. He's come to life."

The unfinished head stood in the attic which she planned sometime perhaps to make into a workroom for herself. But as yet she had no feeling of need for a room for herself alone. This was her home, this small house at the end of the street where she had played as a child. Looking out of its front windows she saw what had been familiar to her all her life, the rows of small white houses, the green of the campus at the far end, and out of the tops of trees the cupola of the main hall of the university where her father taught and where she and Mark had gone for four years. She had at once loved and despised it, knowing it to be small and provincial, and limited by its trustees who were two successful farmers, a lawyer and the president of the town bank, and yet loving the fierce rawboned quarrelsome poverty-stricken faculty, each of whom she knew not only as the dogmatic passionate person who taught her, but as the person, too, of whom her father growled, as he did of Professor Sanford, after faculty meetings, "That fellow Sanford's a crank. I don't care how good he is in astronomy. He can't see anything but stars."

Poor Professor Sanford! It was quite true he lived among the stars. But they all lived somewhere else than in those small houses, where their pale wives struggled to be cultivated while they bore babies and did housework and had no maids. She knew them so well, and she never looked from her front windows now without comprehension sweeping over her again. She loved them and ached a little when she thought of them. They were all trying so hard to live as they felt it beautiful to live, and their houses were so small—too small and too close, so that they had constantly to hush the crying of their children and their own laughter or anger or weeping as well. They had only silence to keep them private from each other. And they

29

needed privacy, since they were not ignorant people and since decency was a necessity to them. They could make a joke of poverty and did. But one day little Mrs. Sanford had clutched her hands together—one day at the faculty reception to the seniors. She wore the drooping black lace dress she wore every year. And she had looked up at Susan, a little timidly, to ask, "What do you plan to do, Susan dear?"

"Everything," Susan had said gaily, and then Mrs. Sanford had clutched her two water-sodden little hands together again, her hands with clean, broken fingernails. It was Monday and in the cellar that early morning she had done the family wash and slipped out to hang it up quickly, not looking at other yards where other wives were doing the same thing.

"Oh, Susan!" she had said. "You frighten me, dear! It's so dreadful to know all that one wants from life and not be able to have it. Sometimes I think it's better not to know—not to be able to read, than to be able and have no books, for instance, or wanting terribly to sing and not being able to afford the training."

She had not known what to say, and then Mrs. Sanford had smiled and patted her arm. "But you're so talented, dear. I know you'll be successful."

Someone cried out, "Now I just know Mrs. Sanford will sing for us," and Mrs. Sanford called back, "Oh dear, nobody wants to hear me sing!"

"Yes," Susan said, "yes, please, Mrs. Sanford. I love to hear you."

"Do you, dear? Then I will."

They had stood listening while she sang in a small wistful breathy voice, *Kennst du das Land.* Susan had heard her sing it many times, so why now should she want to sob when she remembered it? . . . Every time time she looked out of the front windows she remembered how Mrs. Sanford had looked that day while she sang.

But the west windows looked out into Tramp's Woods. She and Mark had become engaged there. He had said that day, "Where shall we go, Sue?" And she had said, "I've always wanted to go into Tramp's Woods! Let's go!"

They had not played there as children, because of a childish superstition, told from one generation of playfellows to the next, that the ghost of a tramp was there, who had hung himself long ago, over his own solitary campfire in plain sight and sound of a street full of homes and families and children. The lights from their windows must have twinkled on him as he ate his supper—there had been a can of beans, half empty, so he could not have died hungry. And there was a little stack of wood if he had wanted to keep his fire burning. There was even enough money in his pocket to bury him, provided it was without fuss. It was in an envelope, and he had put on the outside in a pencil scrawl, "To bury me—no funeral." There was no reason why he should have hung himself there in plain sight of people. It was so queer of him that mothers were really relieved he had done it, since it was not as though they could have helped it. They said above their children's heads, "It's just as well a person like that is out of the way. One never knows what he might do." And the children, catching the tone of their voices, made a ghost out of the tramp and never went near the woods where he had died.

But she and Mark had gone there that afternoon to be alone together. They were sure of being alone in Tramp's Woods.

"Are you afraid?" she had asked him, laughing.

"Not with you," he had answered, and laughed back at her.

Now that her own little home turned partly to these woods she found it a place beautiful and untroubled, and sometimes in an afternoon, waiting for Mark to come home, she wandered among the outer trees, half remembering the old story, but not afraid of it any more because she and Mark had made it

31

their own. It was a strange wood, so silent, the wild flowers untouched. She never saw anyone else there.

But even she did not go there often. For there was always something to do to her house. It was never really done, though the day after they came home, when all their friends came to see them, they had said warmly, "I don't see how you've done it, Sue." "Why, it looks as though you had lived here years!" And she and Mark, laughing, hand in hand, were drenched in their own profound simple happiness, and they received this admiration as part of it. They had done nothing extraordinary, because everybody got married, and their home they knew was small, and yet they felt successful beyond all their fellows.

When everybody was gone that first night they made a tour of the whole house together, to make sure, to see it all again— living room, dining room, kitchen, hall, the stairs, two bedrooms and Mark's little study and the small yellow-tiled bathroom. Mark was going up the attic stairs, but she stopped him.

"Don't let's go up," she cried. "There's nothing there. I haven't even thought what I'm going to do up there yet."

It was true she had not even been there since she had carried up the unfinished head and her working tools. So they turned and went downstairs again, and to see if the chimney in the living room really drew, Mark lit a fire. It was not necessary, for the night was so mild they left the door open, and down the street they could see the lights popping out into the darkness, the lights of the homes of their friends. It was lovely, lovely. She felt a gayety that rose from the walls of her life, lights and friends and home and Mark, her husband. Down the street, around the corner, were her parents and Mary and all her happy childhood, her so nearly quite happy childhood. She was very lucky. Why had her father said goodbye to her? She had not had to leave anything behind when she came away with Mark. It was all there. If she wanted to, she could run down that street, turn that corner, open the door and be back in her childhood.

But she did not want to go back to anything. She turned to Mark eagerly, fully. "I'm happy!" she whispered. They sat down before their fire, warmed and fed. "Oh, that will be— glory for me—" she sang under her breath.

Mark laughed. "The first time I ever heard you sing that," he said, "you were five years old and you were making a dress for a doll, on the top step of the porch."

"Was I?" she cried. "You darling, to remember!"

"You don't know when you sing it, do you? Any more?" he asked.

She shook her head. "It comes out of me," she answered.

To part in the morning was such pain that they dreaded it from the moment she poured Mark his second cup of coffee. Then he looked at the clock.

"Ten minutes," he said solemnly.

She flew to turn the clock around so its face could not be seen, and then she pushed her chair against his. At this moment she felt the house would be intolerably empty without him. "If only you did something at home," she said wistfully. "If you were a painter or a writer—"

"You've married an everyday chap," Mark said soberly, stirring his coffee. "I'm afraid I'll be going to office as long as I live, Sue."

"There's only one of you in the world," she said quickly, and bent to kiss his hand. She looked at him acutely, intensely. "I have to remember you for three and a half hours," she said.

"Can't even be sure I'll get home for lunch today," he said sorrowfully. "Someone wants to look at the old Grainger place."

"Oh, Mark," she wailed, "all day!"

"Afraid so, darling," he said, and got up and turned the clock back again.

The moment of parting was agony, the moment when he had turned the corner desolate, and yet, after they were passed, life closed about her warmly in a hundred things she had to do. She darted about the house, creating cleanliness, shaping their possessions into a basis of order. And then she went into each room as though she were painting its portrait, seeing each in its whole, studying every detail, the pattern a chair made, the line of a curtain's fall, the splash of a picture's color, the emphasis of a flower. The house was a whole, made up of the separate perfection of every room. But the perfection was not static, it must be alive, faithfully partaking of her life and Mark's. It must be their house, lived in by Mark and by her. She made the study a place like Mark, the long sofa where his tall body could lie, the pillows flat because he liked to lie flat when he was tired. The desk was solid and uncluttered, the pictures clear and simple. It was strange that she could see his background better than her own. She changed her own possessions every other day, sure of nothing. Did her toilet table look better here by the window, or here opposite the bed? The flowers here or there? She was dissatisfied, and pondered, trying one thing and another without being able to find what she wanted.

Before she knew it the clock was at noon and she was guilty that the hours without him were so soon gone. He was there almost before she had missed him. She heard his voice calling from the hall.

"They didn't come, after all, honey! I'm home!"

"Oh, Mark!" She flew into the kitchen and started everything at once. It was fun to see how fast she could do it all— the chops, the peas, the salad—set the table in between—put on the bowl of flowers—no artificial flowers in this house!

"There!" she said in fifteen minutes.

"There's nobody like you!" He pulled out her chair.

"Oh, nonsense!" she said. "Don't—I don't like you to say that."

34

"No, but look," he said eagerly, "what have I done? Washed my hands, brushed my hair, changed my tie—I found I'd dropped something on that tie, how—"

"I'll see to it," she said quickly.

"And by the time I get downstairs, you've got lunch ready. Now you know there's nobody like you!"

She smiled and did not answer. Why, indeed, did she not like him to say there was no one like her? It made her feel lonely. She wanted to be like everybody else. But Mark was talking eagerly, happily, eating with hunger.

"They 'phoned up just ten minutes before twelve that they didn't want the Grainger place," he was saying. "I started to ring you up, and then I thought, 'I'll get there as quickly as I can get her.'"

"Why didn't they want the Grainger place?" she asked curiously. "It's a beautiful old house."

"Too far out for servants," he said.

"Perhaps they'd like the Marsey summer place," she said.

"Is it for sale?" he asked.

"It seems to me I heard they were going to live abroad now that Mr. Marsey is dead," she said. "I don't know where I heard it, but—"

"You have a memory like flypaper," he said. "But why didn't I think of it myself?"

He got up and went to the telephone quickly and she waited. "The boss said, 'Swell idea,'" he said, sitting down again. "I said, 'My wife's.'"

"Oh, Mark," she said with reproach, "it just happened I thought of it. You shouldn't have told him."

"It's all right," he said curtly, "it also happens that I didn't think of it."

She looked at him, her heart shrinking in fear. "Have I done something wrong?" she asked. "Why, Mark, you look angry with me!"

He got up abruptly and came over to her and kissed her. "Why do you sit so far away from me?" he asked, and pulled her chair beside his. "Let's sit side by side, always."

Somewhere she had read that love was a force which expanded the being. People who had not known they could do anything wrote poems or music or undertook great tasks when they were in love. But it was not so with her. She drew Mark's love about her like a close and warmly enfolding cloak, and did nothing great, even in dreams. She did not once go to the attic or think even of her modeling. Her hands were satisfied to do the work of this house she loved better every day. When she had made it fresh and had added to it every beauty she could devise and imagine, setting forth every possession into its most perfect place, then she would go into the kitchen, and poring over a cookbook, she would plan and make. When everything was finished, she waited, full of content, and satisfied in her own being, until Mark came home. She built his love about her like the walls of the small house on the edge of the wood.

Of the wood she was always aware. It was a deceptive wood. It seemed, at the end of the street, like a shallow spread of trees, but once entered it went on for miles, unexpectedly tangled and deep, over ground too rough and rocky to tempt clearing for a farm. There was a stream, after a while, running darkly at the bottom of a chasm of wet black rock, and then the wood went on again.

Mark hated the wood. She had led him there last Sunday afternoon and he had tramped doggedly along beside her in silence.

"Isn't it beautiful?" she said, lifting her face to the shadowy trees, dark now with midsummer fullness.

"It makes me feel queer," he said. "How was it I didn't see it that day when I asked you to marry me? I didn't see anything that day but you."

36

A loneliness fell upon them, although they were walking hand in hand. They came to the stream and looked down upon it, flowing upon black rock.

"It must have taken a million years for it to cut a gash like that in this hard rock," Mark said, and immediately the loneliness of a million years was added to them. They stood staring down and suddenly a crash and a roar burst up from the chasm. A little further down the bank, where the stream curved, a loosened rock had fallen into the stream. It settled, trailing lesser rocks and earth and small trees, and after a boiling moment, the water parted smoothly and flowed on either side, and the rock stood as though from ages.

"Let's go home," said Mark. "We've come too deep into it. I've always heard stories about this place."

"You said once you were not afraid here with me," she reminded him.

"I'm not afraid anyway," he retorted. "Only why not walk in the sunshine?"

So they had turned homeward. When they came out of the twilight of the trees, the sun was still high in the street. They could see people coming back from golf, from picnics. A few blocks away Lucile and Hal were coming home, Tommy walking sturdily between them. Lucile waved and Hal shouted, "Missed you folks at the club today!"

Mark waved his hat and Susan her hand and they went up their own steps.

"We ought to get around to the club once in a while," Mark said. "We don't want folks to think we're stuck up."

"Oh, they wouldn't," she said warmly. "They know us."

She forgot them and went into the kitchen singing, and set about supper.

"All the same," said Mark a few minutes later, "it's easy to get folks thinking you're stuck up, Sue, especially when you're the sort of person you are."

She stopped her slicing of an orange for fruit salad. She had been thinking how exquisite was the making of an orange, the segments of tiny drops of enclosed color. She stood, holding nothing but an orange, staring at Mark.

"Why, what do you mean?" she asked, wondering.

Her face was flushed and she felt a little angry with him.

"Nothing, except that sometimes the way you do things—the way you go ahead—sort of—people don't always understand."

She went on slicing the orange. He had hurt her, but she would not tell him.

"Oh, everybody knows me in this little town," she said quietly. "They've always known me—Lucile and the girls and all the boys." She felt suddenly far away from Mark. Once when she was quite small, she had heard a teacher say to another, "Sue is a strange child, isn't she? She's not like the other children."

She snapped on the light and he saw her face.

"I guess I don't know what I am talking about," he said slowly. "You— I want you to be yourself."

"I can't be anything else," she said. "Come, Mark—sit down."

And when they sat down, he said, "This is the best fruit salad I've ever tasted, Sue—you're a wonder of a cook."

A handful of words flew out of her brain and hung on the end of her tongue. She almost let them flick out at him like the barbed end of a serpent's tongue. "There's a bitter orange in it, Mark—take care!"

If she spoke them, he would look at her innocent and surprised. She withheld them. She was too easily hurt. She had learned long ago to withhold the flick of her words when she was hurt. She learned, when she was quite a child, that she could make her mother look afraid when she spoke out what flashed from her brain. The first time she had seen the fear in her mother's eyes she went away into her room and cried. "I must never—never—never—make anyone afraid of me because I am hurt," she told herself passionately, and remembered it forever.

"Have another helping, then, my darling," she said to Mark and filled the plate he held out to her.

But they went no more into the wood. Mark did not want to go and she would not go without him. But suddenly, for no reason, she remembered something. Upstairs in the attic was the unfinished head. Though she went to the attic sometimes to clean and dust, she did nothing else there. Now, because Mark had hurt her, she went upstairs the next day and she stood, looking thoughtfully about the empty room. But she did nothing to furnish it. She still did not even lift the cloth from the unfinished head.

"You have everything a woman could want," her mother said one day, looking around the living room. "A good husband and a nice home in the best neighborhood in town."

"Yes, I have everything," she said, smiling.

"Mark's so steady," her mother went on. She had refused to take off her hat. "I've got to get right back," she always said. She might sit an hour or two, but if she had her hat on she felt she was going at any moment. "The work's piled up waiting."

"I'll come back with you," said Susan. "I'm all finished."

"Oh no," her mother said quickly. "You have your own house now. I wouldn't want Mark to think I couldn't manage—"

"I'm just coming home to see you," she said, laughing. "Besides, I have everything in our house just about finished—all except the attic, and I don't know yet what I want to do to that."

"It looks lovely," her mother said wistfully, looking around on the shining order. "You keep it wonderfully—you always had a knack."

"It keeps itself," said Susan, "it's the easiest house in the world. It lives along with us. Things just run back into their places—like this!"

She waved her hands and lifted her eyebrows. But her mother did not smile.

"It's all right now," she said with meaning. "Later, you'll find you have to have help. Well, I must go."

"I'll get my hat," said Susan.

"It's a real sweet house," her mother said, pausing on the new sidewalk to look back. "The only thing is, I shouldn't care, for myself, to live on the edge of those black woods."

"I like them, somehow," Susan answered, "though Mark feels as you do, I think."

She walked with her mother, her feet familiar with the way. But she was free of her mother now. When she went home again it was of her own will. She entered into the house and began instantly the old habitual round of dishes to be washed, the downstairs to be swept and dusted.

"I just left everything this morning," her mother murmured. "I wanted to get to the store early, since it's Saturday and people pick over things so, and then I thought I'd go round by your place because it's such a lovely day. Well, I'll make the beds if you're down here."

She went heavily up the stairs and Susan tied a clean towel over her hair and flew about the rooms. It was pleasant to make order and freshness. She sang as she worked. When she was a girl this had seemed sometimes nearly drudgery, day after day, when her mind had been full of other things she wanted to do. But it had never been quite drudgery because something in her was satisfied as she worked. She was creating and changing. The rooms assumed a shape and an atmosphere under her hands.

When she was nearly finished, at the top of the house a door banged.

"Is that you, Susan?" her father's voice roared down the two flights of stairs.

"Yes, it is!" she sang back.

"Come up here!" he shouted.

And when she had run up the stairs to him he stood leaning over the banister, his hair tousled, smoking his old cherrywood pipe.

"I want to hear that Sibelius thing," he said. "Mary'll never be able to play it. She picks at it so. And it's got me by the ears these days so I can't get that tune out of my head."

She sat down at his old upright piano, smiling, and opened the pages of *Finlandia*. He stretched himself on the couch and threw his arm over his eyes.

"Go on," he commanded her.

She played it, fully and deeply, forgetting everything else, as she could not help doing in anything she did. Yes, she could not help forgetting even Mark. She was building a structure of music, filled with stern ineffable pain. She knew how so to fill it. Being so young, pain was still beautiful to her. Though she had never suffered in her life, she knew by an instinct deeper than experience how to make pain. When she finished she was trembling.

She waited a moment and then turned to her father. His arm had fallen from his face, and he lay, his eyes closed, his lips clenched white about his pipe.

"Father!" she whispered.

"Go away," he muttered. "Go away—go away!" Under his black eyelashes she saw the brightness of tears. "That music—" he muttered.

She went away, down the stairs. The house was still. She paused a moment at her mother's door and listened. She could hear nothing. She opened the door softly and looked. There on the bed, still unmade, her mother lay asleep, her breath coming peaceably as a child's. She shut the door softly and went away, out of this house, back again to her own.

II

SHE stopped one day when the morning was half over and looked around her living room. Everything was finished in this house. There was nothing more to do. The house looked back at her brightly, the windows clear, the floor shining, everything in its place. There was no room for anything more she could make. The last cushion, the last curtain was done, and one more would be too much. Her small linen closet was full of linen she had embroidered and hemstitched. Outside, the garden was tended and blooming with midsummer. Mark was to make the garden, but she had run out on sunny days and weeded and planted. Yesterday afternoon she had even mowed the lawn. But he was angry at her for that.

"I was going to do it tonight after supper," he said. "I looked at it yesterday—it didn't need it badly."

"I just did it for fun," she coaxed him. "I hadn't anything to do this afternoon, and I didn't feel like going away from home—so I just did—"

"Don't do it again," he warned her. "It's not woman's work."

She looked out of the window and did not answer. It had been pleasant, shaving the long even rows of green.

"I won't do it again," she said.

But today there was no more to do. She went to the window and looked out. She felt restless with nothing to do. Down the street Lucile was wheeling a baby carriage onto the porch and then she went into the house quickly. Susan could hear the screen door bang. It was Lucile's second baby, born six weeks ago. "I'm furious!" Lucile had cried. "Another baby—and

43

Tommy just getting to where I can take him with me! It isn't as though Hal could afford me a maid. Men are so selfish!"

She had not answered Lucile, remembering Hal, docile and always tired. It did not seem possible he could make Lucile do anything she did not want to do.

Behind her the house was orderly and still. It looked at her when she turned, with the bright and placid look of a well-tended child. Now what should she do? Yesterday she had taken Mary's new dress to her, wrapped in tissue paper and tied with yellow satin ribbon. She had worked on it every day and she had made it of pale gold metal cloth, buying the stuff out of Mrs. Fontane's money. She had made it straight and smart. Mary's eyes had lighted to more warmth than had ever shone in them.

"It's lovely, Sue," she said. And without knowing at all why, Susan felt tears hot against her eyelids.

"Do you really like it?" She longed to hear Mary say it again. Perhaps someday she and Mary could grow close.

"I do, I love it," Mary said.

"Well, I should think so!" her mother said, sighing. "It's a handsome dress, Susan. I don't see how you got it all done."

And her father, pausing at the door, put in his head. "Good heavens!" he cried. "I'm not paying for it, I hope!"

"You ought to be ashamed of yourself," her mother said. "Susan made it."

"Did you, Sue?" he said. "You've made her look like a daffodil." His eyes were as mischievous as though there had never been tears in them.

"They liked it," she told Mark last night. "Mary looked pretty in it."

"Well, they ought to like it," Mark said. "It was beautiful. I don't know how you do it, Sue."

His voice was tender and his eyes humble as he looked at her, and she shrank a little.

44

"It was an easy pattern," she said, not knowing why she needed defense, except from his humility. She did not want Mark humble before her. No, no, for then it made her different from him. . . .

Up the street floated the sound of Lucile's baby girl crying. The baby cried so much. If she had a baby she wouldn't put it out and let it cry and cry. She turned suddenly and opened the door and walked quickly down the street. She could say she was just going to see Lucile. She ran silently up the steps and looked into the carriage. Why, the poor little thing was all twisted in the net! She put the net back and lifted the baby out and straightened her skirts. The cap strings were stiff organdy and cut the tiny chin and she loosened them. Then she sat hushing the baby softly, rocking back and forth. A huge blind tenderness rushed up in her as she felt the soft helpless body. Holding it like this in her arms, the small body curved again to the shape of the womb. This helplessness was too much—it was sad. How helplessly life began! She looked down into the small face. The baby had stopped crying now and was looking at her, her little mouth moving. If she modeled a baby face, how could she express what was there?—this naked helpless patience, this submissive patience, as though the newly born child already knew the eternal helplessness of its whole life, not only now but forever.

"Why, Susan!" Lucile's voice cried sharply. Lucile was at the door. "What on earth—"

"She was crying so," Susan said humbly.

"Well, of all—but she's supposed to be having a nap!"

"I'd finished my work, and I thought I would just run down—"

But Lucile was taking the baby away from her. She put her back into the baby carriage and pulled down the net. "Come in, do—the child will never go to sleep at this rate, and if she doesn't sleep she's cross all day."

45

In the bright sunlight Lucile's face looked hard and hostile.

"I'm sorry," Susan faltered. "She was crying so."

"Well, I don't see what business it is of yours, I must say, Sue."

"No," said Susan quickly, "no, of course, it wasn't any at all. . . . I won't come in this morning," she added. "You're not through yet."

"I never get through, with two children," Lucile said. "You might as well come in. By the time I get things cleaned up, it's time to feed the baby."

"No, I'll come this afternoon, maybe," said Susan. She smiled and turning at the foot of the steps waved her hand. Lucile was an old friend. She mustn't mind Lucile.

But when she reached her house she stood a moment uncertainly. That long deep look in the baby's eyes—it was a racial look. It was not the solitary look of one soul. It was a human look which the baby was not yet individual enough to combat. Later when she grew more into her own being her will would strengthen and hide this nakedness. But now her eyes were microscopes, magnifying and revealing the beginning of life.

She sat down on the top step of the little front porch and hugged her knees and stared into the garden, seeing none of it. She had already forgotten Lucile. She was remembering the child, feeling it, sinking her being into its immensity. And desire stirred in her, deep and blind, the intolerable, sweet, dark, solitary desire which she knew so well, which she could share with no one. She rose to her feet and she went slowly upstairs, past the bedroom door, up to the attic. She began mixing fresh clay and out of the clay she began to shape and mold a newborn child from whose minute unfinished features breathed an immense inexplicable helpless patience.

The house fell away from beneath her feet and the attic roof was gone from over her head. She remembered no one

46

and nothing. All the past months never were. The very years of her own life were lost. She was standing here making a child out of clay—out of clay shaping its life. She curved the clay into the shape of a new-born being, the bondage of the womb still upon its crouched back, its updrawn legs, its feeble entwined arms. Only the solemn head was large and free, lifted a little, looking out at unknown life with the awful patience. When it was finished she stared at it, half frightened. She did not know what she had made. She was afraid of it. This face, turned to her, was asking, "Why was I born?"

"I don't know," she answered aloud. Her voice echoed in the empty room and suddenly she felt the dusk about her. She looked out of the window and there beyond the wood she saw the dark sunset, too red. . . .

"I've worked all day," she thought, dazed, taking off her smock and smoothing her hair. Then she thought, "Mark will be coming home!" Mark! She had not once thought of him. But now, thinking of him, she felt the house was under her feet again, the roof over her head. She did not look at what she had made. She ran downstairs.

She felt, hurrying to get Mark's dinner, that she had been away for a long time. Up in the attic the thing she had made remained, a presence. It was there, a part of herself and yet separate from her. She felt exhausted, lonely, and yet content. She was suddenly impatient for Mark, hungry to feel his hand, his lips, to know he was there, solid and hearty, in the house, because she had been away from him so long. She flew about making ready for him. And when at last he came in and she heard his loud eager call, "Sue! Where are you?" she ran to him and flung herself upon him and held to him hard.

"Oh, Mark," she whispered, "oh, Mark—" What would she do if Mark did not come home at night?

"What a long day!" he said. "When I can't get home to lunch, it's awful!"

But for her the day had gone like a gust of wind. She thought, her face buried in his neck, "Today is a blank in our life." She had not lived it with him at all. She did not want to live a day without him. She must stay closely knit to him. She lifted her head impetuously. "Mark," she cried, "please, please, I want a baby!"

"Well, of all things!" said Mark, astounded. He stared at her, touched, smiling a little. "What a girl you are!" he said unsteadily. Then he laughed. "Anyway, let's wait until after supper!" he said.

"Grand supper," he said, and leaning back, he filled his pipe. "Let's go out on the porch."

They went out and found a new moon hanging over the wood, and they sat down in the light of it. He took one of the two new wicker chairs, but she sat on the top step and leaned her head against his knee. The moon was so sharply bright it dimmed the lights of the houses. He bent and turned her head suddenly so that the light of the moon fell full upon it.

"What made you cry out to me that you wanted a baby?" he asked abruptly.

She shook her head. "I don't know—perhaps Lucile's baby. I held her a little while today and she curled into my arm."

He smoothed back her hair. "Lucile has made me afraid to let you have one," he said. "Hal is so worried by the way she feels. He says both their children were accidents. Tommy came before Lucile was ready. They had decided not to until he could afford a maid. I can't—yet, you know, Susan. You've got to be sure—"

"I wouldn't let whether we had a maid or not decide what I want in my life," she said quietly. He did not answer but she could hear the deep puff of his pipe. His big steady hand smoothed her hair and touched her neck. They were very close, so close that she nearly said, "I modeled a little baby today, Mark—perhaps that—" But before she could say it he spoke.

"Sometimes I wonder why you married me," he said. The old hateful humility was thick in his voice.

"Mark!" She turned instantly. "I love you."

"I can't see why," he said wistfully. "I'm a very common sort of fellow."

"You're not!" she cried.

"Yes, I am," he said. "This street's full of fellows like me— Hal, Tom Page, Bob Shaplin—we're all off the same piece."

"Oh, don't," she said. "You're not a bit like them."

"We're all good honest hard-working fellows and we'll be nothing more when we die. I'll be just like my dad—worrying along in the same little house on the farm he and Mother began with, always expecting to be better off, but never being so. We're all the same. Hal said today as fast as he got a raise—"

"But if I love you? And I don't love Hal and Tom and Bob—"

"I don't see why you love me—you're different—you're not like Lucile and—"

"I'm not different! I'm just the same. I don't want to be different!"

"You can't help it."

"Oh, don't—don't—it makes me so lonely—"

She put her arms about his knees and held to him. No, now she would not tell him how the day had gone. She would never tell him.

"Let's have a little baby," she whispered. "I don't want anyone to help me. I don't have half enough to do. I want to be busy."

"Do you mean—now?" he asked. She could feel his hand trembling on her neck.

"Yes," she whispered, and held his hand on her throat with both of hers. She could feel her heart throbbing there against his palm. "Now—now—" she whispered.

He waited a few minutes. He bent over her, looking at her. She looked into his young angular face, all lines and planes in the moonlight. He did not speak, and she waited in his silence, a long time, turning her head away, gazing into the dark wood beyond. Then suddenly he rose and drew her to her feet, and his arm about her, they went into the house. Down the street they could hear somebody's radio singing, "For you'll tak' the high road, and I'll tak' the low road!" He shut the door and locked it and in silence they went upstairs.

She thought sometimes of that curved figure in the attic, its questioning head uplifted away from its womb-shaped body. But she put away the thought quickly. Once, remembering Mark's humility, she went upstairs determined to destroy it, to break it into bits and send it back to its first clay. But when she stood beside it she could not. It had become a creature. It had a life of its own which she could not destroy. It was strange to make an idea in her brain into a creature which could not be destroyed because it had life. She looked at it a long time, pondering on its face. And within her own body a shape was now being made as surely as her two hands had molded this clay. There was no understanding one more than the other. Here in the bare attic she could not even tell which was the greater creation. Could the child of her body be more sentinent than this creature out of her brain? She left it quickly, eager to be rid of it.

For now she wanted to be only body. She took joy in the quick leap of her body to creation. Immediately her body seized upon the seed of life which had been given it and at once she was with child. She was proud of this and she boasted to Mark one morning, "I've begun, Mark!"

"What!" he cried, "already! Why, I thought— I'll have to begin counting my cash."

They went over their money carefully that night. Mark had had a five-dollar-a-week raise—take that off, say, to pay the doctor. She sat by him, her chin on her hand, while he counted pennies.

"We can just do it," he said at last, lifting his head from the sheets of paper covered with small figures. "I'm glad of that. It would have worried me if we couldn't have paid the kid's bills by the time he was born. But are you sure fifty dollars will cover the clothes and things?"

She nodded. "Perfectly sure." She would see that it was enough. She would make everything herself, and spend no more.

"It would be easy enough for me to earn a little, somehow," she said.

"No," said Mark. "No, sir! I'm going to provide for my own child."

"Mine, too," she murmured.

"You know what I mean," Mark replied with sternness, and he gave her the paper.

"Those are your running rules," he said. "Within those limits you have complete freedom, my girl."

And the next morning, after she had the house looking back at her with its clean docile morning look, she sat down by the window and studied the figures closely. Fifty dollars—within those limits she had complete freedom. It would be rather fun to see what could be done, what fine stuffs bought, what materials made into delicate small shapes—it might be fun. But she had already wandered into special departments in stores and she knew that fifty dollars— "Our children will have to take what we have to give them," Mark had said last night, shutting his lips hard.

She sat alone this morning, looking into the deep green wood.

And what had she not to give? There was really no reason why she should not give all she had, too. Why should it be only Mark who gave to the uttermost? A woman gave more of her body, more of her time, than a man could. And why should she withhold what she could give in other ways? She could make the small sunny back bedroom a nursery, the furniture miniature and suited to his needs. There need be no makeshifts. It would not be fair to him, if she could make money and did not. She rose abruptly. Mark was limiting her and limiting the baby. He would have to see that—she would make him see it. . . . And after she had gazed for a long time into the wood, she went upstairs and changed into her green tweed suit, pulled a small brown hat over her head, and walked firmly and quickly to Mrs. Fontane's house and rang the bell.

"Mrs. Fontane, please," she said resolutely to the white-capped maid.

"Mrs. Fontane is in the garden, with guests." The maid was hesitating, but Mrs. Fontane had swept in through open French doors, her arms full of roses.

"Oh, why, here you are!" she exclaimed. "We were just talking about you. My dear, everybody is mad about my little Cupid! I'm going to show it to David Barnes the minute he gets here. Come out into the garden. Dora, put these into water!"

She felt Mrs. Fontane's arm thrust through her own, and she was swept along on Mrs. Fontane's warm voice, in which there was no doubt now of her Cupid, now that everybody was mad about it. "They all want Cupids, my dear!" Mrs. Fontane waved her other arm energetically at the women sitting indolently about the pool, their dresses splashes of blue and yellow and red against the hedge of dark evergreen behind them.

"She's here—the Cupid girl!" Mrs. Fontane called. And when she drew near they lifted kind, well-bred faces to her, and she shook slender soft ringed hands, and their voices said warmly, "I love that little boy looking at himself in the pool!" "You've made more than a Cupid!" "What will you make for me?"

"What do you want?" Susan asked abruptly. She would not tell Mark she had come here.

"She calls herself Mrs. Mark Keening," Mrs. Fontane was booming in her big voice, "but really she's Susan."

They took her at once, gaily, carelessly. "Oh, Susan, come and see my garden and make me something—a fountain, perhaps."

"Susan, do you do heads? I've an adorable child with a head like a young Christ!"

She promised them, drawn by their lovely warmth. "Yes, of course, I'll come and see your garden. I'd love to see your boy."

It became like a page from a story book, this garden, this soft September air, these pretty rich women. Why were the rich so warm, so kind? She thought of poor eager anxious little Mrs. Sanford. But Mrs. Fontane was saying, "She has an extraordinary gift—someday she's going to do something to surprise us."

She looked up, half frightened, to see Mrs. Fontane's assured kind smile.

"Oh, I don't—" she began.

"Yes, you will," Mrs. Fontane said positively, fanning herself with her hat. "Some day I'll point to that Cupid and tell everybody, 'Yes, that's an original early Susan Gaylord. She used to live here, you know. Her childhood home—' Oh, I have a rose thorn in my thumb!" She winced and put her thumb to her mouth.

"Let me," said Susan, and taking Mrs. Fontane's hand, she put her own thumb and finger delicately together and pulled out the thorn.

"Look at those hands of yours!" Mrs. Fontane said suddenly, seizing her hands and turning them over and over. "Ever see hands like those?"

They bent over her hands in breathless interest. Not even Mark had looked at her hands like this. "See those fingertips?" Mrs. Fontane demanded. "Broad and strong and still delicate as antennae! You can bend them any way." She bent Susan's forefinger backward like a spring. Susan sat looking at her own hands as though they did not belong to her. Was there indeed something in her hands? Mrs. Fontane laid them on Susan's lap gently, with a pat.

"When you brought me that Cupid I knew what you were," she said firmly. "I don't mind saying I was afraid at first you would do me something impossible—talented daughter of a local citizen, you know. But when you brought the Cupid I knew it didn't matter in the least where you were born or who your parents were or whom you married or anything. Some day—"

"I wouldn't think of leaving this town," Susan said quickly. "It's my home—my friends, my family—I couldn't think of living anywhere else."

Mrs. Fontane smiled and yawned. "You're a child, Susan Gaylord," she remarked. "Oh, dear, I'm sleepy. I wish you'd all go home! Susan, take them away and see what they want."

They were all laughing at once. Two of the women were quarreling good-naturedly over her. "Come to my garden first, Susan."

"No, now, Diana, you know Michael's got to begin school in a fortnight."

"I'm sure I can do them both," said Susan. "I work very fast once I see my shape."

"Well, then, Michael first, and then my garden."

She was put into a car and driven away, Mrs. Fontane murmuring, "You've begun, Susan. God knows where you'll end."

And they drove miles into the country to stop before a huge white house, the kernel of which had once belonged to a mortgage-ridden farmer, and she stood in an ivory panelled hall and went into a long chintz-curtained room where a big curly-headed blond boy of fourteen or fifteen was slouched in a chair over a book.

"Michael!" his mother cried, and he thrust out his head.

"What?" he said. His voice was surly but his head was an angel's.

"There!" his mother cried. "Do you blame me for wanting it in stone or bronze or something?"

"No," said Susan. The old frightening beautiful desire was rushing up in her like water from a sealed fountain, opening. "No, it's beautiful."

"Shut up, you," the boy muttered over his book.

"Shut up yourself," said Susan. "Let me see your head. Your mother wants me to make it and I will."

"I won't have it," said the boy. "I get so sick— *She* talks like that at school even—before the fellows. I won't have my head made."

"You can't help it," said Susan, laughing. "I'm going to do it. And I'll show you exactly how I do it. It's fun. You can mix some clay, too, if you like. I shall do it in clay and then in bronze. It ought to be bronze," she said to his mother.

The two women stood by. She felt their quick admiration and was made strong by it.

"Come to my house this afternoon," she said to Michael. "At two o'clock. We'll work in my attic, you and I together."

He looked at her doubtfully. "I'll ride over on my horse," he said.

"All right," she said, and turned away from him. "Now where's the garden?"

"You do know how to manage him," his mother whispered. "You've no idea how difficult Michael is! I'm always glad

55

when he goes back to school. Goodbye, Susan. When am I to see the head?"

"A week," said Susan, "—in clay, that is."

"And, oh, dear, I almost forgot. How much will it be?"

Susan breathed deeply and leaped off. "Two hundred dollars," she said firmly.

Michael's mother looked at her a second, and then said quickly, "Two hundred—very well, Miss Gaylord."

It was impossible to tell whether she thought it much or little. It did not matter, Susan decided, in the garden.

"You see," Mrs. Vanderwelt's light hard voice was saying, "the shrubbery makes a natural arch there, so that a fountain would be quite nice."

"Yes," said Susan, and stared at the arch. A fountain—she'd always had ideas about water and stone. The things people bought and called fountains were so ugly. Water should be used as part of the whole, not as a thing in itself. "Will you let me think about it?" she said. "I want to make a picture of stone and water, not just a fountain."

"Will you?" said Mrs. Vanderwelt. "That sounds fascinating. And how much do you think—"

"I haven't any idea until I have my picture," said Susan. "If you care to set a limit—"

"Well—shall we say five hundred dollars?"

"All right," said Susan. "I'll remember that."

She was driven back alone, and when they reached the steps of her little house, the colored chauffeur opened the door and she got out and walked up her own steps into her own house.

In the living room where she had sat a few hours before she now sat down again, her hat still on her head. On the table was the sheet of Mark's figures. Fifty dollars he had written, and in brackets he had put "(Susan's limit)." She had gone out this morning and made seven hundred dollars. At least she could soon make seven hundred dollars. But it was not that which now frightened her. It was something else, more large, more limitless, than money could ever be. The frail walls of this house, Mark's house, which he worked so hard to keep around her—she had pushed them away from her this morning. She had gone beyond them. This room looked small as a closet after the big room where Michael had sat. Ah, but she loved this room! She and Mark had made it to live in together. She got up resolutely. There was no reason why she shouldn't say to Mark quite plainly, "Darling, since there is something I can do, why shouldn't I do it?" And then she'd tell him about the money.

In the kitchen she pondered over bread and milk and an apple for lunch. It was not the money—yes, it was the money—that made it hard to tell Mark. Well, then, if it was only money, it was nothing. No, but it was more than money—much more. And then, alone in the quiet house, everything went away from her except a boy's head, except an arch in dark shrubbery. She forgot even that she wanted money for her child. Water and stone—what could they do together against the stern green of old yews, druidical even in a rich woman's garden? She took the kitchen pad and pencil and began to sketch. The doorbell rang sharply across her dreaming, and she hastened to the door. Michael stood there, slender and tall, against a background of a brown horse, held by a groom.

"I didn't come except to see your clay and stuff," he said belligerently. "Where's the attic?"

"At the top of the house, of course," she replied, and led him upstairs.

Was he going to be a difficult boy? She opened the door of the attic to him doubtfully. He stood looking about.

"There's nothing here," he said.

"You and I and the clay," she returned. "What more do you want?"

She rolled up her sleeves and put on her smock and turned her back and began to mix the clay.

"That's a queer baby," she heard him say.

"It's only just born," she replied.

He did not speak. When she turned, he had lifted the cloth from Mark's unfinished head.

"Why did you make a dead man?" he asked, his voice full of horror.

"He's not dead," she said quickly, "only not finished."

"Don't you ever finish anything?" he asked, still staring.

"Of course," she said. "I'm going to finish you. Come— here's the clay."

He covered the head and came over to her and looked at the mass she had mixed upon the table.

"I don't like getting my hands mucky," he said.

"Then you'll have to do something else," she said, "this is mucky work."

"I could draw," he suggested. "I draw a great deal."

"What?"

"Well, horses mostly."

She wiped her hands and rummaged among her things and found drawing paper and pastels and tacks. She put the paper up on the wall by the window and handed him the crayons.

"You can stand there and draw your own horse," she said.

He took the crayons and began without a word to draw. And she, seeing how the light fell upon his young head, began quickly to mold and shape her stuff into its likeness.

It was a difficult likeness to catch, full of fleeting tender angles and unexpected childish turns. The cheeks were childishly round, but the mouth was wilful and hard, the mouth of a young man, for all its soft full lips. He did not once look at her, and she worked in silence for nearly an hour. Then he threw down the crayons.

"I've done enough," he said. "I'll finish tomorrow."

58

She stopped and came to him.

"Why, you have only drawn the woods," she exclaimed. "I thought you were drawing your horse."

"I shall be galloping into the woods on my horse," he explained, "so I drew the woods first, under that bright cloud, because tomorrow the brightness will be gone. And besides I shall be very small, in front."

He had drawn the mass of the wood, dark against the bright sky.

"It's good," she said, "it's really very good."

He accepted the praise without answer, and went over to the head.

He asked, "Is that me?"

"It will be," she said. "Do you like it?"

He shook his head. "It looks mucky. But I don't know how I look. I want to go now. I'll come back tomorrow and finish the horse."

"I'll expect you," she said. He was gone. She caught one more flashing line of profile and pressed it firmly into the clay. Then she wiped her hands and went to the window. He had mounted his horse and was riding away. She looked at his drawing again. It was surprising how well he had caught the shadows of the wood against the evening sky.

It was hard to say to Mark, brightly, as she had planned, "Mark, I've made some money today." Any other woman she knew would have shouted it to her husband. Lucile, winning two dollars at bridge, always boasted, "Hal will be tickled pink—I've won nearly twelve dollars this month—almost enough to pay for the girl who comes in to stay with the brats while I'm away." But she had made too much, too easily. Mark would ask, "How much is it?" And then when she told him, the dark dead look she dreaded would come into his eyes and he would say, "It's more than I can make in three months

—maybe, four." She was ashamed to be able to do more than he could do. She could not bear to abase him. And there was that thing beyond money which she could not tell him because she did not know how, that desire, the strongest she knew, that need, that solitary fulfilment which separated her from him, she did not understand how, except that then she was alone and wanted to be alone, because she needed no one, not even him. She could not tell him that. She could tell him about the money but not about that.

In the kitchen, moving swiftly from stove to table to closet, she prepared the dinner that would please him. But it occupied only a part of her brain, it was only play for her hands. Even her hands were not working as they worked when she was modeling. Above the small business of chicken pie made from yesterday's cold chicken, above an aspic salad and a dessert her mind went on pondering, reasoning. It was no good refusing any more to face the sort of woman she was and the sort of woman she wanted to be for Mark. Mark must be happy first, but how could she keep him happy, being what she was? There were the brackets he had made, "(Susan's limit)."

She stared out into the sky above the wood outside the kitchen window. The sunset was gone, but the sky was glowing dark, and there hung the evening star, enormous in its nearness. It hung there, large, still, solitary and full of meaning. She suddenly felt quite alone with herself and yet she was not lonely. She looked about the kitchen and it was strange to her for a moment—a transient place, as though any day she might go out of it. She pulled it about her quickly.

"I must tell Mark everything," she decided quickly. "Mark must know everything about me. It's the only safety." Then she thought, "But why is it I don't feel safe?" She drew down the shade sharply and shut out the one star and the sky. She shut herself into the kitchen. And then Mark at the door said, "Do I smell something burning or not?"

And she ran to the stove and drew out the pie. One edge was crisping brown.

"You came just in time," she cried. "Oh, Mark!" She put down the pie and ran into his arms.

He was so kind and so good. Why had she thought it would be hard to tell him?

"Promise—promise you won't be hurt if I tell you something," she begged him after dinner. It was almost too cold now to sit on the porch in the darkness, but he had wrapped his old tweed coat about her, and pulled a sweater over his head. "The stars are all out now," he said. "When I came home there was only one big one over the woods. Come on out for one more night. Winter will be here soon enough." And then he said, "Do you think you could tell me anything that would hurt me?" And she said, kneeling before him, looking into his face, dim in the starlight, "I can hurt you more than anyone else, and you can hurt me as no one can, because we love each other." He stared back at her, and she could not see his eyes, but only the planes of his cheek and his chin and forehead, his dark brows, the line of his nose and his mouth.

"What is it?" he asked.

"Will you promise?"

"You can't hurt me because I know you."

"Ah, promise!"

"All right, but I don't have to— Come here and sit on my knee."

So she sat on his knee and felt his arm strongly around her.

"Mark, I thought over last night—and I still feel I want to do my share—do what I can, that is—and I thought of my modeling, so I went to see Mrs. Fontane, and luckily she had some friends there and they gave me two jobs."

"Here—sit up a minute," he said. "I want to light my pipe."

"The Cupid really looks lovely, Mark," she said, sitting

upright. The match flared out, he drew hard once or twice, and pulled her back.

"Well?" he said.

"I'm to do a head for one of them, and a fountain for another."

"Summer people?" he asked.

"Yes," she said.

"How much?"

"Mark—please don't mind—seven hundred."

"Seven hundred!" he cried. "Why, Sue—"

She put her hand on his mouth. "Don't say it—it doesn't matter. Oh, Mark, let me please make a nursery out of the back bedroom and get a really good carriage and a crib! Why not, if I can?"

He pressed her hand against his lips, kissed it, and took it away and put his pipe in his mouth. She leaned back, her heart lightened. He was not going to be angry. Why had she thought it would be hard?

"This rather brings something to a head that's been in my own mind, Sue," he said. He knocked the ash out of his pipe and put it down carefully on the porch.

"You promised you wouldn't mind," she said quickly.

"It's not a case of minding," he said, "it's a case of what's fair to you, darling Sue. I want to be fair to you and I don't know how."

"Only stay as you are to me, Mark," she begged him. "I love our life."

But he seemed not to hear her. He had his arms about her tightly.

"I want you to do what you want," he said in a whisper. "Go on and fix up your attic. That's what you really want to do. I've seen it all along."

She sat up, struggling out of his arms.

"But I don't want to fix up the attic," she said, astonished.

62

"I want the things for the baby, not for myself. I don't know what you mean."

"Now you are hurt—it's you who's hurt!" he cried. "But all I want to say is I don't want you to think that because you've married me that you can't do what you want. I mean, if you have things you want to do, things I don't know how to do, go on and do them."

"Why, Mark—" she began, and stopped.

"I don't feel I'm satisfying you," he murmured, his voice miserable.

"Oh, darling, darling, darling!" she cried, and reached for him in the darkness.

"I know you're different," he muttered into her breast, "I've always known you were different. What right have I—"

"Hush," she whispered, "don't—it's like sending me away to say such things. I'll never touch my hand to clay again or to a brush."

"Yes, you will!" He lifted his head. "Now, see here, Sue—that's not fair. I've just been telling you—"

"You've been saying one thing and feeling another. You're hurt to the bone about something, but I don't know what it is. I've got to find out what it is and stop doing it. Is it the money?"

"No," he said hotly. She was standing beside him now, her hand on his shoulder. "At least, it isn't only money—"

"Would you rather I didn't use any of the money on the baby?" she persisted. "Mark, I've got to know the truth."

"Well," he said doggedly out of the darkness, "a man would rather provide for his family himself. It makes him out a poor fish if he can't buy necessities for his own baby. But—"

"I'll stay in my limit, then," she said resolutely.

"Oh, there's no use my feeling so," he broke in. "Besides, I don't know that it's that—I don't know what it is—I can't tell how I feel."

"If you can't tell, how am I to know?" she asked.

He did not answer. A long moment hung between them, silent and full of terror. Then he began speaking again, quietly and quite himself.

"Look here, Sue, my darling heart, I'll have to find out how I feel. And I haven't any right to say I won't let you do things for the baby because I can't. Let's go fifty-fifty. I'll swing my half of it—" He was feeling for her hand.

"Will you tell me if you don't like even that?"

"Promise," he said, pressing her head down to his shoulder.

"It's not to last a moment if you don't," she said. "You're more to me than anything."

He was feeling for his pipe again.

"I'm not at all sure it's the money," he said. "Sit up while I light my match."

"Then what?" she said, sitting up.

"Darned if I know," he answered. "Here, lie back—I want you close."

But lying in his arm again, she could not give herself up to him.

"I must find out for myself," she thought. But she said nothing, and Mark did not speak, and she was lonely in his arms. There was no moon now. It had set. Light after light in the houses along the street went out, and the night grew dark. But darker than the night was the blackness of the wood under the stars.

"Let's go upstairs," she said, restlessly. "I'm tired, I think."

"You mustn't be tired," he said gently. "It's not like you to say that you're tired."

She did not answer. She let him half carry, half lead her to bed. She wanted to lean on him tonight in any way she could. She let him help her to undress, he drew her tub for her, and when she was in her nightgown he brushed her long hair. She did not often let him brush her hair, though she knew he loved to do it, because she did it so deftly and easily herself. His slow big hands irritated her and without knowing it his clumsiness pulled at her too delicate skin. But tonight she let him. And he was trembling and passionate.

"It's such lovely stuff," he whispered. He buried his face suddenly in her hair. "It's such lovely, lovely stuff!" And after a moment he murmured, "I don't believe even now I know what color it is—brown, chestnut, gold—it's everything." He drew her to him, and she was still lonely, though not alone. Perhaps because she never felt alone with Mark any more she felt the more lonely, the more apart from him, as though she were busy in something which he could not share.

Yes, she and Mark seemed never quite alone any more, and least alone in those times when they had been most deeply together before. Perhaps, she thought in the night, it was knowing that the child was growing, shaping, taking on his separate being hour by hour. This child must share even their passion, so that she grew shy of passion and somehow shy of Mark.

"It's the child," she murmured, drawing away from him.

"You must never do what you don't want to do," he said, and allowed her to draw away.

So there was no way of knowing what it was that changed between them. There was nothing to do but go on living every day and finishing what she had promised. She finished Michael's head, working slowly and with more care than she had yet used on anything she had made.

He came now quite naturally to the attic and went leaping up the stairs without calling her. When she got there he would have tacked up a fresh piece of drawing paper, and with no more than a "hello" he would be laying on his colors. He never touched the clay, and each picture he made was different from the others. The first one still hung tacked to the wall by the window. He had worked on it for three days in intense silence, and he had made the wood large and dark and looming, and in

65

the foreground was the horse galloping toward it, and himself the rider, hair flying, face lifted, body strained to the wood. Horse and rider were very small, but he had caught them in speed. He had done nothing else with so much finish. Everything else he had drawn largely and with uncertainty, not knowing exactly what he wanted to do. And she did not once ask him, "What are you making?" She left him alone, and worked in her own silence, absorbed in his face.

Then he went away to school and she worked a few days from memory, finishing the head. Once or twice his face slipped from her mind and she could not remember it at all. She went then and looked at his drawings, pondering them, not understanding them or trying to understand them, and his face came back. So she finished, and his mother came to see what she had done before she sent it away to be cast. She stood before it, staring at it from under her wide hat.

"It looks exactly like him," she said at last, "only—I can't think what he's doing exactly. It's a look I don't understand. What's he doing, Susan?"

"He's riding toward the dark woods," Susan said.

"How odd!" his mother murmured.

Susan did not answer. She covered the head with its cloth.

But when she was alone again, she went back and lifted it. She stood looking at it a long time, not thinking so much as allowing feelings to rise in her like mists, to swell and melt and swell and sweep her along. And then, in the silence, she heard Michael's voice crying quite clearly from the lips of clay, and even though she heard only sound and no words, it was enough. She knew it was finished and well. And yet, listening, she felt suddenly afraid and separate from everyone—from Mark. She turned and ran downstairs, and going to her desk, she sat down and wrote to Mrs. Vanderwelt that she could not now make the fountain for her shrubbery. It was best if what she had to give the baby more nearly matched what Mark could give.

66

When she had written and sealed the letter, she sat thinking, and she put away the things she had planned for the child. It was not so important for him to have things as it was to have beneath his life the love between his parents unmarred. Love was a strange thing, sensitive to every change and situation. She had once dreamed of love as robust as life itself, enduring as time. But now she knew it must be sheltered and nurtured and guarded. Two people who loved each other were never quite free and natural with each other. They had always to be careful of their love not to hurt it or make it less. Love was so fragile, so easily, irreparably damaged and in such intangible ways. Now that Michael was gone she would not go any more to the attic.

She had indeed spent more time than she should have upon the perfecting of the head. Since she had decided against more money, she needed time to make instead of buying what she wanted. As the autumn closed down into winter she bought materials and began to sew and she bought skeins of clear blue wools and began to knit. Her mother brought over a suitcase full of old baby things, yellowed and clean, and one day Mark's silent mother took her into Mark's small old empty bedroom of the farmhouse where he had been born and opened a drawer and said, "If you need them—"

But Mark was an only child, and Susan saw his mother's eyes clinging to the few garments left of that one babyhood, and she said, "I shan't need them, dear. Keep them safe."

"I want to help you," Mark's mother said.

"If I need help, I will remember that," Susan replied quietly.

Mark's large-boned, almost speechless mother never left her own house, so Susan said to Mark often, "Shouldn't you go and see your mother?" For Mark had grown away from these two old people in a sort of anger at their unchanging clinging to what had always been. "They're so proud of you—go and

67

see them, Mark," she urged him, and he said with impatience, "I go there and it's always the same. They have nothing to say to me nor I to them."

Looking now at the large bare head of Mark's mother, she thought, "It would be a wonderful portrait in stone—rocky skull, deep eyes, wide mouth." Then she put the thought away. She was not going into the attic again, not for a long time, perhaps never.

"Why don't you go to see your parents more often?" she asked Mark one night.

"What did they ever do for me?" he asked. "I've done everything for myself."

"They gave you life," she said.

"Bare life's not much," he retorted. . . .

Bare life, she thought, remembering Mark's mother—it was all she had been able to give and Mark did not think it enough. But still it was the most precious thing a woman could give. . . . If it was all a woman had to give, it was the most precious thing.

She gave birth to John in the narrow cell of a hospital room. The doctor laughed at her.

"You're as expert at this as the mother of ten!"

She knew this was not true. But she had made up her mind, walking about the cell restlessly, waiting for him to be born, that she would not scream or cry aloud. In another room a woman was screaming, "Oh, am I going to die? I'm afraid I'm going to die!" She wanted the child, she had made him, and he was about to be born. She heard that silly screaming and kept her lips shut when the last moment came.

"How are you, sweet?" Mark's white face was at the door.

"Splendid," she answered shortly, her eyes shining with pain, her hands wet. She passed through the next hour in silence.

68

"Why, you practically had no pain, Mrs. Keening!" the nurse said.

"Silly fool!" Susan thought.

She was lying back now. John was born. She was still swimming in pain. The nurse had for a moment held up a dark-headed little thing wrapped in a blanket. No one knew what pain she had had. She was drenched in pain. But she was glad she had not cried out.

Mark, tiptoeing in to kiss her, whispered, "The doctor said he'd never seen such an easy birth."

She smiled, not able to speak. Only now was the pain ebbing, leaving her body weak and washed upon the shore. She slept almost without waking day and night for two weeks and woke at last, as drained by sleep as by pain, to return to her own house. Before she left she had locked the attic door, and when she went back, she did not unlock it.

John's room was the heart of this house, although it was empty except for his crib, a table, a chair.

But after a while she grew used to the bare room, and forgot it in discovering the child, John. She had never lived with a tiny child before, and now she found that he was a person from the beginning. She could never ponder this enough, how in giving a shape one gave also being. She could perceive in him not the slightest likeness to herself or to Mark, or indeed to anyone. He had gone back into the unknown past and drawn from among those long dead a square compact frame, square short-fingered hands, a round head and very bright hazel eyes, and a mouth so smiling and composed that she laughed at its wisdom in this baby face. Once, sitting with John on her lap, she remembered the child of clay in the attic, and she was compelled to go and see it again. She would look at nothing else, and she would come away quickly. She went, and staring

69

at it, she saw the clay had cracked a little in drying and over its face were small fine wrinkles which gave it a strange premature age. But its head was still lifted in the old question, "Why was I born?" She covered it quickly and went downstairs.

But as he grew John turned to Mark more than to her. All day she tended him and took care of him, but he never leaped to her arms as he soon did to Mark. And Mark doted on him. Now when he came home he did not, as he always used to do, go to find Susan. He went straight to the nursery, and sometimes the sound of laughter was the sound by which she knew he had come home. There was something close and warm between the two of them, and often, hearing their laughter, she did not go in, but went on with her work in the kitchen. At such times she paused and looked out of the window and the walls of the kitchen fell away from her and she seemed to be plodding alone through the wood yonder. She had been more lonely rather than less since John was born. It was as though she had finished something and begun nothing else. The days went on in a routine of work for her hands and her brain waited.

"I've been neglecting my friends," she told Mark one night at the table. "I'm feeling a little out of things. I'm going to have a party, Mark."

"Swell," he said. "It's an age since you saw anybody. Sure you feel able?"

"I feel stronger than ever," she said.

It was quite true that she was restless with some energy which even John's coming did not use. Her mother said mournfully, "Don't overdo, Susan. It's time you had help."

"Oh, John's so good he takes almost no time at all," she said impatiently.

And her father stopped in one day. She heard his stick pounding the hall floor and when she hastened out, there he stood, his cap over one ear.

"Sold a poem," he said. "I got twenty dollars for it. Your mother says you're overworked." He was fumbling in his pocket.

"Oh, my goodness," cried Susan, "do I look overworked? I feel I haven't half enough to do. Look at me!"

He looked at her and grinned. "You look about as overworked as the Statue of Liberty," he said. "Well, then, why don't you come and play for me again?"

"There's John," she said.

"Bring him along," he replied. "Why not? It'll do him good—let him hear some music."

"I will," she said, after a moment. "Why not?"

And she fetched the child and took him with her, and in his own attic her father made a nest of pillows for him on the cot.

"There—you can forget him," he said. "Now for the music."

And playing, she forgot him in the music.

But the music only increased the restless loneliness in her. "Perhaps I do need people," she thought. "I must have a party."

"Are you all right?" her father asked abruptly when she closed the piano. "Happy, and all that?"

"Oh yes," she said, smiling. "Why not? I have everything—Mark's doing awfully well—he sold the Grainger place the other day—to a sculptor—isn't that interesting?"

"Everything's not always enough," her father said.

"Susan, Susan!" her mother called up the stairs. "Are you coming down?"

"Yes, yes!" she called back, and picked up sleeping John.

Downstairs in the bedroom, her mother sat with him on her knee, rocking him. He slept easily and deeply.

"You're lucky he's so healthy," her mother whispered. And then she said in the same breathy whisper, "I'm glad you have him. A married couple needs something else after a year or two, 'specially the woman does. At first you're all wrapped up in each other and getting started, but then when your house is all settled and the man's coming and going regularly, you feel the need of something more." She paused awkwardly. "—That is, I suppose you and Mark are like everybody else."

"I don't know," said Susan, and then she said, "We're very happy."

"You should be," her mother said. "I know Mark's people are plain, but they're solid. I think that kind of man makes the best husband. I always felt your father would have been happier if his father hadn't been a professional musician. It's made him unsettled in his mind all his life, and that hasn't been easy for me."

"What was grandfather really like?" asked Susan. She remembered in her childhood an angry voice, a huge white tangled head, and darting, incessantly moving hands.

"I've about forgotten," said her mother. "He died years ago. I never cared for him and he didn't like me. I never understood what he said. He always talked so you didn't know what he meant. I like things to be plain."

Upon her knee John opened his eyes and smiled amiably at them both. They laughed back at him, forgetting their talk, for the moment agreed in him. Then her mother sighed.

"It's no time till they're grown. . . . Susan, Mary will have it that we send her to some other college, though she knows her tuition won't cost her anything here with her father a professor. She's so much harder to manage than you were."

"She doesn't know what she wants," said Susan, "and that's always hard. Let her go, Mother."

"Well," said her mother, doubtfully, "I don't know if we can manage it. She's so silly in why she wants to go."

"Why?"

"Why, she says she doesn't want to go to the same place you

72

did and feel she has to keep up to what you did and be class president and valedictorian and all."

"She doesn't have to—"

"Of course, I told her so. But she says she wants to go where nobody knows her."

"She'd better go, then." Susan picked up her baby. "I must go home. Mark will be waiting."

"You think we'd better let her go?" Her mother followed her to the door.

"I certainly do," Susan returned. That deep foolish ache in her deepened a little, causelessly. For of course it was foolish to be angry with Mary because she wanted to be free of her older sister.

The next day she called them up one by one, her old friends, to come to her house.

"I haven't seen you all for ages," she cried into the telephone. "I miss you—I'm lonesome for you. Besides, John's practically grown up!"

For a day her home was full of speed and business. She hurried with John and she flew about her kitchen, singing.

"It's fun being so busy," she cried to Mark joyously at lunch. "I believe I don't have half enough to do!" But she had taken time to make his favorite lunch and he ate it with pleasure.

"I expected nothing but scraps today," he said.

"It doesn't take half an hour," she said, "and it's all fun."

She had left until the afternoon the pleasure of flowers in vases, and to this she gave herself with pains, making of each a small perfect picture. Then she dressed herself, and lastly upon John she put a pair of minute blue linen rompers. And at three o'clock she held him in the crook of her arm and opened the door to her friends, and they came in and the quiet house was full of talk and laughter, and little sudden

73

screams of joy and surprise. It was the height of this one day, her friends, filling her house full.

"Have a good time?" Mark asked, picking up a sandwich and munching it. Everyone was gone and the house had returned to its stillness.

"John was awfully good," she said busily over the dishes. The house had been so noisy with their voices that now the silence seemed dead.

Mark took up a dish towel and began wiping the plates as she washed, rapidly and deftly.

She paused and then turned to him, her hands still in suds.

"I have the queerest feeling that they didn't really like me," she said in a low voice.

"Why, girl!" he cried, and came to take her in his arms. But she shook her head.

"No, Mark, don't—my hands are all soapy. Besides, I can't think why."

He began wiping again. "Did they say anything?"

"No—no—they admired everything—they loved the sandwiches and cake—we had wonderful bridge—" She paused, pondering. "I kept feeling all the time that they didn't like it because I'd—managed—alone—with John, and all."

"Forget them," said Mark sharply. "They feel guilty. Most women are a lazy lot—yelling for help whenever they have a little work to do."

"Lucile said a strange thing. She said, 'Girls, I think we ought to boycott Susan because she's making labor conditions harder for the rest of us. She's a scab.' Of course she laughed when she said it. They all laughed."

"Forget it, I say," Mark repeated. "Say, Susan, maybe we won't stay here all our lives. Sometimes I think it's better to get away from your home town where everybody knows everything."

74

But she went on. "I told Lucile, 'You have two, Lucile. I'm sure when I have two, I'll need help.' But I don't think I shall, Mark. I want to be busy—busy—I don't have half enough to do."

"Forget it," said Mark. "You suit me." He came over to her and took her in his arms and she felt his body against hers, solid and good, and she was grateful.

After all, she had Mark and John. She expected too much of people like Lucile. She would be content with what she had, with Mark and John. For the moment she was a little less lonely. Perhaps if she drew the walls closely enough about her, if she made her house big enough only for these, she would not be lonely. It was dreaming that made people lonely.

Then one day the doorbell rang and when she went to it there stood Michael in riding breeches and a blue shirt, inches taller and broader.

"Hello," he said gently, and smiled.

"Why, Michael!" she cried.

"I saw that head of me you did and I decided to look you up," he said. "It's better than ever. What else have you done?"

"Nothing," said Susan, "unless you call a baby something."

But he had walked past her and was going straight upstairs to the attic.

"You mean that unfinished child I saw once? I've never forgotten it."

"No, I mean a real one," she said.

"Oh, that," he said carelessly. He was at the attic door, shaking it. "Why, it's locked!" he cried impatiently.

"I keep it locked," she answered.

"Open it," he said, and she opened it and they went in together and he looked at his own drawings which she had left upon the walls just as he had put them.

"Those old things," he said. "They weren't so bad for a kid,

75

were they? Do you know, I believe it was working here with you that showed me I really wanted to paint."

"Have you gone on?" she asked eagerly.

He nodded. "I've had lessons ever since. I shan't go to college—it's a waste of time for me to do anything but paint. I'm going to Paris. But I shan't do any French stuff. I only want to learn how to use paint. Then I'm coming back to paint —gosh, the things I see every day to paint! You know, hardly anybody's painted America. That woods is not bad, is it? I might paint you, you know." He was so at ease, so sure, so full of energy that she felt small and left behind. "Now what have you done, seriously?" he insisted.

"I tell you, nothing!" she replied brightly, hardily.

"Not a thing?"

"Not one thing!" she said. She did not now mention John because she did not think of him. It seemed to her she had been completely idle.

He stared at her, his blue eyes accusing. "You ought to be ashamed," he said at last. He went and looked at the figure of the child, and then at Mark's head.

"Just as they were," he murmured, "unfinished."

"Unfinished," she repeated.

"And you," he said, turning on her, "you're happy, you're satisfied to have done nothing at all?"

He was staring at her, piercing her, his long young forefinger stabbing at her, and she could not lie to him.

"Not quite," she said faintly. And then, as though he were a grown man, she began humbly, "The circumstances of my life—"

But he was not listening. He was not interested in the circumstances of her life. He began to talk as though she were not talking.

"There's a man—David Barnes, the sculptor—who's taken a house near here—the old Grainger place—and last night he was at our house for dinner. He saw that head you did, and he just shouted when he saw it, 'Who did that?' And when Mother told him, he said, 'Tell her to come and see me.' "

"Oh, Michael—did he really?"

"Yes. Partly that's why I looked you up today. Will you go?"

"I don't know."

She was looking at his picture, the wood dark against the sky, the small figure on a horse rushing toward it dangerously.

"Yes, you will."

"Will I? I don't promise."

"You'll go tomorrow."

"I don't know."

"You'll be sorry to the end of your life if you don't."

She turned to deny it, but she could say nothing at all. Her eyes were full of tears and her heart was dismayed with feeling she could not understand.

"Goodbye," said Michael gently. "I shall call up Dave Barnes tonight and tell him you'll be there tomorrow at three. You know David Barnes— He made that enormous statue last year which won the Chicago prize—early Titan, he called it."

Then Michael was gone and she stood in the attic alone, lost in a yearning so huge, so deep, that nothing she had ever known was like it.

"I can't leave John and I can't take him," she thought, but underneath she was planning quickly. "I could ask Mother to come and sit with him a little while. Then, if I have to, I can make arrangements later for someone regularly—"

She went downstairs, bathed and fed John, and made the dinner carefully. And when Mark came she said nothing at all to him of what she knew now she would certainly do.

She pulled on her gloves quickly at the door of the living room, glancing about it. Everything was in order. Upstairs

77

John was asleep. Her mother sat in the big chair, her shoes off, her feet on a footstool, a magazine in her hands over which her eyes roved.

Susan said, "If he wakes before I get back he can have some orange juice and a piece of toast. But I'll be back soon."

"Shall I do anything for your supper?" her mother asked, staring at the picture of a lurid salad.

"Everything's ready to put on the stove. I'll be back long before then."

"All right," her mother said, and she turned the pages to a story and her face grew vacant as she began to read.

Susan closed the door behind her and went out into the bright spring afternoon, and walked down the street to the bus stop. She would ask the driver to drop her as nearly as he could to the gate of the Grainger place. And then she would go up the path under the drooping old hemlocks, and then, and then—she had no imagination of what would happen. But she would go into the house where a great sculptor did his work, and she would hear him talk of what he did and she could ask him all the questions for which she had no answer alone, and whom no one she had ever met or known could answer. All her life she had been like someone wandering in a dark wood alone, and now she was coming into light. She was going to learn, to know how, to make what she saw to make.

But when she stepped down before the Grainger gateway she stepped upon other ground. And she was afraid. What was she beginning, and what would be the end? She might have turned and climbed the steps of the bus again had it not roared on in a cloud of dust. She might have turned and walked away if she had not lain awake those hours last night, imagining this moment, dreaming of it, still forbidding it to herself, although she knew it would come because she wanted it too much to refuse it to herself.

"What's the matter?" Mark had asked out of his sleep when

she turned on the light, not able to bear the reality of her dreaming. She had to make sure of the room, of her bed and chest of drawers.

"Nothing," she said, and put out the light.

She walked now, as she had dreamed, straight through the gate, between crumbling red brick pillars, up a wide winding sanded path to the columns of the old colonial house. She mounted the steps to the door and rang the bell. Nothing yet had been done to stay the decay. The steps were loose, and the floor boards warped beneath her feet. But her dream stopped at the door. She had no dream of what was beyond it. He would be perhaps tall, rugged, large, like his own work, a sort of Titan, creating Titans.

But the door was jerked open and a small man with a heavy black beard stood there. He was inches smaller than she was, and his figure was paunchy, his shoulders round. She saw in the same flash his hands, square and strong as a miner's hands, grimed at the nails.

"What do you want?" he said.

"I am Susan Gaylord," she said. "Michael sent me."

He stared out under bushy black eyebrows, under rough black hair. He was as hairy as a gorilla.

"You're that girl," he said. "Come in. That was a good head, abominably cast. You could have cast it better yourself."

"I don't know very much," she said, ashamed. "I got the name of that place out of a sculptor's handbook I saw advertised somewhere."

He did not answer, and she followed him into what had once been the great room of the old Grainger house. It was full of crates and boxes and figures half unpacked.

"Sit down," he said, and she sat down on a crate, seeing nothing.

"Well, what do you want?" he asked abruptly.

"I don't know," said Susan. "I'm not sure I want anything."

He rubbed his broad flat nose with a thick forefinger.

"You'd better stay here and look around until you do know," he said, irritated. "I'll be back after a while. If you're not here I'll take it you don't want anything of me."

He rolled off the crate where he was sitting and walked out of the room as clumsily as a sailor, and she was left alone. But after a little while she perceived that she was not alone. The figures of marble and of bronze which had been nothing when she first came in now began to come alive, each with its own meaning. Voice after voice, as she paid heed to one and to another, began to speak. There were two dancers, a man and a woman, rising up from the swath of wood and sacking in which they had been packed. They were people of some savage island, their bodies long and narrow, their faces flat, and the eyes oblique and full. The woman was crouched, her head flung back, and the man was springing over her. They spoke to each other, not to her, but she could hear them murmuring in words she did not understand. She stood before them a while, seeing how their smooth slight strong muscles were moving, or about to move, under the dark supple smooth skin. He had seen them somewhere like that, in a temple or upon a shore by a hot sea. She moved on to the figure of a woman, a silent waiting woman whose hands were locked together in waiting, her head bowed. But under the delicate brows the eyes were anxious and waiting, and from the warm marble of her body she was asking, "Has no one seen him? Has no one seen him coming to me?"

Behind her was a full-length figure and looking at it, Susan saw it was Michael, his beautiful body bare, his hands clenched. And all about her were packed crates, and she could feel presences bursting from them. She could scarcely keep from tearing at them to let them free, that she might see them.

There was a mass of clay thrown upon a table and she went over to it restlessly, and broke off a piece and rolled it in her hands, impatient, hungry, craving the textured mass of it in her hands. She crushed it together in her hands and then opened them. It lay in her hands, marked with her finger prints, and she began to press it quickly into a shape.

"What are you doing?"

She heard his voice so sharply that she leaped and there was his bearded face at her shoulder.

"I don't know," she said, and held out the clay.

He took it from her and looked at it a long time. There roughly was his own face, and he recognized it.

"What shall I do for you?" he asked.

"Teach me what I must know," she begged him.

He put down the lump and began to move among his own figures, so much larger than he was.

"A woman!" she heard him muttering in a whisper. "Damn, damn, damn, that it's been given to a woman!" He stopped and turned on her and stared at her furiously.

"You're strong, anyway," he said. "You look as strong as a man."

"I am," she said.

"You've got to be—and stronger," he said, and pulled a frowsy brown tweed cap out of his pocket. "Well, come on!" he shouted.

"But where?"

"Wherever you keep your things," he said. "I've got to see something more than that abominably cast head. I'll have to teach you from the ground up. Look here, you've got to learn how to do it all yourself, casting, everything. They all think they're too grand for that nowadays. They shape out their little bits of models and they pat out little lumps of mud and send them off to be finished! *I* don't! My stuff is mine from beginning to end. That's why it's what it is."

"I haven't done anything to show you," Susan said.

"You must have done something," he roared and jerked off his cap and put it in his pocket again.

"No, I haven't," she said miserably. She forgot all the rooms she had swept, the meals she had cooked, the beds she had made. She forgot Mark and John, and she said at last, "I've made two small things, a head and a child, and both are unfinished."

He pulled his cap out of his pocket again and flung it on his head.

"All this delay!" he muttered, and stalked out of the room, and she followed him.

There at the bottom of the steps was a small very dirty car, and he clambered in and waited an instant until she was beside him and then with a frightful clatter of gears they were rushing down the drive and up the road toward her own house.

What time it was she did not know, and it did not matter. When she opened the front door, her mother was asleep in the living room, her magazine upon the floor. She led the way past her and upstairs. From the nursery she could hear John calling to be taken up, but she went on to the attic. Behind her came tramping heavy footsteps. He was panting a little as she opened the door to the empty room. She swept her arm about its emptiness.

"You see I have done nothing," she repeated.

But he did not answer. He went up to the child, curled in its primeval shape and now covered with dust, and stared at it for a long time, and said nothing. Then he went to Mark's head, and took off the cheesecloth covering.

"Ha!" he said, after a moment, "you didn't get that."

"No," she said.

"You tried to make it from life."

"Yes."

"Maybe there wasn't enough to make," he said. "It's a queer thing that you can't make anything in our trade unless there's something permanent to be made."

She could not answer, not being able to say, "It's my husband." But it did not matter to her at this moment who it was.

He turned away abruptly and said, staring at her, "Look here, I'm going to Paris at the end of the summer. You'd better arrange to go with me. Meanwhile come to me twice a week. Begin tomorrow."

Still she could not speak. For he was commanding her to the impossible, which she knew she must perform.

"Don't come down," he added, and tramped to the door, and there he turned again and looked about the empty room.

"You ought to be ashamed of yourself," he said. His voice was cold and his red-brown eyes were angry. Then he was gone.

She could hear John's voice, now turned to wailing. She ran down into the nursery and picked him up from his crib and held him. But he could not at once be consoled for neglect. He cried loudly, and soon she heard her mother's hurried step on the stair and the door opened.

"Why, you're home! I didn't hear you come in," she said, surprised.

"I'm only just back," Susan answered, hushing the child in her arms.

"Is there anything wrong with him?" her mother asked half guiltily. "I guess I must have dropped off—I didn't hear him until just now."

"I'll wash his face and take him downstairs," said Susan. "He's just hungry."

Her mother yawned. "Then I'd better go on home and fix your father's supper."

"Yes—and thank you, Mother."

"I didn't do anything—it's kind of nice to sit in somebody else's house for a while. He is a good little boy." She gazed at John with dim affectionate eyes. "Well, goodbye, dear."

"Goodbye, Mother." Susan's mouth was full of safety pins

and she held the child firmly while she pinned clean diapers about him.

And then she went downstairs with him in her arms and gave him orange juice and a cracker and put him in his play pen among his toys, and she began Mark's dinner. The child looked at her doubtfully every now and again and went on quietly playing with his toys. After a while Mark came in and kissed her and picked the child up and tossed him about in play, and then he gave him the bread and milk she had mixed in a bowl. They went upstairs together, and together she and Mark bathed the child and she curled his hair on top of his head in a long tunnel on her finger, and they laid him in bed, rosy and clean, and put out the light.

She and Mark went downstairs again and she brought in the meal she had prepared and he sat down in solid obvious comfort to eat. He began talking at once of what had happened to him during the day, of time he had spent with people who could not make up their minds about homes they saw, and of a mistake in an account which he could not trace for an hour or two and of how his boss had said that the business had trebled in two years and if "things kept going so good—"

Everything was exactly as it had been every night, and she sat listening and tending to his needs quietly. But suddenly he looked at her.

"Say," he exclaimed, "you haven't heard a word I've been saying. And you aren't eating! I feel as if you hadn't been here at all!"

"Yes," she said quickly, "yes, I'm here, Mark. . . . Mark, do you mind if I take some lessons in modeling?"

"Why should I mind?" said Mark, cheerfully. "Go ahead, sure! It'll amuse you, won't it?"

"Yes," she said.

"You don't get out enough," he went on kindly. "It isn't

as though you ran around to other women's houses. When have you and Lucile had a visit?"

"No, I don't seem to care to," she agreed.

"So," he concluded, generously, "go right ahead."

"I'll pay for them," she said.

"Oh, well," said Mark carelessly.

Ever since John was born they had not talked of money. He did not ask her anything, merely turning over to her each week all his salary except five dollars which he kept for himself. He did not want to know what she did with his money, so that he need not know whether or not it was enough, so that he need not know what she added to it. And he talked a great deal more than he used to do, and she sat listening and listening. "So, as I was saying, Susan, the boss—"

His voice was going on and on, and she fixed her eyes on his face. He grew a little thinner, perhaps, and he was going to be bald before he was old. . . .

Tomorrow she would see if she could get somebody to come and sit with John for an hour or so, twice a week, someone whom no one on the street knew, a stranger who would say nothing because she would not care. She would go to the agency.

And Mark, having finished his dinner, helped her with the dishes, and then he said abruptly, "You haven't really kissed me since I came home tonight. We both got so busy with the kid—"

He took her in his arms and she stood in silence while he pressed himself to her. She had an impulse to pull away, to sigh and say, "Oh, I'm tired, Mark." But he had buried his face in her neck, and she saw the curve of his head to his shoulder, as helpless as the droop of a child's head, and she held him hard. Indeed, indeed, she loved him very much.

"Oh, Sue," he said breathlessly, "you're all that makes the day worth while!"

And standing thus, holding him, she knew what he said was

true. She must never forget how much she was to Mark, how much he loved her, or that she loved him.

She found a white-faced, half-frightened English woman and engaged her to come twice a week to stay with John. She had looked about the roomful of desultory women and girls at the agency, passed hastily all who were chewing gum and gaudily dressed, to meet a pair of pale blue timid eyes set in a thin white face.

"I'd like to speak to that one," she said to the thick-bodied woman at the desk.

"Jane Watson, come here," the woman said, and Jane Watson came forward. She was dressed in a black cotton dress and on her hands were black cotton gloves and she carried an umbrella.

"Lady wants somebody twice a week to nurse," said the woman.

"Oh yes," Jane Watson said eagerly, "I'm that fond of a child!"

"Her husband's just died," said the woman to Susan. "She hasn't had a job before. You'll have to bear it in mind."

So Jane came, slipping into the house like a shadow twice a week, hanging her things in the kitchen closet, tying a white apron over her black dress. She was as silent as though she were dumb, but she did not once fail. And she was a presence in the house, a guardian to whom Susan could entrust the part of her life which the house held while she fled down the street to that other part.

"Where do you keep yourself?" Lucile called to her. "Come in a while, Susan! I haven't seen you all summer!"

She only waved and smiled. "I'll be coming in soon," she promised. One day she would stop to see Lucile again. But now she hastened, her heart flying ahead of her. And on the porch Lucile stood looking after her, her pretty face a little shrewish.

86

Sometimes David Barnes was in the big studio which had once been a ballroom, and sometimes he was not. It made no difference, because she had begun to work on an idea for the fountain. He had sniffed at it a little.

"Fountain!" he snorted. "Garden truck!"

"I've always wanted to see what I could do with water and stone," she said abashed. "But if you think—"

"Go on if you want to," he said. "What's my thinking got to do with it?" So without further talk she had begun on a fountain, which was to be a thirsty adolescent boy, holding his cupped hands to catch the water gushing strongly from a rock. But the boy's figure troubled her. She needed a model and she had none. She knew only the lines of Mark's body, and remembering them, she began to hew out the marble of the block she had chosen from those in the studio.

She had never before worked in anything except clay. But there had come to her now like an unquenchable thirst, the desire to carve instead of to mold. She spent hours watching David Barnes hewing at his Titan. Then she said, "I have to work in stone. I've been wrong to touch anything else."

"Hm," he grunted. "Mud's lots easier, especially for a woman."

"I haven't any money to buy stone," she went on. "But I could sell my fountain for enough, maybe, when it's done."

"Pick your piece," he ordered. "You can pay me. It's the best marble—I get it from Kinnaird. Know Kinnaird?"

"No," she said.

"Marble man," he said.

He had taken her from one piece to the other.

"Choose your own," he said again. "Not too quickly—feel them all over, get the texture and the colors—every block is different from every other—some are warm, some are cold—and some have a vein of rottenness right in the heart. You have to take your chance of that."

87

So for hours she had brooded over stone, pondering upon each piece. Finally she chose a small warm white block and touching it she asked him, "Have you chosen this one?"

He shook his head and went on with his own work, sending a fury of small chips about his head. These were the years he was doing his Titans, and this was the tenth—the figure of Galileo. It would be one day a gallery of history in stone. And half hesitating, having watched him, she began her own figure.

At first it was simple enough. She saw quite clearly through the intervention of the marble, the figure she wanted. She had made a sketch, then a dozen, and finally under his scorn, she had finished a complete and careful painting of what she wanted.

"Sketch—sketch—sketch—" he had muttered through his beard. "A sketch is nothing but laziness. Put down what you really mean."

She had put it down in careful lines. And he said, "The body's too stiff. It's the body of a bank clerk or an insurance agent or a salesman. It's a real estate man or a critic or a sergeant in the army." He was twinkling at her over his beard, and she laughed. "You can't make fountains of such lumps," he said harshly.

But she did not know how to change it, and so she began, driving off the outer layers of her stone. And then she grew bitterly dissatisfied with her picture. She put down her hammer and chisel and stared at the painted figure a long time. It was exactly Mark's body and it was not Mark who stooped to catch in his hands the water from a spring. Where could she find a boy's body, a boy not quite a man, a boy lovely and light? Not here—the townspeople would think her insane.

"What's wrong?" he asked gruffly, and the endless swift tapping of his hammer paused.

"I don't have the right body," she said. "I dare not go

closer to the figure in the marble until I see it. I don't like this one." She tore her picture in two.

"So, why don't you get what you want?" he asked.

She would not say she did not know how to do it. She would do it somehow. What did it matter what people thought? She would hire a student in the wretched little university—they were all poor. But she could not imagine any of them with a beautiful body, since they were children of the poor. And besides, there were the townspeople. And at that moment she heard a clatter of horse's hoofs and outside the French window, open upon an old dilapidated terrace, Michael was leaping from his horse and dashing up the steps. They looked at each other.

"Why not?" said David Barnes carelessly. "Michael— Michael!" he roared, and the door opened and Michael thrust in his head.

"Hello," he said politely. "Say, Susan, Mother wants to see you. She's got someone who wants you to do her kid."

"I shan't do anything just now," said Susan.

"Come in here and take off your clothes," Barnes ordered. "She needs your figure."

And Michael came in, cheerfully obedient, and tugged at his belt and his open shirt collar and kicked off the shoes from his already bare feet.

"Can't stay long," he said amiably.

"You'll stay half an hour at least," Barnes ordered him. "Now then, Susan Gaylord."

But she was already drawing as fast as her pencil would fly.

"You're bending to drink from your hands at a gush of water from the side of a rock," she said, and Michael stooped carelessly, gracefully, and cupped his hands.

"Gosh, I am thirsty," he said, his lips parted. "It's getting hot out. Barney, I want to finish my picture of you. You've got to come and sit for me this evening."

"An old ape sitting in fading candlelight, that's what you've made me in your damned picture," he growled. "Every time I look at it, I'm afraid my beard'll catch on fire."

"I'll expect you," said Michael, laughing.

She did not hear them. She was catching every line of his hard young body, of his beautiful turned head—no, but she knew the head—no, but it was larger, different, changing. And his hands—she must get them right—thank God his knees were smooth and straight as a girl's and his flanks were narrow. She looked at him, seeing his body marble, his head marble, the curve of his waist and bent thighs marble. This was the body inside her block of stone. She turned away from his flesh and blood and began to work certainly at the stone, shaping as she searched. When she looked up again and stopped the noise of the mallet, the room was silent. They had both gone away and she was alone. How long she had been alone she did not know, but the yellow evening sun was lying across the silent terrace and she must hurry home.

But the marble was no longer a block of stone. Out of it was coming a warm white human figure outlined before a rock. She took up the chisel and she put it down again, dazed. . . . She must go home to put John to bed and to make Mark's dinner. That was the work she must do.

When Mark came home his dinner was ready and John, bathed and in his night clothes, was finishing his supper. And when he had played with his son a while she and Mark put him to bed, and ate their own dinner and he told what had happened to him all day. When he had told all he could remember he said pleasantly, "Did you have a good time at your lesson?"

"Yes, I did," she answered.

"What did you do?" he asked.

"I hammered stone all afternoon like a convict on the road," she said.

90

He laughed and she laughed with him, and he did not notice in their laughter that she said nothing more than that.

The summer passed and she did not know it. Jane came stealthily earlier and stayed later and when Susan came home in the evening, always hurrying because she was too late, she found vegetables washed and meat ready, and the table set, and John bathed and eating his supper.

"I haven't anything to take my time, Mum," said Jane. "It's somethin' to do—you needn't pay me more than reg'lar."

And Susan, knowing the house and the child safe, stayed into the summer dusk, while the light lasted, timing herself only against Mark's homecoming. Michael sat for her several times more until she had his body by heart, and then she departed from it, making the figure more slender, more young even than his own, so that it was not he, but a dream. All the time David Barnes was beside her, paying her no apparent heed.

But he saw her, sidewise from his own work, and he was silent, or he shouted at her suddenly, furious at a line gone wrong or at a slip of her chisel. But for nothing was he so angered as when she failed in power.

"You're not making a damned candlestick!" he roared, "you aren't a gift-shoppy artist. Pound it in—pound it in! Straight and hard and clear!"

He would not touch the figure himself, not even to show her what he meant. But he was merciless upon her, sparing her nothing because she was not a man.

"Forget forever that you're a woman, will you? God forgot it. Pound that line deeper, harder— That's it—that's it—that's it!"

She swung her arm down, pounding.

"Don't let me hear any tinkling," he said, savagely. "When you're finishing you feel the chisel point like the end of your finger—now it's muscle you want."

At night her shoulders ached until she could not sleep. But she wanted no mercy because she was a woman.

When the fountain was finished he glanced at it carelessly.

"It's good enough for a first piece," he said. "But you've got to dig out your anatomy. You've photographed a body very neatly. You haven't made it from the skeleton out. When we get to Paris this autumn I'll send you to a friend of mine—a surgeon—he taught me when I was a kid like you. I watched him until I could have performed a major operation myself. You've got to know your insides or you go on doing nothing but photographs."

She stood in silence, listening. The fountain which had seemed so beautiful to her a few minutes before, so nearly what she meant, was now worthless.

"Sell it—sell it," he said harshly. "It's good enough to sell."

"Shall I put my name on it?" she asked humbly.

"No," he growled, "it's not good enough for that."

So she sold it to Mrs. Vanderwelt for five hundred dollars. But when it stood in its place against the dark yews she loved it a little.

"It's mine, even if it isn't perfect," she thought, and she scratched her name small and deep and secret, in the palm of the outstretched hand. If years later she were ashamed of this, the water splashing so long in the hands would have washed away her name.

"Don't sign anything," he said one day in August, "until you have been in Paris two years. Then if I am satisfied, you may begin to sign. You won't know enough until then to know whether what you do is good or not. Everything you do looks beautiful to you at first. You've got to know when you've done something bad."

"I haven't said I was going to Paris," she said quietly. "The truth is I can't possibly go."

92

He was blocking out Leonardo da Vinci, his eleventh Titan, that day. He had a man sitting whom she had never seen before, though why he wanted a model she did not know since he seemed never to look at him. He had told him, "Walk about, read, do anything you like except bother me. I don't want to hear your voice or know anything you think. I'm only paying you for your body. Your mind's nothing to me. I've got the mind to put behind your face."

Now he turned on her as she sat drawing the detail of a foot, and shouted, "What are you talking about? I've already written to my own master about you. I want his opinion on you before I go on spending time on you. If you're only plastic I won't bother with you. Carving's the only thing. That fountain didn't tell me anything—too pretty—might as well have been made out of mud."

"I have a husband and a child," she said.

He turned his back to her and worked furiously for fifteen minutes. Then he threw his beard over his shoulder and shouted above his own din.

"Any woman can have husband and children. What have they to do with you?"

He did not turn his head to look at her, but he half paused for her answer, though he pretended to be studying a line before he proceeded.

"I love my husband and my child," she said clearly.

He started pounding again very loudly and would not speak to her, and at the end of the afternoon she went away a little early.

"Goodbye," she said, but he did not answer.

It became a quarrel between them as the summer drew near to its end. He ceased being angry with her when he saw she was not afraid of his anger. Instead he spoke kindly to her, explaining his own reasons.

"Susan, I've seen a lot of 'em, but I haven't seen the authentic gift before. You have it. You may not want it, but you can't give it away. You can't throw it away. It's in you, it is you. Now just because you didn't know it, because you went and married yourself off young and had a baby, doesn't mean you have the right to neglect this thing a silly God has gone and given you."

"I may be able to give it to my child," she said.

He grimaced with rage and forced himself to calmness.

"Listen to me, Susan. Will you grant that I know more than you do?"

"About some things."

"About this one thing—my own trade?" He would never say art, hating the word.

"Yes," she said, "that one thing perhaps."

"So far as I am concerned, it's the only thing," he retorted. "And it is with you, too, though you don't know it. Let me tell you something. You can't give it to your child. Who gave it to you? Was there ever a sculptor in your family? Or even a painter?"

She shook her head, but before she could speak he was pounding at her with his words.

"No, and no one gave it to you. You may go on and have a whole nursery full of brats and they'll all be just like any other woman's—no better. Why, you won't even make them a good mother! A woman like you can't make a good mother—you're thinking too much about something else."

"I can be a good mother," said Susan grimly.

"Don't think I don't know all about this business of children, for I do," he went on. "I've had 'em—I've got three boys and a girl and not one of 'em knows how to pick up a chisel or wants to."

"Their mother?"

"Three mothers!" he shouted derisively. "Three different women I've had 'em by! And the brats are all alike!"

She did not answer and she would not talk with him any more. For what could he know of the little house by the wood at the end of a lighted street, and the safety of Mark loving her and telling her she was what made his day worth living to the night? If she went to Paris—but she would not go to Paris, not with John waiting for her, warm and clean and rosy in his high chair in the kitchen. She could not go.

At the end of every day she knew she would not go to Paris. But in the morning when she was sweeping and cleaning she wished she had not that five hundred dollars in the bank for the fountain. And David Barnes knew she had it because he would take nothing for his marble. She had tried to give it to him and he had said angrily, "I don't want your money. Keep it. I've got all I need."

"Your children—" she began and he burst out at her, "Hell, I don't give them anything."

"Not your children?" she cried.

"I don't want 'em."

"You had them," she accused him.

"I didn't—their mothers did." He chuckled and then bellowed with laughter.

She gazed at him a moment, unbelieving, amazed at such a heart in a man so passionate for beauty.

"Where are they?" she asked.

"I don't know," he answered. His voice was indifferent, but his eyes grew suddenly warm.

"Look, Susan!" he whispered, "Look!" She looked at the line of his finger drawn along a rough edge of marble. "That's how the head bends. I haven't seen it until now."

His face was tender, alight, and though she had hated him for a moment, now she leaned forward, seeing.

"The marble lies to the curve," she whispered.

"Yes," he said. "You see it?"

95

She nodded. They looked at each other with a perfect comprehension, forgetting everything.

They took up their quarrel again next day. For there was the money in the bank. So she could not say, "I have no money." And she could not say, "I want to spend it on my family. They need it." For she was no good at telling lies. She said to him plainly, "I cannot go, because none of them would understand —my husband, my mother, my friends—no one would understand," and then she added, "unless perhaps my father."

"What of it—what of it?" he roared at her, wringing his blunted roughened hands. "What the blazes does it matter if they understand or don't?"

He was quivering, but suddenly he stopped short, and sat down and leaning forward with his hands on his knees he began to speak in a gentle voice. "Susan, does it mean nothing to you that you may become one of the great of your generation, perhaps of all generations?—No, I won't put it on that—Susan, you have a deep desire in you, deeper than love and mating, deeper than motherhood. It is to create, in that way peculiar to you, the things you feel and see. No one can do it but you —no, wait—that doesn't matter—the thing is this, you'll never be happy, not even happy as a woman, unless you are satisfying that desire.—No, wait—you're not to speak. I won't ask you again. See here, I've made a reservation for you—third of September—not my boat—I'm going next week—I know gossip. But you can tell me before I go. No, I don't want one word."

He got up and rolled out of the room, and she put on her hat and walked homeward. On her porch Lucile was sitting with her third baby in her lap, and Susan stopped a moment and went up the steps. It was a little boy.

"I'm glad it's a boy, anyway," said Lucile, her voice proud and discontented together. "Women have too hard a time in this world for me to want to bring any more here."

Susan stooped, smiling, over the small grave pink face. She

96

slipped her hands under his body and stood holding him to her. What was there in a baby's body held like this to the breast? She stood a moment, confused and feeling. Then she put him down and kissed Lucile's cheek and went away before she saw the surprise in Lucile's eyes. At the end of the street was her own house waiting for her, and John would laugh when she came in the kitchen and Jane would say tenderly, "He's been that good today. Shan't I stay and serve your dinner, Mum? I 'ave it all ready." And Mark would come home. She hurried as fast as she could and ran up the steps, her heart hot to be there.

She did not go to the studio for a week, and he did not write her or seem to notice it. She was quite happy, she told herself, very happy at home. The day before he was to leave she went once more to tell him goodbye, and there he was, working alone. She came in from the door open on the terrace as she always did. He was kneeling before the Titan, the afternoon sunshine falling across the figure. He was hammering swiftly, sure of his creation. And when she saw him her little house shook upon its foundations.

"Well?" he said, looking up. For her shadow had fallen black upon the marble.

"I came only to say goodbye," she said. She knew exactly what she wanted to say.

"You are not coming?" he said gently, so gently that it was the voice he might use before one dying or dead.

She shook her head, and he rose to his knees and put aside his tools and went over to the table and wrote an address upon a bit of paper.

"If you ever know you are wrong," he said, "you may write to me there. But do not write me for anything else. I have no other interest in you." And he went back to his work, taking up his tools and kneeling again before his Titan.

She went home then through the afternoon light and did not know whether it was night or day. She had the bit of paper in her hand and she went upstairs and put it under the statue of the child she had never finished. Then she stood looking about the still empty room. It was emptier now than ever, and it would always be empty. And as she stood, she heard Mark's step in the hall, and his voice calling her.

"Susan? I'm home early!"

She ran downstairs to him and threw herself upon his breast. "Mark—Mark—Mark—" she cried, over and over, clinging to him.

"Why, Susan—why—darling—" he said, frightened.

"Oh, Mark," she said, and then laughed and drew away and wiped her eyes. "I didn't expect you so early. I've never been so glad to see you."

"Is anything wrong?" he asked, still troubled.

"No—no—" she said. "I love you—I love you—"

They clasped each other close and kissed as they had not in many months. And that night she turned to him resolutely in the dark and said, "Mark, it's time we had another child. I want another child."

And he said, longing and afraid, "Sue—are you sure?"

And she answered steadily, "Sure."

She slept dreamlessly, and woke to sunshine streaming across her room, and when Mark was gone she plunged into her house with pleasure that, for the moment, was complete. She felt satisfied, as though a hunger had been fed. She went upstairs gaily and began turning mattresses and beating pillows. She swept and mopped and dusted and then, sitting on the sills, she washed the windows, her hair blowing in the autumn wind. She worked with joy, delighting in the making clean, in the order, in the freshness. Yet all the time only part of her was working and she knew it. She ran downstairs when the door opened at noon and John came in holding Jane's hand, his cheeks rosy, his brown eyes full of peace.

"Milk," he said, "an' bread."

"You shall have your lunch," she promised him.

"Shall I give it to him?" Jane asked, her pale eyes begging. But Susan shook her head. "I want to, today," she answered.

"I'll come again this afternoon," Jane said, and went out, shutting the door softly behind her.

Left alone with the child, Susan washed him and put him in his chair and fed him, and he ate, thinking as he did so, of all he had done.

"I made a house," he said, "a big house."

"Yes, darling?"

She dwelt on him with adoration, loving him to pain. He was beautiful. He was what she had dreamed, her child with Mark's eyes and her mouth. When he had eaten she carried him up to bed and undressed him and tucked him in for his nap. He looked up at her with Mark's faithful pleasant eyes, and she was faint with love for him. But even then, and even though she ardently wanted many children, she knew part of her was waiting and not in all of this. She pushed the knowledge away from her and drew her chosen life about her, close and warm.

She had thought at the end of the summer, aching a little, that she would miss David Barnes very much, miss him and what was given her there in the huge old ballroom studio. The night when she had cried to Mark for a child, she had been desolate in one part of herself. But the days closed around her quite happily without David Barnes and with no other work done than caring for the house, for John, for Mark.

Mark said with content, "I've been too busy this summer, I

guess, girl. It's good to have time to talk again. People don't buy so many houses in the autumn and winter."

He had not known that she also had been busy apart from him. But then he had had another increase in salary and he felt happy and successful and overflowed in detailed accounts to her of all his day's doings. Sitting together over a meal or under the light of the lamps, she sewed and listened, quite content. Yes, she was quite content, except sometimes in the midst of fire-glow and lamplight, when the wind howled in the wood. Then she lifted her head and listened. Upstairs John lay warm and asleep. All was well. They were safe, and one day followed another in the old safe pattern she had known all her life. But when she heard the sound of the wind in the night she felt, and she knew, without knowing how, that there was more than this, although with this she was perfectly content. Even when she and Mark went upstairs together, his arm about her, hers about him, in true love, she could see corridors, wide and empty, stretching before her, down which she had not yet walked.

But she seemed almost all the time, even to herself, like any other woman. By Christmas she knew she would have another child, and she was glad. She told Mark, and he took her hand gently and held it.

"It comes over me like a dream sometimes that you bear my children," he said. "I have such a feeling that you could be anything you liked. I'm not good enough for you."

"Don't say that," she answered sharply. "I can't tell you how I hate to hear you say that."

"Even if I feel it?"

"Even if you feel it don't say it," she begged.

"Why?"

"I don't know."

But she did know. It was because she must feel him equal to her. She must have the sense of complete comradeship. For when Mark's bodily presence was not there, or John's, immediately she was alone. She wondered if other women were as she was, so that she must put out her hand and touch solid flesh, meet eyes, hear a voice and words spoken, or else feel the world dropped away and herself alone. But she could not ask anyone.

"It would do no good if I did," she thought, pondering. "I am as I have been born, and what others are can't change me."

But looking ahead with that prescience which came over her at times she saw herself walking through the unreached spaces of her life, and she was always alone. Mark was not there, nor any child, nor friend. She hung back from that lonely march, occupying herself with this bright present. That vision meant, perhaps, nothing at all. In any life, perhaps, the years ahead looked different, more formidable, than the known present.

She must be, she was, like any other woman. She cooked and sewed, she read and played the piano and listened to Mark. She took care of John and began to tell him his first stories, to which he listened with eager half-understanding. She let Jane talk to her with sad pleasure of her life as a girl in London, a kitchen maid in a big household, whose master came during the war to Canada, because he was too old to fight, and having married late he had no sons to give to England, and he decided to emigrate with all his daughters and servants.

"Twelve servants in all," Jane said with mournful satisfaction, "and he nigh burst a blood vessel, Mum, over the war because he was too old to go. So we left England, and he brought the carriage and horses as well, because he thought the motion of motor cars was bad for babies. He had his ideas, Mum. And then he lost his money and suffered somethin' terrible, Mum. I do feel that sorry for the rich. The poor, Mum, we're used to nothin'. But it's cruel hard for the rich to be poor. It's best to be used to nothin'. Then you're thankful for the little you get."

She looked at Jane's meager honest face and felt guilty because she had so much.

In January the postman brought her a thin blue envelope stamped in Paris.

"A furrin letter, Mrs. Keening," he said.

It was from David Barnes, a curt question scrawled across the page.

"What are you wasting all this time for?" he demanded, his writing square and black across the blue paper.

She smiled and crushed the letter in her hand and threw it away. Her child would be born in June. John was growing. Her home was tended and her garden in the spring would be filled with flowers so that to those who walked up the street the brightness of the flowers shining against the wood would be as gay as flags flying. Now that she was at home all day her old friends came in, dropping onto the couch by the grate fire, or in the spring, which came so soon, upon a garden bench Mark had made, talking and gossiping, sighing over work to be done. She listened to them, smiling, saying little. Though they were women, they seemed still to be the children she remembered them, eager to be done with duties, eager for simple play at games, at the pictures. She loved them with compassion, talking with them of their problems, half ashamed that she had none to offer in exchange. The winter slipped away and it was early spring. And still she was resolute in her happiness.

Lucile said gratefully, "It's nice to have you at home once in a while, Sue. Last summer every time I ran in you were away."

"I was taking some lessons," Susan answered. She was digging around a pansy bed and Lucile was sitting in the new grass, idle beside her.

"Was that what you were doing!" Lucile's small gray eyes grew shrewd.

"What else?" asked Susan simply. "I went to David Barnes every day all summer.

"I knew that," said Lucile. "I must say we all wondered. He has the worst reputation."

"I don't know anything about that," said Susan.

"Oh, my dear!" cried Lucile. "Don't you know about Vannie Blaine? Why, everybody says she was his mistress! That's why she left her husband. They say she thought of course he'd marry her. But he didn't, though there was a child. That sort don't marry anybody. Artists don't behave like other people, I guess."

"I don't know anything about it," said Susan.

David Barnes was a pair of hands, sensitive, blunt, moving, strong. He was a brain looking out of sullen dark blue eyes. He was an angry voice crying to her out of his own wilderness.

Jane was coming in the gate. "Well, you're lucky to have help in the house," said Lucile. "I've got to go. The baby'll be awake. I wish I could get a girl. Mark must be doing awful well."

"I pay for Jane," said Susan, and wished she had not. What did it matter who paid for Jane? But Mark would not like anyone to think he did not pay for everything.

"You can't keep that up," said Lucile with decision. "You'll find that out when you have two. Besides, Sue, you want to be careful not to spoil Mark. Goodness, things have come to a pass if we have to earn the money and have the children, too!"

"I want six," said Susan, smiling. Under her fingers a crown of yellow pansies stood up in a gay circle.

"You're crazy," said Lucile. "I have three, and I never have a moment to myself. Well, goodbye, Sue."

"Goodbye, dear," said Susan, peaceably.

Alone again she pondered over Lucile. The town was full of Luciles. A little fatter, a little thinner, old or young, she was everywhere. How did women grow so alike? Or if they were different, they were like Mark's mother, silent and alone, and seemingly friendless, or they were like Mary, sullen and young. Her own mother was only a sort of Lucile. And all these Luciles lived childish, haphazard years, disconnected from life as it really was, clamoring for a romance which bewildered, harassed men did not know how to give them.

Last night Mark had sighed against her shoulder. "You're so restful. I sink into you somehow and you're still and deep and warm. You never demand anything, Sue. Sure you're happy?"

"Sure!" she had said. . . .

For every moment of life was her own. "Not a moment your own," Lucile had said. But all her moments belonged to her life. This moment, for instance, her hands warm in the soft moist earth, was part of her life. In an hour she would be cooking luncheon and that hour also was her own life.

Jane was bringing John out of the house, and she hesitated.

"I want to ask you something, Mum," she said.

"Yes?" said Susan.

"When the little one comes, shan't you be wantin' me reg'lar?"

"I don't think so, Jane," said Susan gently. "We haven't much money and it isn't as if I didn't love to do my own work."

"I thought maybe you'd be sculpturing again, Mum."

Susan paused. "I don't know," she said. "I can't say now."

"Ah, well," said Jane, "I'll just wait. It'll come to you."

She stooped and took John's hand and together they went out of the gate, her long black skirts flapping against her thin legs in the spring wind. But Susan, lifting her head, saw the old flash of long empty corridors, ahead. The street, the house, the budding trees, were suddenly as unreal as the painted backdrop in a theater. Then she struck her trowel resolutely into the earth and it all grew real and so she held the moment still her own.

On the tenth day of June she gave birth to a daughter, whose name, she had decided, was to be Marcia. And Mark, tiptoeing into the hospital cell in creaking shoes, found her smiling.

"You look like a million dollars," he whispered. "If anybody had told me you were a woman who'd just had a baby, I'd laugh!"

She pulled back a blanket and showed Mark the small girl, dark and black-haired. "I have the technique now," she boasted, laughing. "I know exactly how to do it. There are going to be four more, Mark!"

"I'll have to hustle for them," he said.

He sat a long time staring at the tiny face, deep in contented sleep. She did not ask him of what he thought, not caring quite enough to trouble to know. Besides, she knew him so well. Mark would not be thinking anything very strange. She was drenched in easy content, steeped in it. Some double instinct in her was nearly satisfied, more satisfied than she had been in many months. She had felt the solidity of Marcia's shape with more than a mother's content. It was a beautiful and perfect body, every line right, and she had made it. She sighed, smiling, and fell asleep.

Waiting quietly to be allowed to go home, she thought, hours upon end, of everything and of nothing. She lay receiving into herself anything that stopped, like a wandering bird flying past, to lodge itself in her brain. It was the pause that comes after creation. There would be something else. One day she would get up out of this narrow white bed and go back to all that had been, and the more that she knew waited for her. But until then she could be as she was, receptive, waiting. Her mother and father came each day, never together. Her mother said little. She sat and held Marcia with a simple pleasure, broken only to ruminate aloud after long pondering, "She doesn't look so much like you as she does like Mary did when she was born."

And her father, glancing at Marcia, said briskly, "I suppose she's like any other child. Still, here's a poem—To Marcia on Her Birth." He cleared his throat and read it aloud. When he had finished he said, "Question is, would you rather have the twenty dollars they might pay me for it, or would you rather have the poem?"

"Oh, the poem!" said Sue, laughing.

"Might as well have both," he replied. "Take all you can get, I say—there's precious little, all in all. . . . Sue, when I retire I'm going to the South Seas, whether your mother will go or not."

She laughed again and reached for the poem. As long as she could remember he had talked of going to the South Seas. As a tiny girl it had troubled her because her mother believed him and had cried every time, "Oh, Danny, what would I do there?" And in her mother's alarm she had trembled with insecurity. But as years went on her mother ceased to hear him.

"I'll put this among my precious things," she said.

He was pleased, but he only growled, "I have another copy, anyway."

And Mary came in the last day, home from her first year in college, and bent over Marcia, a new composed Mary, very mature and detached, in a dark blue suit with a white blouse and a small dark hat.

"She looks healthy," she said carelessly, and sitting down she lit a cigarette with ostentation.

"Dad said anything about me?" she inquired, her eyebrows lifted.

Susan shook her head.

"He will," said Mary. "He's furious with me."

"Why?"

"Because I don't want to finish college. I want to get a job. College is so bourgeois now."

She blew a ring of smoke, and another, and another.

"What does Mother say?" Susan asked cautiously.

"Oh, Mother," said Mary. "She hasn't an idea in her head." She flicked the ash with her little finger. "It isn't as though I'd be content just to settle down and marry," she went on. "I want to get out into life."

Susan looked down at Marcia, now curled in her arms.

"This is life, too," she said.

"Oh, well," said Mary, "but not my sort." She got up restlessly, a straight dark girl with a cold clear exact profile and the small tight red mouth. The shape, the look, of her mouth never changed. In childhood she had had the same shaped mouth. It was not larger now, not fuller, nor more passionate. "Susan, I'm not asking favors, but if Dad says anything, just say I know my own business, will you?"

"If you're sure you do," said Susan doubtfully.

"If I don't, nobody else does," Mary said. "Well, goodbye, Sue! It's a swell baby!"

She lay a little exhausted after Mary was gone. Mary used up the very air about her.

A day or two later her father said moodily, staring at Marcia, "I'm not sure I don't wish you hadn't another boy. Women are damned hard these days. Your sister's got radical notions—wants to live her own life and go to New York and get a job. You can tell a boy to go to hell, but you can't tell a girl that, and I don't know what else to do with Mary."

She said nothing, not knowing what she ought to say. In a flash of memory she heard Mary striking the wrong note again and again on the piano, with determination, not knowing she was wrong.

So their lives drifted in upon her and out again, and she was bound to all of them partly and to none of them altogether. She got up at last, and with Mark beside her, carrying Marcia, went back to her own home. John and Jane were at the door for welcome. The house stood sturdy and accustomed and dear to the sight and she entered it gladly.

But the instant she was there, in the midst of all the familiar and the warm possessions, her heart fluttered in her breast and something moved in her, as Marcia had moved before she was born, a creature confined in her and yet apart. She was not restless at all, she was happy, for she had a nature made for happiness, being easily absorbed in every passing object. An unexpected yellow rose open on the vine over the porch was as absorbing to her as the news in the paper last week of the award to David Barnes of five thousand dollars for his new Titan, Christopher Columbus, which the city of New York wanted to buy. She was as enchanted by these things as she was by the news of the discovery of the North Pole, or as she would be by Marcia's first tooth. But she knew, not so much by knowledge as by instinct, that she could comprehend infinitely more happiness than she now had in everything, and that she was capable of a profounder peace than the peace of this life with which she was nevertheless quite content.

Out of this instinct came a movement as blind and as inevitable as the instinct of a tree to branch, and of a branch to leaf. Out of perfect happiness she began to need her own further growth. Once as a child sitting in a church she had heard the minister speak of one bereaved and he said, "Whom the Lord loveth he chasteneth," and he said, "Sorrow is sent to teach the human soul and fit it for larger things." But she had known no sorrow at all. Mark was simple goodness in his love, her children were healthy and undemanding, and the days were not cumbered by anything. Even Jane said darkly, "Enjoy everything while you can, Mum. The end comes fast enough." But all such sayings meant nothing. She had never seen death, and it seemed to her that life was endless, and she was glad to have it so. But her content was like earth which nourished seed, and the seed grew by its own health out of the earth. Her very content forced her to creation again. And the beginning was her restlessness.

She had not enough to do. However busy she was, she knew there was an energy in her still unused, a primary function unperformed. She began to feel beyond what her eyes saw in the shape of a tree whipped by the wind, in John building his block houses, in Jane bent over pots, in Jane looking up to answer her at the door, in Jane half startled, wiping her hands on her apron. Jane—Jane—Jane had no curves at all. Her body was cut as simply as a slab of granite—and yet every line had been made, not born, but made by the inwardness of Jane—her straight sad mouth, her stoic chin, her knotty hands, her thin strong shoulders and flat big English feet.

"Jane!" she cried one day at the kitchen door.

Jane looked up, startled, and wiped her hands on her apron. "Mum?"

John was playing in summer sunshine in the garden. Marcia was asleep in her crib.

"Yes, Mum?" Jane said again.

"What are you doing, Jane?"

"The pots and kettle, Mum!"

"Then come upstairs!"

She heard Jane's plodding big-footed tread behind her on the stair, following her into the attic. She stood in the door, still wiping her wet arms, looking anxiously at Susan.

"Just stay like that!" Susan said. For suddenly she saw this essential Jane, looking out from among pots and kettles, humble, fearful, living moment by moment in another woman's contented house, in a timid precious peace, borrowed for a moment from a troubled and tragic life. She stared at Susan with her frightened, habitually pleading look, and Susan, mixing her clay quickly, began the shaping and the making, in frightful silence, in swift sure movement, of this creature. It had been so long since she had fed this strange hunger. But her hand could not forget the cunning with which it was born. All these months the cunning had not been used, or needed. This morning it was here, more strong than ever for being pent. She worked with fierce speed and Jane's eyes grew more frightened, though she was speechless. And Susan was humming in a sort of fervent whisper, "Oh, that will be—glory for me!" not knowing that she made a sound.

As the time passed, Jane began to make little broken movements, and Susan, disturbed in the passing of hours, cried out, "You're tired! I've kept you standing too long. Why, what time is it?" The noon sun was blazing hot upon the roof and she felt her face wet with sweat.

Jane said anxiously, "It's not that I'm tired, Mum. But I hear the baby cryin' and Johnnnie's bangin' to be let in."

"I didn't hear them," Susan said, half ashamed. She listened and now she could hear Marcia's clear loud crying and John's shouting, "Janie—Janie! I can't opie the door!" But Jane was already gone.

Susan closed her eyes a moment. She need not hurry. She caught the deep hard beat of her heart. Then she opened her eyes to see what she had done. There, life-size, roughly and crudely enough, but serenely true, her clay still wet and dark, stood Jane, wiping her wet arms. But this was more than Jane. Here were all women like Jane, humble women who crept about the hearths of others, cleaning and cooking and sewing, receiving dazedly beyond a small wage such scraps as were given them. And out of these socket-like eyes, out of the half-open drawn mouth, from the whole drooping fragile yet somehow unbreakable figure, Susan could hear a voice. It was not a clear cry as the child's had been, asking why it was born. There was no question here, for the possibility of question was long dead, since to question is to be able also to rebel, even a little, and there was no rebellion in Jane against anything. No, it was a voice, murmuring in a monotone of pots and pans, of meat to be cooked, of kitchen floors to be scrubbed, of children crying to be fed—nothing more. Only death could cut this murmuring short. One day there would be a sigh, and what had been life nearly dumb would become a simple silence. This was Jane, thousands upon thousands, and Susan, realizing her, went to the window toward the wood, and stared out into its summer greenness. There was sunshine everywhere, the street was brilliant in sunshine. Through the window she could hear the creak of a hammock next door. Now the house was still. Jane had taken Marcia up, she had fed John. But Susan stood by the window, weeping, her body a blaze of pain she could not comprehend, except that she was somehow weeping for Jane.

She did not again want any Jane, in flesh and blood, to pose for her. It was not necessary. She saw clearly what she was doing, and day after day she came upstairs and finished the figure, working more surely than she ever had. Those hours with David Barnes a year ago had taught her sureness. She had, without knowing it fully, learned how to model strongly with her thumbs as he did in the rare times he used clay, how to be bold and hard with her material, striking away what she did not want. But upon Jane's face she worked with such delicacy that it was as though she felt the features out of the clay. Her eyes were half closed, and her fingers went feeling, feeling, into the clay, pressing out each bony plane and surface. Each day when she opened the attic door it was to open it to ecstasy and when she shut the attic door behind her, she shut it as upon that secret ecstasy. She was alive throughout her being. And she told no one. There was no one to tell.

One night she wakened. She felt in her sleep a light pressing unbearably upon her eyelids, and she woke suddenly to find the brilliant moon, setting full and bright as a sun, in the sky outside the window, opposite her bed. She sat up, startled, and Mark spoke, his voice clear of sleep.

"You're awake, too. It's the moon."

And after a moment he said, "Sue, may I come over to your bed?"

And she said—for when had she ever denied him anything?—"Of course, darling," and fell back on her pillows. She yawned drowsily, but still she was conscious of pleasure in the warmth of Mark's body. And when he said in a low voice, "Hold me tight, Sue," she put her arms about him warmly, feeling him dear and not repellent. Thus, following sweet habit, she was not prepared for the sudden chill that crept over Mark's flesh. In the moonlight she felt his hands falter and the warmth pass from him. He lay quite still a moment, then he kissed her gently and tucked the sheet about her.

"Go to sleep, dear Sue," he said gently. "I shouldn't have disturbed you."

She came instantly out of her half sleep.

"But, Mark, I was loving you!" she protested.

"That's all right," he said in the same gentle voice. Now he was getting up, putting on his dressing gown, feeling for his slippers. "Guess I'll read a while. This darned moon keeps me awake."

She stared at him. His voice was cheerful, but she felt him changed to her.

"Mark, something is wrong and you are not telling me."

"Nothing is wrong," he insisted. "Now you go to sleep." He

was reaching for the light, and then began fingering the books on the little shelf by his bed.

"Mark, you never have lied to me," she said. She was now so awake that she felt she could sleep no more that night.

"I love you," he said, not looking at her.

"Of course you love me," she replied, "and I love you. So what's wrong?"

He looked at her then and she saw his lips trembling.

"Why, Mark!" she cried in terror. She had never seen Mark weep. She leaped out of her bed and went to him and pulled his head down upon her shoulder.

"Mark—Mark—" she whispered, and holding him, she felt his body tremble and grow stiff against his weeping. "What can be the matter?" she demanded. "Come, Mark, I can't bear this."

"Nothing," he gasped. "It's nothing—only I feel you're changing to me somehow. I'm not enough for you."

For a moment she felt as if she were the man and he the woman. She had listened to other women speaking thus of their husbands. Once at a bridge party at Lucile's house Trina Prescott had thrown down her cards, crying, "I can't go on, girls— I'm so miserable! Rob doesn't care about me any more. He's changed." And they had talked it out, pityingly, and she had taken Trina home at last, and Lucile had come over next day to talk it all over again and say, "Women are so soft, Sue! I'd just like to see Hal act different to me! It would mean just one thing—he's thinking about some other woman, and that's one thing I won't stand! I'd tell him where to get off! Didn't he promise to cleave to me only?"

She had listened in silence to this behavior of women, knowing it impossible in herself toward Mark. But she had not heard before of a man, his head bent upon a woman's shoulder like this, crying out that he had lost her. It made Mark a stranger, and no more the cheerful, simple, single-hearted comrade in her house. She saw in a terrifying second the far corridors ahead of her, to which this present was but one entrance. But she did not want this life to change. She and Mark had been married four years and she had not dreamed he was not happy. She was frightened.

"Sit down, dear," she said very gently, and like a child he obeyed, clinging to her. "Now, tell me. I've done something to hurt you. But the dreadful thing is I didn't know what it was. So you must tell me. I love you so."

But it was a long time before he could speak. He had not put into words even for himself what she now asked him. He had been suffering deeply, dumbly, against his will, not knowing why he suffered.

"You've been perfect," he said over and over. "I'm crazy, that's all. It's me, not you. Why, you keep a beautiful home for me—you're perfect to the children—" He paused and went on. "You're always dear and lovely to me. I hear other fellows jawing about their wives. Hal doesn't dare to be ten minutes late or Lucile wants to know why—and she snoops around his pockets, she's so jealous—why, she's jealous of the shop stenographer, even! I hear them all and say to myself, 'My wife's not like that, thank God!'"

She listened, smoothing his shoulder, feeling its quivering under the thin stuff of his cotton pajamas. "It's nothing you've done."

"Then it's something I am," she replied.

He did not speak for a moment. Then he pulled away from her, and walking about the room, he found his pipe and lit it and sat down on the windowsill and stared out into the moonlight.

"Maybe it is," he said, "perhaps that's it."

Her heart flickered in fear. "That's much worse," she said very quietly. "I could stop doing something that hurt you, but it would be very hard for me to stop being what I am. I wouldn't know how to begin. I don't think I've ever thought how I am. I've been so busy all my life, and so happy."

He got up and drew down the shade against the moonlight and sat down on the bed.

"I never meant to get started on this," he said. "I can't tell you what I mean, so I shouldn't say anything. But I feel all the time that you aren't here—not all of you. You do everything so well, so much better than anybody else—I know that—"

"Oh, Mark, don't!" she begged him. "What do I care how I do anything except to make you happy? If what I do doesn't make you happy, it's no good. I've failed!"

"You do make me happy," he said stoutly. "I'm a fool to say a word. I'm comfortable and cared for and you don't leave anything undone—except—" he paused, and after a second he said, "except perhaps give yourself to me straight through."

"What do you mean?" she asked. "When have I refused you anything?"

"You don't—I'm a fool—but I feel as though I never quite had you. See here, Sue—when I'm talking to you, I tell you everything that happens to me, I tell you everything, see? There isn't any more to me. But there's so much you don't tell me. You listen, but only part of you is listening. I think that's it—I'm only married to part of you."

He looked down at her earnestly, his face anxious with effort to make her understand. And she did understand, and for the first time in her life she wanted to shrink away from him. For who had the right to ask her to give him the uttermost recesses of her being? To give everything was not within her power. She gave as he was able to receive. She was about to open her lips and say sharply, "If you want all of me, you must be able to take all. If I have held back anything of myself, it is a thing I can't help."

But Mark was speaking unsteadily. "It's as though I held out a cup to you—"

She could have said, "The cup's too small." But before she could say it, he cried out, "That sounds terrible—I don't mean it. The trouble is I'm just not enough for you. The cup's too small, maybe!"

She did not say anything. She could with a word have made him weep again, have made him afraid lest he lose her altogether. But she would not because it would have been to wound herself more than him. She wanted never to wound anyone. That was the great sin—to wound another person. All her life she had held herself back and she had hidden her true powers because she did not want to shame or wound anyone. But she ought not to need to hide herself from him. Yet she had, she had, and in some blind way he knew it. She was dazed. She would have to think it over, all he had said, and see what it really meant. But now the first need was to comfort Mark, to make him realize, through her love, that he was enough for her and therefore for himself. Whether he was enough for her was not so important as to have him think he was enough. She smiled at him richly, warmly, putting aside everything except that one thing.

"Come here to me, my darling," she said, her voice firm and clear. "You are talking nonsense, you know. I'm so happy— you are my best and my dearest. You're the center of my life." She drew him down upon her breast. It was quite true. He was the center. For she had to have someone like Mark, faithful, immediate, close, for a center from which her life could radiate into all its own ways. He was her earth. Her roots were in him, dark and close and strong, and what flowered above him depended on that. She drew him to her with warm compelling arms, laughing a little, teasing, making love to him. He gave himself to her mood, excited and persuaded. And she closed all her other doors and lived in this one room of their own house, in this secret hour of the moonlit night. She was for the hour as persuaded as he, as swept. There was this difference. At the end of the hour the dream held for him. He lay with his head on her arm, half asleep, smiling, his eyes shut.

"Forget what I said, sweet," he said. "I was tired, I guess. It was a hard day in the office."

She raised herself on her elbow and looked down at him.

"Do I love you?" she demanded.

He looked up at her.

"Yes," he whispered, his eyes humble before hers. "I don't know why, but you do!"

"Promise me you will never forget it!"

"I promise," he said, as willingly as a contented child.

She looked at him. "Now go to sleep," she commanded him. "No, don't move! Stay in my bed, and I'll go over to yours."

But he was already asleep. She slipped her arm from under his head and went to the other bed and drew the covers about her. His breathing came and went in a quiet rhythm, but she could not sleep. She lay in a fierce tense determination. Her will was demanding her heart, her brain, her being. He had been right, but he must never know it.

"I'm not going to fail at anything. I can do it all, wife, mother—and myself." She had been careless and even lazy, letting Mark be hurt through her absorption in something apart from him. For there was that in her which must be apart from him. He had come blindly upon something in her which was true. She would manage better. She would take thought how to give herself more completely, to live more wholly where for the hour her life was.

But in spite of herself, choose as she might how to realize herself as here and now, in this room, in this night, ready and wishful for sleep, the door shut. In her mind one door and another opened, silently, and she wandered forth, quite alone, while Mark slept sweetly sure of her presence. She lay on, motionless, realizing herself as she never had.

Why should she not be as she was born, and why should she not do and be everything?—not openly or with fuss, as some women did, declaring to themselves the right to freedom, not in fact to do, so much as to be. It was quite true that Mark was not enough for her. But she could not do without him, for nothing was enough for her in itself—not the children, nor the house, nor her parents, nor the town, not the beauty of woods and sky, and still she could not live without them all. Not even her work was enough. If it were possible to live as David Barnes did, all day long carving and shaping and making, at the end of the day she would know, even after hours of forgetfulness of all else, that this also was not enough. For in his own way David Barnes was as limited as Lucile Palmer, and in his way he lived as little of life. Though beauty was his soul's food, it was not all beauty for which he hungered, but only one kind of beauty. He could see no necessity in childbirth and in growing children, in cleaning and cooking, in planting and singing and in making love to Mark. So much of all this as he could sort out, grasp, and translate into a fistful of clay, or discover in stone, so much he understood. But she— she needed to be as well as to create. Indeed, in her the two were not separate. She could spare nothing from her life, and no one, not Lucile or Jane or Mary and certainly not her children or Mark. She could spare nothing and no one.

"Greedy!" she said to herself solemnly while Mark slept. "I'm greedy as hell!"

But why not? Why should she not have all she could take? The moon waned and she lay in darkness for an hour, thinking furiously. No one could have quite all of her all the time, no one—not Mark, not David Barnes, each clamoring after his fashion. Yet to each she would be what he needed, because she would be herself to the top of every bent. Where she herself most was, she did not know or care. She would have all she wanted of everything. Nobody should limit her, not by love or by blame. The universe was her universe, with all its hours, its lands, its gardens, its skies, its children, its music, its painting, its people, its stars. What could stop her? She would crowd her life full to perfection. She would be all she could be, and she could be what she would. When the room grew light with dawn, she watched the coming day with joy. She did not need to choose between one thing and another, between the old ridiculous finalities of women. She wanted and did make a home, and she would begin, now that Marcia was well born and thriving, to work.

In the ease of this confidence, she suddenly fell asleep to wake two hours later to Mark's cheerful shouting, "Hey, you girl! Going to sleep all day?"

She woke, and the sunshine was streaming in the window. Mark was dressed, and from downstairs came the hungering smell of bacon. Jane, surreptitiously coming earlier and earlier every day, was making breakfast. There was no noise from the nursery. That meant Marcia had had her early bottle, and John was in the kitchen. But she did not speak of any of this. She remembered Mark in the night and she reached for him and drew his head down to her breast. He murmured, "Forget all that silly stuff I talked in the night, will you, Sue? I don't know what came over me."

"I will!" she said. She pressed his head, kissed him, and then leaped from the bed.

"Two minutes for a shower, and I'll be down," she cried. Her eyes were clear and bright as a child's eyes, she was smiling, and when he seized her in his arms for a moment, she was yielding and willing. She would never forget Mark in the night nor a word of what he had said. She would never

119

again cut a single moment short. She put on a fresh blue linen dress and ran downstairs and sat behind the coffee pot and beamed at him. And he adored her and she knew it and held it precious. She must keep him adoring her. And when John came in she caught him in her arms and nuzzled him until he gasped with laughter.

"Mummy—Mummy, I like you so when you're funny!" he sighed. Well, then, for John she would be funny. She followed Mark to the door and together they sauntered down the garden path and she stood waiting, John's hand in hers, until he turned the corner of the street.

"Now what would you like to do this morning?" she inquired of John seriously.

He considered and replied weightily, "I s'all make mud pies today."

"Very well," she agreed. "I'll tie an apron around you, and we'll fetch water in a pail. Only please save all your pies to show me."

"All wight," he promised.

And there was Marcia to bathe and feed and she gave herself to this with joy. Every moment was hers to live.

When the house had thus begun its own day she went resolutely upstairs to the attic. For this house must be large enough to comprehend all her life, and this, too, was her life, though Mark and the children did not come here. She shut the door behind her and looked around. There was no reason why she should not make this place into a room in which she could really work. It had been until now an occasional place, where for a few hours, months apart, she came to work at fever speed upon a hasty secret thing. She would work so no more. If she gave herself fully to the others, she would give herself fully here also, that she might be fulfilled. It would not be so much a room of her own as simply one of her many rooms, without which her house would not be complete. She took stock quickly of her materials. They were shamefully lacking. She would make a list of everything—new crayons—she had only the ones Michael had made into stubs—fresh sheets of paper, new tools, there was a new kind of clay David Barnes had told her about —it would have to be clay and not marble here. She would get a couch and an easy chair—there was nothing here to sit upon but a box. She would get a rug and curtains. She needed more light, and the northern gable could be made bigger. As she planned, she found herself possessed by a mounting hunger, which she had scarcely noticed before because she had been denying it. She wanted now to make something more than fountains and small figures. She might make a big thing, a group of figures.

But the house was too small, the room was too small. Well, she could make a small model of the idea first. The idea need not be small. If she wanted to, she could do it life size later. Some day she might want to move out of this attic altogether— build a studio, perhaps, or rent something. When she thought of this she had again that sense of infinite largeness in herself. She could do anything. Why not?

She sat down on the box, thinking quickly, dreaming in great leaps of fancy. If they moved out into the country somewhere into a farmhouse there would be plenty of room for her to work and for the children to play. They had not thought of such a thing, she and Mark, when they were married. A little house on a well-known street near people they knew was what most people wanted. It was what Mark wanted. She stood up restlessly. Suddenly she felt there was no use doing anything to this little house. It was too small for her. She wanted a big house, with room to grow in. She could scarcely wait for Mark to come home that night. All day long it seemed wasteful to do anything to this house. She felt finished with it.

"Mark!" she cried the instant she saw him, "let's move into the country."

He stopped, his hand on the gate. "Leave this house?" he asked, staring at her.

"Yes," she answered impatiently. It took so long for Mark to catch up with her thoughts. But then she had been thinking all day and he had not. "I want more room. I need a real place to work—and the children—"

"You never have really fixed up the attic," he said slowly.

"It's too small even to begin in," she said. "I want to do a big thing this summer when David Barnes comes back. I want to do life-size work. Besides, the children—"

"There's an old house with a barn," he said, considering. He suddenly looked very tired, and he began to walk slowly to the house. "Just wait until I've washed," he said.

"Oh, darling, yes!" she said. "I'm too quick, always."

"I'm slow," he murmured.

She went into the kitchen, contrite. She would wait until he spoke—wait until after the meal without mentioning it. She would say nothing until he did. He came into the room slowly and sat down, and she smiled at him quickly and his eyes warmed.

"If you really want to move out," he said, "there's an old house on a hillside, about a mile to the south of the town, with a creek."

"Could we go after supper and see it?" she asked, and stopped herself again. "No—we'll wait. You're tired."

"We could go," he said. "The evenings are long now."

"I think of the children, too," she said.

"Of course," he agreed.

"John wants to play in the woods all the time now," she went on, "and I'm so afraid of that deep ravine."

Mark looked up suddenly.

"That's so," he replied. "I'd forgotten about that. Well, we'll go tonight. I do want time to think it over, Sue, though what I said holds good. You're to have what you want."

"We're not deciding anything," she agreed. But she felt herself already out of this house.

In the clear twilight they drove out of the town southward, and down a country road through trees to an old house built of rough field stone. It stood heavy and sound against the tawny evening sky. There was no light in its windows, and when they reached it they saw the blinds were shut and crossed pieces of wood had been nailed against the door. Without a word Mark tore them away and forced the door open, and they entered, walking about the rooms. Every room was empty and clean except for quietly gathering dust. Susan stood a moment in each, pondering, feeling. Could she live here? Was this her house? They did not speak until they went out on the long pillared porch.

"The barn is over there—it's stone, too," Mark said. He pointed to the right and she saw it, huge, under a sloping roof.

"That would be room enough even for me," she said. Instantly she longed for it. Blocks of marble, blocks of granite—the barn was big enough for hugeness.

"I like this place," she whispered. "Look at the hills—and the old trees! Is that a well over there?"

"We're not deciding tonight," he said abruptly.

"No," she agreed, "we'll come and see it by daylight."

They drove home in the dusk, and when the car was put away they sat upon the porch of their small house.

"I feel," said Mark, out of silence, "as if we hadn't lived in this house yet to the full."

"We won't go unless you want to," she answered quietly. But she knew they must go. For this house had no room for all of her. Mark's wife, the children's mother, could live here happily, but there was no room for Susan Gaylord. She thought, "I'll go alone tomorrow and see it for myself."

The next day when she went alone to the stone house she

knew it was her home. She walked through the rooms, planning.

"Mark," she said at noon, "I must have that house."

He looked at her with his humble faithful eyes.

"All right, Sue," he said. "Whatever you want."

Even Mark said, when the moving was over, that it was a good home, better than the other.

"Look at the children!" said Susan. "It's worth it just for them!"

John was running across the meadow to the brook. Jane came in, her face wrinkled with pleasure, carrying Marcia.

"Mum, there's brambleberries in the back garden," she said. "I shall put up jelly."

Jane, living in a little room over the kitchen, was perfectly happy. " 'Twould be nonsense for me to come and go," she had said when they moved. "You won't notice me, Mum, I promise you that."

"It is you I think of," said Mark to Susan.

"I can do my work here," Susan answered simply, and he was silent.

In the big empty barn she set up her materials and her tools. The size of the place possessed her. Far above her were the cobwebby rafters. There were the bins which had once held the harvests of earth. Now they were to hold what she made. They were great enough to hold the largest figures she could make. She threw open the great barn doors to the hills. Upon the space of their greenness was John, a tiny moving mote in the sunshine, and beyond the hills was the sky.

And she in the midst of this spacious new universe felt stirring in her the old enormous need to take clay and make it into shape and form and create being. She began to draw the figures of a man and a woman, and between them she put a child, and after a while into the woman's arm she put a baby. These four were the unit in this universe. She drew them over and over again, day after day, covering huge sheets of paper, spending endless hours upon a hand, a mouth, upon eyes looking. But the woman escaped her. At last, unsatisfied, she put aside the pencil and paper and took the clay. Perhaps out of the solid stuff she would move toward the clearer shape. She made them far smaller than life, experimenting, trying out each movement. If the woman came right she would use this as a model, and perhaps even cut them out of final marble when David Barnes came back.

Two or three times through the two years he had been away she had had his scanty letters. And last week he had sent her a postcard, "I am arriving July the fifth."

She worked, as the summer days went on, seeing no one, stopping only when Mark's car, at evening, turned the corner of the lane. Then she put aside whatever she was doing, though a line lay waiting to be shaped from thought to the reality of clay. Stone! One day perhaps she would work only in stone. She turned away and washed her hands and was there at the gate to meet Mark.

"What have you been doing all day?" he always asked, when he had kissed her.

"Oh, nothing much," she always answered.

They walked to the house, arm in arm, and she followed him upstairs.

"Busy day for me," he said. He went into the bathroom and washed and came out again, his brown hair wet and spiky.

"These summer people," he said cheerfully, brushing his hair before the mirror, "certainly are making good business for me. I could have sold this house three times over just since we took it."

"We'll never sell it," she answered. "I don't see how we lived in that other one."

125

"We didn't know that when we were in it, though," he said. "It was all right as long as we thought it was our home."

But she did not answer. She sat quietly watching him put on a fresh tie. She knew Mark very well now. She knew how to make him happy. She was sure, nearly all the time, that he was happy.

The man and woman and children were finished. The woman had suddenly capitulated and came out of the clay. She stood, docile at last, clasping the child, her head turned a little away. When she was finished Susan cried out of the barn door, "Jane! Jane!"

She had to show someone what she had made. And Jane came running with Marcia, John after her, compelled by the joy in her voice.

"Look!" she said solemnly as they came in, and they looked, standing together before the dark clay figures.

"How you can do it, Mum!" Jane whispered.

And John said, shyly, "Who are they?"

"They are people," Susan replied. "I don't know them. I only made them."

She looked at them, half awed by them now that they were separate from her. When Mark came home in the evening she would bring him here. After all, Jane was ignorant and the others were children. She hungered to see Mark's face when he saw what she had done. She could not hide them now. She wanted eagerly to share them with Mark.

All afternoon she stayed by them, looking at them, pondering them, seeing them approach her more and more closely. She could hear their separate voices. She could hear them speaking to each other and as she gazed at them she could see them about to move, though she knew she had locked them as they were. She thought, pondering, that she would free them if she knew how, but she did not know how.

When she heard the sound of a horn, blown three times, she rose and went to meet Mark, walking without haste.

"Come and see what I have made," she said.

"Have you finished something already?" he asked.

"The shape is finished," she replied.

They went hand in hand to the barn, and she said nothing.

"Well!" he said, and then, "Why, Susan!"

He stared at the four as John had stared.

"Who are they?" he asked.

"Only people," she replied.

She stood waiting while he looked at them.

"They are not looking at each other at all," he said. "Why did you make them like that?"

"What do you mean?" she asked. "I made them as they were."

"They are looking away from each other," he said. "Especially the woman—see her! She's looking away from her baby. A woman would look at her baby, I should think, Susan, or at the man."

"Does it seem wrong to you, Mark?" she asked anxiously. "I had a hard time with her. I couldn't get her right until suddenly she seemed to fall into that pose."

"Are they us?" he asked abruptly.

"No, of course not," she replied.

"Where did you get the models?" he asked again.

She hesitated. It was true that for the woman's body she had stood naked before a mirror, studying every line of her own body.

"The woman certainly looks like you," he went on.

"Nothing but her body," she said quickly.

"More than that," he said. "There's a whole look about her that is like you. And the eyes—I've seen you turn your head exactly like that and look at the woods beside the little house. Sometimes when we were at meals and I was telling you something, you'd turn your head like that and look away off, somewhere, out of the window, into the woods."

"If you are going to imagine everything I make is us," she said impatiently, "then I must stop making anything. I can't take the risk of hurting you every time."

"Of course I don't—I wouldn't," he said.

But a strange bitterness was creeping over her like a chill. "Don't you see," she went on, "that I must be free from the fear of hurting you, or I can't work? I have to feel free. I can't keep thinking, 'Will he like this?'"

"But I do like this," Mark insisted. "Come here, Susan." He put his arm around her. "I think it's wonderful. I feel so humble before you. I don't understand how you do it. It's like magic. But—"

"But?" she asked him.

She stood in the circle of his arm, not leaning against him, not knowing that the woman she had made stood thus also, apart, within the circle of a man's arm.

"It's—I can't express how I feel—but you seem somehow to escape me. It's the old trouble—I can't forget it. I'm not good enough for you—it comes to that."

Mark's arm dropped. He put his hands in his pockets. She stood alone.

"I can break this thing to pieces in a few minutes," she said slowly. "Then it would be gone from between us."

"Susan!" he cried, his face horrified. "Why, you've spent days on it—weeks!"

"I could break it in a moment," she repeated.

"Look here, Sue—I'd never forgive you. I'd be miserable—I couldn't be happy if I thought you were not doing something you wanted to do."

"But if I make you unhappy—"

He broke in. "I promise you—I'll never say a word again about us."

"I shall know if you are even feeling it," she said, "and the knowledge will be handcuffs on my wrists."

"I won't—I'll think about something else," he said fervently. "Sue, please kiss me!"

She turned toward him and saw his beseeching anxious eyes. She took him in her arms and felt his arms about her. He was afraid of her. Why was he afraid of her? There was something about her that made people afraid, and when she felt their fear she was frightened. She pressed herself against him.

"Hold me close," she whispered, and obediently his arms enfolded her. "Close—" she whispered, "closer than that!"

She strained against him for a moment. But he could hold her no closer. Then she said quietly, "Come, darling, let's go and find the children." Mark turned with her and she locked the barn door, and they went together to the house.

When she came in she went upstairs and hid the key in a little box in her desk. "I shall never take him there again," she thought. She was wounded somewhere, somehow—no, perhaps she was only very tired. She brushed her hair freshly and put on a yellow linen dress that made her eyes darker than ever. Then she went quietly downstairs.

On the sagging porch Mark was sitting, smoking, with Marcia on his knee, and John was on the step beside him, hugging his knees as he talked, exactly as Mark often did.

"I tried worms, Daddy," he was saying, "and one kind of fish don't like worms."

"Flies, then." Mark's voice was warm with interest. "You must study the sort of fly that is in season, son, and use that for bait."

"M-m-m," Marcia was humming, under her breath. She held a small rag doll with no arms. Their voices made her reality again. These were her real world, these three.

"Well, my darlings!" she said warmly, deeply. She went out to the porch. "Ready for supper?"

John leaped to his feet and Marcia dropped her doll. Her eyes met Mark's and they laughed. They were very close now, with these two children. He rose and put his arm over her shoulder and all of her life was suddenly here. The thing she had made was cold clay.

The house was full of the sweet heavy odor of brambleberries and sugar, cooking. She was in the kitchen with Jane making jelly. The children were out in the sunshine but again and again John was drawn to the kitchen.

"It smells so good," John said.

"You're like the bumblebees," Susan laughed. The bees were drumming against the screen door, frantic at the sweetness they could not reach.

John stood before the glasses of the dark jelly. "I could eat it all up," he cried.

"You shall have some this minute on bread and butter," Susan said gaily. She fetched one of the loaves of brown bread Jane made.

"Marcia, too," said John earnestly.

She cut the bread and buttered it thickly while they watched her. She looked at them and there fell upon her again one of those moments of intense reality. Time paused and held everything for the moment as it was, the big kitchen with its clean rough floor and small bright windows, Jane at the stove, letting the purple-red syrup drop from the long pewter spoon, Marcia in her high chair, John waiting, his eyes upon her hands, herself— She handed him the bread and time began to flow again.

"There," she said, "eat it and you will feel better."

"Shan't we give the bees any?" asked John. "They want it dreadfully."

She poured a little of the hot jelly into a saucer.

"Set it down on the step and see what happens," she said.

He was gone and she and Jane were filling glasses again, one by one, and setting them aside to cool and jell.

"As I was saying, Mum," Jane went on where she had left off, "my husband was as good as gold. He never drunk nothin', except on Fourth of July a glass of beer, which he would to keep the Fourth, Mum, he used to say, just to show me he was independent, him bein' American and me English. It was only a joke, Mum—for he worked steady and he never hit me once, and what more could you ask of a man, I've always said."

"What, indeed," Susan murmured.

"There's plenty who haven't the luck that you and I have, Mum," said Jane mournfully. "Mr. Keening's the same, isn't he, Mum? Never takes a drink, and just the same, day in and day out. It's a wonderful disposition in a man."

"Yes, it is," said Susan.

And when her world was happily encompassed by the walls of the house, by the rim of the hills against the sky, she heard one day the clatter of a car. She was making a pink linen frock for Marcia, because Marcia's eyes were as dark as her own, and the doorbell rang. She heard Jane's voice, and then, harsh and impatient, she heard David Barnes say, "I've had the devil of a time finding the place."

She rose at once and put down the dress, and at the door of the room Jane said, "There's a gentleman downstairs. He's in such a bad temper, Mum, he must be somebody!"

"I'll come at once," said Susan.

But she did not go down at once. She stood a moment after Jane was gone. Then she went into the room where Marcia was taking her afternoon nap. She was waking, yawning and stretching her plump legs. Susan gathered her into her arms and put on a fresh frock and brushed her short dark curls.

"Somebody has come to see us," she said, and with Marcia in her arms she went downstairs into the living room where

David Barnes stood staring out of the window. He was thicker than ever, and burly in his rough tweeds.

"I've kept you waiting," she said brightly, "because I wanted you to see Marcia. She wasn't born when you were here."

He turned, holding tightly in his hands a short heavy blackthorn walking stick. His cap stuck out of his pocket and he shoved it down impatiently.

"Is this all you've been doing?" he demanded.

"It's enough, isn't it?" she replied, her eyes hard and shining.

She sat down with Marcia on her knee, but he stood bluntly before her. He had changed, she thought. He was older.

"Have you worked at all?" he demanded.

She did not answer. Marcia was struggling down and when she was free she cried, "Janie!"

"Let her go," said David Barnes. "She doesn't want you. Who's Janie?"

"She helps us," said Susan.

"The child prefers her to you," said David Barnes. "You're a rotten mother. I told you you would be."

"I'm not!" Susan said in a low voice.

"What have you done?" he demanded. "—If you have done anything."

"I have done something," she said.

"I want to see it," he said sternly.

There was nothing left to her now except what he chose for her to have. Home, Mark, her children, were gone. There was only this fierce short figure, this voice, these angry eyes, demanding her powers. She rose and went and fetched the key which weeks before she had put into the little box, and without a word they went to the barn which she had not entered since she stood there with Mark.

Mark had said many times, "Aren't you going to work at your figures again, Sue?" and she said each time, "I don't think so, darling. Somehow I want to be with you and the children, these days." Once in the deep soft stillness of the country night she had said to him, "Let's have more children, sweet—Marcia's going on two." But he had said, "No—not yet. I don't want you to unless you're certain."

"I feel certain," she murmured. His shoulder was beneath her head, flesh and blood, warm and sure.

"No," he said, "no—not yet. . . ."

She opened the great stone barn door and David Barnes strode in and turned, as he might toward light, to where the figures stood, and looked at them. She stood beside him, waiting. The wet clay had dried slowly under the great sheet she had spread over them, and now when she drew it aside, they stood unmarred, dried to a pale and tawny silver.

He looked at them without a word. It was a long time, but she waited. Above their heads was the rustle of pigeons nesting in the rafters, and a few feathers fluttered softly down and settled on them.

"You still won't study anatomy," he growled at last. "It's so damned good you don't deserve your luck. But the skeletons aren't right. I tell you you've got to study skeletons and muscles. I won't have any more shilly-shally from you. I know a fellow in New York and you've got to go and work under him three times a week. He does nothing but anatomy."

"I can't," she was about to say and did not.

"How can you tell?" she asked, wondering. "I copied my own body."

"Copy—copy—copy—" he roared at her. "I tell you you've got to stop copying! A sculptor builds from the inside out—he makes his people the way God does!"

"Perhaps I'd better stick to making babies," said Susan, but she knew instantly what he meant.

He did not hear this. "The only advantage you have in being

a woman," he was saying, "is that you can let a man feed and clothe you while you work. I had to make stuff to sell so that I could keep myself alive to work."

"You don't understand me," she said hotly. "I'm not like you—I'm a human being—a woman who wants—"

"I had to make a fool of myself over a woman, even," he went on without listening to her. "Poor as I was, and eaten up wanting to do my work, I had to go and itch after a woman and persuade her to run away from her husband and then I thought I'd never get rid of her. It took me years to see what I know now—that nobody, nothing matters except your work. I wish to God somebody had taken me and beat me over the head and told me what I tell you now, nothing matters to people like us except our work—a few of us are made so—and we do the world's work. The rest of 'em can only stand and stare at what we've done."

He snatched her out of the world and she stood beside him, bodiless and a flame.

"Shall I break this into pieces and start all over again, after I know anatomy?" she asked.

"No, no," he said impatiently. "It's good—too good not to be better, and plenty good to finish."

"I was going to do it in marble," she said.

"No," he said. "Keep marble for your best. I let you cut that fountain just to see how you handled it. Some day or other you'll put clay aside and never touch it again. You're made to carve—not to mold. But this'll go into bronze—I'll send it away for you. And look here, I'll enter it for a competition. There's a man I know who's been wanting a thing for his father's hospital—this'd do. I'll speak to him."

He walked around the figures, whistling softly, nodding his burly head.

"You've made something," he said at last. "You've photo-

134

graphed the rotten detail, but then you've forgotten yourself and made something. The woman's very fine, gazing off like that—clever of you to have seen she wouldn't have been looking at the man or the baby. Oh, Lord—most people would have said she'd be staring at the baby, the fools!"

He pulled his shabby cap to his ears. "Be ready to start your skeletons on Tuesday," he said, and in a moment she heard his car whirling up gravel on the drive.

She said to Mark very casually in the evening, "David Barnes came to see my figures today."

They were sitting side by side on the wide sagging porch. The evening was like every other evening, and she wanted it so. She would keep it so.

"What did he say?" Mark's voice was pleasant, a little cool. She moved closer to him and curled her hand into his.

"He said it was pretty good, but I don't really know enough. I haven't a foundation."

"He's a big stiff!" cried Mark. "What you made was wonderful! I want to go over and look at it again."

"He says I copy people's bodies, but I don't create them."

"What's he talking about?" Mark growled.

"He wants me to go to New York on Tuesday and begin some work in anatomy. Would you mind? I'd be back by the time you were."

In the dusk she could hear the sound of Mark's pipe, puffing. He said at last, "You know I want you to do whatever you like. But I'd make sure that fellow knows his business."

"I would only go twice a week, and Jane's wonderful with the children," she said.

He did not answer. But she had said what she must. After a moment she got up and sat upon his knee and curled herself small into his arms and he held her. For a long time they were silent.

"You're sweet," he whispered at last. "When you're like this you're so sweet."

As soon as Mark left the house on Tuesday she went upstairs and changed her flowered morning dress. He had forgotten it was Tuesday and she had said nothing to him. He kissed her and said as he always did, "Exactly ten hours and I'll be home again."

"We'll be at the gate, all of us," she said. And John had said, "It's nice Marcia can walk a little, 'cause she can go to the gate, too, on her own feet."

They walked down the cinder path to the gate with him and waved at him as he went away. And then she had turned quickly to the children. "John, Mother's got to go away today for a while and you must help Jane take care of Marcia."

"Where you going?" he asked.

"To New York," she said.

"What for?" he asked.

"To work."

"Are you going to work every day like Daddy?" he asked anxiously.

"No, no—only sometimes," she replied, and she had left them in the sunshine, staring at her, bewildered by more than they could understand. But she had to go.

It was only a mile to the railroad station at the south end of the town. Mark could easily have driven her there, but she had not wanted to have the morning different from any other. She would walk.

She was able to do everything. . . . Yes, she was even able to do this. When she was taken into the brightly windowed spotless room she thought for one quick moment, when she saw the long shape under the sheet, that she could not.

"I can, though," she said to herself. "I can do it."

And a gentle-faced, quiet-voiced man came toward her and said, "Miss Gaylord? Creighton is my name. My friend Dave Barnes was telling me about you."

She shook a clean slender nimble hand.

"Will you just come this way?" She followed him into a small room. "Now if you will take off your hat, and put on this—and the gloves—it's very important never to cut yourself at this work."

She obeyed, her heart faltering in her breast. He looked at her sharply.

"Is this the first time you've done this?"

"I've never even seen anybody dead, before," she answered, and was ashamed of her small voice. She cleared her throat and spoke more loudly. "I am a sculptor, and Mr. Barnes says I must know more anatomy."

"My God," he said gently. "It's like Dave to plunge a girl like you into this right off. Why don't you start in an anatomy class, or something mild?"

"I can do it," she answered firmly.

"Well," he answered, doubtfully, "if you feel faint—"

"I shan't feel faint," she replied.

She was glad, when he turned back the sheet, that this quiet body was a beautiful one. If it had been old and gross—but it was young and very beautiful. Once it had been a young man.

"Why did he die?" she whispered.

"There is some strange disease hidden in his brain," Creighton replied.

"And his family—do they mind?"

"He was a foundling child who was never right. He spent his life in a state institution, a ward of the state. His brain will be of some use, at last."

It was quite true, she saw when she looked at the face, that it was smooth and empty.

137

"He looks all right now," said Creighton. "But I saw him twice when he was alive, and his face was in agony."

"Pain?"

"Who knows?" Creighton said. "He was never able to speak. . . . Now I'll go on with my work, and you had better begin—like this."

He cut quickly, accurately.

"There's no blood," she said, amazed.

"No, it's been prepared," he replied. "Now, you see—and here's the manual. I'd advise you to begin like this. Read a page—to here—and then proceed. Ask me anything. But I'll go on. Sure you're all right?"

"Yes," she said.

She sat down and read slowly, forcing her mind to attention. She read carefully to the end. Then she rose to her feet and took the thin sharp knife, delicate and strong. . . . She was glad no blood flowed. The flesh was clay. The touch of it was like clay. All flesh was only clay. She could touch cold clay. And clay knew no pain or distress. . . . The skin was so thin. And when it was laid back like this, the flesh was there, striated. How the muscles wove into each other, fitted to the bone, pulled and moved! And there were the wonderful delicate nerves, and the exquisite lacery of veins and arteries. . . .

"Aren't you about through?" he asked at last. "It's time I shut up shop."

She looked at him dazed.

"I did not dream that was the way an elbow is made," she replied. "Now I know."

In the night she lay awake while Mark slept. She could not sleep. "I shall have to find out how it is all made before I try to make anything again," she thought. After a while she got up and barefoot she walked out of the house upon the grass and stood under the sky. There was no moon and the stars were clear and enormous. Under her feet the grass was wet with dew. In the stillness of the night she stood, feeling everything.

"I am going to the very heart of creation," she thought. But she was not afraid.

She could not tell Mark anything at all of what she was learning. It had become a habit now that twice a week she went to New York. And he insisted on driving her to the station and meeting her in the evening.

"You can't walk that distance in the hot sun," he said tenderly. Once or twice he had asked her, "What do you do when you get there, Sue?" And she had replied, "Just work at anatomy."

Once he had pressed her a little.

"How do you do it?"

"Oh, I just learn how muscles and bones work," she answered.

"Must be sort of dull," he said, and she had cried, "Oh, look, Mark—there's a blue heron in the creek!"

It was quite true that once or twice a year a blue heron, in passage, drifted down an aisle of air into the stream. And this morning there was one. And Mark stopped the car because he was excited about birds, and together they watched the heavy graceful creature dip its beak and flutter its wings in the running water and climb again, lap upon lap, into the air.

"I could believe God sent it!" she thought, and smiled. She could not possibly have made Mark see the ecstasy of discovering week after week how the curve of a thigh was made, how the arch of a foot, of uncovering the beautiful mechanism of a hand.

"Creighton says you should have been a scientist," David Barnes said one day at the end of summer when he came into the laboratory to see what she was doing.

"You have a wonderfully sure touch, Miss Gaylord," Creighton said, smiling.

"And a cold heart," growled David Barnes. "Thank God she has a good cold heart. I'll bet she hasn't once tried to flirt with you, Creighton."

Creighton's fair skin grew bright red, and Susan smiled. They knew nothing about her, these two. Yes, they knew part of her and Mark knew part. But nobody knew all of her.

"She's going to be a great sculptor, this girl," said David Barnes. His blunt hand was on her shoulder, strong and sentient. "She can't be wasted on science. When are you through here, Susan? The summer is over. I'm going back to Paris, and you're coming with me."

"No, I'm not," she said.

"Not through?"

"Not coming to Paris," she repeated.

"Why not, damn you?"

"Because I can't leave Mark and the children."

Creighton was looking at her astonished.

"Yeah, she's gone and got herself married," David Barnes growled bitterly. "Here she is, born with the greatest thing a human being can have, and she goes and gets herself tied up to somebody—what is he?—real estate or something—and actually has children by him. She's got to leave 'em, but she doesn't know it yet. But God will make her!"

Creighton was silent. He was busily washing his delicate instruments, examining the fine edges, wiping them carefully.

"What you don't understand is that I have to have everything," said Susan. "Part of me would be dead if I hadn't married Mark and had the children. I'd only have been working from part of me, and my work would have been no good."

"You don't have to spend your life in jail to know what it's like," said David Barnes. "A couple of nights is enough."

She did not answer. There were things she could not tell

David Barnes, just as there were things she could not tell Mark. No one could understand everything. . . . But putting away her instruments that night she suddenly felt finished here. She knew what she wanted to know. She was ready for something beyond.

"Goodbye, Mr. Creighton," she said when David Barnes was gone. "I shan't be back."

"No?" he asked quickly. Then he smiled a little dimly. "Well, it's been very pleasant, Miss Gaylord. Some day, when you're famous, and I see a statue of yours standing somewhere, I'll think, 'I helped a little in that.'"

"Indeed you have helped me," she said warmly. She had worked beside him all summer, and she knew him, but he did not know her.

"It's been very pleasant knowing you," he said again, wiping his hands on a towel. "I never dreamed, of course—I guess I never knew a married woman who was interested in anything else. You're not like anybody else, though, I guess."

The familiar words woke long echoes in her. When she was a little girl in pigtails she had heard someone say to her mother, "Susan's different, isn't she?" And her mother had said, "Sometimes I can't make her out, myself." And she had crept away to cry for a little while, vaguely, without knowing why she was crying except that she felt lonely.

"Goodbye," she said, holding out her hand to Creighton. "You've been kind."

"Not at all," he murmured, and she looked into his wistful, somewhat startled eyes for a moment, and felt his dry clean hand. He hesitated a moment. "I suppose," he said, "you think this isn't very constructive work, this tearing to pieces all the time. But it's so somebody else can go on. I try to remember that. It's foundation work."

"Yes," said Susan.

She went out and shut the door behind her, softly and finally. "I'm going on too," she thought to herself.

David Barnes was sitting on the front porch, thumping his stick upon the old boards while he shouted at her.

"I want you to see the big fellows working—you haven't seen anybody yet but me."

"Why should I see anyone?" she broke in calmly. "I have to work in my own way. Besides, I want to do American things, not French."

"Good God, you're as ignorant as one of those cows over there!" he bellowed, pointing his stick at the hill. "Nobody's heard of you here—you've got to say you are a pupil of somebody well known."

"Oh, well," she said peaceably, "you're well known."

"But you need Paris!" he groaned. "You don't understand art if you haven't been to Paris!"

She did not answer. Marcia was coming up the garden path, dancing, ahead of Jane. She fell and lay a moment, doubting whether to cry, and decided against it. She struggled to her feet, dusted her small hands together, and began to climb the steps again nimbly. They watched her as she reached the top step and turned a beaming face toward Susan. And Susan opened her arms and took her and set her on her knee and looked arrogantly at David Barnes.

"Wait till they're grown up," he said harshly, "wait till they're gone—and they'll go the first minute they can, because they're selfish as all human beings are and you'll be left with nothing to show for yourself. It'll be too late, then."

"What you don't see," said Susan, "is that I am not giving up anything. I shall have everything—see if I don't!"

"You can't," said David Barnes. His voice was gentle as she had never heard it. "That's what you don't see now, my dear. You've got to choose in this life. There isn't time for everything." He clumped his stick and rose. "Well, some day I'll see you in Paris. I hold to that."

"Perhaps you will," said Susan, smiling. "Didn't I say I was going to have everything? Perhaps Paris, too."

"You can't, I tell you." His voice was inexorable. "If you're in Paris, you won't have this. No, don't argue—wait! I'm never wrong."

She laughed, and he walked down the path and out the gate and down the road, his short body rolling from side to side.

She watched his solitary figure. It disappeared and she sat, rocking Marcia in her arms. In a little while John would come home from fishing in the brook and Mark would turn the corner of the lane. It was nearly sunset and there was a chill of autumn in the air. Marcia was getting to be so big. Soon she would be two years old. It was nearly time for another child. But did she want another one just yet? She was not sure, after all. She wanted first to use this knowledge which was fresh in her. It seemed a long time since she had made anything at all. There was no haste about children. She was young and there was plenty of time for everything.

The gate opened and Mark came in. She heard his step upon the path and her ear sharpened. She knew the rhythm of his step as well as she knew the rhythm of her heart's beating. It was changed. His step dragged.

"Mark!" she called. She stood up and put Marcia down.

"Yes, Sue," he answered. His voice was tired. But then he was often tired at night. His tall frame looked so strong, but he had not much real energy. There was not in him the tirelessness of her own resilient body.

"Is anything wrong?" she asked. He came nearer, and she could see him smile faintly.

"No, dearest," he said. He stooped to pick up Marcia, and came up the steps heavily, holding her, and sat down. "I keep thinking I am going to feel less tired now the summer is over. But I don't," he said.

She looked at his white face and into his eyes, deep set with fatigue.

"I am going in to make you a good strong soup," she said and forgot everything but Mark.

"I'm all right, Sue," he said in the morning at breakfast. "There's nothing the matter with me. It's been a hot summer."

She was about to say, "Has it? I hadn't noticed," but she did not.

"Sure you're all right?" she asked. He smiled and nodded his head and the old quiet faithfulness in his blue eyes and big-featured homely face smote her to the heart. She leaned toward him.

"I love you more than anything," she said earnestly.

"Do you, dear heart?" he said simply, and she saw tears rush to his eyes.

She got up and went to him. "Why, darling," she cried softly, and put his head against her breast.

"I'm all right," he muttered. "Just tired. We mustn't scare the children."

John and Marcia were staring at them with large bewildered eyes. She went back to her seat.

"You're going to have a vacation," she said firmly.

Before he could answer Jane came in, holding out an envelope to Mark.

"It's a telegram, sir," she exclaimed, horrified. "Somebody's passed on, I doubt."

"Who could it be?" Sue exclaimed.

Mark tore it open.

"What's this?" he said. "Sue, it's for you. It's from Barnes."

She took it from him quickly and read, "Hurrah for Susan Gaylord stop your group considered best in Halfred Mead contest stop can you meet me here New York their office eleven o'clock today stop postponing sailing on your account Barnes."

She looked at Mark, breathless. "I never dreamed—of course, I won't go—"

"Of course you will!" cried Mark. "Hurry up and get ready! I'll be late for once."

"I shan't be easy a moment with you not well," she protested stubbornly.

"I'm all right, I tell you!" he cried. "See here—you come back on an early train and I'll meet you and stay home and rest—go to bed if I don't feel just right."

"Promise?"

"Promise!" he said gaily, and she ran upstairs.

"You do look all right," she said from the train window. "If you didn't, I couldn't go, Mark."

"Of course I am," he said, looking up at her. "You look lovely, Sue—you always do."

She smiled and blew him a kiss and then said practically, "I think the children will be all right for the day. I planned everything with Jane."

"You're a perfect mother," he said. She felt his eyes adoring her. The train began to move. "Forget us all for a while," he said. "Have a swell time, darling!"

She waved as long as his tall loose figure was in sight. Then the train curved about a hill and he was gone.

She could put them all safely out of mind now for a while. Out of mind did not mean out of heart. They were always in her heart. She sat by the window, gazing steadily out to the passing country. Her mind ran ahead over the hills. Soon there would be the suburbs, and then the Jersey flats and the sculptured towers of the city. Her mind played about them. She might sometime make a group of men, working against the tops of the towers. She pondered it, planning, weighing the

145

relation between the human beings and those towers they had made. The figures might be larger, in the foreground, or they might be very small, shadowed, bent, crushed by what they themselves had made. She put the idea away, undecided, into her brain's storehouse. She wanted next to do not a group but a single human figure, pliant and swift with life running electric through bones and muscles, through veins and nerves. David Barnes had been right. The knowledge to which he had compelled her was precious, a source for creation. She smiled, remembering that all summer Creighton had not understood what she was doing. But men only understood women as far as their own wives went, and Creighton's wife, if he had one, would be a small mouse of a woman, worried with house and cooking, who could not bear his work. Susan could hear her say primly, "My husband's a scientist." But in herself she would be saying, "I can't bear dead bodies. I won't think about them." Susan laughed a little to herself, softly, seeing her.

The train began to swerve through streets and a faint sour swampy odor drifted into the window. Far ahead she could see the pearly towers, rising against a misty blue sky. She breathed deeply, her hands clasped tightly together. She was glad she had put on her russet dress.

All the way through the traffic, while she sat in the taxicab, her heart was thumping in her breast. It seemed another creature in her. She was sitting quite composed, holding in her this heavily beating heart. She was not in the least excited, except for this excited heart. And when she entered a quiet, deeply carpeted office, it swelled and quickened to suffocation in her throat.

"What name?" asked an indolent voice from behind a telephone switchboard.

"Susan Gaylord," she said.

A blond head appeared above the board, and a girl's startled face looked at her.

"My word!" she exclaimed. "Just a minute—sit down, please."

She cried into a mouthpiece, "Miss Gaylord—Susan Gaylord—yeah, sure!"

Susan sat down in a plushy chair and waited. Across the room the girl's unwinking blue eyes stared at her. And in a moment a fresh-faced young man came rushing to her with both hands held out to her.

"Miss Gaylord! We were waiting for a telegram from you. We've just called Dave Barnes to come right over. He's been fuming about."

She rose to her feet. "I didn't think of sending a telegram," she said shyly. "He sent for me, and I came."

But the young man seemed scarcely to hear her. He was holding her by the arm, guiding her down a passage into a bright square room, filled with dark-toned furniture.

"Sit down, sit down," he was saying. "I'm Jonathan Halfred, by the way—my father's son, only nothing more. Now, tell me everything about yourself. I can't tell you how excited we are over your work. It's simply perfect, you know. The memorial hospital to my father is to be opened at the New Year, and we wanted a big group in the huge square entrance hall, and nothing was big enough. I don't mean cubic feet, you know—I mean in feeling—and then Barnes sent us your marvelous piece. Of course, it's got to be in bronze—huge, twice the size of life, at least."

She was rushed into the torrent of his warmth, his enthusiasm, his frankness, his beaming looks.

"I'm so glad," she kept saying. "Of course, I am glad." And then she interrupted him to say, conscientiously, "I think I ought to tell you that we—Mr. Barnes and I—don't think it is my best work. I have learned a great deal since I did that. I've been studying anatomy all summer."

"It cannot be improved upon," he assured her.

She smiled, knowing it could, but she let him pour out his tumbling praise. Praise could not deceive her when she had in herself, in the feel of her own hands, the knowledge of what was good.

And then the door opened and David Barnes came in.

"Well!" he said, and pushed back his brushy gray hair. "You don't deserve all this luck, but you've got it, and I'll see you through. You can bring the whole kit and caboodle to Paris, now—not that you'll get any real work done until you park them somewhere for good."

She did not heed him.

"Can I see the place where it's to stand?" she asked Jonathan Halfred.

"Of course!" he said heartily. "We'll just run over there." He took up the telephone. "Tell Briggs to pick me up on the Avenue entrance in five minutes," he ordered, and in five minutes they were stepping into an enclosed car, through whose sides no sound of the city could penetrate. She had never seen such a car.

The two men were talking but she did not listen. She was saying to herself that if, when she saw them again, her people, if they did not seem good enough, she would simply do them over. She must have this first thing she did right. She turned to David Barnes, interrupting him without knowing it.

"If I think they're not good enough," she said, "I shall do them over again. I can do them."

"It's good enough to sell," said David Barnes. "But you can make up your own mind."

She said no more, sitting tensely, waiting until they reached a shining new building, still unfinished. She followed them to

148

the bronze doors and stood at the entrance of a great hall, whose light fell from a round window in the roof.

"Here it is," said Jonathan Halfred. "We set it here just to get the effect. Of course it's far too small as it is."

He pulled off the sheet and she saw them, standing in the glare of the light. She saw them as though she had not been their creator. She saw them as creatures in themselves, and she turned to David Barnes.

"I've got to do them over," she said.

"Oh, now—" Jonathan Halfred began, but she did not hear him. She was talking to David Barnes.

"They're made to look like people," she said, "but they're not people."

He said, looking at her, "Not many passing by will know the difference."

She said, "I'll always know it and it will make me miserable in the night."

They gazed at each other steadily. Jonathan Halfred was looking from one to the other, dazed, as though they were speaking a language he did not understand.

"It must be much bigger," said Susan.

"You're a silly fool," said David Barnes, between his teeth, "you're a silly fool and nothing can stop you, because you're right. You don't need me at all—I'll go back to Paris."

He turned and stumped down the steps, and Susan said to Jonathan Halfred, "Promise me to have it destroyed, and I'll send you the real one."

"But—but—" he began.

"No, promise me," she commanded him. "I'll have it here in time."

"It seems folly," he said at last, still dazed, "but I'll promise."

"Now I want to go home," said Susan.

"Oh, you must stay for lunch," he exclaimed.

"No," she said. "I must go straight home and begin. I see exactly what to do."

She had known instantly what was wrong, she thought calmly, sitting in the nearly empty train, and she knew how to make it right. She remembered now that Mark had told her to telegraph him her train, and she had meant to do it, and then had forgotten. He would not know she was coming. It was much earlier than she had expected to be ready to come, but there had been no use in staying after she saw what she had to do. She wanted to be home, to go straight to the barn and begin work. Her mind was already in the barn, shaping the new clay.

It was early afternoon of the September day when she stepped from the train, and she turned straight homeward. The air was dry and cool and she could walk fast. A half hour and she would be home. She planned as she walked, minutes for telephoning Mark, minutes for seeing the children and hearing Jane say, "John's gettin' that lively, Mum, and Marcia breakin' herself to be the same. Today I says to 'em—" And then, and then, she would slip into the great cool barn and mix the clay and take it into her hands—no sketches, no pictures. She had the feel of it ready in her hands. She closed her eyes and bowed her head and saw again the square noble hall, the place in the light where her people would stand. She could feel the power in her gathering to make them as they really were.

The train stopped at last, and she stepped upon an empty platform and went through the empty station and down the road on the south edge of the town toward home. She could not remember anything she had seen all day. Her mind was filled with this surging need in her to make, to shape, her waiting people. She walked quickly, and took off her hat and carried it in her hand. Twenty minutes, fifteen, ten—she was at the gate, and she lifted the latch. There was a strange car at the door, a small dusty gray car.

"John—Marcia!" she called, and went toward the porch.

The door opened, and her father came out.

"Why, Dad!" she cried cheerfully.

"My dear," he said gravely, "Mark is very ill."

She stared at him from the steps. "He was all right," she said, her breath catching in her throat, "he was all right this morning."

"Hal brought him home at noon," her father said. "You weren't here, and Lucile came over, and they got him to bed and sent for the doctor. Your mother and I came over right away. It's typhoid."

But she was pushing past him, up the stairs, into Mark's room. It was already not his room. A strange nurse sat by his bed, and he lay, his face very red, his eyes half closed.

"Mark—darling!" she said, and the nurse stood up as she came in.

"Mrs. Keening?" the nurse asked, but Susan did not see her.

"Dearest, I'm back," she said. She knelt beside the bed and leaned toward him.

And he opened his eyes slowly and turned his head toward her and said in a drowsy, thick voice, "Have a—good day?"

"Why didn't you tell me this morning, darling?" she cried. "I'd never have gone!"

But Mark did not answer her. He passed his dry tongue over his dry lips.

"Water," he whispered to the nurse.

She brought him a cup with a little water in it and he drank and closed his eyes again.

"How long has he been like this?" Susan asked. Within her body her bones were weak with terror and she felt a nausea of fright creeping over her like a cold fog.

"He should have been in bed days ago," the nurse said in a

clear useful voice. "He's dragged around until now he's down he's collapsed. The doctor's downstairs and wants to see you, he said, as soon as you come in. You'd better go on and let your husband rest."

She took up a basin and began sponging Mark's forehead and hands, and Susan got up slowly, gazing at this fevered Mark, whose hot swollen face looked strange to her.

She went into her room and smoothed her hair and washed her face and hands and went downstairs, and all the time she was taking her world and forcing it to the catastrophe of this hour. Her mother came out of the kitchen, her round wrinkled face puckered.

"I've sent Jane and the children home," she whispered. "Johnnie kept crying."

"Yes," said Susan loudly. Why did people whisper as soon as somebody was ill? Mark was not going to die. She went into the living room, and there with her father sat the doctor, a young, sharp man whom she had never seen, since the old doctor died who had taken care of her when John and Marcia were born. They were all so healthy. They never needed doctors.

"Mrs. Keening, your husband is a very sick man," he said, rising quickly and sitting down again.

"It's very sudden," said Susan. "This morning—"

"The symptoms have not been recognized," said the doctor. "I imagine he is of an uncomplaining nature."

"Mark never complains," she said. "But I should have noticed."

The doctor coughed behind his hand. "There is some source of infection about," he said. "Have you had your well tested? These old farms often have impure wells."

"No," she said, looking at him very directly. "I never thought of it."

152

"Ah?" said the doctor. She could feel him thinking, "It is your business, I should say, to think of such things."

"I wouldn't have thought of it myself," her father murmured.

"I should have thought of it," she said. It was as though she had stabbed herself. "It was I who wanted to come here," she went on ruthlessly. "If we had stayed in the house where we were, we'd have had the town water supply, and this wouldn't have happened."

The doctor coughed again.

"Now, Susan," her father said, "there is nothing more absurd than such talk, when the thing's already done."

"I wanted to come here so I could do my work," she went on in the same voice.

The doctor did not speak.

"It doesn't matter," said Susan quickly, leaning forward in her chair. "What shall we do for him?"

The day was gone—no, more, it had never been.

"He must be taken to the hospital," said the doctor. She could feel him enjoying his power over her. He rose. "I'll send the ambulance at once," he went on ruthlessly. "Meanwhile, you must all take precautions. I'll let you know."

He was gone, and she looked at her father.

She rose abruptly. "I had better go and see what's to be done," she said restlessly. She paused on her way to the door and kissed the thick white hair on the crown of her father's head.

But there was nothing for her to do.

She hung about Mark's bed a moment.

"Oughtn't we to—" she began, and the nurse said firmly, "He's quite all right, Mrs. Keening. I will see to everything."

She went downstairs again, into the room where her father was. He had not moved, sitting there quietly by the window as she had left him. She went over to the deep windowsill, and sat down. The window was open and the wind of the cool late September evening blew in. She gazed into the garden and after a while she looked at her father.

"Have I been wrong?" she asked. "Should I have given up the half of my life? How do I know it would have saved him?"

"There is no use in such questions," her father said. He put his beautiful hands together, fingertip to fingertip, and contemplated them. "When you give up the half of your life for any reason," he said quietly and clearly, "you then become an entirely different person. You do not merely become the half of what you might be—the sacrifice twists you and deforms you into another creature." He waited, and then went on. "Your grandfather lived only for his music and he was one sort of man, and his wife and children nearly starved. And I swore I'd never treat a woman as he treated my mother. Your mother was a pretty baby when we were married and I was twenty-two, and promised to take care of her. And because she was afraid when there was no salary coming in every month, I took a job teaching instead of trusting to my luck writing. I think in the end I've done worse by her than my father did by my mother. I'm not pleasant to live with, and no pleasanter for knowing it."

She did not answer. What would she have been if she had stayed in the little house and put Susan Gaylord quietly to death, hour by hour, every day?

"What people don't see," her father went on, his fingertips fluttering apart, "is that it's not a question at all of the work. The world can live without the bit of music or poetry or what not that people like you and me feel we have to make. The point is, what about you and me?" He paused again, and pressed his fingers together firmly. "My advice to you is, give up your life if you can. If you can do it, you can do without it, and everything will be simple. People will understand you and like you better if you're not different from them. God, how people hate any person whose head stands higher than theirs!

154

They'll keep you down if they can—they'll cut off your head to do it."

He was silent, and she sat watching the delicate spare hands, saying nothing, hearing over and over again in the confusion of her mind what he had said. She could not now know what she should have done or been. She had lived as naturally and unconsciously as children live, from every part of her being. And the woman she was had been the woman Mark loved. So much she knew, and no more.

The house was so still that the noise of the pounding of the machines that were digging a new well only made the stillness deeper. She had had the old well sealed at once. No one should ever drink from it again. She had moved to her parents' house until it was finished.

"Stay until Mark comes back," her mother begged her.

She could come at night to the house where she had been a child, but in the morning she wanted to be in her own house. For now the days were nothing but blank hours between the visits she could make to Mark. Morning and afternoon she watched the clock until she could open the door of the small white room in the hospital where he lay motionless upon his bed, smiling drowsily when she came in, but scarcely speaking. Every day at one of the times she met his father or his mother. They could never come together because of cows to be milked and chores to be done.

"How does the boy look to you, Susan?" his father always whispered hoarsely, and she always answered clearly and loudly, "Mark will get well!"

But his mother seldom spoke. She took Susan's hand and held it hard, and gave her the smile that was so dimly Mark's own. Sometimes they sat together by Mark's bed for the half hour allotted to them, and Mark spoke to neither of them. When the time was gone and they came away together and out again

155

into the strong autumn sunshine, Susan said, "It's a lovely day, isn't it! I am glad the weather stays fine for his sake. The very air is lively."

And his mother agreed. "The air makes a difference." And they smiled at each other and parted because they could speak no more.

And day after day she refused to believe anything except that when Mark could gather his strength together he would do it and get well. She needed him and he knew it. She told him over and over.

"Darling, everything is stopped until you are home again. We are all waiting."

When the letter came from New York she put it on her desk and did not open it. She could not think of a moment of her life away from Mark. If she could not be with him, she must at least think of him. It was impossible to turn to her work, lest she forget him.

"What a wicked woman I am," she thought. "Even now I could work and forget him whom I love."

So she would not work. If against the dark emptiness of her brain the figures stole forth, the figures she could make, she sent them away again. Let there be no one there but Mark. She felt a strange superstition rising in her. If she could think only of Mark she could keep him alive. If she never let him slip out of her mind, then he would not slip out of life. She could hold him to life. She believed this at last, and was not afraid. She could save him. She had always done everything she wanted to do. The doctor said gravely, "I must tell you I am not at all pleased, Mrs. Keening. He is putting up no fight at all." But still she would not let herself be afraid. Everything had always come right for her. She would not let Mark die.

"It is a strange case," the doctor said at last. "It is not running its proper course to a crisis. He is not getting better."

"He's no worse," she said stubbornly.

"There is no standing still for a human being," the doctor retorted. "If he isn't getting better, he is getting worse."

. . . One day, causelessly, Mark was better, and on that day he died. He had talked a little when she came in.

"How are the children?" he opened his eyes to ask.

"They are well, except we all long for you," she answered. They were alone for a few moments.

"I'm still—tired," he said, very faintly.

"Yes, and rest," said Susan comfortingly. "You're to rest as long as you like, my darling. Only don't forget us."

He smiled, and after a while he asked, "What are you making now?"

"Nothing," she said quickly. "I can't do any work until you come home. I must have you well and home again."

He said in his slow fainting voice, "What shall you make—then?"

"I am going to do my group over again, darling," she said gently. "But only when you are quite well."

"The woman was looking away, wasn't she?" he murmured.

"Yes," said Susan softly.

He did not speak again. He closed his eyes, and then suddenly as she sat gazing at his silent face, he turned his head away from her toward the wall and quietly he died.

How could he die so quickly, so quietly? If she had dreamed that death was in his mind she would have seized him and held him, cried out to him, and forced the thought of death away from him. When she screamed it was too late. He had already gone. The nurse had run in.

"Why—why—" she had said, startled.

"Quick—" Susan gasped.

But it was no use. He had escaped them effortlessly, not by swiftness or by speed, but by simple weariness.

"I saw him look so very tired," Susan said, her throat tight

157

and hard. She could remember now every instant of Mark's last look. "Then he closed his eyes and turned his face away."

"He just gave up, that's what," said the nurse resentfully. "I've had 'em do that on me before. You work and work on 'em, and then some fine day they just get tired and quit on you."

The doctor was there. His quick hands were touching Mark's breast and eyes, his pulse, his hands. He drew the sheet over his face.

"You had better go home, Mrs. Keening," he said quietly. "Shall I call your father?"

"No," she said, "no."

She could not move. She could not think what to do.

"Come and lie down in the other room, dear," said the nurse.

"No," she said again.

"Shall I call a cab?" asked the doctor. He was kind, but she could see that for him there was no more to be done here, and he wanted to be about his business.

"No, I have my car," she said.

"You needn't worry about—details," he said. "I'll ring your father. I'm very sorry, Mrs. Keening. We did all we could, you know. I think there was a certain stamina lacking, perhaps —one doesn't know—well, if you'll excuse me—"

She was able to turn at last. She went down the hall steadily and out into the sunshine of the rich October day. She climbed into the small gray car and drove to her own house. She would tell no one. Let others do the telling. She wanted to go home, to go upstairs into the room where she and Mark had lived together, and there she would shut the door against everyone else. He could not be quite gone yet from the house where they had lived.

Everything was still when she drove to the gate. She missed a rhythm of noise without being able to remember what it was she missed. She stopped a moment, in the path, trying to remember. Why was the windless brilliant air so silent? And as she stood there a laborer in rough blue overalls came around the house.

"Well, Ma'am!" he shouted in a loud joyful voice. "We struck water, Ma'am, half an hour ago! Yes, Ma'am, two hundred feet down, fifty feet into rock, there's a regular run of the clearest, sweetest water you ever saw or drunk!"

He held out a cupful of water to her.

"It's too late," she said.

She left him staring after her and went quickly into the house and shut the door.

She had telephoned for the children to be brought home, over her mother's wondering, hurt protest.

"Susan, you ought not to stay in that house. Come home for a while."

"No," she had said, "no. I want to stay here tonight—this very night. I want the children to come home. It's quite safe—we've pure water now to drink."

"You're not crucifying yourself, I hope, Sue," said her father. "You're not taking comfort in suffering as much as you can?"

She thought a moment. "I don't think so," she said at last. "No, it's not that. It is only that I feel better here than anywhere else."

So Jane had brought the children home, and she had eaten supper with them quietly and helped Jane put them to bed.

"Shall we kiss you good night for Daddy, too?" John asked, his voice bright with interest.

"Yes," said Susan.

Their kisses fell upon her heart, but she did not weep. Jane was weeping steadily, silently, her face turned away as she worked. . . .

She read far into the night that first night. When she had bathed herself freshly and braided her hair as she always did, she laid herself down on her bed and took up a book and read, carefully, hour upon hour, word after word. She had not wept and could not weep. She turned the pages one by one until she was weak with weariness. Then she closed the book and looked at the clock. It was three o'clock. Mark had been dead exactly twelve hours. She looked over to his empty bed, and blindly she rose from her own bed and went desperately into his and curled her body into the hollows his body had made and put her face into the pillow where his head had rested. And suddenly, like a river breaking out of rock, she felt tears rush at last to her eyes.

People were so strange. They felt that their presence, their very number, could comfort her, or at least could keep her from remembering that he was dead. They crowded to see her, to chat carefully about other things. Hal came every day, and over and over again he said, "If there's anything I can do—any job at all around the place—"

"Thank you, Hal," she said. It was better to finish with weeping in the night because then one's eyes were dry in the day, when people kept coming. "I'll tell you," she promised.

But she did not miss Mark in such things as Hal meant. Mark had not been one to do much about the house. She had not depended on him for such things as women usually depend on men to do. Without thinking, she had done things herself, so that Mark had not even known of them. It was always easier to do things herself and get them out of the way. No, she missed Mark in ways no one could supply for him. She missed him nightly coming home. She had not known, when he was living, how the day rose to the peak of six o'clock, when he came home. Now, knowing he would never turn the corner of the lane again she grew tense with hopeless waiting.

"He isn't coming," she said to herself resolutely. "I'm never going to hear the three notes of the horn again." But she listened as though she would, until six o'clock had come and gone. Then the evening stretched endlessly ahead. She took as much time as she could, helping Jane put the children to bed. And each night they kissed her gaily for Mark. That kiss kept him alive for them, and so she suffered its pain.

And every evening people came to see her. Lucile came down almost every evening, leaving Hal with the children. She chattered industriously of her day, of what "the girls" were doing, of what Susan ought to do, "to take her mind off herself."

"Of course I know you don't feel like it now, Sue, but just as soon as you can I think you ought to join the bridge club again. All the girls say so. There's lots of things you can do to fill up your time, Sue."

"Yes," said Susan vaguely. There was a huge moon tipping the edge of the barn, the first full moon since Mark died. They had always sat together and watched it rise. Even on cold winter nights they had put on coats and run out, shivering and gulping the cold air and laughing. "Let's do it as long as we live, Sue!" Mark had said. . . .

Lucile was asking her something.

"I didn't hear—I'm sorry," Susan said.

"I just said I always wondered how you happened to be in New York that day Mark was taken," Lucile said. "He kept saying over and over that nobody must call you because it was so important."

And instantly Susan could see Mark, desperately ill, insisting that she must not be called because of him.

"I didn't want to go that morning," she said, "but he wanted me to. He said he would come home early and rest, if I would go."

"Well, he said it was awfully important," Lucile repeated.

"It seemed so that day," Susan said, and added, "It doesn't seem important enough to talk about now."

Lucile was silent a moment. Susan could feel her wondering what to say next.

"You are all so kind to me," she said gently. "I'm better and I think I'll sleep tonight."

And Lucile had got up quickly and kissed her warmly on the cheek.

"I'll say good night, then, Sue, dearie. And see you tomorrow! Say, there's a grand new serial started in one of the magazines. I'll bring it along."

She shut the gate briskly and Susan could hear the gears of her car jerk as she pulled away. Then, as it did at the end of every day, night fell upon her. There was the long night to live through before day could come. She sat watching the swinging moon. She could go to bed, but it was easier to sit awake here, easier to think of Mark here than shut into the intensity of loneliness in that room. She remembered again every line of his face. . . .

And as she remembered, she thought of the modeled head which she had never finished. She had not thought of it in months. But now in the night, she wanted instantly and intolerably to see it. She wanted to feel in her fingers the lines of his face. She went into the kitchen and fetched an oil lamp and matches, and then she crossed the patch of moonlit grass into the immense darkness of the barn.

She lit the lamp and put it on a box. Then she went to the shelf which he had put up at the end of the barn and felt along its rough length until her fingers fell upon the shape she knew so well. She carried it to the light and took off the cloth she had wrapped about it, and there in her hands lay his face. She knelt, holding it, gazing at it. It looked exactly like him now. Death had made it look like him. It was finished at last. She knelt, holding it, and after a while she bent her head and laid her cheek against the cheek of clay. It was cold against her warm soft flesh and the lips were still. She wrapped it up again and holding it in the hollow of her arm she took up the lamp and went to the shelf and put it back.

It was at that moment she caught sight of the curved shape of the new born child. And there fell upon her a knowledge of fresh death. There would be no more children, now that Mark was gone. She had not even thought of it, but now this child she had shaped out of clay made her remember everything. Instantly she became aware of herself alone in the huge barn. She put down the lamp and stood terrified because of her loneliness. If she called, no one could hear. There was no one to hear. Jane and the children were asleep, and they would not wake. Her voice would not reach anyone. There was no one to care, as Mark would have cared, where she was. He would not have thought of letting her come to the barn alone at night. There might be a tramp, like the one who hung himself in the wood. She looked about, possessed by a childishness of fear. Above her were the long angular shadows of the beams. She stood in a little circle of dim light, but all around her were shadows and the blackest silence. She wanted to snatch the light and run. But where would she run? There was no one.

"I am a fool," she said aloud. Her voice echoed in the emptiness. She heard the echoes knocking against each other hollowly. "I've got to do something," she thought. "I've got to do something with my hands or I'll go really mad."

She looked about her and there on the shelf before her was the patient clay, waiting. And she took it up and mixed it and slowly the familiar stuff began to make her remember. She had promised that she would make the people over again. There was a little pile of letters on her desk. Several days ago there had even been a telegram which she had read and not answered. She began to remember everything gradually, while she worked. She had not wanted to work. She could not begin. She could not think of it while she was keeping Mark alive. Now, through the feel in her hands, she began to stir out of a sleep. Her body had not slept, but something in her had slept as though it were dead. But not dead as Mark was dead. For now, up from her hands, through bone and vein and nerve and muscle, desire was moving, the old voracious desire, electric still. She began to work fast and with a terrible energy, as though for a long time she had been hindered and now the hindrance was gone. She forgot she had ever been afraid. She forgot everything again, until the dawn came.

And when the dawn came she could work no more. Then she walked back to the house slowly, her ankles wet with dew and mists in her hair, and she bathed and lay down and slept for a while as though she had drunk too much wine.

But when she woke she could not work again. There was no desire in her. She was cold with lassitude, though it was impossible to lie in bed. There was nothing to do except to get up and dress and let the day begin again.

"Sue, you're looking downright sick," her mother kept saying. "If you won't come home, I shall come and stay with you. Mary can look after your father a week or two."

She had taken the children there one afternoon before Christmas, because suddenly, at three o'clock, she realized she was already watching the hands of the clock move toward six. Her father had come downstairs when he heard the children and now he was whittling a little ship for them. He whittled beautifully, each stroke true to the design in his mind. John stood at his knee, silent with pleasure, but Marcia was whirling around and around, singing, "A little boat—a little—little boat—"

"I don't want to be left with Mary," he growled. "Every time she comes home from that business school in New York we have less to talk about. If anybody's going, let her go."

"Yes," said Susan eagerly, "why not? Let her come, Mother."

"Well, if you want her," said her mother with her habit of reluctance.

She did not really want Mary. She wanted no one. But Mary would be better than her mother. Mary would be thinking about herself, and not about her. Mary would not notice if she were pale in the morning. . . . When would she really sleep again, long deep hours of sleep instead of little torn fragments of unconsciousness from which she woke to know again and again that Mark was gone? . . . And Mary would not notice her and cry at her, "Susan, you're eating nothing." When would she know hunger again?

"It's very good of you to spend your holiday like this, Mary," she said when Mary came in with her bag. Mary was different every time she came home. She had grown very tall and her sallowness had changed into plain, dark, thin good-looks, and she was learning how to dress herself.

"I don't mind coming," she said carelessly. "Where's my room?"

Jane had made the small guest room fresh, and Susan had brought a yellow rose and put it in a vase on the dressing table. Now she led Mary upstairs and hesitated. Mary was at once familiar and strange. But Mary dismissed her. "I'll be down after a bit," she said, and Susan went downstairs.

It was still hard to talk to anyone. She had grown used to Mark's easy talk of small and pleasant things. He had talked without waiting for her to speak first or to answer, and she had fallen into a habit of listening to him and dreaming as she listened, because what he said did not fill her mind. But it was comforting and pleasant, and now when people waited for her to talk she did not know how to begin.

But Mary did not talk, either. It was almost like having no one in the house. She sat reading for hours, and then she would fling the book aside and put on her brown tweed coat and stride bare-headed across the fields. And at night she went upstairs early, making no demand of Susan beyond her short, "Good night, Sue. See you in the morning!"

Then Susan was left alone with the night again. There were many small things to fill the day, the children, the house, bits of sewing. Marcia's dresses wanted lengthening and she lengthened them. John wanted a red sweater and she knitted it. Mark used to watch her fingers and say, "I like to see your hands at work. They know exactly what they are to do and they do it quickly." She smiled, being secretly a little proud of her nimble, strong fingers. But now there was no value in swiftness, since there was no hour toward which she worked. Yet she could not stay her hands because they were used to their own quickness and worked as they would without her.

She could read a little, and sometimes she walked home to play on the piano, until one day her father said, "I'm going to have that piano sent to you. I have my own upstairs, and nobody in this house cares for music since you're gone."

"Susan can have it, of course," her mother said half resentfully, "but I don't think you ought to say I don't like music, Father. I'm fond of a good tune."

He had not answered, he never answered her, and the piano came. It was a way to spend hours out of a day and Susan was grateful for that.

But whatever she did the day was over, and there was the long night in which she could not sleep. And in despair at its endlessness and her own intense wakeful empty mind and without any desire for work of her own, she put on her old blue coat and went across the frosty grass to the barn and lit the oil lamp and without any desire still she began to shape again the dark mass of clay which was slowly taking form. The first hour she worked doggedly, against her will, aware always that Mark was gone and that she did not care what she did. Then out of the deeps of her brain, deeper than thought, deeper than knowledge, the old slow fire awoke, and she began to go beyond work into creation. Then only could she forget that Mark was dead. And the habit of the nights grew until at last as soon as her hands touched the clay, she could forget, and it was as comforting as dreamless sleep, and so she ceased to be afraid all day because night was ahead.

The one night she now still feared was Christmas Eve. She could not forget how she and Mark had kept it every year. Now without him she and Mary put into the small stockings the toys she had gone out alone to buy. They did not talk of what they did, beyond a few words.

"That knife is for John," Susan said. "He wants to whittle things as his grandfather does. He'll cut himself, I suppose."

"He'll cut himself anyway, sooner or later," said Mary. "Of course the doll is for Marcia."

"Marcia doesn't like dolls any more either," she answered.

"I never liked dolls," Mary said, yawning. "But you always did."

Susan nodded. "I suppose that's why I keep giving them to Marcia," she answered. In a few minutes it was all finished. Mary yawned again.

"I'm going to bed," she said. "I can't get enough sleep since I came home. I've been sitting up late in New York. There's everything to do there. It's so quiet here."

"Do you like your life?" Susan asked.

"I love it," Mary answered passionately. "I hope I can stay there forever. I can, I suppose. They practically promise us jobs when we finish. I'm going into designing—gowns and hats—" Halfway up the stairs she looked down, a tall, angular, smart young figure. She said carelessly, "I might be able to help you, Sue—if you want to make fountains or figurines or something like that. I might be able to place them for you."

For the first time since Mark died Susan felt another sting.

"I shan't be doing any small things," she said proudly. "I

never told any of you that Jonathan Halfred chose my model for the memorial to his father. I'm working on it."

"Halfred of Halfred-Mead?" Mary asked in her cool voice.

"Yes," said Susan.

"That's very nice," said Mary. "How long have you known?"

"Since the day Mark went to the hospital," Susan answered.

"It's not like you to keep a thing like that to yourself." Mary's voice dropped the words, one by one, like bits of ice.

"With Mark gone it didn't seem to matter," Susan said.

They looked at each other. Something hung trembling between them, some old instinctive difference with which they were born. Susan waited, defensive, for Mary to put it into clear cold words. It might be well if it were put into words so that each could know what it was and the mists between them be cleared away. They might be nearer afterwards, in that clarity, than they were now, each not knowing what the words were.

But Mary turned her head away. "Good night, Sue," she said in her neutral way. "See you in the morning."

She went upstairs, her heels tapping sharply.

Susan crossed the dark lawn that night, angry, and in anger she began to work with energy and at once.

"Mary hates me," she thought. "I don't know why, but she hates me because of what I am. Nothing I can do will make her like me."

She stopped a moment, thinking. Once in the night Mark had said that something she was came between them and made her remote. And she had put herself aside and given herself up to him.

"I am so glad I did that," she thought, wistfully. Then abruptly she began to work again.

There was no wistfulness in this knowledge of Mary's dislike. There was nothing but anger, and anger was healing because it made her forget. She worked twice as fast and as well as she had done before, and when at four o'clock she went to bed she fell asleep immediately and slept without dreaming and without pain.

On Christmas morning Mary watched John with cool dark eyes while he struggled with his new knife, and she sat without a smile while Marcia undressed her doll, dropped it, and began to open every package. Mary seemed not to see them. All through the Christmas Day at her father's house she was apart from them, as though she were a stranger, tolerating the Christmas tree and her father's old jokes over the turkey and the blazing plum pudding. Susan, acute with anger, saw and felt her, and her anger made the day pass without the despair she had so dreaded.

But still she said nothing to Mary. She remembered Mary's pale dark stubborn childhood, and when her father growled to her aside, "Is Mary suffering secretly from cancer or unrequited love or something?" she laughed and answered, "She's only trying to be grown up." Mary's grave face was childish still, her profile so young, when she turned her head unexpectedly over her stiffly held shoulder.

The day after Christmas Susan, at the piano, heard the doorbell pulled without mercy. Jane flew to see who it was. Susan could hear her say stiffly, "Please to take off your things here, sir." In a moment Jane tiptoed in to whisper indignantly, "It's only that young feller that used to come ridin' to the other house—what call he's got to pull off the handle to the doorbell, I don't know, Mum, but he's done it." She held the old-fashioned brass knob in her hand.

Now Michael's voice was shouting from the hall, "Susan, where are you? I'm sorry!"

She went out and there he stood in a brown fur coat, looking

169

enormous and changed. But when he flung the coat off, he was still slender, though inches taller.

"We're here in the country for Christmas," he explained, his face beautiful and amiable. He bent and kissed her lightly on both cheeks. "Now let me come in by your fire and tell me how you do—don't tell me anything sad, for I know all that, but tell me what you are working at."

He was pulling up the blue chair by the fire, and talking in his faintly foreign way. He had been away so long that it was hard now to know where he belonged in the world. But he made the room warm and bright and gay. She leaned forward to put a fresh log on the fire, and before she could do it he had it and was mending the coals, the tongs skilful in his firm quick hands.

He was real, he was fresh and young, and he made everything about him leap with reality, this room, this house, the children's voices floating down the stairs, the flying flames, the lamplight, the drawn curtains. And whatever he talked about became real.

"I saw Dave the other day in Paris," he said, and Paris shone before her eyes, a city of living people. "He's expecting you one of these days."

She smiled and did not answer. It had not come to her that she could leave this house where she and Mark had lived together. But Michael brought the world into this room with his easy voice and his talk of everything. And Michael had never seen Mark.

"I went over to Constantinople," he was saying, "just for a holiday, and last winter I was in India to paint the Himalayas. I wanted to do mountains—not Alps, because people are crawling all over them these days, but snows where feet have never trod and all that, you know. There are mountains in the Himalayas which simply won't let people reach them, Susan.

You can see them lifting their heads higher and higher when you start climbing them."

She was leaning forward, listening. No one had really talked to her for so long. He was throwing the world before her to see. She had forgotten there was a world. "Then I shipped my canvases home and went to China and painted again—people, this time—not the old gorgeous mandarin stuff, Sue, but women like arrows, like odalisques—like—like thin ivory statues—modern women. There's nothing so wonderful to paint in the world—wait till these old fellows in the Academy see them! The world hasn't discovered them yet."

He stopped short to stare over Susan's head. She turned, and Mary was standing in the doorway in a close, smooth, dark coat of red, buttoned high about her throat, and on her head a small red hat.

"Come in, Mary," Susan said. "This is Michael Barry."

He was on his feet, waiting for her. "Michael, this is my sister," she said.

Mary put out her narrow dark hand. "How do you do," she said calmly. "Sue, I'm going for a walk before dark."

"When will you be back?" Susan asked.

"I don't know," Mary said. If she knew Michael was staring at her she made no sign she knew. She stood pulling the small red velvet hat on her head, and he stood staring at her. She turned, indifferently, without haste, and went out, and after a moment he sat down.

"You were talking about China," Susan said.

"Yes," said Michael and lit a cigarette and smoked it quickly. "She looks rather Chinese, your sister. You didn't tell me about her, Susan."

"I never told you about myself at all," Susan said quietly. "I have two children as well, and a father and a mother."

But he was not listening. He crushed out his cigarette and stood up again. "I'll be going along," he said abruptly. She

171

followed him into the hall. "Awfully good to see you," he said hastily. He plunged into the great fur coat and slammed the door.

Jane, setting the table for the children's early supper, peered out of the window. "A nasty conceited young man," she muttered, "not at all the sort a woman'd want about."

Here in her house she saw with wonder the swift onrush of instant love between Michael and Mary. Their love was weaning her away from herself, pulling her out of the stupor in which she had let the days pass since Mark died. It was not like any love she had ever seen, and she knew it was not like the long, slow-growing love between herself and Mark. She had known Mark from her babyhood. There was no time in her life when she had not some memory of him. He was always the same, pleasant kind little boy, shy pleasant lad, and he was strange only for a night, when he became her lover. But there had been no madness in him even then, nothing but the endless reaches of his loving kindness. Love was a wide gentle sea which she had seen scarcely disturbed.

But this new love was a sharp, narrow, angry river, hemmed in between rocks. There was no gentle approach to it. Michael came every day in the morning.

"Where's Mary?" he demanded. "I've got to see her."

"Mary?" Susan called upstairs.

Sometimes Mary answered and sometimes she did not. If she did not Michael waited, fidgeting and talking. The first morning Susan had opened Mary's door.

"I only want to tell you Michael's here," she said.

Mary was lying asleep in yellow pajamas, her head on her arms, her body straight. She opened her eyes and looked at Susan.

"Why should he wake me?" she said and turned and closed her eyes again.

172

Susan shut the door and went downstairs to Michael.

"She doesn't want to wake up," she told him.

"She's got to wake up," Michael said. "We have only a few days."

"I won't wake her," said Susan gently.

"I can see she has a damned bad temper," said Michael gloomily. "But I don't care."

He shouted up the stairs. "Mary! Get up! I'll come up if you don't! I won't wait for you."

But he waited. Mary came downstairs coolly at last, yawning a little.

"You put your coat on and come with me," Michael ordered. "I've got my car."

"I shan't go anywhere until I've had my breakfast," Mary said, and she sat idling over coffee and toast and a cigarette, and would not hurry though he stood glowering over her.

Love grew between them like a sharp wind in spring, and they made no secret of it.

"I'm silly about her," Michael told Susan one day. "I can't eat, I can't sleep. It's not as if I didn't know about women. It's Mary—I'm hit to the heart."

"I ought to be glad but I'm not," Susan said slowly. "I can't see you happy with her. She has to have her own way."

"So do I," he said quickly. "I'm going to marry her. I shall ask her today, because she's going tomorrow." He was standing by the fire, waiting for Mary, at ten o'clock in the morning. "Then she won't be going back to that business college. It makes me crazy to think of her in offices with a lot of men. I want to paint her—I want to paint her all the time I'm making love to her, but there isn't time to do both. When we're married, I'll do nothing but paint her all day long."

"Does she love you?" Susan asked. It was impossible to know whether Mary was in love.

"Of course she does," said Michael impatiently.

She watched them in the car, flying down the gravelly drive, down the hard frozen road, across the wintry country. They scarcely spoke when they were together, and if she had not known they were in love she would have thought they hated each other.

They were gone all day. It was twilight when the door opened and Mary came in alone. She went upstairs and Susan went to the piano and played quietly, waiting. She felt strange and sad, as though she were old and her life was over, though she was not yet thirty. But life was not according to one's years —it was according to what one had. Tonight what she had was not enough, and she felt old.

She heard Mary's footsteps come down the stair and into the room behind her. Mary's hand was on her shoulder, cool and light.

"Well, Sue," she said in her clear voice.

"Well?" asked Susan. She went on playing, softening the music to a whisper.

"I'm all packed," said Mary. Susan turned and looked at her. Mary took her hand away and sat down in the blue chair and crossed her long slender legs.

"You're not—you didn't—" she said.

"I'm not going to marry Michael Barry," said Mary, looking back at her straightly. "I suppose that's what you're talking about."

"Don't you love him?" Susan asked, astonished.

"Yes, I love him," said Mary, "but I simply will not be married. I've made up my mind to it. I know what I want."

"You're wrong," said Susan quickly. "You'll be sorry."

"Why?" Mary's voice was clear and hard.

"It's life," said Susan slowly. "You can't refuse life and be alive."

Mary looked around the silent room. Outside was the darkness, falling upon the stillness of the winter's night.

"There's not much life in this house," she said. "You don't know what life is, Sue, shut off like this."

"I had Mark," said Susan. "I have the children."

Upstairs John and Marcia were asleep. They had played outdoors in the cold sunlight until their cheeks were scarlet.

"I don't know why women think one man and a couple of children is all of life," said Mary.

"It's the earth out of which life grows," said Susan. "If you refuse marriage, Mary, you'll never have your roots deep."

She could not say what she meant. But she knew, though Mark was dead, that death could never take away what he had given her.

"I don't want deep roots," said Mary. "I don't want to grow anywhere, in a house, tied to it. It's no good your talking, Susan. We'll never see things the same. You've always been rather obvious, with all your ability. You take this little town seriously—you keep on with the girls you always knew—that awful Lucile!—just as when you were in college you loved being president of your class. You waste yourself. Mark was all right but he wasn't half good enough for you."

"Don't talk about him," Susan muttered. She clenched her hands on the edge of the piano bench.

"I don't want to talk about him," said Mary. "It's simply that you're an example to me." She paused, looking at her narrow pointed nails. "You've thrown away your gift," she said. "You shut yourself up here—why, you ought to get out and travel and see people, make connections! You'll never get anywhere like this. Nobody knows you. If I had half your gift, I'd be miles ahead of where you are—of where you'd be if you hadn't stopped to marry Mark and have the children and fuss over the house like any ordinary woman."

"I have to have everything," said Susan. "I can't narrow myself the way you do. I had to have babies. I had to feel life pouring in on me—not just overhead, like rain, but deep, like a well bubbling up. You won't understand. Poor Michael!"

"Oh, Michael and I will keep on," said Mary. Her clear voice was passionless. "Nobody refuses a man nowadays—absolutely, that is, unless of course he's sickening. And Michael's really sweet. I want him, in a way."

"Mary!" Susan protested.

"What?" asked Mary, opening her eyes.

"I shall warn Michael," Susan said firmly.

Mary smiled and got up. "I'm going to say good night before we quarrel," she said. "Poor Susan!" She bent and kissed Susan's hair quickly. "I used to be so jealous of you, Sue. You were always much prettier than I, and you could always do everything a hundred times better. But I'm not jealous any more. I'd rather be myself, at last. I know what I want." She was going upstairs as she talked, as positive as a sword, young and hard and inexorable. "I'm alive," she said, "and you are dead."

She was gone, but the words remained, and Susan heard them echoing over and over again. She dead, who had been suffering as it was not in Mary to suffer! Dead people could not suffer. She was alive at this moment as Mary did not know how to be alive. She felt everything, the falling coals of the dying fire, the music she had been playing, the white stars in the black sky. She lived in every instant of her being, wherever she was, whatever she was doing, as Mary had no power for living. All this life she had chosen and lived was only the beginning for something, the foundation for something to come. For what was to come! She put on her coat and went out of the house, across the frozen snowy ground to the barn. She lit the lamp, and put a match to the wood in the big sheet-iron stove she had bought and set up. It made quickly a circle of warmth and in this she stood. She worked until midnight without a moment's rest, feeling the power flowing from within her, down her arms, from her hands. She had made these creatures with knowledge, this man, this woman, these children. She knew their bodies intimately, and she created them as though their surface covered flesh and their flesh bones and organs of life.

At midnight she stepped back, and pulling forward a log she sat down and looked at them. They were now to be clearly seen, for she had made their shapes. There remained no more to be done except the finishing of what was already plain. And as she looked, she saw that out of her own life she had made them. The man, not aware of what she had done, she had made to look like Mark, and she knew the turn of the woman's head for her own. She got up quickly and went and stood under the man's figure and looked up. Yes, it was Mark's face. How strange a thing it was that when he was alive she had not been able to make him seem alive, so that the head on which she had worked then was a death mask now! But here, though he was dead, was Mark alive. The look she knew so well was in his face, a look half shy, a little hesitant, not bold but kind and good and with the strength of goodness in it. But the woman was looking away still.

If Mark were here beside her, she thought, he would be bitterly hurt again.

"You've made them us," he would say slowly, and then he would ask, "Why do you look away from me, Sue?"

But he was not here. He would never be here again. When the stab of bright pain died into the dark she remembered to think, "He will never be hurt again, either." And she thought again, "I would have hurt him again and again, because I have to make all I do out of my own life. It's my only material."

Yes, this was what Mary could never understand. Travel, the casual come and go of strange faces, people for whom she cared nothing and who did not care for her, these were not her life. She had to live not in that passing world but in her own deeps.

She put out the lamp and smothered the coals in the stove with ash and covered her work with the old sheet and went out. The sky was black but the snow shone faintly in the darkness. There was no wind. She stood a moment, aware of intensest loneliness.

"Am I born to be alone?" she asked herself. She felt the air cold and dry as she trudged across the snow. The house was as silent as the night, and alone she crept up the stairs and into her solitary room. She lay awake a long time. Mark, it had come to her, was safe from any hurt now that she could give him. She need not have to think again, "I must be careful—I must not say what I did yesterday. I saw his eyes cloud—I must wait." She could go on unthinking, along her own road, because love was laid in its tomb and could not any more be hurt by what she was. If she were sometimes desolate still, sometimes, also, she was only free. And in this freedom she finished her people. And so she accepted loneliness.

III

HER figures were finished and she was ready to send them away. She was glad that her work was craft as well as art, because there ran in her veins more than the blood of the musician who had been her grandfather. Her mother's father had been a carpenter and a builder of houses, and his sturdy knowledge of tools and their use gave her the perception of wood and stone and a value of fine tools. She had not many tools, but she had never bought a cheap or worthless one. And the more she worked the more she knew what tools she lacked and which she would buy first, when she could. She was satisfied that her power was to take rough and common material and hew it and shape it with her hands as well as her brain. She had to know not only how to build the human body in its fleshly shape, but she had to know what skeleton of wood, what armature, was of size and strength enough to hold upon its frame the huge mass of final clay. She had to know how to saw and hammer and nail and how to twist wires together and of what proportion a base must be. She had to calculate with numbers as well as with dreams.

She was wrapping her figures in swaths of coarse sacking upon soft old rags, ready to ship. She was standing on a step-ladder, reaching the heads of the man and woman. She had called in a carpenter to make the crate, which stood in two halves ready. When she had every part protected, she would put the crate on like a shell and nail the halves together with strong strips of wood. She was singing under her breath, "Oh, that will be—glory for me—" and paused, to think, startled,

"It's the first time I have sung that, and I didn't know I was singing." Then she heard the clatter of the barn door, and when she looked down there stood Michael looking up at her, his head thrown back over the collar of his fur coat.

"You didn't tell me you'd made such a huge thing," he cried reproachfully.

"You didn't ask me," she flung down on him.

"I wish you'd unwrap it so I can see it," he called.

"I won't," she replied cheerfully. "It's done and it's going."

And indeed she could not bear to delay it a day. It was late. She had written Jonathan Halfred at last, and he had answered quickly that she was to take what time she needed. The space was waiting for her. She had telegraphed him this morning in triumph, "My people are coming," and he had telegraphed back, "They shall be met with honors." She tied the last bond and came down the steps.

"It has to be cast yet, but if you go to the Halfred Memorial Hall, a few months from now, you'll see it."

"I'm going to live in New York, as a matter of fact," he said casually. "Here, let me help you lift that."

He lifted one end of the crate with her and then the other.

"Just hold them together a moment, until I get the first strip across," said Susan. The sound of her hammer rang out, quick and clear, hitting each nail true. Mark had said once, "You're the only woman I ever saw who can hit a nail square every time."

"Saw Mary in New York the other day," Michael said, raising his voice.

"Did you?" Susan answered.

"We had dinner together and went to Central Park and rode round and round in a hansom cab in the moonlight."

Susan held her hammer in mid air.

"Did you mind that Mary wouldn't marry you?" she asked.

"I don't know," said Michael slowly. "Perhaps I don't, if she will let me hang about as much as I like."

"Will she?" Susan asked curiously.

"Yes," said Michael in a low voice.

She began to hammer again quickly. Michael was changed. He was not any more the bright-haired boy whose head she had shaped, so that his mother could remember forever how beautiful he had once been.

"Are you staying here in the country?"

"No," he said. "I came down to get all my stuff. I don't know when I'm coming back."

He helped her finish the crating, and then he took a brush and a pot of black paint and drew in bold swirls the address she gave him.

"Andrew Kenley, The Kenley Foundry, Mount High, New York."

He helped her fit casters under the crate and roll it to the door of the barn. Tomorrow morning a farmer whom she knew would stop and take it in his truck. As far as she could she had finished it. They walked through the twilight to the house.

"Will you come in?" she asked.

"No, thanks," he said. "I want to get back to town early tomorrow."

He was full of impatience. She could feel it an edge in his voice, in his look, in everything he did. She saw his head and profile clear and black against the sky behind the open door where she stood.

"Then goodbye," she said.

"Goodbye," he answered.

If she did his head now, no one would know it was the same. She was not sure she knew enough about him now to do it. She stood, letting him go. He was not her life—no, not now. She missed something, some clear pure quality he had been able once to pour out like a radiance. He was full of Mary and the radiance was gone. She stood watching him leap into his car and whirl away, and then she went slowly into her house.

When she saw the crate set into the truck and go swinging down the dusty country road it was as though everyone had gone away and left her behind. In the morning sunshine of an early spring day she stood in the pause of a new loneliness. John and Marcia had run out to see the truck and they stopped beside her. Then she heard John say to Marcia, "Let's go back to the boat."

"What boat?" Susan asked.

"We're making it," said John.

"Where?" she asked.

"In the orchard," he said impatiently. "You don't ask such a lot of things every day, Mother!"

He did not wait for her answer. He was hop-skip-jumping across the grass, according to some secret pattern of his own.

"I go wiv John," said Marcia, and trotted away.

She stood looking at them, proud of them, half sad, cut off from them somehow. She would not be able to take Mark's place with them, however she tried. She had not Mark's power to enter into their small busy world. And they could not enter hers. Perhaps there was no real companionship in children. She had wanted them desperately. She did not forget that she had begged Mark for them. If he had lived she would have again and again wanted a child, because when she was carrying a child in her body there was the satisfaction of creation going on in her being. But children were born and they grew and went away. Whatever she made was completed by the very law of its being, and went away from her and ceased to be a part of her. And each time she was left alone again.

She went into the barn and slowly and with pains she polished her tools, oiled them and put them away. Then she cleared away the refuse of her work, dusted and swept and ordered. She took stock of her materials and made notes of what she must order freshly. When she left the barn at noon, everything was ready for the next work she would do, and she did not lock the barn door.

She was already looking restlessly into herself for what she must do next, for mere work was now a necessity to her. She took a long walk in the afternoon, and all she saw she looked at through a light of question—a farmer ploughing a field, a hawk tearing a dead rabbit, a pheasant startled from the nest. The nest was there at her feet, a shapeless hollowed heap of grass, holding two tawny eggs. But it was all useless to her. There was no meaning in photography of these outward shapes. Meaning came from within herself. She might do the children for mere beauty, or she might as she had often thought of doing, carve the portrait in stone of her father's irritable, beautiful head. But even these would not be integral in themselves if they did not come out of the inner necessity of her being.

She had wandered toward the far edge of Tramp's Woods before she knew it, and now she plunged into its thicknesses. Above her head the young leaves already were dark enough for shadows, and fresh mosses were green under her feet. She stooped to pick a fern, its tendril curling and soft as a baby's hair, and then she walked on toward the ravine. She came upon it soon, not where she and Mark had stood, but at another point where she had never been before. She looked down, still afraid, but she did not draw back as once she had. There was no one now to whom she could turn, whatever her fear. She sat down on a rock and gazed steadily down into the narrow green river that ran among the black rocks. But still she saw no meaning. These were not her materials, these trees and clouds, these fragile ferns at her feet. She must work in sturdier stuffs. Her material was people, not their bodies but their essence, of which the body was only the shape.

"I must go out and find people," she thought, and there

183

flew into her mind all those worlds of people of whom Michael had told her, whom she had never seen. "I've seen very little," she thought. "I wonder why I've been so happy." Mary had said she was as good as dead in this little town, and she had said, believing it, that life was wherever you were living.

"But I'm not living just now," she thought. "Nothing is happening to me inside, and if nothing happens inside, my hands have no work to do and then I shall really die."

She stood up, frightened. She must get out of this wood before night fell. She began to walk quickly and soon she came unexpectedly out of the trees at the street's end where she and Mark had once lived. There that first house stood. It was closed and neglected and the garden was full of weeds. No one had come into it after they went away. She stared at it, seeing it strangely with different eyes.

"How did I ever live in that small house!" she thought, wondering. But once it had been enough for her.

Then, suddenly, as she stood there all the life she had led until this moment seemed to shrink into this closed house which she had outgrown. The town, the people, the friends she had had, the years she had spent, everything gathered around the memory of Mark and was folded away with him. And all was past. She alone, she and the two children, remained, with nothing except the future. And toward that future she must now move.

She walked quickly down the twilight street. Once she turned her head aside and saw Lucile's house. The shades were up and they were all sitting about the table at supper. Lucile was standing, cutting slice after slice from a loaf of bread. Susan looked away and went on her own way.

That night she wrote David Barnes, "I want to go away—" She paused and looked out of the window and saw a delicate young moon. "And it may as well be Paris, because you are there," she added.

184

When the letter was finished, stamped and sealed, she walked down the lane and put it in the rural delivery box and set the little tin flag flying so that in the morning the postman would stop. Then she walked back through the pale night and slept as she had not slept since Mark died.

In the morning she woke to a light excited heart. She hummed a little as she dressed and when she went downstairs she said to Jane, "We are all going to Paris."

Jane looked up from the kitchen stove. "I'm sick as a dog on the sea, Mum," she said, "but I suppose I won't die of it, though I've wished I could. Paris! I can't talk the langwidge, and however will we get the shoppin' done?"

"A ship—a ship!" John cried.

"Who'll live in our house?" asked Marcia solemnly. They were eating their breakfast at the kitchen table.

"No one," said Susan. "We'll lock it up."

"Aren't we ever coming back?"

"I don't know—yes, of course we are."

"I should hope so," murmured Jane, searching for the pan holder, "the raspberries and all—"

After her own breakfast she went to tell her parents. They were still at the table, and her mother said, "I wish you'd leave the children with me, Susan. Those foreign countries have such queer food."

She considered a moment. What would it be to go off, free and alone, to work! But she could not leave them. At night she must come home, and they were now her only home.

"I can't do without them," she told her mother. "Even if they're safer with you, they must take their chances with me."

"Paris!" her father kept saying, "Paris! I always thought I'd get there some day, but I never have."

The news flew about the little town. Lucile gave her a bridge party and she listened to their exclamations. "How you have the courage, Sue!" "With those children!" "I envy you, I must say!" "Paris is so fascinating, I've always thought—" "We'll be wanting to hear all about it, Susan!"

"What'll you do over there?" Lucile asked. She was growing stout and she pouted a little as she cut a dark cake and licked a bit of icing from her forefinger. Then she forgot Paris. "There, girls!" she cried. "That's a good cake, if I do say it as shouldn't!"

They all forgot Paris, Susan, everything not in their own lives. They screamed and cried, "You always make grand cake, Lucile!" "Oh, Lucile! M-mh!" Lucile, smiling and flushed, forgot what she had asked. "The whole secret of it—" she began. "No, I won't tell!" she declared. "If I did, you'd all be making it, and then I wouldn't have anything special to give you when you come to my house!"

"Aw, you meanie!" "Isn't she mean?" "I've a good mind not to eat your old cake, anyway!" they cried.

Smiling, silent, trying to be one of them still, as she had tried to be when she was a child, Susan was as lonely as she had been the other day in Tramp's Woods. Not one of them was living. If she should put one of them into stone or marble the strong stuff would crush them into nothing, for they were empty in themselves. There was no material in them for her needs. If they had known what she thought, they would have hated her. And she did not hate them at all.

She sat listening, watching, admiring their pretty frocks, their pretty hands fluttering among the cards. She had often paused in her morning's work to watch a flock of small birds gather and pour out a chit-chat of varied noise, not musical, not strong enough for speech. She watched them, half amused, half tender, understanding their small intensities which were none of her intensity.

"I must remember to put out crumbs for them," she always thought, and sometimes she remembered. . . .

"Of course, I'll remember to send everybody picture postcards," she promised at their gay importunings— "Oh, all the wonderful things you'll be seeing, Sue!" And she answered, smiling, "You must all write me and tell me how the babies are growing and everything that happens in the town."

"We will, Sue dear," they promised. "Good luck, Sue—oh, dear, I must hurry! Larry will be home!" "Heavens, is it six o'clock? Tom will be starving! Goodbye, Sue!" "Goodbye, dear Sue!"

"Goodbye—goodbye!" she said to them all.

They set forth for New York, a little company of four, and she was their captain. They looked to her and she led them, looking back wherever she went, to see Jane's faithful dilapidated figure, a child's hand in each of hers, and her eyes dogged and anxious.

"I'm too big to hold your hand, Jane," John muttered, tugging.

"I'll not leave hold of the two of you till we get there," Jane answered fiercely, perspiration cold on her upper lip, and he subsided.

Susan left them in a hotel room while she bought tickets and learned about ship's docks.

"Lock the door," said Jane grimly. "John's that good at arguin', I don't want it so we can get out before you're back, no matter if he argues me head off the way he does."

So she locked them in and put the key in her handbag and went about her business until everything was done. Then in the few hours before the ship sailed she took them to the entrance of the Halfred Hospital and half shyly she said to them, "There under that great round window is where those people I was making are going to stand."

"Well, I never," said Jane vacantly, staring around the great space.

"Look, Mother," John cried, "there's a man with balloons!"

"Where?" screamed Marcia. They were darting toward the street.

"There! There!" John cried.

"I'll get them for you," said Susan quietly, and turned away to buy the balloons. Of course it could be nothing to them where her people were to stand.

On the ship, leaving the last land she knew, she counted her money carefully. Alone she would not have troubled to know what she had, but these three looked to her for everything. She counted the bills and looked to see if the traveler's checks were where she had put them. Jane was stalking the decks, her hands still clutching firmly the children's frantic little fingers.

"I'll keep a-hold as long as I'm up," she had told Susan, "for once we cast off, I'll have to lay for good."

"I'll go down and get things unpacked, then," Susan had said.

So she had come down into the cabin and unpacked pajamas and tooth brushes and counted her money. She had her prize money, and she had drawn half of Mark's insurance money from the bank and it was enough, she reckoned, with Jane's managing, to live for a year. In that year she must earn for another year. Her work now must be more than art, more than something to satisfy her own desire and need. It must be bread to feed the children and a roof beneath which to live.

The last moment, when she had stood ready to close the familiar door, swept back into her mind. For that moment she had been half afraid. She was leaving shelter, the only shelter she possessed, to go out, for no particular reason, into the world she did not know. Yet she did not want to sleep another night in that house. She wanted to wander, she must wander.

"Am I afraid?" she asked her heart. She was not afraid. "I'm strong enough." she thought steadily. She was brushing her hair before the mirror with swift long strokes. Her face was brown with country winds and burn, and her body was firm and full of power, and since the day she had determined to go to Paris, the lack of will which had kept her weary since Mark died, had left her. She felt able for anything. A year! She could do anything in a year.

The door opened and Jane stood there, a pallid green upon her face.

"We've left," she said faintly. "I've got to lay down." She thrust the children in. "You won't forget 'em, Mum, and get to dreamin'?"

"No," said Susan, "I won't get dreaming."

"You have to keep a-hold of 'em," said Jane, clutching them both, and leaned her head against the door jamb.

"I will," Susan promised. She looked out of the porthole. The ship had cast her moorings and was sailing slowly toward the sea.

"Well, Susan Gaylord," said David Barnes, "you're here at last!"

The train had slid to a stop in the gray of an early Paris morning, and immediately his head had appeared at the door. "Kit and caboodle," he added. "Well, come on—I've got a room at a pension for you and I daresay we can get another. I thought you'd be alone. Never dreamed you'd drag your pups along."

"I had to come like this or not at all," she said.

He did not answer. He was roaring at a blowsy porter to take their bags and then he stumped ahead of them through the crowd, digging his way with vicious jerks of his elbows.

"Keep straight behind me," he ordered.

He led them to a gate and put his fingers in his mouth and blew a sharp whistle and a taxicab rushed out of the mist.

"Here, bundle in," he said, and when they were all in he

squeezed himself by Susan and roared an address at the driver.

"Everything's ready for you," he said to Susan. "You'll go every morning at eight o'clock to the studio—here's the place— I wrote it down for you, and you will work all morning with this man. He will teach you the million things in which you are still ignorant. And in the afternoon for the present you will come to me and work as an apprentice. I haven't made you work before. I have treated you pretty much as a woman until now. But from this moment you aren't a woman. You are a sculptor. You shall complain of nothing I set for you to do. You shall learn everything. Have you ever seen a foundry?"

"No," said Susan.

"Ha!" said David Barnes. He stared at the children. "Why did you bring them?" he asked.

"They are my home," she said.

He grunted. "You don't need a home!"

She did not answer, but she was not going to be afraid of him. At the door of the pension she turned to him and held out her hand.

"You have been so kind," she said. "Now there is nothing more you can do for us. I will go to the studio tomorrow morning, and in the afternoon I will come to you."

"Here is my address," he said. He gave her a bit of paper. "I wrote everything down. These French names have nothing for the mind to hang to. . . . You're all right, are you?"

"Quite all right," said Susan quickly.

"Well!" he grunted, and turned away and stumped into the mist.

"Where'll we go, Mum?" asked Jane. She interrupted the stout dark Frenchwoman who had come to receive them.

"We'll go in and have breakfast," said Susan. "Then you shall keep the children, and I'm going out to find a place for us to live." They were following the woman up a clean dark little stair, into a large bare clean room.

"One moment!" the woman cried. "A little breakfast, my dears!"

"What's she sayin'?" asked Jane with suspicion.

"She's going to bring us breakfast," said Susan brightly. "Now, Jane, don't look at her as though she were a murderess."

But Jane was looking at the small ewer of water set in a basin. "We'll not keep clean on that," she said. "The French are a dirty people."

"We aren't staying here," said Susan. "Only today. I've got to find something today, because tomorrow my work begins. Jane, I have to work as I never have before."

"All them raspberries goin' to waste in the garden at home," Jane muttered. She was taking off Marcia's hat and coat tenderly. "Now, lovey, we'll wash and have a bite of breakfast, and then you shall have a sleep after such a night. Such trains, Mum! John, you've not cleaned yourself proper."

"You shall all rest," said Susan gently. "I'm going to find a pleasant place for us to live and we'll go this afternoon."

She had no idea of what she could do, but she must do it. Today was her one day. She would ask no delays because she was a woman with two children. In her stiff college French, while Jane spread rolls with butter and honey, she asked the large dark woman about a place to live. "Near a park, if possible, for the children, but not dear," she added.

"But certainly," the woman said briskly. "I see it exactly. Madame is an artist, but there remain these children. Ah, yes, there are houses, flats, apartments, assuredly, and some not dear, if Madame does not mind poor people—clean, naturally, as all French are clean. With us poverty is not filth—no, no, we are not like the English, thank God. As a matter of truth, there are such places in this very street—how large a park do you require, Madame? At the end of our street there is a bit of ground where they have set a statue of an old provincial general. It was presented by his province, you understand, Madame, and naturally is not good enough for Paris. But what would you?—it is a gift. We are nothing if not courteous, we Parisians. So the authorities set it here among the poor. There is not a park, but the sparrows come and sit so sweetly upon his poor old shoulders. He is quite gray with their little excrements. And there is a bench and a bit of grass and a tree, and the street is wide."

"I'll go and see," said Susan.

But when she turned at the door to say a last goodbye, she saw Jane was terrified.

"If anything should happen, Mum," said Jane, "I can't speak a word."

Susan laughed. "Nothing could happen to me, but here is David Barnes' address." She gave Jane the bit of paper and went out alone. And going down the strange street and from one strange house to another, seeing nothing but strange faces, to her too his name and address scrawled upon the leaf from his notebook was comfort.

She went into every house on the long winding street that announced itself to have a vacancy. She listened to long effervescent explanations of how sunlight fell through such a window, so, even in winter, and how here one did not hear the noise of the carts at dawn or of vendors shouting, and of this room, which though seeming dark, was miraculously cool in summer and warm in winter. She could not see any of them as home. There must be something in rooms to receive life, and these did not receive her.

She walked at last to the end of the street. It was better to see the bit of grass for herself, and to know if it were enough for a park. She came upon it suddenly. The tall narrow houses, so closely pressed together, their roofs jagged as cliffs, here stopped short and encircled a tiny square of green. There, truly enough, sat an old general in gray stone under a single large chestnut tree. She crossed the street and stood in front of him. Someone had carved him out of natural granite, someone who did not know very well how to use his tools, but who had loved the man. The uniform was stiff and ugly, but the face was tender and kind in its lines and every medal was on the proud old breast. It was quite true the sparrows had made him their own. They sat in droves upon his head and shoulders and in the crook of his arm a pigeon had built a nest. Here in this bright busy neglectful city the old man sat an exile, and only the birds gave him heed.

"I'd rather like living near him," she thought. The children could play here, and the bench was empty and Jane could sit and sew. Across the streets on four sides were little shops where she could buy their food. She crossed again and searched among them carefully. Above a little patisserie she saw a sign of rooms to rent and she went in. A small clean white-haired woman nodded brightly above long shelves of breads and pastries, and led her up a straight narrow stair beside the shop door and opened a door. Four small clean rooms, joined one to the other, lay before her. She walked to the window and looking out saw before her the proudly bent head of the old general and his gray covered shoulders, and the chestnut tree made a spray of green across the panes.

"We can live here," she thought. "May we come at once?" she asked the old lady.

"But yes, Madame," she answered simply. "It is for rent, is it not? The sooner the better for you and for me."

There were two bedrooms, and Jane could take the big one with the children, she would put up a screen for John—and she would keep the small one alone. The place would do very well. She opened her purse and paid her first week's rent into the old woman's pink, wrinkled palm.

From the turmoil of this small crowded house, from the merriment of the chatter over the tiny breakfast table drawn to the window, from sparrows on the windowsill, gobbling the crumbs the children put there, from Jane, in perpetual gloomy pleasure over the evil ways of foreigners, from the noise and shrillness and energy of the square, stirring into its morning life, she took each morning a bus to the huge silent studio on the edge of the city where the famous sculptor worked. On the first morning she had presented herself, a woman in a peasant's dress and cap had taken her card, and had said in a rich deep voice, "Enter, if you please, into the foyer and wait."

She had come into a small stone-floored hall and waited, standing, until the woman came back, her face composed, to say again, "Enter, if you please, into the studio and wait."

She entered into a long room full of swathed and marble figures. The moments stretched endlessly as she waited. She walked back and forth, waiting, but no one came. The windows were high and she could not see more than green treetops, and the walls were so thick that there was no sound from outside. The woman did not come back, and it was as though she had been put there and forgotten.

She sat down and then got up restlessly, and walked to and fro among the figures again, and then as she waited, she grew half angry and half determined to walk out of the door and away from this house. But at the end of the room was a great scaffolding. She had not seen it at first because the room turned sharply at a right angle and ran along another side of the house. She went up to the scaffolding eagerly and saw within a huge block of marble, partly carved, with an enormous, bold head. Head and shoulders of some giant were blocked in rough sure lines. She looked up at it, awed by its immensity, not seeing what it was to be, and then, because she was not able to deny herself, she began to climb the ladder up to the top of the scaffolding. There on the topmost board she found, laid in exact order, a set of tools. Her heart leaped at them, and she took them up carefully, one by one. These were real tools, fine, tempered beyond any sculptor's dream. They were a master's tools, beautifully strong and light, sharp and tended. She took a chisel and a mallet. They fit the palms of her hands as though the maker had measured her for them. She leaned over the immense head, compelled to feel the edge upon the marble, and then she chipped delicately, once and twice. It was like painting with a brush, the edge cut so true and fine. Where, where could she buy such tools?

"Come down," she heard a voice say. It was so gentle and quiet a voice that she was scarcely surprised. It stayed her hands but did not startle them. She looked down through the scaffolding and saw an upturned face, huge and bearded.

"Come down," he repeated. She laid the tools down carefully and came down and found herself face to face with an enormous old man in a brown smock. He was brown as a seal, brown skin, brown eyes, but his spreading beard was white. His voice burst out of him, suddenly enormous, so that she jumped.

"So, Mademoiselle," he bellowed, "you finish the head for me, hein? A young lady I do not know, whom I receive only because of my friend Barnes, comes in and condescends to finish my head for me. I thank you, Mademoiselle!"

His hands were in his beard, pulling and twisting.

"Where can I get such tools?" Susan asked. "I must have such tools."

"Ah, now you would take my tools!" he cried. He turned and addressed the figures. "My friends, the tools—where are they? She demands them of you, the tools that made you— give them to her!"

"Please," said Susan.

He breathed fiercely and coughed and said, suddenly rational, "Well, my dear, why have you come?"

"To learn—nothing else," Susan said stoutly. "I shall learn everything you can teach me."

"In that case," he said gravely, "the task is endless." He paused, twisting his beard, his eyes sparkling. "Climb up again," he commanded her. "Bring down the tools. Let us begin with tools."

She climbed up and brought them down, one by one. "Now observe—" he began, and for two hours he told her about tools.

"You're late," David Barnes growled at her in the afternoon. "What did you learn?"

"I learned where to buy tools," she said, and then she said, "I shall have to earn quickly, Dave. I spent half my money today on tools, half my children's bread!"

He was standing by a sloping desk, drawing a short bold squat figure. He looked up.

"I told you you weren't any sort of a mother," he said in his harsh barking voice. But his eyes were shining at her.

She was doing nothing but drawing, nothing but learning how to make armatures, how to mix clay, how to make plaster. She forgot that she had not a man's body, and she learned how to bend iron and twist heavy wire, how to calculate the strains and stress of a huge figure of clay. All she had known now became nothing—she had so much more to learn.

"Compute!" the *maître* would command her. "If the Laocoon were to be made in clay, of what size and shape would the armature be to support it?"

She sat for hours like a schoolgirl, computing, wetting her pencil in her mouth, muttering multiplications to herself, and when at last she brought her drawing to him he roared with enormous laughter.

"The serpents!" he cried. "The serpents—everything would collapse into earth again."

And she stood, staring at the swift lines of his black pencil on the paper.

"So!" he said. "And so—and so—" She felt the strong black lines eating into her brain.

. . . She had given the rest of her money to Jane and Jane

was hoarding it, spending it as hardly as blood for rent and food.

"Tell me when there is only enough for a month," Susan said to her. But Jane had not told her yet. . . .

"First a craftsman," he said, "and only then the artist—perhaps never the artist," he added, "for it depends on what you are within, Mademoiselle, as to whether you are an artist. One does not become the artist—one is or is not."

She would not ask him the words in her mouth, "And I, am I?" It was not for anyone to answer except herself. When she knew her craft she would ask herself the question and answer it.

"The soul," he said, sharpening delicately a narrow chisel, "it all is in the measure of the soul. A little talent and a great soul are better than great talent and a small soul. When talent and soul are equally in great measure, ah, then—once or twice I have seen it so."

He looked up at her sharply, his eyes bright behind his bushy brown brows. "You ask me no question?"

"No," said Susan steadily, "I ask no question, yet."

He went on sharpening his chisel. Then he stopped and brushed up the ends of his mustache. Between his mustache and his beard his lips still shone full and red.

"You are not a woman, you know, Mam'selle," he declared. "A woman does not pursue art as you do. With women art is an escape only. It is a thing to do when life does not give what they want most. But I can nearly believe it is what you want most. Ah, your heart is cold and clear! I feel it is so."

She smiled and did not answer. He talked a great deal to her. She knew quite well that if once she let her eyelids flutter or her hand tremble, he would pounce upon her with those hot red lips. She had heard fragments of stories among the pupils in the studio before he came. This model was his mistress and that. But she had not listened, for she cared to hear nothing. Now she could feel the essence of what he was, a hot, molten creature, still fluid with warmth, forever burning to ready passion anywhere. But still she cared no more than she had cared to use time to hear the stories about him. She looked at him with wide and candid eyes and her hand never faltered.

"You are a little stupid, I think, sometimes, Mam'selle Gaylord! Your eyes are as stupid as a child's!" he said.

"I am not at all intellectual, Monsieur," she agreed peaceably.

"So, you do not work out of your brain, eh?" he demanded.

"No," she said, "not out of my brain."

"And you have no heart," he said abruptly, staring at her.

"None," she said, pleasantly.

"So!" he shouted. "You work out of your stomach, perhaps!"

She thought about this. "Perhaps I do," she agreed again.

"Ha!" he snorted. "You don't know anything. You don't know anything about yourself."

One afternoon in his studio she said to David Barnes, "How shall I know what I am?" She was working on a flat surface of bronze, rubbing in acids, studying the patine.

He replied, "If you can be satisfied with tools and materials, be satisfied. You are not then an artist. Learn your craft, and if it is enough, let it be enough."

He stopped and began to whistle.

"What then?" she asked.

"You will be a good marble-pointer for sculptors like me."

"That would never satisfy me," she said quickly.

"Very well then, Miss!" he retorted. "Discover what it is that satisfies your soul. If you are satisfied with less you will be surfeited with more."

He was sitting at his great drawing table. All about him were big sheets of paper upon which he was drawing.

"I shall have to go to America next year," he muttered. "I shall have to do that Edison next." He looked up at Susan.

"To discover who these Titans are, that is the difficulty. It is easy to make them once they are found. But where are they? It was easy to choose among those who have already made our history. Death has sorted them out. But life is not so clever. Among the living who can say this one is greater than that?"

Susan did not hear him. For weeks she had been working with her hands rather than her brain. Tools and materials, the making of plaster casts, the preparation of marbles, the textures of bronze and the methods of casting—these had been all her interest. David Barnes had hired a carriage and driven her down a cobbled road to a spreading old foundry to watch a white-bearded French foundry man and his two sons cast his Napoleon from the plaster. She had stood by David Barnes when this plaster model was being finished. Now while they waited, she saw a pulse was beating in his jaws and that his eyes were grim. He caught her look and said, "I never can pass unscathed through this moment, when my clay model is destroyed. It is the work of my hands. When it is taken from me by these men, even though I know it must be so, I give unwillingly to other hands—it's the core of my being for the moment—the thing I've made. What if they make a mistake? I shall never be able to do it again exactly right."

"Have you ever had to do it over?" she asked.

"No—but I suffer always the same," he replied. "And yet when the bronze comes to me from the furnaces, it is rebirth—my own is come back to me, completed and permanent."

He would never, as other sculptors did, allow the craftsmen to finish his bronzes. He held the gas torch himself, or he made her do it, and he brushed the acids into the hot metal. He could not eat until he could discover if what he had done were successful. Together they rubbed the smooth surfaces inch by inch until they glowed and shone, and only when all was finished he roared that he was starving. Then putting his hat on askew he would rush out and bring back a great round of beefsteak which he cooked over charcoals and made her eat with him.

. . . Tonight she went home late, as she often did, walking through the lonely Paris streets, holding her look steadfastly ahead because of the solitary figures that came out of the darkness and brushed against her. Her garments were too poor to tempt a robber, and her intent unwandering eyes held no lure for the casual. If a man stood in her path, drunken, she pushed him aside with one hand. Her mind was full of what she was learning.

Day after day now she was at the foundries, watching the stirring molten metal in the crucible, the pouring of its hot white stream into the mold. She pressed forward, forgetful of the sparks and the smoke, until the mold overflowed. Someone leaped forward to knock away the surplus, and the white intense moment was over. She longed as she had longed for children, to be able to make entire a figure from the clay to its final bronze. To make the clay models was only to conceive. She wanted to work through the whole creation from original clay, through the plaster mold, to the final smoothed and polished bronze. But no one did such things, not even David Barnes. And the other sculptors whom she came to know through him never thought beyond the plastic clay. To conceive an idea and put it to clay was enough for them. They sent them away and received them again, not knowing how it was they went out in clay and returned in metal. But she was incomplete unless her hands had moved to perform each step. . . .

"Am I craftsman or artist?" she asked herself aloud in the darkness of the street.

The *maître* kept saying to her loudly that women were never artists. Women were too passive, they lacked the cold desire for perfection, women were lazy, they could not give themselves, women were machines and not creators, women had no imagination. She listened, pondering what he said. But she was not like other women. Once she had told Mark most passionately that she would not be different, but now she knew she was different. Other women did not carry about in them this unceasing desire for perfection in the shaping of clay and the carving of stone. Other women did not leave their homes and come across the sea, searching. She knew now that had Mark lived, one day she would still have come, and if he had not come with her she would have left him and come alone. And that would have broken his heart. It was better that he died than that she should break his heart. Then she was shocked that it could ever seem well to her that Mark was dead. She was ashamed and still she said to herself doggedly, "I have to do what I was made to do."

She reached the square and in the blackness the old general's figure lifted itself, still more solid in blackness, and she opened the door of the straight steep stair that led to home. Now she left the unanswered question outside in the night. Upstairs Jane sat beside a clean lighted lamp darning John's sock drawn over her hand.

"How have they been?" Susan asked quickly.

"They'd a wunnerful day," said Jane. "I took 'em on a bus to some gardens the policeman told me about. There's a policeman at the end of the street who can talk almost Christian, Mum."

"You mustn't get lost," Susan said. "How would I ever find you?"

"I'll not lose them," Jane answered. "I always look which way I'm goin' and come back the same."

Susan tiptoed into the big bedroom where on the two cots they lay asleep. She drew up a stool and sat down. Asleep or awake they gave her something which she did not try to understand, but which she must have. Their bodies, their voices, their talk and laughter, their whole being made a foundation of reality to her life. She had not seen them all day. She had scarcely thought of them. But at night she came home because they were here. In the faint light of the night lamp she could see John's head, his cheek upon his hand, quiet, ordered, as John was. But Marcia lay in a sprawl, her arms flung wide, her hair tossed as sleep happened to catch her. If there had not been these two to make her home, to what would she come, who must come home at night? David Barnes had a cot behind a screen in his studio and he did not care whether it was night or day. He slept when he could work no more. But she had to open a door into a room and see a lighted lamp and a table set for food and know that her children were safe and sleeping. She tiptoed away, content.

Jane rose to fetch her supper and Susan sat down in her place and drew John's sock over her hand and began to weave the thread in and out. It was good to feel the familiar homely work in her fingers.

"How long his foot is growing!" she said to Jane.

"He takes eight-year-old things reg'lar now," said Jane. She set down a bowl of soup. "It's a soup I learned off of Madame downstairs whose name I can't never say," she said. "But the soup's good. I smelled it one day when I ran in. 'What is it?' I says, sniffin' you know to show her, on account of her bein' slow in the langwidge, and she takes me behind and shows me. Carrots, onion, a bit of cabbage, whatever meat you've got handy—"

"It's good," said Susan. She forgot food hour after hour, and came home to find herself ravenous at the smell and taste of food.

"Perhaps we ought to send John to school," she said to Jane who was bringing in a salad.

"It would maybe be good for 'im," said Jane, standing to

wait, "though it's a pity if he has to learn his books in such a langwidge as they've got here."

"I think I'll take tomorrow to find out about schools," said Susan. It was a long time since she had spent a day with the children. A hunger for them stirred in her. She had every now and again to renew herself with them. "They mustn't forget I am their mother," she thought jealously.

And for a day she was everything to them.

"I want Mother to button my dress," Marcia cried. "Go away, naughty old Jane!"

"Mother, I drew some birds," said John eagerly. "I want to show you my birds."

After their breakfast she took them with her to see Mr. Withers, the English clergyman who had come to call on her once.

"We want a school for John," she told him. They were sitting in the proper little English drawing room which looked out on a winding old Paris street, and Mr. Withers' faded little wife was saying, "Would you like a biscuit, dears?"

"Cookies, she means, Mother," John explained in a whisper when she had passed the jar.

"Let me see," said the clergyman.

"French," said Susan.

"Ah," said Mr. Withers, "I doubt the wisdom of his learning his letters in a foreign tongue."

"Ah, no," cried Mrs. Withers softly. "Don't let them become foreign. It is such a temptation. One succumbs, scarcely knowing. I feel odd myself, sometimes, when we go back to dear old England. If it weren't that Mr. Withers' flock is in Paris—"

But in the end she put John into a small day school nearby where the children of the neighbors went. It was not a school which Mr. Withers had ever heard of nor would he have approved it. But neat little French boys and little girls in cotton aprons went there every morning, and she had stopped on her way home at noon from Mr. Withers.

"But yes," the fresh-faced school mistress cried, "why not, Madame? We do not object to little English boys if they will learn to speak French! Ah, small one, you are six? A big boy! The English are so big—ah, he is American! They are bigger, even, than the English. Yes, yes, tomorrow—why not?"

In the afternoon she took them to the Louvre. They stood before the Venus de Milo.

"Can you make them just like that?" John asked.

"I don't know," she answered. All day she had forgotten the question she had asked herself the night before. Now it rushed back to her. How smooth were these surfaces, the planes how flowing! There were no angularities to disturb that harmony of shape.

"Look, John," she said eagerly, "feel her!" She lifted him to touch the smooth body. "See how the lines flow as though they were made of water! Do you remember the curl of the wave at the prow when the ship cut into the sea?"

They were looking at her with large uncomprehending eyes.

"Come, it's time to go home," said Susan. And when they were home she fed them and bathed them and put them to bed.

"I can bathe myself," John protested. "Jane always lets me."

"Let me just dry you," she said when he stepped out of the tin tub Jane filled with water from a can. She dried him, feeling the lean firmness of his body. The roundness was disappearing. He was growing in lines and planes. She saw him for a moment like a statue, the turn of his shoulder and thigh, the poise of his head. . . . She had been with them all day. They had been happy and she had been content. Again and again through the day she put out her hand to touch them, to caress them, to hold their hands, and now she was assuaged in one part of herself and now she was hungry in another.

When they were in bed she said to Jane abruptly, "I'm going for a walk before I sleep."

And when she opened the door there was the question she had left there, still waiting for her. She crossed the little square and sat down in the shadow of the old provincial general. Along the outline of his shoulders she could see the ragged headless shapes of sparrows, their feathers ruffled in sleep, their heads under their wings. She sat there a long time, until Madame had closed her little shop and her black-haired boy had put up the boards for the night. At night the square was as still as a field at home, except for a little café at the far corner. But even there the tables were being deserted. A man passed by with a woman and he drew her into the general's shadow and kissed her deeply and long.

"*Alors!*" he cried with a loud sigh, and she clung to him a moment and then they stepped out into the street again and went on. They had not seen her because she had shrunk away between the old general's knees. But she had watched them as eagerly as though she had known them. She had felt the woman in the man's arms, she had felt on her own mouth the pressure of his lips. She sat dreaming of them, of people like them, of all people everywhere, and of how their indestructible life forced itself into being. What she wanted to do was to catch this life into her hands and make it live forever. Those two figures, man and woman, had stood together as motionless as marble. Life at its every height was still, instinct with pure feeling. Marble alone could contain that noble stillness, toward which all movement flowed. Every end is still.

She rose, feeling a power rush into her. She knew her tools now and she was master of her materials. But tools were not enough and materials were only means. Marble, stone, and bronze, flesh and blood and bone, these were still only her means.

"I want to make people," she thought. She was suddenly

done with numbers and metals, with casting and with foundries. She knew her craft. She had now to find her art.

"I want my own studio," she said to David Barnes. "It's been very nice of you to let me stay here, but now I want really to work, and I need to be alone."

"I don't know what makes you think you know so much," he muttered. He was very short-tempered these days because he was more and more convinced that he must go to America for his next Titan, who had to be a living man. Until now they had all been in Europe and England, great men who were dead. But he had caught up to his times.

"I've got to go to America," he groaned. "Edison won't come here. You can have this place to yourself."

"No," she said, "you'd always be here. I'd never rid myself of you."

"You're a weak woman," he said. "If you were strong enough you could work anywhere. Look at me! I work where I happen to have my stuff. I've got my hands along with me and clay's easy. One of the best things I ever did was in an English public house with all the chaps standing about making fun of me."

"I could do that," she cried, his scorn lighting her anger like a torch put to tinder. "But you're so damned domineering. I feel you here even when you're gone."

"I never interfere with you," he shouted.

"Only by being yourself," she replied.

It became a challenge to battle between them.

"I dare you to take my studio and go on with your own stuff!"

"I could if I knew what my stuff was," she replied. "But I'm only trying to find out. Your ideas, your words will hang about here like echoes after you're gone. I don't want them."

"I'm going in a week," he said. "Make up your mind, you woman."

To be a woman was such a burden that she had become sensitive to the word. She replied instantly, "Very well, I'll take it. And when you come back, you'll find it so strange here you won't want to stay."

But before the week was out Jane said, "I've only money for a month, Mum. You said to tell you."

She had forgotten. "Well," she said, and drew a deep breath, "I shall have to get some more, Jane."

She felt a sudden terror. She would be completely alone. There would be no one to whom she could turn when David went to America, and if she could find no food for her children— She was glad that she had not known before Jane told her. She would not now tell David Barnes. She could manage her own life. She helped him to pack and endured the last day of his frenzy. He packed his tools meticulously into beautifully made cases, each chisel point wrapped in chamois skin, and took an immense supply of a clay he had mixed himself.

"That American stuff," he growled, "it dries before you're half done—it's their cursed facility. Clay ought to stay soft as flesh until you're through with it. I've got a secret I'll tell you sometime, Susan, but not until I'm dying."

"Suppose you fall out of a plane or something?" she asked.

"You're to look inside that Adam over there," he nodded his head at a small primeval figure in plaster. "It's sealed inside of him, on a bit of paper. Nobody knows.—There now, I'm ready to go."

"But where are your clothes?" she asked.

He looked at her.

"Damn!" he said, and pulled an old Gladstone bag from under the cot and opening a chest he pulled out garments. "Once I went without 'em," he said busily, "and didn't find it out until I was at sea."

"What did you do?" she asked.

"Wore what I had on," he replied briskly. "There—goodbye, Susan." He opened the door, roared into the hall, and a boy came and heaved the box of tools to his shoulder, and he seized the sagging bag. She felt the stiff brush of his gigantic beard against her cheek. "Goodbye," he said again, and stopped at the door. "There's some mixed clay there in the closet," he said. "You might as well use it, I guess."

"All right," she said.

Now he was gone. From the window she saw him throw his bag into a cab and go swaying down the narrow street. She stood a moment, and then she turned firmly and quickly and opened the closet door. There was the clay.

She had not time each afternoon for more than a moment's realization that this was David Barnes' studio. His smock hung against a door. The first studies of his Titans stood under the shadows of the eaves. She did nothing except to clear a small circle for herself. Indeed she could not. Day was passing day, and like catastrophe she saw the month's end when Jane's hand would be stretched out to her empty. She had the children to feed and alone. If she let herself, she could be afraid. This city seemed suddenly too foreign for her. She had been so busy she had not thought of it as foreign before. But now, looking out of the long windows northward, she thought of Tramp's Woods. The streets were strange, the people sharp and alien. She turned away, summoning her old power in herself. She would not allow herself fear. She could do anything that she must and would.

She would use these very people to earn her children's bread. She turned and began quickly to model her clay. She would make little figures of such people as she saw every day; old Madame Jeure in the downstairs shop, the corner café proprietor with his barrel stomach who drank his own wine all day, the children playing about the knees of the stone general, a taxicab driver asleep at a curb in the early morning, slumped behind the wheel. These strangers trooped through her mind and her fingers flew. She would make them and cast them in plaster and offer them for sale in a certain little shop she passed every day. She had seen women going in and out with bundles, and in the windows were many small things for gifts. These were only toys she was making, and yet even now a certain content came creeping into her breast, warm and sweet. She was humming under her breath and she caught it and held it to hear what she was singing. "Oh, that will be—glory for me—" It was her old song. She had not sung it since she came to Paris, and where had it come from now, except from this familiar ecstasy in her hands?

"I've enough money for a week more, Mum," Jane said without urgency. She had been out to early market and now she was back, her small thrifty purchases in a round French basket. She was not in the least alarmed. Money came from somewhere, somehow. It was only her duty to spend it as sparely as she could. Susan was seeing John off to school, straightening his tie and finding his cap.

"Goodbye, son. Don't forget you're American."

"Mother! You don't suppose I ever forget that!"

"No, but remember you're the only American they know and when they look at you they will think of all America."

"Mother, I *am* sort of forgetting America! Did we have apple trees and a barn?"

"Yes, darling—we still have. Goodbye, goodbye!"

She watched his tall slight figure running down the street, looking so different from everyone else. And Marcia, jabbering a mixture of English and French, was wanting to cut paper dolls.

"Mother, Mother, *où est le* scissors, Mother?"

209

She found the scissors and settled Marcia in the sunny open window.

"Now Mother must go to work, darling."

Marcia did not mind. Marcia was already singing in a high sweet small voice a song Madame Jeure had taught her when sometimes she ran away from Jane to see little rolls come out of the oven.

"I don't know just when I'll be back, Jane," Susan called from the door.

"No, Mum," Jane said at the kitchen door, wiping her hands on her apron.

"I'll probably bring some money today," said Susan.

"Yes, Mum," said Jane.

Susan stepped out into sharp autumn sunshine. Every angle of the many angled crowded houses stood out clear and hard, and the cobblestones, wet with carrying of water, glittered. She turned right and went, as she did every morning and evening, past the little gift shop. She stopped. Two of her little figures were gone from the window, Madame Jeure and the little schoolboy. She hurried in to find the old shopkeeper.

"Monsieur," she cried, "Monsieur, *est-ce-que*—"

"A-ha!" he replied merrily from behind his counter. His white mustaches quivered with pleasure. He dipped his hand into his drawer and held it out to her. There was a handful of francs.

"*Mes Américains!*" he cried roguishly. "They adore the small dolls!"

"*Merci—merci—*" she said, smiling.

In the street she counted the francs. It was good enough—he had taken his commission, of course. She put the money into her purse. It was pleasant to know it was there, though it was very little, really. Little dolls would not pay all the rent and all the food and the cheerful schoolmistress and Jane's wage.

The days were growing chill and soon she must think of coal. She went steadily on toward the studio where she still spent her mornings, learning in any way she could things she did not know. It was not so much as she used to learn. She had grown skilful at many things now. But she had not yet the large thing she needed. She did not know what she wanted to do next.

She opened the door of the square hall to the studio and there she took off her hat and coat and put on her brown smock. Then she went into the studio. Sometimes there were other students working there, but Monsieur taught no classes. If certain young persons of gift, he would say, shrugging his thick shoulders, wished to come and watch him and learn, he would ask them questions sometimes and discover their ignorance for them—nothing more. But no one came every day as she did, early, before he had finished *petit déjeuner*. She came in every morning and took up the task she had left off the day before, the making of an armature, the shaping of a plaster mold, the preparation of a bronze. He came in, wiping coffee and honey from his mustaches.

"Ah, Susanne, you are here!"

"Yes, *Maître*. What shall I do when I have finished this?"

"Let me look at you—you are pale!"

He had her by the shoulders, her face turned to the window.

"I am quite well."

"You do not eat enough. You do not play. In the evenings you must go out with the other students and play. You go home—what do you do at home?" he asked her.

She smiled, not answering.

"You are not in love?" he asked her.

She shook her head violently. In love! These French thought of nothing else.

"No, you mustn't be in love, Susanne. It is a great curse to work. Once, yes. Everyone must be in love once, to discover it is not so much. You have been in love once?"

She hesitated, and then said quickly, "Yes, once." Had she not been in love with Mark?

His hands dropped from her shoulders.

"Then go to work," he said abruptly. And he himself turned to the huge block of marble which he was measuring and studying. He was beginning a new piece, a commission, a statue of Clemenceau. Susan had been watching for days the sketches he made.

"How to make the body crouch behind that great head," he had kept muttering. "The man's body is nothing—an appendage, merely, to the ferocious head." He had not been satisfied with anything and for a week he had been prowling around and around the great block of marble, fretful with discontent. Now suddenly he shouted at her.

"Ha, Susanne! I forgot something!"

"What is it?" she asked.

"What time is it?"

She glanced at her watch. "Nearly ten."

"Then he will be here—that fellow!" he complained. "As if I am not sufficiently troubled with this old monster, today I must have a new pupil from Barnes—a genius, Barnes tells me, he cables me, if you please, a genius of the modern! And Robert cannot come—today when at last I see how my monster lies in the stone, today when I wish Robert to begin the preparation, Robert has cut his hand upon some trivial play of his own! Robert cannot wait patiently for the monster—no, he must hack at something for himself and have his hand infected and hanging in a sling, and I am desolate. Unless—shall I make the new pupil—no, he will ruin the monster. The monster is old—primeval. I have told Robert many times, 'You are a marble cutter—an excellent marble cutter—never a sculptor, do you hear? Leave the tools alone!'"

She had often watched Robert, the marble cutter, a large, dark, amiable fellow, chipping off the first flakes of marble, breathing hard as he bent over sketches, measuring with pursed lips, depths and angles from the model in clay or plaster which stood before him.

"I could do it," she said aloud.

He stared at her and pushed his mustaches up from his red lips.

"Ha," he said, "only perhaps!"

"Try me," she said, and then she thought of her children and she said quickly before shame overtook her, "Will you pay me what you pay Robert?"

There, she had said it, and now she was ashamed, but she had said it. Robert made a living wage at cutting marble.

"Money—money," the old sculptor growled at her. "You Americans! And what if you spoil my marble?"

"I'll pay for it," said Susan. She was picking up the mallet and chisel.

"No—no," he cried, frightened. "Well, then—yes, wait— only when I am in the room, do you hear? I shall watch every stroke!"

Two or three French pupils had come in and were beginning to work, watching them curiously. She did not know them. Sometimes one or the other had invited her to go out with him, but she had shaken her head. "I have no time for pleasure," she always said quickly, and added unwillingly, "Thank you."

She began to knock off an edge, a corner.

"Oh, my God," the old sculptor groaned, "so fast?"

"I see it," she answered calmly. But she was not calm. Inside of her a feverish eagerness rose. She saw coming out of the stone the crouching negligible body, propelling the huge fierce beautiful head. She had only to proceed thus—thus—these two great corners off, left and right, but the base must be left square for the figure squatting on its pedestal.

A door opened and someone came in. But she did not turn. She never turned when the door opened. "Ah, you are here, Monsieur," she heard the *maître* say—now she must cut—carefully—where under the stone the shoulder would round, thickly, sullenly. She must not forget to look at the model. Ah, but the model now was wrong! The neck was too long. The shoulders must be hunched. She turned, forgetting everything else. She cried out, "*Maître*, the model is wrong—here—see? The shoulders must be so—" She began chipping again strongly.

He leaped to her side. "Stop—no more—let me see—you will ruin me—"

He seized her hand, and before she could pull free her gaze passed into a man's amused gray eyes, very cool, very level, very handsome under straight black brows. She did not see them. She clung to the mallet and chisel the *maître* was pulling from her.

"Leave me alone!" she cried. "I see what I am doing. I see him—Clemenceau! He had no such neck. See!" She put her chisel and mallet safely into her left hand and seizing a pencil she began to draw quickly. "He is so, *Maître*—like this!"

"Ah, *hè!*" he groaned. "Is it my Clemenceau or yours?"

She stared at him and began to laugh. She put down the mallet and chisel.

"I am not a marble cutter," she said proudly. "I was wrong. You must wait for Robert."

"No—wait—you are so quick," the *maître* murmured, troubled. "Wait—what if you are right?"

She stood waiting. She knew she was right. But it did not matter whether she was right or wrong about this. The substance of the marble under the chisel, the instinct of her hands, guiding the tools, had loosed the old dark wild desire. She wanted to make, she must make, a thing of her own, a big thing—

"Yes, you are right," the *maître* said suddenly. "I see what you see. Go on—"

"I asked for money," she said. "I take it back, *mon maître*. I do not want money. If I do Robert's work, will you give me a piece of marble for my own?" She must have the marble. She would make more little clay people for money, but if she had marble—

The old sculptor stared at her. His eyes looked suddenly sunken above his mustaches.

"And why are you a woman?" he inquired sadly. "A woman tells *me*— Barnes is right, when he says to me, 'God grows careless nowadays, throwing his gift anywhere.'" He sighed, shrugged, jerked his mustaches. "Yes, what do you want? A piece of my marble! Well, you shall have it on one promise— no more ideas of your own. From now on you will follow the model. And leave off within an inch, I tell you. Do you hear? You will be finishing it according to your headstrong fashion. You are that abomination—a woman with a mind! I hate such women. Why does God send me such a gift by a woman?"

She paid no heed to all this.

"May I choose my marble today?" she asked. Her eyes were bright upon him. "When I have finished for today, I mean?"

He growled into his beard and stalked away. She took up her mallet and chisel, in a triumph both gay and grim. She would have the marble. And then she would begin at last her own work.

"You seem to have the old boy frightened," said a fine voice, full of laughter.

She turned, startled, and saw a tall, rather young man, in a gray suit. It was the man with the gray eyes. She had forgotten him.

"He's only upset because I wanted to change his model," she answered shortly. She turned and began chipping bits away now from the arms she could see folded under the stone.

215

"I am Blake Kinnaird," the pleasant clear voice said again. "David Barnes told me to look for Susan Gaylord."

"Well, here I am," she said. But she did not stop for one instant the knocking of her mallet, the diligent slip-slip of her chisel. She was thinking . . . and when she found exactly the right marble, she would feel what she was to make. The marble would tell her. She would go among all the pieces until she found it, as large a piece as she wanted. She wanted to make something big. She was a sculptor, not a modeler. She wanted no more clay—well, only the small figures for bread until she could sell a big thing—she wanted to work direct in stone— no drawings, no models, nothing but feeling out the thing in the stone. . . . She did not hear the voice again, nor did she look over her shoulder to see where it was gone.

She had been so long alone that she was startled every time he spoke to her. He broke upon her silence and each time she came out of her natural silence, startled at the sound of his voice. She looked at him, answered him, and went back into the silence in which she lived. And every day she worked, carving the Clemenceau to the last inch of the model. There, though longing to finish it, she forbade herself.

"I could do it as well as the _maître_—perhaps better," she thought and was not ashamed because she felt in herself the power not yet used. She was sure, now, as she was sure of life, that she would do some great thing even though she did not know what it was. She only knew there was all this power in her which nothing had yet consumed, which no one had plumbed. There was so much more power than her life had yet used. Mark had needed only a little and the children needed a little. Sometimes, longing to spend, on a Sunday, on a holiday, she poured herself upon them.

"John, Marcia—see, let's play together, all of us. I'll play,

216

too. Let's play we are traveling around the world on the clouds and winds. No one can see us, but we can see everybody."

But they went with her only a little way. They grew weary of her too full fancy, her too swift planning even for their pleasure. They wandered away from her.

"I don't want to play any more, Mother," John would say.

"I don't like this game, Mother," said Marcia.

"I think I'll whittle," said John.

"Let's all whittle," she said, not wanting to be shut away from them, longing to pour out this power of her love and have it used. But the speed of her skilful fingers discouraged them. She whittled a row of little birds on a branch and John said in discontent, "I'll never be able to make such nice birds. I wish you wouldn't make them, Mother."

No, and she could never love them fully enough to use her love. Sometimes when they passed her she could not keep from putting out her arms and seizing them and holding them in her great embrace.

"Ah, but your mother loves you!" she would cry. But her love was too much for them.

"You hold me too tight, Mother!" Marcia cried, and John struggled away from her. She learned to kiss them quickly and let them go. . . .

Only the marble was large enough for all her power. She spent hours choosing the piece she wanted. When one could only have one piece it was precious. The *maître* had been generous. He was pleased with her, and he said, waving his square hands, "Take what you like. You are not Robert, and you shall have more than his wage. What would he do with marble?"

She wandered among the pieces of rough marble, feeling for her own, touching, pondering each. Each was a prison for some shape. She was full of the strange familiar silent happiness which came when she was ready again to create.

"Shall I help you?" his voice broke into her silence again.

She looked up angrily to refuse. "I know a lot about marble," he went on. "My father is an importer of marbles. This piece, for instance, has a black rotten vein running through it. You would be half finished before you found it."

"Now how do you know that?" she asked, and forgot to push him away from her.

"Do you see this creamy thread?" His quick nervous thin hand was feeling the marble. She had to bend close to see what he felt. There it was, almost invisible in the roughness of the unfinished stone.

"This—and this—are not good pieces," he said, rapidly rejecting two more, "and these two are very fine, and this one is best of all."

He chose a rounded block, and she looked at it, wanting it and wishing he had left her alone to choose it for herself.

"Do you work in marble?" she asked, unwilling to accept it from him. She would not decide until he had gone away.

"Lord, no!" He laughed. "It's too slow for me. I model—and let other people do the work."

She did not hear him. She was thinking about the stone, wishing he would go away.

"David Barnes told me a lot about you," the pleasant voice said.

"Did he?" She started, and looked up at him and away again. His eyes were gray as the sea under clouds.

"He thinks you're a great genius."

"I don't know yet what I am," said Susan. "I don't think anyone does."

Blake Kinnaird laughed. "I don't think so, either," he said. "Are you going to let me try?"

She shook her head gravely. "You can't," she said. "I shall have to do it alone." He was intolerably close to her here like this. She had a strange premonitory fear of him. "I must go away," she said abruptly, and went, leaving him standing

218

staring after her. She went out into the street and at a little shop bought a roll and a cup of hot milk for her lunch. . . . She really wanted that piece of marble, only she wished he had not . . . "I shall just forget him," she decided quickly and firmly, and did.

But he would not allow her to forget him. He was at the studio every day, arguing over his work, laughing when the old sculptor snorted at the figures he modeled so quickly and easily.

"But I am modern, sir!" he said over and over again. "I make my own technique, if you please! I work in planes—*à bas* with realism! I am not realistic, and you are!"

The old sculptor, his hands clenched under his waving coattails, was shouting, "And who has seen a human face like this? A smudge, a platter, a tea tray, but not a human face—*non!*"

Blake Kinnaird, all good humor, took him firmly by his thick round shoulders.

"If you stand two inches from any human face it will look either like a teapot or a tea tray. Stand here, sir, where the light falls so— You see, sir, I use light as one of my materials."

"Susanne!" the old man roared from under the two strong young hands. "Come here—see with your good honest eyes— is this a human face?"

She left the corner where her marble now stood and came to them and studied the clay he had been modeling so rapidly and with such seeming carelessness for several days. Half of his time he had spent twenty feet away in staring at it. Then time and time again he had gone back to move it an inch this way or that.

"It's a girl in autumn," he said. "The wind's blowing her hair."

Then she saw the girl, a thin shivering creature, shielding her face with her hands. It was true the wind was blowing.

"Do you see her?" the old man demanded.

"Yes, I do," she said slowly, "but it's like a dream. You're not sure—it almost escapes you."

"Look at this!" He let go the old man's shoulders and went and moved the pedestal. Instantly there was only a mass of planes and angles.

"Why, she's gone!" Susan said.

"She was never there," said the old man cynically.

Blake Kinnaird turned the mass slowly, exactly.

"I see her again!" Susan exclaimed.

"Well, a very little," the old man admitted. "If I look at it quickly and away again—"

"Look at it again and again," said Blake Kinnaird, "and each time you will see her more clearly."

"There is something wonderful about it," Susan cried with excitement. "I don't understand it, but I see it."

"So long as you see it you needn't understand it," Blake Kinnaird said.

"You two—" mumbled the old man, stumbling away, dazed. All around him stood the honest classical statues upon which he had spent his life, bodies with sound full arms and legs, rotund trunks and noble heads.

"Thank you, Susan Gaylord," Blake Kinnaird said.

And she went up again to the girl in clay and studied her, wondering and puzzled and charmed.

"To use light like that!" she said. "I never thought of it— But of course you are right. Light is a material—it can't be treated as a constant. The planes lay hold of it."

"You see that!" he exclaimed eagerly.

They were very near to each other. She had forgotten that she did not like him near her. She wanted to talk. She had not really talked with anyone since David Barnes went away.

"Let's have lunch together!" Blake Kinnaird said.

"Yes, let's!" she answered eagerly. "I want to talk about

this whole business of realism in work. I want to know what you think. I've been trained in realism, but I feel it a prison around me, sometimes. I want to leap out of it."

They left the studio, and he took her to a table on a sidewalk and he pulled out her chair.

"Realism is the end," he was saying. "No, Susan, you aren't just going to eat bread and milk—I'm going to order your lunch. Here, *garçon!*"—he ordered quickly under his breath and turned to her again—"the trouble is in making the means realistic. When the means and the method are realistic, literalism and not realism is the result, and literalism is false. The literal truth is only half-truth, and perhaps not even that. There are all the tones and supertones, unexpressed. It's not what's said that is important—it's what is meant."

She was eating something hot and delicious, but she did not know what it was. She was talking, listening, seeing him in flashes between talk. He was beautiful in a tall angular spare fashion. His hair was black. His hands were long and very delicate, much more delicate than her own. She rose abruptly at last.

"I must go back to work," she said.

"Where do you work in the afternoon?" he asked.

"In my own studio," she answered. "That is—in David Barnes' studio—he's lending it to me."

"May I come there sometime?" he asked, smiling, and when she hesitated, he said quickly, "I'd like to see his things. He said I could."

"I suppose I have no right to say you cannot," she said slowly. Then she said quickly, "No, no—if you please, don't come!"

She could not have him near her when she was working on her marble. As surely as he came near her the thing she saw receded.

"Go away—go away, Blake!" she cried at him in an agony in the morning if he came near. She had to be quite alone. She could endure the *maître* stepping softly about her sometimes as she worked, for he said nothing. But Blake had always to speak to her, and at the sound of his voice the image fled into the marble and hid. Worse than his voice was his touch. If he put his hand on her arm—he was always touching everything—she groaned against him.

"Leave me alone, Blake—"

And once when carelessly he ran his hand over the marble, she winced and threw it off.

"Don't touch me like that," she cried at him.

"I didn't touch you!" he shouted at her.

"You did—you did!" she cried. "I can't bear to be touched!"

"Susan, you're crazy!" he said, astonished. "I swear I only touched the marble!"

She wiped her face with her smock.

"Blake, please go away when I'm working."

"Will you let me come to your studio this afternoon if I go away now?"

He was smiling at her, mischievous, wilful. But she was looking at her marble.

"Yes—yes—anything, if you will only not spoil my work."

Then when he was gone there was the blessed, acute loneliness. She missed him when he was not there. But when she was alone the thing she saw came creeping out of the stone again. It was a woman, a shy woman, kneeling, young, eager, waiting, innocent. When Blake came near she went away. But when he was gone she came straining out of the stone. Then Susan cut and carved, quickly, surely, seeing her plain.

In the studio, making her little figures to sell, he was no interruption at all. He was enchanted with her little figures.

222

"Susan, your loaves and fishes—" he said, "they are charming. I will buy them myself."

She would not allow it. "No, you must go to the shop like anybody else."

"But you'd save the commission," he protested.

She shook her head. "I couldn't be sure you weren't helping me," she said firmly. "I've got to know I am doing it myself. Of course, I can't forbid you the shop."

"I hate independent women," he declared.

Susan looked up from the tiny creature in her hands and paused. She had not thought of herself as a woman with him. But when he said this he made her a woman. She saw she was wearing her old stained brown smock, and that her hair was stuffed into a beret to keep it out of stone dust, and her hands were calloused and grimy, and her nails worn away with feeling rough stone. He hated independent women, such as she was.

"I know," she said humbly, "all men do, don't they? But I can't help it—I'm made so."

"Susan!" he cried. "You're not serious? You don't think I meant it?"

He had dropped to his knees in his impulsive habit of quick affection to which she could not become accustomed. Now he clasped her wrists.

"Oh, yes, you do," she nodded her head vigorously. "I know how you feel—everybody feels that way to me, I think." She freed her hands and snatched off her beret and smoothed her hair.

"I admire you with all my heart," he said in a low voice.

"I think people don't like people they admire so much," she said, faltering. "In school even, I wasn't liked so much—when I took prizes, you know."

"Susan, Susan!"—he was laughing at her, wasn't he?—"You're a little child! Where have you been all your life?" He seized her wrists again.

223

She looked at him with embarrassed dark eyes. What did he mean? She had been married, she had two children, whose bread she earned.

"Look here!"— Only why didn't he let go her wrists when he talked? His hands were tight as manacles. She struggled to get free.—"No, I'm not going to let you go. You're always going off alone, even when I'm talking to you, you slip off somewhere by yourself secretly. I'm going to bring you to life."

She stared down at his thin tense face. Bring her to life! "I am alive," Mary had said, "and you are dead." Her house had once been full of that strange hot rushing love between Michael and Mary. She had felt it, an unknown flood, like a swirling river upon whose banks she stood as it swept past her. She had hated it and felt it. What sort of love was it that did not make Mary want to marry Michael? . . . Blake was talking to her. His breast was against her knees. He was holding her hands now, clenched in his, against his cheeks.

"Susan, did anyone ever tell you you're beautiful, beautiful? Did anyone ever say your hair is the loveliest hair in the world, of a color even I can't understand because sometimes it is dark and sometimes it is gold? Did anyone ever tell you it is sure magic to have dark eyes with such hair—eyes so shy when you're a woman and so bold when you're a child? Did anyone ever tell you anything at all about yourself, Susan?"

She was being drawn out of something hard and cold around her. She was coming out, shy, quivering, alive.

She shook her head slowly, her lips parted, her eyes still upon his. His face was close, too close—

"No," she whispered. Her breath was hot and tight in her throat. "No—I don't want to—"

She bent her head.

"Don't want to what?" he whispered.

—Why did they whisper? No one was there.

"I don't want to come out of the stone," she said aloud, and pulling her hands away she leaped to her feet and ran out of the studio.

It was cold in the street. The afternoon was later than she had dreamed. What had they been doing all afternoon? She had neither coat nor hat, but she would not go back. She went straight homeward, her head held high against the wind. People stared at her, but she did not see them. . . . Was he making love to her? But she did not want it. She never wanted to see him again. She wanted only to get home to John and Marcia and Jane. She had a home, a home to which to go. She had been wise to know her need of a home and keep it about her. She needed nothing more. She had had everything—she had everything now, except Mark who was dead.

She ran upstairs and into the room. Jane was setting the table for supper. The children were carrying in the plates.

"Why, Mother!" John cried. "Your hair—it's blowing all loose!"

"Where's your coat and hat, Mum?" asked Jane.

"I must have come without them," Susan said. She stood with her back to the door, looking at them all. They were all the same and yet they looked at her so oddly. They were strange. No, it was she who was strange to them.

"You'll catch your death," Jane reproached her.

"I had to come home," she said. "I didn't know it was so late. I just ran out as I was—"

Marcia gave a high tinkling silvery laugh and put down her plate.

"Mother, you're so funny!" Her voice was full of tolerance and pity.

"I know it," said Susan humbly.

She went into her own room and brushed her hair and washed her face and hands. She sat down with them and ate the soup Jane had made and the vegetable and the bread pudding. She was safe at home and he could not find her here. He did not know where she lived. But all the time she was eating, all the time she was listening to their voices, safe in the warm circle of the lamplight, her heart was still running and running, down the streets, away from him.

She rose very early and went to the studio and worked on the kneeling woman hours before he came. He slept late and it was mid-morning before she heard the *maître* complaining against him.

"*Eh bien,* another piece of triangles! And what is it now, my fine sculptor? No, I will guess—a maiden at her bath—no? Ah, then, a woman washing clothes—no? I confess I see nothing."

"It is a tiger," Blake said tranquilly.

"A tiger!"

"I haven't finished the light yet," Blake explained, "but you'll see."

"Ha, thank you, Monsieur. I am not so sure."

She heard his voice a moment later asking anxiously, "Do you see how thin the poor old chap's mustaches are getting? He's so exasperated at me he's fairly twisting them off."

She felt him coming near her. She would not look at him. "Blake, you promised—"

He had promised he would not come near her while she worked, if he might idle about her in the afternoons.

"No—I'm good—I'm going— But, Susan darling, she's swell! I can see her on her knees, the blessed lovely thing! I can't wait for her face—"

She was trembling under his voice. "Oh, go away, Blake, while I work!" she was crying silently. "I want to work—when you are here I can't work. I keep listening to you. I want to be free." But she said nothing. She would not turn around. She

226

would not look at him. She waited until she heard him sigh.

"Cold heart—Susan, Susan!"

She waited until he was gone. And then with her mallet and with a chisel of cold fine steel, as narrow as a pencil, she began feeling in the marble for the face of the kneeling woman.

There was nowhere she could fly from him in all this alien city. She must work in the afternoon for her children and there he could always find her. She did not stop when he came in. No, she worked on more quickly than ever. And sometimes she thought perhaps that she only imagined that she needed to fly from him. He was so pleasant and so cool. Sometimes he did not try to catch her hands, he did not once call her "Susan darling," he did not talk about her "lovely big mouth, as red as holly berries at Christmas, Susan!" He stretched himself on the couch, indolent and kind and detached.

He said, "This old man can't teach me anything, Susan. I'm going home. He doesn't understand modern America. I'm too new for him."

And then when she saw he was not thinking about her, out of a strange perversity which astonished her and made her afraid, she wanted him to think of her. She hated herself because she said wilfully, "I don't want you to go, Blake."

—Ah, but in the morning she wanted him to go!

"Shall you miss me, darling?"

"A little, Blake."

No, but loneliness was good. One worked when one was lonely.

"A great deal," he was saying arrogantly. "You shall miss me a great deal, my darling, because you are beginning to love me."

"I am not!" she cried, furiously. "I've had all that!"

He would not allow her to talk of Mark. He laughed when

227

she said she had been married. "You've never been in love in your life," he said, and laughed again.

"I have, I have!" she said, summoning Mark to her with all her strength. But Mark was dead. She could not see him. She could only see the head she had made of him once and she had left it at home in the barn, wrapped in its shroud. And here was today. Blake was coming toward her here in the warm studio bright with the quick sun of a winter afternoon. She stood still, looking at him.

"You've never been in love like this," he said, and he lifted her against him and turned up her face, his hand under her chin. "You don't even know you're a woman," he said. His eyes narrowed. "But you are!" he said, and his voice suddenly strangled behind his clenched teeth. He kissed her and she did not move. How hot was the sun in which they stood, how still the room! But it was not silence. He had broken into her silence and it was gone. Instant by instant she gave herself up. At first his lips touched hers closed. Then his mouth pressed into hers. He was entering into the great silence of her being, where no one had ever entered. Until this moment she had been alone all her life. He drew away from her at last.

"I don't believe you've ever even kissed anyone before," he said, amazed, a little amused.

She did not answer. She was looking at him, her eyes enormous and filled with tears. She was trembling.

"Don't cry," he said. He put his arm about her shoulder. "I'm going to be awfully good to you. Susan, Susanne, you look like a little girl. Why do you cry, darling?"

"I feel afraid," she said. Yes, she felt afraid, and for the first time in her life, helpless. But he laughed aloud.

"You're going to be married to me," he said, and lifting her against him, he kissed her again and again until she was laughing, too, as she had not laughed in years, and crying helplessly through her laughter, "Oh, Blake—Blake—"

"There!" he said, putting her down. "Now get your hat. We're going out for a celebration."

Like a clear west wind he was sweeping into all her life, deciding everything in great instants.

"We shall be married right off," he said, in the middle of the celebration. He was showing her a Paris she had never seen. Her Paris had been quiet winding streets, the old stone general, the little rooms above the patisserie, old Madame Jeure, her little withered face beaming in the morning. There were the Louvre, the Seine and the old book shops, and Notre Dame, huge and silent. These and the people she saw so sharply were her Paris.

But he went on with the celebration, night after night.

"Haven't you seen this, Susanne? But this is Paris!" She stared over a crowd of mad, gaily dressed dancing figures and shook her head. She sat listening to merry naughty dialogue on a stage, laughing and secretly half ashamed.

"If anyone had ever told me I'd be marrying a child!" he said. "Susan, you're a child. You're not very intellectual, you know, my dear. A nice big intelligent child, not at all articulate. What'll I ever do with you? It'll be like having a St. Bernard puppy in my house." He laughed and his eyes shone and she felt stupid and humble.

It was quite true she never knew what to say to Blake. But then she never had talked a great deal. She was always busy doing something. When people talked she always listened carefully, receiving from them not only their words but their gestures and their looks, the sound of their voices, lifting and dropping. If she listened closely enough and let herself feel them, she could feel what they were thinking. So it did not seem necessary to talk.

"Perhaps you are right," she said to Blake docilely.

But then there were good days in the Bois, sunny cold after-

229

noons, when he took off his coat and rowed her in a little boat on the lake, and then she was not so afraid of him and she asked him shyly, after a few times, "Do you mind if we bring the children?"

"No, of course not, if you want them."

Though she did not tell him, she did not quite enjoy herself always without the children. She had been so anxious that Blake should see how beautiful they were. She had explained to him how she had wanted them—how she had wanted many children —and flushing, she had paused to think with delicate inward amazement that now she could have her other children. She had not until now thought of having children with Blake. Even now she did not feel it in her body, but only in her mind.

But he said lightly, "You shouldn't have children, you know, Susan darling." He was stirring a spoon in a tall green glass. They were lunching together as they did every day. "It's sheer waste for you to use your body like that. I'm not going to let you, you know."

"Oh, Blake, you don't understand," she cried earnestly. "Indeed it's not like that. I can't tell you how I feel when I'm having a child—as though not just my head and my hands were working, but all of my being, my blood, my breath—"

"You're in love with *me*, you know, Susan," he said suddenly. Over the green glass his eyes looked stern and a little cold. She was bewildered. "Yes, but, Blake, when people are in love, they want children."

"I don't want children," he said, "and I'm frightfully in love with you, you old-fashioned darling!"

He put out his beautiful long thin hand and caressed her palm under the table and she caught her breath. His touch was frightening, it was so strong, so sweet. But she need not be afraid of it now. She was going to be his wife—only why was she a little afraid? When they were married he would want children. It was only because he had never been married, because he had never really had a home. His mother had died when he was a little boy, and his father had not married again. There had been a great deal of money and much travel.

"I do so want you to love John and Marcia," she had said anxiously. "Marcia has very long eyelashes and John is such a dear good boy."

"I can't imagine them," he had said. "You with children! You've made them up to frighten me."

But she did not want to play.

"No, really, Blake. It's very necessary to my happiness that you love them."

"Then I promise to love them," he said gaily.

It was true he had been very good to them. But she was not sure that he loved them.

He was very good to them in a careless fashion. "Here!" he would call to them, "Catch!" And he tossed francs at them. "Go and buy balloons! I like to look at children holding balloons."

"Must I buy only balloons, Mother?" asked John, distressed.

Blake shouted his high clear laughter. "No, you literal-minded youth! Balloons mean what you like. Only I like balloons."

"I'll buy one for you," said John, anxious to be good in this new situation.

John was a little afraid of him. She could feel his delicate tentative fear. He was very polite, remembering always to say "Good morning" and to say "Thank you" to Blake's small gifts. But more often than not he was bewildered by the gifts. "What shall I do with it, Mother?" he inquired after Blake was gone one day, staring at a grotesque pottery tiger whose head twisted backward to look over its own tail mournfully.

"I really don't know," Susan answered honestly.

"I think it is *jolie*," said Marcia pertly.

Marcia was not at all afraid of Blake. But she was never shy of anyone and she was afraid of nothing. "I like you," she told him at once. "I like you very much."

"Good," he replied pleasantly. "Everybody does," he added, mischievously, "that is, nearly everybody. Sometimes Susan doesn't."

"I do," Marcia replied seriously, "if she doesn't, I do."

She put her hand protectingly into his and looked at Susan arrogantly. It was absurd, a child's arrogance, a child's fondness, but Susan had to put out her own hand and touch him. . . .

"If you don't like the tiger, I will have it," Marcia declared. "Give him to me, John."

"Well," he agreed. "I don't want it."

Marcia seized the tiger. "I will call it Blake," she murmured, stroking it. "Dear Blake, nice Blake!"

"It really isn't at all pretty," Susan said, "although I'm glad you didn't say so before Blake."

"Oh, I wouldn't!" John cried, his eyes large with horror.

"I like it," Marcia insisted.

It was not very easy to tell Jane that she was about to marry Blake. She waited until the children were in bed one night. Then she went into the kitchen and said directly, because she did not know how else to say it, "Jane, I'm going to be married."

Jane looked up from the dishpan.

"Oh, Mum!" she said. "Not to a Frenchman!"

"No," said Susan, "to an American, from New York."

Jane stared at her. She had not yet seen Blake. "Is there an American in this town, Mum? I never see a Christian soul here, myself."

Susan laughed. "He's a sculptor, too."

"It's that one, is it, Mum?" said Jane doubtfully. "The children told me about him, only they didn't say he was Ameri-

232

can. Well, I hope it's for the best, I'm sure. I don't know. For myself I always say let sleeping dogs lie, Mum. It's luck when you've made one good marriage. There aren't so many good men about. They're married a'ready or under ground."

"You'll see," said Susan. "He's coming tomorrow. I want the children nice."

She turned to go away, uncomfortable in Jane's gloom. Jane was ridiculous. She could not run her life by Jane, who always wanted everything exactly the same.

"Why do you look so miserable, Jane?" she said impatiently. "You ought to be glad I'm to be happy again."

But Jane refused to be cheerful.

"Shall we live in New York?" she asked.

"I suppose so," Susan answered.

"All them brambleberries goin' to waste, year after year, at home," said Jane, mournfully.

But Susan had not paid any attention. Now that Jane knew, she must tell the children. She went into the bedroom where the two beds were close together.

"Not asleep, darlings?" She sat down on John's bed and reached for Marcia's hand.

"No," said John.

"I am, though," said Marcia.

John raised himself. "Marcia!" he said reproachfully, "you aren't. She wouldn't know you were here, would she, Mother?"

"My eyes are tight shut," Marcia insisted.

"Never mind," said Susan. "You may wake up because I'm going to surprise you. Darlings, I am going to marry Blake and we are all going to live in his house."

John had not, she saw, the faintest idea of what marrying meant. But Marcia opened her eyes and lay looking at her brightly, secretly, in silence.

"Where is his house?" John inquired guardedly.

"In New York," she said.

"And then what?" Marcia asked in a bright voice.

"Well, I suppose that's all," said Susan, astonished that it was indeed so. "Only he's coming to see you tomorrow, and I want you to look your best. He is your new father, you know."

"I didn't know it," said John.

"I can't even remember my old one," said Marcia.

"I can, a little," said John. "Wasn't he kind of tall, Mother? And he used to play with me when he came home."

"Yes," said Susan steadily. Mark came dimly out of the shadows. At the sound of his son's voice he came out, and she saw him as she had not seen him alone for many months. She could not bear it. Marcia was looking at her still, with bright inquisitive eyes.

"What are you thinking, Marcia?" she asked.

"Will Blake like you best now?" she asked. "Will he like you better than me?" Her eyes were big and her mouth was small and bright.

"He loves me in one way and you in another," Susan said. She looked away from the coldness of Marcia's perfect little face.

"Sleep—sleep—" she said quickly. "Good night."

She was very proud of them, standing so precise, so upright, before Blake. John gave a little sharp French bow and Marcia curtsied. On other days she leaped at Blake, clinging to his neck, her knees tight at his waist. But today he might have been a stranger. She curtsied without speaking. Then they put out very clean hands.

"How do you do?" they said together.

"Thank you, very well," Blake replied gravely. "I brought you chocolates, Mademoiselle, and to you, Monsieur, I bring a box of charming pencils." He presented them with two boxes.

"Thank you, thank you," they replied, and looked at Susan.

"Open them, yes, darlings. It's very kind of Blake," she said.

234

But John hissed, "Have you asked—you know, Mother?"

She did not remember. She looked at them blankly.

"You know—Daddy?" Marcia whispered.

"Oh, yes," cried Susan. "How could I? Blake, what shall they call you after this?"

She smiled at him. It was so sweet of him to bring them gifts—it was so warm to have them all together, these whom she loved. Jane was bringing in tea. It was like home.

"This is our dear Jane," she cried, and Jane ducked.

"Hello, Jane," said Blake carelessly. Jane nodded and went out abruptly. "Well," he went on, looking at the children, "I certainly shouldn't want two great children calling me dad all of a sudden. I'd feel my front teeth would all fall out and my hair drop off. I'd begin to dodder. You'd better just say Blake. . . . I'll have some tea, Susan."

"I wouldn't call you dad," Marcia said suddenly.

"Why?" asked Blake. "What's the matter with you today, Mam'selle? You're as cold as a snowflake."

"You are not my father," Marcia said.

"Right!" said Blake briskly.

John turned to Susan. "Do you mind if I take my tea in with Jane, Mother?" he said. "She's probably lonely in the kitchen."

They went off, their plates carefully balanced, and Susan looked at Blake, laughing, proud.

"Aren't they lovely?" she demanded.

"Very decent kids," he said. "I say, Susan, let's go and look at that exhibit of French moderns." He looked at his watch. "There's just time."

She rose and went into the kitchen. At the table sat John and Marcia, with Jane, in silence.

"I'm going out a little while, Jane," she said.

"Very well, Mum," said Jane. She was gazing at Susan mournfully over a large cup of tea.

235

Susan hesitated. "Goodbye, darlings," she said. "I shan't be late."

"Good night, Mother," said John. But Marcia did not answer. She regarded her mother thoughtfully as she chewed, slowly, her small red lips shut tight.

"There is something wrong with Marcia," she told Blake as they walked in the cold bright evening air.

"Queer kid," Blake said. "In some ways she's older than you are—born old, as some women are—born knowing."

"What do you mean?" she asked.

"Will you forget them?" he answered impatiently. "You are with me, Susanne."

She loved them, she loved them. But when she walked out into the street with Blake, she left them behind.

But he was very kind to them in his abrupt, gay fashion. It came to be usual that though in the evenings they were alone together at some place of amusement, or alone in the studio, on Sundays they took the children and Jane to the Bois or to a theater or even to Fontainebleau as spring drew on.

He never pretended that he was not happier alone with her.

"There now," he said heartily when the door closed on the children, "your duty is done. Now, Susanne, you will please think only of me."

"Ah, but I am always thinking only of you," she answered ruefully. "When I am with them, I am impatient to be with you. When I am working I look to see what time it is—I who never used to think until it was too dark to see what I was doing!"

He seized her and laughed with triumph.

"You are in love with me!" he cried, and the certainty in his voice made her tremble. . . .

"What goes wrong with you, Mademoiselle?" the *maître* asked in the morning. "You who were so hot to work now waste your time staring at what you have already done. How shall you finish in time to send it to the Salon? You are so nearly finished and you do not finish."

Blake, overhearing, came striding over to her as soon as he was gone, while the French pupils stared at them secretly, curiously.

"Finish!" he commanded her in a low voice. "We are going to be married and go home."

"When?" she asked, astonished. He said every night, "Marry me soon—soon—" but the next word was lost in his kiss.

"Why do you decide so quickly?" she asked now.

"I am through with this," he answered impatiently. "I want to take you home."

She did not answer. She set soberly to work finishing her marble. She caught, at the last, a few moments of her old rich loneliness. She forgot Blake for fragments of hours while she finished the eyes, the hands, the line of hair. Then she cut small and deep, into the pedestal of rough marble, the words. "The Kneeling Woman," and smaller still her own name.

The next week, the day before they sailed, she and Blake were married quietly in a clerk's office. She went home afterwards exactly as though it were any other day. She said to them, "Blake and I were married today."

Jane put her hand to her mouth.

"Oh, Mum—not right off, like that!"

"We both wanted to get it over," she said.

"Mother!" John cried, and Marcia looked at her and went on eating her supper.

"I am not changed," she said quietly. She stooped and kissed them both. Then she went into the bedroom and took off her hat and smoothed back her hair. It was the last night in this small room. Blake had said, "Let's get it over with. I hate weddings." It had not been a wedding, only a contract, signed by their two names. Blake had said tensely, "Come to my rooms, Susanne—tonight. Why not?" But she had shaken her head. "No, Blake, I couldn't leave them—they've never been alone at night." So she came home.

He did not persuade her, although she had braced herself against it. The tenseness cleared from his face. He lit a cigarette.

"All right, Susanne," he said. "It doesn't matter—today or tomorrow." He smiled. "I've taken the grandest suite on the ship, just for fun."

She sat thinking. She was in complete love with him. She knew now that Blake had found a woman in her who had been sleeping until he came. When she was with him she was all that woman, shy and quivering, eager, alive, alive. Covering after covering he had stripped away until he had come to the core of womanhood. He did not care in the least that there was power in her to do or to make. It was nothing to him that she was a sculptor, great or small. He laughed whenever she said soberly that she must work.

"Why need you work when you have me to take care of you?" he said. And before she could speak he cried passionately, "Susanne, do you know there is a dimple just to the left of your mouth? Wait—don't move—I must kiss you."

And she waited, forgetting. . . .

She wanted to do exactly what she had done. Then why did she keep thinking of her Kneeling Woman and what her fate would be, alone and left behind in the hands of old academicians?

"Susanne, Susanne!"

The day began with his voice. She was sleeping as she had not since she was a child. His voice called her out of sleep. "You are so beautiful when you are asleep that I must wake you to tell you!" She woke, and the stateroom was full of fresh sea air, of sunshine and the sound of his voice. And she felt

238

herself beautiful, lying still half asleep, beneath his gaze. She was a beautiful woman, nothing else, and it was enough. "Susanne, do you remember last night? Every morning when you wake up your eyes look as though they remembered nothing."

She nodded quickly and shyly. She remembered everything. In his detailed love of her body she felt as though she were marble and he were carving her free, as though she were clay and he were giving her shape. His hands, touching her, defined her. She had not seen herself until now.

"Susanne, let me feel this line of your shoulder, down your back and your lovely thigh, your knee, your ankle, your exquisite foot. Your body is so strong. I hate fragile women."

"I have to be strong for my work," she had said once. And he had answered quickly, "No, you are strong because it is beautiful to be strong."

In his adoration of her he was creating something she had never yet been, a woman conscious and aware of herself. It was not in the least like marriage, and it stirred no memories. It was much more like being his mistress, lovely and beloved. And their love did not go beyond each other. There was no desire for homemaking or for ordinary life together. There was only this intense exciting closeness to each other, hour by hour. . . . He lifted her out of bed and put a lace wrap about her. The closets in their room were full of such garments as he had chosen for her.

"Go and wash your face and brush your hair," he commanded.

When she came back breakfast was ready in the little drawing room. They ate together in half-laughing passion. He made her forget everything.

Once she said, "I ought to go and see how the children are."

"No, you ought not," he said. "You ought only to love me. You have no other duty—and no other pleasure."

He swept her into his arms and she gave herself to the

moment again. Each moment was a life, a new and shining life. She laughed, she was always laughing. The ocean was a bright and dancing blue, day after day, and there was a full moon. The children were happy and good. She scarcely saw them or thought of them.

Every detail was as absurdly perfect as a too cleverly directed play. Blake took joy in perfect details. But there were the full moon, and the windless sea, the procession of extravagantly colored sunsets, for which he could not have planned.

"Although," she said, leaning her head against him one midnight when they stood together at the bow of the ship, "I feel as if you might have ordered it all, sun and moon and purple sea."

"I did," he said gravely. "I said to God, 'Turn on your works. She's going to cross your old ocean.' And he was as meek as anything."

They laughed and he seized her and held her and kissed her.

"Blake," she whispered, her breath tight in her throat, "Blake, I half believe that about God."

She had an intense realization of this moment, she and Blake, pressed together, held together, by moonlight and the smooth dark sea.

"It can't possibly be as perfect on land as it's been these days on the sea," she thought, watching the towers on the shore loom in the sky. She felt her heart cooling in her bosom, slowing its dancing pace. There was a subsidence in her blood. They had not been living in the world at all. Now she must think soberly of a house, of servants, of a sort of life she had never had in a great city. Blake's life would be very strange to her. She knew him so closely well, and she knew so little about him. Alone she knew him as she had never dreamed of human knowledge. And then, stepping out of the door of her room, he was suddenly another man, debonair, a little impatient, quick to be critical, even of her.

"Susanne," he said at the cabin door when they were ready to go, "your hat is wrong with that brown costume."

"Is it, Blake?" She hated herself for her humility before him. She ought to say quietly, "I don't agree with you, Blake." But she could not say it now. Perhaps after a while she would be able to say she did not agree with him.

"When we get home, get another hat," he said, "a larger one. You should avoid small hats." Then he said with the secret warmth which could so excite her that instantly she forgot what he had not liked, "You're beautiful—everything you wear must build into your beauty." She had never thought of her face, her body, her eyes, her hands and the garments she must wear for beauty. He created her and he made her feel herself precious. That was why, perhaps, she humbled herself before him and listened to him. "Am I growing vain?" she asked herself, astonished. Blake was making out of her a woman she had never been. How strange to be vain!

But Blake was saying something. The ship had docked. "This is my beautiful Susanne, Father," he was saying. "Susanne, he never leaves the country, so this is for love of you."

A delicate-faced tall old man, very thin and narrow in a pale gray suit, took her hands in both of his. She felt the dryness of his palms, his lips were dry on her cheek, the look of his old pale eyes was dry and light upon her. His voice when he spoke was high.

"I have hoped my son would marry, my dear, for a long time. I had a very happy marriage myself. Now I am glad he waited."

She smiled, liking this tall, slightly trembling old man.

"These are my children," she said, her hands on their shoulders.

"Yes, yes," he murmured, looking away from them. "They

241

must come to Fane Hill and spend the day." But he did not take the hands John and Marcia put out, tentatively. Behind them Jane stood, in her decent black. She was very pale, and Susan thought in a parenthesis of her mind, "I ought to be ashamed. I never even thought of her being seasick." But before she could speak Blake packed them into a huge car and they were driving through city streets bright with evening, until at last they reached a quiet quadrangle of houses by the river. The car stopped, a door on the street opened, and a man in livery came out.

"Are you coming in, Father?" Blake asked.

"No," said old Mr. Kinnaird, "no, I'll go back to Fane Hill. You'll be fatigued. Besides, the city fatigues me. And the peaches are very fine. Linlay will bring you some in the morning. One of the terriers is ill. I must be getting back at once."

They came out of the car and it drove noiselessly away. The children stood bewildered. She was suddenly strange herself, upon a strange street in a city she did not know. The moment lagged. She felt dazed, not knowing what next must come. Then she felt herself lifted quickly off her feet and set inside the threshold.

"You are in my house now, Susanne," said Blake. She stood looking down a wide hall, very bare and beautiful. At the end was one of Blake's paintings, an Indian woman standing alone in hard white sunlight in a square of bright desert. The sunlight seemed to stream from the canvas. Outside she could hear Marcia's voice clamoring, "Lift me, too, Blake! Lift me into the door!"

But Blake shook his head, laughing. His arm was about Susanne's shoulders, and he was hurrying her into the rooms. She looked back and saw the children hesitating in the hall.

"Come, darlings," she cried.

But Blake commanded her. "Susanne! Here are your rooms."

They were going upstairs. Behind her the children walked soberly, tiptoeing up the white marble stairs.

And Blake was saying to John, "You and Marcia and Jane are on the next floor."

"Come with me, then," Jane said, pushing them along before her.

Blake opened a wide door and Susan stood looking into the rooms he had made for her, enormous rooms, beautifully bare, graciously empty, the furniture pale and straightly built, the corners windowed, the light tempered.

"Nothing small or fiddly for my big Susanne," Blake said. "I designed everything."

"When?" she asked, staring into this hugeness.

"Oh, almost at once—I think I began the day after we met," Blake said, smiling at her, watching her.

She could not think of anything to say. She stood gazing about her.

"Do you like it?" Blake asked.

"Yes," she whispered, "it's strange to me—but it's beautiful." She waited a moment, and then she said simply, "I do thank you, Blake, for loving me."

IV

EVERYTHING in the house, she thought, looking down the long narrow drawing room, was now in order. She had lived in Blake's house weeks enough now to know when everything was ready for the day. At the end of the drawing room was a small formal garden and beyond the garden was the East River. Linlay, the Scotch gardener, came up from the country once or twice a week and saw to the plants around the pool. The chauffeur was to water between his visits. She had just been listening to Linlay's complaints.

"Bantie don't water half that he should, Ma'am. With your leave, I'll speak to the maister."

"Oh, no, Linlay," she said quickly, "please don't trouble my husband. I will speak to Bantie." Next time—this afternoon when she was driving to the Metropolitan, she would remember to lean forward and say to young Bantie— She went alone almost every day to the Metropolitan. It was cool and empty and she could sit as long as she liked, pondering what she saw.

The house itself was very still in midsummer. The children had gone away to camp. Blake, in the first week, had said to her restlessly, "Don't children go away to camps in the summer?" Certainly they should not be kept in town. Blake had been wonderfully generous about doing over the west end of the house for them, but it was hot. Besides, there was the morning she had found Blake in the drawing room holding his head in his hands, because John was leaping down the stairs.

"John!" she had called sharply, and had gone into the hall

to meet him, flying at the last step. And then because of the innocence of his inquiring eyes she had not scolded him.

"Would you like to go to a camp?" she asked instead.

"Jane said she might take Marcia and me home," he said, his voice tentative.

"This is home," she said.

"Yes, I know," he answered gently. "But I mean—you know —our real home."

"No," she said quickly. "I'd much rather you both went to camp and learned swimming and things."

She worked with Jane for a week, getting them ready. Blake had been very good. He gave John an expensive fishing rod and explained about flies. There was almost nothing Blake did not know. But last week John had written to her privately: "Will you please send me an ordinary fishing rod and don't tell Blake as the fellows say the ordinary kind like everybody has here are better, and we use worms." So without telling Blake, and she would not for anything have told him, she had gone alone to a sports shop and sent a very ordinary-looking rod. Marcia was too young to write for herself. Every other week a prim official letter came announcing certain facts about Marcia, that she was quite well, that she was going to be a naturally good swimmer and rider, but that her appetite was capricious and she was a little wilful. Susan asked, "Does Marcia seem at all homesick?" "No," the prim letter replied, "Marcia speaks occasionally of her new father, but actually we should say she misses no one."

And Jane, when they were both gone, said very firmly, "With all the help in this house, Mum, you don't need me until the children come back. I'll just go home and clean up good and put up the brambleberries to jelly."

So she and Blake were alone in the house.

"Do you want to go away, Susanne?" Blake asked her.

"Do you?" she asked.

"No," he said. "I love it here. I love this house—I love this city. Besides, I've some ideas I want to work out in terra cotta. New York is a wonderful place in the summer. Everybody is gone."

But the city was full of people. She watched them often from her windows above the river. She was idle, idle. She was given up to loving Blake.

Blake was, in his moods, tireless in work. The top floor of the house was his studio and he had said on the first day when he led her there, springing ahead of her, "You're to use it, too, Susanne—if you want to go on working, that is."

"Of course I shall go on working," she had answered, amazed. But she had not. . . .

Then he had not seemed to hear her. He was showing her everything. He was proud of his house, and most proud of his studio which he had designed. There were the great windows whose curtains were so cunningly controlled by silken ropes and pulleys, the endless cupboards where his materials were kept, the drawing boards and tools—she had never in the bare barn or in the old *maître's* haphazard useful studio dreamed of such luxury. She went upstairs often to watch him, but still she did nothing herself. With everything about her she could think of nothing she wanted to make.

Indeed, why need she hurry? It was sweet to live in Blake's house, to feel herself Blake's wife. It was nearly enough. When she had been married to Mark she was continually thinking of things beyond which she wanted to do. Now, even if Blake had been poor and she compelled to cook and scrub, she would not have wanted to do anything but be what she was, Blake's beloved. But she could not imagine Blake poor.

"I still don't feel I'm your wife," she said again and again.

"It's negligible," said Blake in his gay voice, "a mere accident, allowed for convenience simply. The only reality is that you are my love."

He piled the cushions on the great studio couch, and there she lay watching him work. He worked at such speed, whistling incessantly scraps of songs, stopping to mix a drink, to throw himself beside her for a passionate moment into which he could go, out of which he could come with such suddenness that she was left helpless and bewildered. His passion fled ahead of hers.

She wondered at times, watching him, that she was content. She seemed to have no more desire to create, or if she had, perhaps he satisfied it with what he did so swiftly, so blithely. Beside him her work would seem thick and slow. He was then making what he called his gallery of moderns. Once or twice a week, when she opened the studio door he had a model there, young men or young women with thin dramatic bodies. He drew them off rapidly in a series of irregular concave surfaces, at once absurd and real.

"I don't in the least understand how you do it," she told him. "But I feel it is art."

"It is the only art today," said Blake carelessly.

She looked at him. She ought to contradict him, if he were wrong. And he was wrong. There was no one art in any day.

"The only live art, that is," he added, and whistled a shred of melody out of a rhumba they had danced on a roof the night before. He took her somewhere every night, among people they did not know, and together they looked down from among the stars upon miles and miles of little threaded lights on the earth beneath them.

She asked Blake, "I ought to go and see my parents. Why don't I want to go? I thought I loved them—I do love them."

He said, "I'm making you an honest woman. You never have really wanted to see them, but you've thought you ought to want to. Children naturally hate their parents."

"I don't believe it," she said, surprised. She thought about it, puzzling. He could hit a truth sometimes, carelessly and accurately too.

"Then why don't you go to see them? Why do I live perfectly contentedly without my father? Why won't he even spend the night with us? Why are John and Marcia quite happy away from you?"

She did not answer. His face, when he was working as he was now, was very hard, as hard as the sharp-lined creatures he was making.

"You're hard, Blake," she said. "Why?"

"You don't get anywhere unless you're hard," he answered, stepping back to stare at the mass he was striking into shape. "That's the best thing we've got, we moderns—we're hard."

"No, but why?" she insisted.

"Ruthless love of beauty!" he said. "Pure beauty is hard."

No, there was no softness in him. Even at his most passionate he was ruthless. Even his tenderness was hard. . . . What had his life been? She did not want to know. He never asked her of her life before he came, nor did she ever speak of it. They lived as though this were all. Perhaps it was.

She went to her own room and shut the door and wrote a long letter to her parents. "I am perfectly happy, darlings," she wrote at the end, "and I'm coming home for a long visit one of these days." Then she added, "Of course Blake is anxious to know you," and then in a final postscript she added an old childish sentence, "Don't forget I love you. Sue." It was such a letter as she would not for anything have let Blake see.

Blake liked Mary at once.

Susan had written to Mary as soon as she came to New York and had no answer. Then suddenly at the end of weeks Mary came in casually, like any visitor. She sent in her name and sat waiting in the long drawing room. Blake, coming in, found her there and went to find Susan in her room, reading.

"Girl downstairs by the name of Mary says she's your sister," he said. "Good-looking girl—not a bit like you."

She went out and there was Mary, all black and white, her pale hands crossed on her knees.

"Hello, Susan," she said. "How ridiculous for you to be married to Blake Kinnaird!"

"Do you know Blake?" Susan kissed the cool smooth pale cheek Mary turned to her. Mary never kissed anyone. She merely turned her cheek to be kissed and looked away.

"No, but Michael does," Mary said.

"Where is Michael?" Susan asked.

"We're just back from Norway," Mary said coolly. "He's been painting rocks and water and things like that. He admires Blake immensely, but he laughed when he heard he'd married you. It must be rather different for you now, Susan. Michael said he couldn't imagine Blake really marrying anyone. Well, at least you'll be independent—he won't want children and all that."

Blake had come in, lighting a cigarette, and looking sidewise at Mary out of his long gray eyes. "What's that about me?" he asked.

"I said Susan could keep her independence, married to you," Mary said, as easily as though she had always known him. There was no shyness left in her now. She would perhaps be silent with women, but not with men.

"None of you understands Susanne," Blake said. "She's not in the least independent. Are you, Susanne?"

Mary smiled. "No more theories, Susan?"

"None at all," said Blake for her, boldly. "She's the most female of her species."

"I always suspected it," said Mary, her small mouth twisting. "Don't trust her! She'll sneak up on you yet and have a baby. She was always wanting babies."

"It'll be grounds for divorce if she does," Blake declared. "I married one woman named Susan Gaylord—not Susan Gaylord et al."

They were sparring back and forth, laughing, sharp, absurd. Mary was the sort of woman Blake knew at once, and though she had never seen him before she was completely familiar with him. Susan sat watching them, smiling, aware of bewilderment, as though they were laughing at her. She felt clumsy and slow-witted and dark. When Mary was gone she asked Blake humbly, "Why did you marry me, Blake?"

"I haven't the faintest idea," he said, his eyes teasing.

"Do you think Mary is pretty?" she asked. The room was twilight and she could not see his face.

He reached for a cigarette and the light of the match flared on his narrow handsome face, set into sudden cautiousness.

"Is she?" he mused. "I don't know. She'd be easy for me to draw. She has lines. But she's not a bit like you."

She wanted to cry out, "She was an ugly child, you know, Blake." She wanted to say, "Mary was really a horrid girl when she was young." Then the discovery of such ungenerosity in herself frightened her. Loving Blake made her strange to herself. She had never had such thoughts before about Mary. It was terrifying to see what she really was. She did not speak. Instead she sat thinking quickly, "I can give Mary something pretty now—something really expensive and pretty. Blake is so generous to me with money."

"Let's have the lights." Blake leaped to his feet. "I hate dark rooms."

The room burst into light. He leaned over her chair.

"What are you thinking about?" he demanded.

"I was thinking I would like to give Mary a nice present," she said simply.

He laughed down at her, but his gray eyes were sharp and bright.

"You've been thinking bad thoughts about her," he said. "You are ashamed of yourself!"

"How did you know?" she asked, opening her eyes very wide.

"Simple Susan!" he said, and laughed again.

"Am I simple?" she asked humbly. "Too simple for you, Blake?" She wished he would stop laughing. Why did he laugh at her so often?

"Good people are always simple," he declared. He was still leaning over her, looking into her eyes.

"Mary—" she began.

"Mary," he said, "is like any other woman. You are not. And that's all."

"Marbles—" old Mr. Kinnaird was saying. She and Blake were at Fane Hill for a week in August during a sudden swelter of heat. Blake had turned one morning in disgust from the clay.

"Everything sticks to my hands," he said. "Get ready, Susanne. Fane Hill's better than this. The house is big enough so the old boy won't trouble us much."

"I'd like to know him better," Susan said. She leaped to her feet. The thought of trees made her pant.

"Oh, you can't know him," said Blake. He was washing his hands meticulously and he put a little scent on his palms because clay left an odor he disliked.

They were gone from the house in an hour, and she was sitting under a great elm tree, a cool glass in her hand, listening to old Mr. Kinnaird. Blake was lying on the grass, his eyes shut, his arms and legs flung in graceful exhaustion.

"Marbles," old Mr. Kinnaird said, stirring his tall glass carefully with a long-handled silver spoon, "cannot be understood in a lifetime. I suppose I know as much about marbles as any man living. I do not simply sell—I keep the finest back, to study them, to understand them, to give them at last into hands that know."

He might have been made of his own marble, she thought. He sat there under the trees, in the shadows moved by the gentle wind, very thin and upright in his creamy flannels. Across one long narrow white shoe lay a small smooth black terrier, cocking an ear in fitful sleep.

"By the way," the dry silvery old voice was saying, "if you wish to work in marble, my dear, I should be only too glad—I have some Italian marble I have saved for years, thinking Blake might turn to marble one day. But he doesn't."

"My stuff won't," Blake murmured, and did not open his eyes.

She felt a faint movement of interest in some vague part of her being.

"I'd like to see it," she said, and added, "that is, some time."

Blake yawned nicely, without looking at all unprepossessing. "I hate the country," he murmured. "It makes me into a dullard. I'm going to sleep."

He threw his arm across his eyes and dropped into light instant slumber.

"Why not now?" Mr. Kinnaird said. There was an eagerness in him that he had not showed before, and she rose.

They left Blake asleep on the grass and they wandered along a shadowy lane.

"I keep all my fine pieces together here," he was saying. "I look at every shipment and choose what I will not sell. These pieces I present—"

He took a key from his pocket and opened the door of a great unpainted wooden shed at the end of the lane. Inside were blocks of rough marble of all sizes.

"All waiting," he said gently. "Would you like to choose

one, my dear? I brought David Barnes here once and he took three—a large one for a Titan and two small ones. He is making his Edison from one of my marbles."

She walked among the pieces restlessly. Within her something stirred again.

"You must not choose at once," he said. "Whenever you are ready, here they are. Marble cannot be chosen quickly."

"I know that," she said. She ought to say more and could not. She was glad when he locked the door, and still she felt the restlessness stirring in her, like prophecy of pain.

"You know Blake is wrong about marble," Mr. Kinnaird was saying. "It's the only stuff for the real sculptor—not clay. It's only the great who can use hard stone. Blake's afraid of it." She looked at him. His face was tranquil and cold as he spoke of his son. "Blake's stuff," he went on, "wouldn't hold up in marble. You've got to have an inward solidity or the marble won't take it. No, marble is only for the plain—that is, the eternal."

She listened, wondering that he knew this. But she did not answer. Deep in her being something was stirring. She was quickening as for child.

On the first cool day of early autumn she went alone one day to the Halfred Memorial Hospital to see the thing she had made. She thought once or twice of telling Blake of it, and then she did not. She was afraid for Blake to see it. She had made it so long ago that she could not trust her memory of whether it was good or bad now. She wanted to see it first alone.

On a cool afternoon in late September she went there and people were coming in and out, and she went in at one of the doors and stood in the hall quietly, looking. . . . They were there, the people she had made, set forever in immutable bronze. Painting could be destroyed by time, books moldered and died and passed away, and music was silenced, but what she made, good or not, had to endure. She looked at them with solemnity, because they were more eternal than herself.

Then, as she looked at them, they seemed clumsy and large. Were they so, or had she grown used to Blake's attenuated slant-sided figures? She had made these people before she ever saw Blake. They were huge, the man's shoulders broad, the woman's breasts full. She could hear Blake say banteringly, "Hopelessly realistic, my Susanne!" Why did they seem so alive, then? The dark bronze shone with their life, the light fell upon them, moving, heaving with life. Two girls came in and stood beside her, staring, chewing gum.

"The woman looks awful sad, don't she!" she heard one whisper to the other.

"Yeah," the other said. "It kinda makes you want to cry."

If Blake had been there he would have laughed to hear them.

She turned away and went home. She did not even ask if Blake were in. She went into her own room and shut the door. She took off her street clothes and bathed and wrapped herself in a satin robe and lay down on a couch. Blake had put mirrors at angles opposite to her, and she saw herself reflected again and again, smaller and smaller, until the room seemed full of pretty idle women, wrapped in ivory satin, lying outstretched upon creamy satin couches. She lifted her hand languidly. It had grown soft and white as her hands had never been. Her hands—her hands! And glancing at the mirror she saw lifted innumerable pretty hands, languid and white. She turned away from the women and buried her face in her arms.

When Blake came in she had not moved. She heard him come in. He stood beside her and still she did not move. Then she felt his grasp on her shoulders turning her over to him. His hands were quick and hard and they always hurt her a little when they touched her, as though they were sharp.

"Why, you're not asleep!" he cried. "I thought you were asleep."

She shook her head, and he sat down. In the mirrors tall handsome slender men sat down and leaned over pretty women.

"What is it?" he asked.

But he did not wait for her answer. His gray eyes flickered as he looked at her. "You're beautiful," he said abruptly.

In the mirrors the men bent and seized the women into their arms. Over his shoulder she looked at them. All the men were Blake, but none of the women was she—no, she did not know the women.

Her life, which had always seemed simple and whole, was now a conglomerate of fragments, all shining, all momentary. There was nothing to link these pieces together. They were not bound together into a life. She walked from one room to another and all the many rooms made no house in which her soul could live. She had everything. There was really nothing to be imagined which she did not have. Blake loved her passionately. She was his beloved. John and Marcia came home and she was their mother and she listened while they talked.

"I caught fifty-six fish and we ate them," John said. "I wish you had come to see me, Mother."

"I swimmed and swimmed." Marcia, brown as bronze, swam around the room.

Jane, returning, brought jars of jelly and fruit. "I left the balance of it in the cellar at home," she said.

"But why, Jane?" Susan asked. "Nobody's going there."

"I dunno," Jane answered. "I felt to do it. I cleaned everything good. It's like heaven there—so quiet."

These walls of Blake's house were suddenly strange around her.

"How is the new well?" she asked.

"Wunnerful, Mum," said Jane. "The water's sweet and cold."

She did not speak. If Mark had drunk that sweet cold water

he need not have died. But then there would not have been all this life with Blake. She could not think of herself now without Blake.

She was Blake's beloved and he was hers.

"Put on your dark gold dress tonight, Susanne," Blake said. They were going out to dance. "You ought always to wear dark gold, my sweet. And let me do your hair. Everybody's coming back to town and everybody wants to know whom Blake Kinnaird has married. You know I always said I wouldn't marry anybody, Susanne—damn your lovely eyes!" And she had gone as Blake's beloved, holding herself proudly, and proud to see these gay and beautiful people surrounding Blake. Blake's arm was about her lightly.

"Susanne, Susanne!" he presented her to them all. Women's eyes looked at her curiously, coldly, but men's eyes were hot. She looked at them all alike and scarcely spoke.

She would never be able to speak to them, she thought, watching them, listening to them. She could not understand what they said. Blake understood. Blake tossed their brittle talk back to them. Women came up to him abruptly, throwing their scraps of glittering talk at him, their eyes ardent. The eyes of all the women were ardent upon Blake. Their eyes made a pool of warmth about him. And he was like a shining silvery thing, darting through their warmth, toward them, away from them, evading, eluding, smiling. None could touch him. They put out their hands while they talked, but he moved away, as though he did not know a hand was about to touch his arm, his hand.

"Blake can take care of himself," she thought. Then she thought, wondering, "But he loves it—he loves every one of these women a little." Sitting there quiet in the midst of their incessant fluttering and darting and preening, she wondered again, without humility, with nothing but pure wonder, why he had ever married her.

"Did you have a good time?" Blake asked her at four o'clock in the morning when they were going to bed. He was a little drunk and he turned back her head and kissed her throat over and over. She lay passive and considered.

"I think I did," she said seriously. "Only the strange thing is I can't remember any of their faces."

"You're a little drunk," he said, laughing.

But she had drunk nothing all evening. She had only watched them, listening, wondering.

"Susanne, come here!" Blake was commanding her. She went to him docilely. She was Blake's beloved and he was hers, though she did not know why. But this, too, was only a fragment. . . .

Once Michael came to see her. He came alone and she was alone, too. He was entirely a man, she saw immediately. All of the beautiful boy was gone. The Christ look was gone as though it had never been. The blond hair was darker and smoother. He wore a small mustache and his body had thickened. He did not mention Mary at all or that she had been with him in Norway.

"I'm having an exhibition—my fjords," he said. "I've done nothing else all summer but rocks and water and nudes—mostly rocks and water. There is something about a woman's soft body on a wet black rock and the surf pounding toward her— You'd swear she was about to be crushed. You want her to be mangled and crushed." He paused. "I keep painting that sort of thing just now," he said carelessly. "One does what one must—" He got up and walked to the window of the long drawing room and looked out upon the river.

"Don't you paint horses any more?" she asked. "You used to paint running horses so beautifully. I could feel the streaming wind."

"I painted some wild horses around a pool in the desert," he said. "Old Joseph Hart took it."

258

"Tell me," she begged him.

"Nothing," he said impatiently. "I was out west and I'd never seen wild horses. People talked about them, but I never saw them. Then one night when I was sleepless I went out of my cabin and climbed a little sandy hill and there they were, nine of them, drinking from a pool at the bottom of the hill. One of them was black but the rest were all white. They felt me somehow. The black one felt me. He was the leader. He lifted his head and whinnied, and they were all off, galloping together behind the black one, in the moonlight."

"I see it," she said. "Oh, Michael!"

But he was lighting a cigarette.

"It will be interesting to see what you and Kinnaird do to each other," he said. "One or the other of you will be changed. I can't imagine his being anything else, though."

"You aren't married?" she asked.

"Lord, no," he exclaimed. "It would be ruinous for me."

"Why?" she asked, remembering how desperately once he had wanted to marry Mary.

"I don't want to let anyone in that far," he said. "I'm not strong enough for it. I see that, now. My entity would be disturbed. I wouldn't feel what to paint." He paused and added, "It's different for you."

"Why?" she asked.

"Oh, well—a woman—" He shrugged his shoulders.

"Yes? A woman?" she repeated.

"A woman is different," he said. "They're basically physiological."

She was about to protest and then she did not. Last night in the darkness when Blake had gone to sleep she had lain quietly, spent and satisfied. Yes, she was still satisfied. She sat looking at Michael steadily, too honest to deny what she was.

She was Blake's beloved.

One day David Barnes came stumping in. She and Blake were alone for lunch, and he made a third.

"You two," he said, looking around the mirrored dining room. Here Blake had set into panels the diagonal mirrors he loved, so that the room was full of the three of them infinitely repeated. "Blake, I thought you'd be doing other things in Paris than getting married."

"Ah, but Susanne," said Blake lightly. "She's the confounded sort of woman to whom you can't propose anything but marriage—nothing else suits her type." He picked the fragile bones of a small bird quickly, cleanly, as he talked. His thin hard hands were always deft. "God knows I didn't want to be married," he went on. "I tried everything else, didn't I, Susanne? But it was marriage or nothing."

"Blake!" cried Susan. "You asked me to marry you from the very first."

"Ah," said Blake, looking at Barnes, "she understood nothing until then. She is a stupid creature, as you know, Barnes!"

They laughed, and when she blushed they laughed again because they had made her doubtful of herself. Had she not understood Blake?

"I know you're only teasing me," she exclaimed. But she was not sure.

And she was not at all sure when after lunch Blake went away and she and David Barnes were alone.

"So you would be married, eh, Susan?" he said abruptly. He lit his pipe and stretched out his legs and cracked the joints of his big grimy hands. "I thought you were through with that and ready for work. Aren't you ever going to begin to work? It's because you're a woman. Women don't want to do real work."

"Something in me wanted Blake," she said honestly.

"Blake won't be like that what's-his-name. He won't be kind and die young," said David Barnes, and his eyes grew grim.

"Blake's going to live and live. He'll let anybody die before he lets himself die."

"If Blake died I would die, too," she said.

"Ah," said David Barnes, "you think so."

She did not answer. In a moment she looked up to find him staring at her curiously as though he did not know her.

"What is it?" she asked. "What is wrong?"

"Don't you feel any sense of guilt?" he asked.

"Guilt?" she repeated.

"Yes, guilt," he said. "Guilt! Your life is passing and you are doing nothing."

She shook her head. "I'm content to live," she answered.

"Live!" he whispered. "You call it living! Then there's no use talking to you yet."

And very soon he went away.

She did not mind. She even pitied him a little.

"David Barnes lives in a box," she said to Blake that night. "He has let his art kill his life. Life must come first, mustn't it, Blake? Out of everything lived it comes at last, a flower and a seed."

"Do you still think about art?" asked Blake. His gray eyes were laughing at her. "I thought you were through with all that—" Before she could do more than open her eyes at him, he said quickly, his eyes lighting, "Susanne, I thought of a gown today that I want to make for you—thin gold tissue on red— you know, the gold standing out stiff like this—and underneath the tight red." He began to draw on one of the little paper pads he kept everywhere about the house. She leaned over him to look. She was beginning to love the clothes he designed for her. At first she had been shy when he dressed her, but now her body was his clay. To such use she gladly put herself. For she was Blake's beloved and he was hers. She went on living her life, one bright fragment after another. It was only long after

261

this that she remembered David Barnes had not once that day spoken to her of his Titans, or indeed of anything he was doing.

Blake said, "Christmas is nothing to me, my dear. Of course, take your children and go and visit your parents. You'll be miserable unless you're doing your duty—whereas I am miserable if I am doing it. So I shall not go and dine with my father. I shall let him dine alone at Fane Hill as he always does."

"What will you do on Christmas, then, Blake?" she asked, troubled. It seemed wrong somehow to leave Blake on their first Christmas. But he disliked anniversaries. "Why do I want to be told about time?" he always demanded.

"There are hundreds of things I can do," he said, "and I shan't tell you any of them. All I say is that if you stay I beg you will not litter the house with trees and tinsels nor allow your children to heap me with gifts I don't want."

"Very well," she replied quietly. She never quite knew whether or not Blake was serious in anything he said. She watched him continually that she might discover by sense or sight all that he meant, since merely to hear what he said was not enough to tell her.

It had come to her for the first time that she wanted to go away from him a little while. She could not bear to be away from him for a single night, yet she was beginning to feel exhausted. He kept her at some pitch that was not her own. She had grown thin, although she lived in this complete idleness. She wanted to go away from him and sit by a fire in a quiet old-fashioned house and hear nothing but homely sounds. Everything in Blake's house was quick and keyed to his necessities. The servants were nervous and too deferential. She still did not know any of them. Even Jane was not herself. She had a little room of her own near the children and she had nothing to do with the other servants.

262

"Jane, we're going to spend Christmas with my father and mother," Susan said.

"John has been prayin' for it," said Jane.

"I want to rest," said Susan slowly, "—though I don't know from what."

Jane opened her mouth, shut it again and went away to pack. Once she had decided, the holidays were almost instantly there and then she clung to Blake again. "I don't want to leave you," she said. Out in the hall John was hopping up and down on one leg, and Marcia had on her new hat and coat. Of course she must go. The children would never bear the disappointment. But had she been alone she would not have gone. Blake was in her blood like a mad drink, like a sweet disease. She had closed her life to everything but him.

"Yes, you do want to leave me," Blake said, his eyes glinting. "You want to go away from me."

"Do I?" she exclaimed. "How do you know, Blake?"

"You are a little different, Susanne," he said, "a very little. I feel it when I hold you. You do not quite yield up yourself. Go away and see how you miss me!"

"Shall you miss me, Blake?"

"Yes, of course I'll miss you," he said. "But I won't mope for you—or anybody. I have a hundred things to do."

He kissed her in his hard quick fierce fashion. "Now, go along," he said. But his eyes fastened on her, sure of possession.

He loved her, but he had no tenderness for her.

She had been so long without tenderness, so long strung to the thin height of passion, that this house of her childhood was a world of comfort. She sank into the shabbiness of its old easy chairs and couches and wide old beds and faded curtains. When she saw her father at the door she suddenly wanted to cry. John went straight to the kitchen.

"It's been a long time since I was in a kitchen," he had said

263

in the car, and Marcia had cried, "I never have been in a kitchen!"

"Yes, you have," he said gravely, "but you don't remember. I just barely can, myself." Marcia ran after him.

She heard her mother's excited laughter, "Well, I never—"

"I have a new coat and hat!" Marcia's high voice cried.

Susan stood clinging to her old father, her lips trembling. "Why, Sue, my girl," he said, patting her back.

"Father, I've had a hard time," she wanted to say. But she had not, she thought, amazed at her untruthfulness. It was not true. It was only that she needed tenderness, that foolishly and vaguely she craved some sort of sympathy, though for what she did not know.

"I don't know why I cry," she said, half laughing, trying to find her handkerchief. "It's so good to see you again, Dad. But you're thinner." He looked frail and old.

"Yes, yes," he said. "Well, your mother's expecting you. Your room's all ready. Marcia's in Mary's room. Mary won't be home for Christmas—got other plans. I don't understand that girl, Susan. Maybe you do. She doesn't belong to us."

"There are a lot of people like her," she said. She did not want to talk about Mary. She kissed her father's brown cheek and went into the kitchen to find her mother. She was at the table by the window, cutting slices of bread for the children, and she turned a softly withering cheek to Susan's kiss. Jane was already peeling potatoes.

"You look just the same, Mother," Susan said. Her mother's stout compact body had not aged at all, nor was there any white in her faded blond hair. Only her face was a pattern of wrinkles, a loose withering of her once fair skin which gave her a look now of childish age, withering but unripe and unmellowing.

"I have my health," her mother said. Then she looked at her. "You're thin, Sue—I don't know as I ever saw you so thin before. Well, you'll pick up. . . . John looks more like Mark, don't he? It's his build more than his face."

"I hadn't noticed it," Susan said. She glanced at John. Mark was too long dead, and she saw only John.

"I don't suppose they even remember him," her mother said mournfully. "His parents never got over it. They've just shut themselves up and don't go anywhere. I don't see them year in and year out, now they've stopped coming to church. They haven't been to church since the Sunday Mark died. You remember he died on Sunday? People say they just gave up their faith when Mark died."

"I didn't know what day it was," she said. She might, she supposed, go and see Mark's parents. But why? When Mark died they had passed from her life. And what faith could she restore to them? She lived in this moment, only in moments of her own life.

The kitchen was hot and fragrant with the odor of spices. There were geraniums red in the window and the sun shone fulsomely upon them. Her mother was spreading brown sugar on the buttered slices.

"I believe I'd like some," Susan said. When she was a little girl she had hurried home from school for bread and butter and brown sugar. She took the slice and bit into it.

"I didn't know you liked bread and sugar, Mother!" cried Marcia.

"Of course I do," Susan answered.

It was good and hearty and she ate it slowly to the last crumb as she went upstairs to her old room. The room was exactly the same, the blue checked gingham curtains and the blue counterpane and the rag rug on the floor. She sat down in the wicker armchair. All through her body she could feel the let-down of nerves and muscles, like the slipping strings of a violin strung too high and shrill. She was coming back to her own pitch. She wanted to sleep and sleep, not to have to speak or to listen to anyone. The children were safe and she need not think of them. Everything was safe in this house. She got up and took off the sable cloak Blake had given her and hung it in the closet. There was her old blue dressing robe, washed and clean. She took off her dress and slipped it on and lay upon the bed. It was deep and soft beneath her, and remembered. She fell instantly and dreamlessly asleep.

When she woke her mother was standing over her. The light was on, and outside it was dark.

"We got worrying about you," her mother exclaimed. "You aren't sick, are you, Sue?"

She struggled to sit up. The stillness was amazing. She had grown so used to noise. "No," she said, "only tired. It's so good to get home."

"Supper's ready, then," her mother said. "I've made a good oyster stew. I let the children start—they seemed just starving. My, but she's a handy soul, your Mrs. What's-her-name!"

"Jane?" said Susan, yawning.

"I can't call a body by their Christian name like that," her mother protested. "Say, Susan, shouldn't she sit down with us?"

"No," said Susan. "She would be miserable."

"Well," her mother said doubtingly. "I suppose you know her. Here, don't get all dressed up, child—just keep on your slippers. We're only home folks."

Around the lighted table they sat down and her father bent his head to say grace, while John and Marcia paused, astonished, spoons halfway to their mouths. She never had taught them about grace. The fragrance of the rich soup was in her nostrils. She began to eat with a whole pleasure.

Nothing happened in this quiet old house. Her parents had little to say to each other or to her. They did not ask her about her life and she did not speak of it. "Blake was sorry not to come," she said, perfunctorily, the first night, and her mother,

266

her eyes roving the table, answered half hearing, "Yes, it's too bad. Maybe he can come some other time."

Blake sent her a telegram every day and she replied and then she did not miss him. She was amazed that this was so, and sometimes dismayed. Surely she would miss him. Some day, some night, the need for him would seize her and then she would say in the morning, "I must go back to Blake."

Day followed day and still she did not want to go away. She waited in silence, wanting nothing beyond its deep rest. She thought once of the farmhouse but she did not want even to go there. Mark's memory would be there and she wanted nothing and nobody. She felt something slowly releasing itself within her, growing back, as a tree bent by a weight grows back when it is freed.

"Don't you want to have some of the girls in?" her mother asked. But she shook her head. What did she have to say to them?

They went to church on the Sunday before Christmas and in a pew ahead she saw Hal and Lucile and three children between them. Afterwards Lucile came rushing at her screaming, "Oh, Susan, it's wonderful to see you! We hear the most wonderful things—don't tell me these are your children! You don't look a day older—oh, I'm a fright—so fat! I began to put on weight after Jimmy. Yes, this is my only girl, Leora."

Susan looked down at a pale, silent little girl, who looked, of all the children, the only one like Hal.

"Once I heard you crying and I went and picked you up," she said. "You don't remember it."

The little girl shook her head and Lucile gave her great bouncing laugh. "Leora's still a cry baby," she said cheerfully. "Here's Hal, Susan!" Hal was there, tall and shy of her, and he was growing bald. Instantly she was overcome with the feeling of Mark. If Mark had lived she would have gone on being

267

one of them all. And she—what would have become of her if Mark had lived? But now she was very far away.

She walked a great deal during these days. The winter was very warm.

"No snow this year, much," her father said when the children were searching the skies for clouds. "The corn husks were thin, I noticed, in the fall, and the squirrels haven't hurried to hide their nuts—nuts lying around everywhere in the woods. That means a mild winter."

Christmas Eve dawned like a day in October, full of still, warm sunshine. She walked that day to Mrs. Fontane's garden. The house was closed and the gates locked, and she climbed over a low stone wall and crossed the leaf-covered lawns until she saw the pool, rimmed in the fallen leaves. There knelt her little Cupid, gazing into the water. She stood looking at it as though she had never seen it before. She had forgotten it for years, as one might forget a child who scarcely lived to draw its breath. It seemed no more than such a beginning. Yet, as she looked, she did not remember why it had been made, that she and Mark might marry.

"It is rather good," she thought, forgetting. "It looks alive, in spite of all I didn't know then. Yes, I caught life somehow, though I didn't know I did."

A wind flurried down a shower of last leaves and they fell past the Cupid, catching, and falling past and settling gently on the silent shallow pool. . . . How long ago it was! She felt herself wrapped into the endless silence.

Even Christmas did not bring her out of her silence. She went through its familiar ways, still apart. When the day was over and she was alone in her room again, in bed ready for sleep, she remembered that Blake had sent her no message. His gift had been on the Christmas tree, a small square watch set with diamonds, but there was no message with it. It had been sent straight from a shop. She half rose to go to the telephone and then she did not. She lay a moment, half deciding, and then without knowing it she fell into sleep.

Her father said, "Come up to the attic and play a little, Susan. I don't get much music nowadays." So she went upstairs and played the things she had not played in many years. He sat listening, his mouth covered with his beautiful old hand. He always hid his mouth when he listened to music.

"Do you ever write poetry any more, Father?" she asked him while she played.

"No, I've given it up," he replied, and sighed.

"You haven't given up the South Seas?" she asked, smiling. In the high sweet upper notes her right hand was wandering, and the soft bass followed, echoing.

"I think a little bit about it sometimes," he said. Then he smiled back at her, shamefaced as a child. "Of course you know I always knew I'd never get there," he said gently. He closed his eyes and she went on for an hour while he listened.

And then, when she had finished playing his favorite Sibelius she turned. He was looking at her, trembling, a look of fright in his blue eyes.

"Dad!" she cried, sharply.

"I took a wrong turn somewhere in my life, Susan," he whispered. "I thought I was going up the main road, and it has been only a blind alley. I haven't come out anywhere."

"Don't," she said. She went and put her arms around him and held him and pressed her head against him. To grow old, to know too late that somewhere one had taken the wrong road, to understand that there was no return, life having been spent in bright fragments—this was the first death. "It's wasted," he whispered. "I've wasted myself. The years fooled me—I haven't done what I was sure I would." She knelt beside him, holding him hard in an instant terror greater than his own, feeling to the depths what he meant.

269

This was what happened. Year followed year, that was all. One day there was plenty of time, and the next day there was none at all. "I don't suppose it matters," her father was saying. "It isn't the world that's missed me—it's I who have missed it. I don't suppose that matters—but it does to me."

"Father!" she whispered. She knelt beside him. "You haven't really missed everything."

"If you don't get what you wanted at the end, nothing seems to count," he said. Then suddenly he shook her off and rose to his feet. "Oh, well!" he said.

He had turned away from her, but the terror was still in his eyes.

And this terror was a light to her soul. She lay awake in the night, and the terror played about her as fierce as lightning and in its clarity she saw that Blake, Blake was what was wrong with her. She who should yield to no one had yielded to him because she loved him. She knew now she had not loved Mark enough and so he had done her no harm. But Blake was strangling her. She was subduing herself to him, letting the years pass over her. She loved him and feared him, and lest he be angry with her she had let him make her what he wanted. That was why she had grown so spent and so mortally weary. She had been shaped as surely as he shaped his figures of clay, and her spirit, now docile, was fainting, though she had not been aware of it until she left him. For the shape into which he was making her was not her own. . . . Once she remembered her father had told her in one of his abrupt, half confidences, "When I married your mother she was a small pink-cheeked creature with yellow hair. I thought she would do anything for me. It was only afterwards I discovered she was the stubbornest thing on earth. She's sweet and stupid and she always knows best and she takes her way. She will crush anyone near her. If I could only stop loving her—"

270

But he had never stopped loving her. The horrible thing was that he still loved this woman to whom he had yielded. He had never gone away from her even for a night, though he dreamed of the islands in the sea and though he had built the cabin by the lake. But at night he came home, loving her, and hating her.

It was when one could not go away . . . She must go away from Blake. But she did not know how because she loved him. Other women might lose themselves and live on, but she could not.

Lying in the dark of her old room, she began to plan, bitterly awake. Blake was a poison in her veins. She had been infatuated with him. She was, still. She would always be, though she was his wife. And this infatuation would be the end of herself, if she did not drag herself out of it. She must lay hold on herself, command her life before it was too late.

"Guilt!" she thought suddenly. "I know what David meant. Of course I am guilty!" Love was wicked when it did what she had let it do. She sat up in bed and hugged her knees. What if she waked like this one morning to find her hair white and her hands too old to work, what if the years fooled her, too, stealing past her silently, secretly, making no sound to disturb her so that she did not know they passed? And then one morning it would be too late. Her hands would be withered and her sight dim.

She sprang out of bed and turned on the light and stared into the mirror. She was still young, still strong. Her hands were still her hands. She could work with them. There was time. She had caught the years at their evil game, and she would march ahead of them for the rest of her life. She stood, looking at herself. She was ruddy with rest and sunshine. Strength welled up in her body. She wished it were not night. She was finished with sleeping and now she was impatient for the morning. And Blake? What should she tell him? What but

271

the one truth, that she had been idle and now she must work? If he laughed at her, if he pulled her back into himself, she would remember the fear of waking to find herself old and life finished.

She could do it. She went back to bed and curled into her own warmth and thought of Blake. She did not hate him, she would never be able to hate him. Some part of her would always be tender and passionate because of him. He had made her for a little while to be nothing but a woman like other women. It was one of the rooms of her life. She had lived in it and now she had come out of it. But the door was not shut. She could come in and go out at her will, only she must never let Blake lock her in any more. No one must ever lock her in anywhere. "I can do anything!" she exclaimed aloud, and the sound of her own voice in the old confident words drove away her last terror. She lay in the soundless dark and at last she slept.

V

THEY went back the day after the new year. Blake was not at home.

"The master reckoned you'd not be here for an hour yet, Madame," Crowne said, looking at her as though she were an unexpected guest.

"It doesn't matter," said Susan.

There was an hour in which she could take new possession of this house. She went with the children to their rooms and together they unpacked and hung up their clothes.

"Oh, I wish we could always live in the country," John said moodily.

"So do I, to be sure," Jane sighed.

"I don't," said Marcia. She was growing into a tall child with a sharp preciseness of speech and movement. She had asked Susan again and again, "When are we going back to Blake?" She admired Blake and adored him, because he paid her such fitful attention. He would play with her and then for days forget her. And she pursued him and talked to him in affected vivacity to make him laugh. Susan thought, "I must send her away from him to school. I don't want her growing into the kind of girl Blake likes." She was afraid for Marcia. Within her a robust and healthy instinct began to rise. There was something a little wrong in Blake. He deadened whomever he loved, whoever loved him. She longed for his footstep and dreaded it. She would stay here with the children and let him find her here.

Then he came, handsome and immaculate, very gay and glad

to see them, and he gave her his quick hard kiss, his hands on either side of her face, his palms cool and smooth.

"Susanne, I'm glad to see you! But how hot your cheeks are!" he said. "I don't care to tell you how the time dragged. I won't let you think yourself indispensable to me, though in your way you are. I do hate Christmas! How do you do, John! Marcia, come here and let me kiss you."

Marcia ran to him and he lifted her and kissed her on the mouth.

"Kiss me again, Blake!" she begged him.

"Marcia!" Susan cried sharply.

"It's only because she likes the way Blake's face smells," said John with scorn. "She told me so." He stood aloof, his hands in his pockets.

But Blake laughed and kissed Marcia again, looking at Susan, his eyes teasing her.

"Have you forgotten all the dance steps, Marcia?" he demanded. He had once taught her little stiff precise dances which he said suited her square-cut straight hair and thin child's shape.

"No, I haven't—not one," she cried, and she began to dance. Susan could see the child's eyes fixed on Blake and her body grow tense to Blake's command. He was singing in a sharp syncopated melody, beating time in a nervous ragged rhythm. When he stopped Marcia was quivering. "More—more—" she begged him.

"No more," said Susan. "Blake, it's bad for her. She is too highly strung as it is."

"She loves it," he said calmly, "don't you, kid?"

He ruffled her hair and she looked at him in ecstasy.

"Yes—yes!" she whispered.

And Susan thought, "What is this power he has?"

. . . "I'm going to send them both away to school in the country," she told Blake that night.

"As you like," he said, his tone careless. He was looking at her. "Put on that new thing, Susanne—the red and gold."

"No, Blake," she replied.

"Why not?" he asked, surprised.

"I'd rather not," she said tranquilly, and chose a soft blue gown she had not worn in a long time.

"I don't like you in blue," he said sulkily, watching her.

"Don't you?" she said quietly. "I like blue."

And she would not notice the looks he threw at her. It was so small a thing, and yet in that moment she felt her body reclaimed. For she would not have done even this if she had not had her terror.

Slow and deep there came out of her with this first small independence the huge need to begin to do her own work. She awoke to it as one awakes again to health after illness, feeling herself well again and her muscles ready and her mind clear and willing. They went downstairs together and Blake put his arm around her, his hand in the warm pit beneath her shoulder. She turned toward him and smiled, and checked the old instant submission of her being, the sweet, half-fainting instant yielding which was once the power of his touch upon her. She had herself again.

She was about to say, "Blake, do you mind if I work?", but instead she said, "I am going to begin to work again, Blake." They were at breakfast the next morning.

"Why not?" he said busily. He knocked the top from his egg with one short quick blow. "Now that the children are going to school I am not enough for you, I know. I felt that last night."

She looked at him to discover his mood, but he was very amiable in spite of his words. "It is quite all right," he said gaily. "You shall have a corner in my studio, and I will explain

275

to you the secret of mixing my clay. No one else knows, and I would tell no one but you."

"Do you have a secret?" she asked, playfully.

"Of course," he said. He was a little lofty with her. "How do you suppose I get those lean creatures to stay together?" he demanded.

"I suppose everybody has a secret," she replied peaceably. "I remember David Barnes said his was in that little Adam he had in plaster in his studio. There was a small square cut in the back, which came out."

"What was the secret?" Blake demanded.

"I never looked," she replied, surprised. "He said I was to have it only if he died."

"You worked day after day with that beside you and never looked?" Blake's fine narrow black brows were raised at her.

"Of course!" she said indignantly, and he laughed.

"Darling Susanne!" he said. "The reason I love you is because you are like no one!"

"Don't you believe me?" she asked.

"I do," he declared. "I always believe you and no one else. And you may have the corner by the window for your own."

He was so amiable and so handsome that she could scarcely go on to what she had already planned. She was beginning to see she had dreaded him when he was not amiable, and that he knew it. That was to be ended. She forced herself to go on.

"A corner will be scarcely enough for me, Blake— I want to work in marble."

"Marble!" he exclaimed. "No, you can scarcely haul a quarry up to the studio. If I am too curious, forgive me—but what, Susanne, shall you do in marble?"

He was not in the least unkind. His voice was humoring and gay. She loved him very much, but she found, feeling her way from moment to moment, that she did not want to tell him anything.

276

"I don't know," she said.

"I thought you didn't," he said. "Let me advise you, Susanne, against carving directly in marble. No one can do it—only two or three very great sculptors try to do it."

Her proud heart reared its head like a lion in her woman's body. "How do you know I am not great?" it demanded. But though she heard it she would not let it speak. She sat silent, smiling at Blake while he talked, and not listening to him at all. Still she was his beloved and he was hers. But she was sorting out her life from its fragments, even from love. . . .

Outdoors on the street she dismissed Bantie, while he stared at her.

"Thank you, Bantie, I'll take the small car myself this morning."

"Traffic's bad, Ma'am," he said glumly.

"You might surprise Linlay this morning and clean up the garden," she said, twisting a smile at him as she took the wheel.

"Yes, Ma'am," he said forlornly. Nothing pleased him more than driving endlessly about the city in the thickest traffic, and he hated the garden.

But she wanted to go alone and discover a place where she could work. There must be a place somewhere to which she could go and where she could forget Blake, a garage she could rent, or a floor of an old house.

The reputable real estate offices had nothing for her, she found. "We could rent you a studio apartment," one plump neat young man after another told her, their voices full of bright professional interest.

"No—no, thank you," she said. "I won't want to live in my studio. I have a house."

She drove home after hours, slowly, by devious ways. Quite near Blake's house were tenements, full of the alien and the

277

poor. A few rich men like Blake had seized upon the river front and, disregarding the poor, had built their homes on a few streets, evading tenements. Bantie always drove in and out by those wide clean ways.

Now alone she found herself in the tangle of tenements. She had to drive carefully because of children, shrilly intent upon play and seeing cars no more than flies in their path. Women leaned out of windows and screeched at them and shook out grimy bedclothes, and men lounged on stained doorsteps. Blake would never come here. She paused at an entrance. A sign was at the window—"Apartment to Let."

"May I come in and see that apartment?" she called to a pleasant-looking man with a dirty face, who stood leaning against the door.

"I don't care," he remarked.

A swarm of boys leaped at her like grasshoppers.

"Watch your car, lady?" "I'll watch it, lady!"

"Why does it have to be watched?" she asked.

" 'Cos," said a dark boy with shining secret black eyes, "if we don't, somethin' happens to it."

"Shall I give a nickel each to ten boys or fifty cents to one?" she inquired.

It was something serious. They went into conference and emerged.

"Give it to Smikey," they clamored, "we can make him divide."

Smikey came forward, a pale child with anxious blue eyes and his front teeth gone.

"Will you watch it, Smikey?" she asked.

He nodded, prodded from behind, but speechless.

So she went in, guided by the dirty-faced man, and looked at the empty apartment. There were three rooms, partitioned lightly from each other out of what had once been a room of noble size. The ceilings were high and corniced and there was a carved wooden mantel now defiled and filthy. Blake would never find her here.

"Would it matter if I took the partitions out?" she asked.

"I'll do it fur yez, Miss," the man said eagerly. "I'm odd job man and janitor here."

"I'd want the walls and the floor painted," she said.

"I cud do it," he answered.

"And the windows washed?"

"Me ould woman," he said.

"Very well," she said. "I'll take it."

"I'll report it to the office," he said proudly.

"When can I come in?" she asked.

"This day week," he said with certainty.

She went down the dirty steps. Around the car a crowd of silent intense children watched for her. She took fifty cents from her purse.

"Thank you, Smikey," she said.

"She done it!" they muttered. "Fifty cents—Jeez!"

They disappeared down the street, sweeping Smikey along in their midst, a bird in the wind.

She drove three blocks and turned a corner into the quiet quadrangle where she and Blake lived among a few rich people.

"You couldn't work here, my dear?" old Mr. Kinnaird was asking. She had gone to Fane Hill to choose the marble he wanted to give her.

"Oh no, I couldn't indeed," she said. "It's beautiful—but I couldn't." She could not possibly work in this remote place under those pale kind eyes of Blake's father.

"It's very quiet," he murmured.

"Yes, it is," she said gently, "it's lovely."

It was very still. Winter was silently passing. The beautiful old house where Blake was born was settled back in its great trees, asleep and dying, even while their new leaves prepared to bud again. She could not work there. She would only sit idle, day after day, dying with all that was dying.

"I wish you'd take all you want," he said, unlocking the door of the storehouse. "I'll have them sent—where shall I send them?"

She gave him the number and the street.

"I don't know it," he murmured. "Is there a studio there?"

"I've made one," she said.

Then she walked among the marbles. Without any knowledge of what she would make, she chose four pieces—a Siena, two Serravezzas, a piece of Belgian black.

"It's treacherous stuff," old Mr. Kinnaird said, his hand white as ash upon the Belgian black, "as treacherous as beauty. Watch it as you go." And then he gave her three blocks of Paros marble.

"These are years of my life," she thought, "caught here and held." The marble stood before her, solid and heavy with promise. The years were stopped.

"You must let me see what you bring from them," he said.

He stood against the light of the open door, slender and fine and pale, as graceful and pure a statue of age as she had ever seen, and somehow never to be loved. She put out her hand, impulsive and warm.

"I do thank you with all my heart."

He touched it quickly with his fingers and drew away. His hand was cold, and dust to touch. . . .

"Blake," she asked him that night at dinner, "do you remember your mother?"

"No," he said, "she died when I was two."

"Did your father never speak of her?" she asked.

"No, except to say they were happy."

"He or they?"

"I believe," Blake said, looking at her hard, "that he always

280

put it like this, 'I was very happy with your mother.'" He cocked a fine eyebrow at her. "Isn't it the same thing?"

She smiled and shook her head.

"Yes, it is," he insisted. "Wouldn't I know it if you weren't happy?"

"Suppose I didn't tell you?" she said.

"I'd know," he said, carelessly.

She looked at him thoughtfully, searching him. No, he did not know, she thought, anything about her happiness.

She said to herself that Blake should not notice the slightest difference in her. No one should feel or see her different. The only difference would be in herself. She had her love disciplined now. It should not longer consume her with hours of idleness. When Blake went to work, she would work. She had told him she had rented a studio not far away and he had said nothing at all. But he began to dally in the mornings. When he knew that she would come to his studio and lie on the couch watching him, he sprang out of bed, full of zest to begin. A half hour was long enough for breakfast.

But now he came into her room early in the morning and delayed her with his love. She bit back her impatience. She loved him, but this was perversity, this was childishness. The day must begin, because night came so soon. Then he cried out at her, "Susanne, what's the matter with you? You're changed to me!"

"No, I am not, Blake," she said flatly.

"Then why do you want to get up?"

At first she put him off. Then she saw she was afraid of him and so she said plainly, "I have my own work to do."

"I'm sorry!" he said, and leaped from her bed.

He stood looking down at her, wrapping his robe about him. His lips were thin and his eyes gray as slate and his voice was so cold she caught his hand.

"You know you are my beloved," she said gently. "Kiss me, Blake!"

He kissed her harshly.

"Don't ever say that to me again!" he said.

"You must love me, Blake," she begged him.

"I do," he said. "But—stay what I love."

He went away and he did not come back as he usually did to see if she were dressed, and she knew he was angry. They met at the breakfast table and though she coaxed him with her eyes and voice, he was wilfully cold to her. Once she put out her hand, but Crowne came in and she drew it back again.

He went upstairs immediately after he had finished, and she stood looking after him. He could be so hot and so cold. She wanted to run after him. Instead she put on her coat and hat and went into the street. Bantie, at the curb, touched his cap.

"I'll walk this morning, Bantie," she said.

She wanted to walk alone this morning to her own studio, not to ride in Blake's car. She turned the corner and went down the street. There were the thousands of people in this city whom she did not know. But she could never tire of looking at them, at dark Italian faces, at brown Greeks and pale Swedes, thick-bodied Czechs and low-browed Slavs. They stared at her as she passed. Some day she would know them. They were friendly, for everyone knew that she had rented lower three hundred and twelve. They had stood open-mouthed when the Fane Hill truck had delivered the great lumps of marble.

"Rocks!" the children had murmured in astonishment.

"I'm a sculptor," she had explained to the ones near the door. "I make things from rocks."

They had nothing to say to this. "Chee!" a single small boy's voice said at last. Then they had disappeared like a flock of birds. Nothing held them long, these city children leaping from one excitement to another. The siren of a fire wagon or an ambulance, a roar and a curse and a policeman's whistle, and they were gone.

Inside the great room was empty except for the marbles and her tools and one chair. She sat down, ready to work. There was nothing here to keep her from her deepest desire. No one knew where she was. She looked about her gratefully. The walls were clean with paint, the bare windows were shining. She rose and moved from one piece of marble to the other, touching them. Yesterday she had gone out and bought herself more of the beautiful tools, the finest, the most delicate, the strongest. The man in the shop had said over and over, "Now this, Miss, is a new thing—it's a short cut, you might say—"

But she had put aside all except the strongest and simplest. "No gadgets, please," she had said.

She sat down again. She must begin, she must think what she would make. And then, here where Blake had never been, away from him and where he could not find her, she found herself thinking only of him. She was not leaving him—no, she wanted to keep everything as it was. But he must see that this could only be when she was most fully herself. They must be two equal creatures, each complete in himself, each loving the other the more for such completeness. She would show him day by day what she meant.

"I can do it," she said to herself firmly, "I can do anything."

Her mind ran back over the years. Nothing had been impossible for her. To think of a thing, to know she wanted to do it, was to have it done. She saw herself as she had once been, that young girl overflowing into a hundred activities which she did well, not knowing which she must discard. In those days she had cried out to Mark that she had wanted everything. Now all that various demand of her too abundant life had clarified itself into this great sole necessity which was her work. She had been away on a holiday with Blake, a holiday of love, and now she was back. Marriage—what was it for her? She did not know.

"Perhaps women like me can't *be* married," she thought. It was not Mark, it was not Blake, it was she who could not make a marriage. Some part of her was complete alone, needing no mating. If this was true, and it was, then how impossible a task for any man she had given to him! And so thinking she fell into the intensest loneliness she had known.

"Blake, Blake!" she cried in herself. She wanted his hand, his touch, his presence, anything to push away this knowledge that she was born a solitary.

"I'd never have been happy if I had never married, if I hadn't had the children with Mark, and if I hadn't known what it is to be Blake's beloved." It was the old story, she thought half sadly. She had to have everything. And then everything was not enough. Still there was herself, solitary at the core.

"I've got to stick this out," she thought. "I know what I am." When Mark died it was her will that first began to work —her will, her will! She took up her tools and put them down, the fine strong mallet, the chisel with its exquisite edge. Pencils and paper—she hung the great sheets on the walls and sharpened her pencils. Then she sat down again, staring at the incomparable marbles, and thinking only of Blake. She wanted to run back to him, to see what he was doing, to make sure there was he. But she would not. She would love Blake with all her heart, but for her love could not be an end. It must build into something which was larger than either of them, larger than love. She could not give herself up, because part of her could never be given, however she willed it. Unused, it remained apart to die, and by its death to poison all of her being. Let her remember that terror.

When she went home at noon she was spent and exhausted, but her will was stirring. She braced herself against Blake's anger. She was ready to tell him plainly, "Blake, perhaps I ought not to have married you. But this is how I am and must be, and if you can't love me, I must still go on being what I am."

But he was not angry at all. He came out to meet her from the long drawing room, and smiled at her with all his earliest charm.

"Did you have a good morning, Susanne?" he asked, and hurried on, not waiting for her answer. "I had a wonderful morning—something inspired me. It does me good to hate you, I think!" His voice was so amiable she laughed with relief.

"Did you hate me, Blake?"

"A little," he said gaily. "Now I love you again. Come and see what I have done!"

He took her lightly by the elbows and walked with her up the stairs. She thought, "Why am I so silly and serious? He forgot me at once. How I shall work tomorrow!"

He opened the door of his studio and there, facing them, stood a hissing cat, in terra cotta. It spurned the pedestal, arched and angry, its claws spreading, full of grace and smartness.

"Oh, Blake!" she cried.

"Isn't it wonderful?" he said eagerly. "I'm going to call it The Female!"

He laughed and pounced upon her with his kiss. She had wasted her morning, thinking of him. She would never do such a thing again, she promised herself fiercely, under his long kiss.

She had begun work first on the great block of Belgian black in spite of its treachery, because a huge Negress had come tiptoeing in the next morning, treading as lightly as a tigress. She opened the door and closed it softly. Susan, dreaming, waiting, saw her as she might see a vision. The woman was pure African. Her skin was glistening black, her mouth like a split blood orange, and all her body was huge and firm.

"Do you want a lady to clean?" she inquired, and her voice was a viola. "I cleans and washes for some of de bettah class folks on de otheh street."

"Come in, please," said Susan. "Tell me your name."

"I'm Delia," said the Negress. She came in and seated herself on a piece of white marble and laughed, her lips folding back over big white teeth. "I ain't evah cleaned rocks before!" she said, laughing.

"Where did you come from?" Susan asked. "Who are you? Who were your ancestors?"

"I haven't no ancestors," Delia answered.

"You must have come from somewhere," Susan urged her. "Your grandfather—"

"My grandpappy was in a fambly in Virginia. He come over the seas, they always said. My pappy he run no'th."

"But where were you born?" Susan asked. How had this African escaped the touch of white hands upon her blackness?

"I was born right heah in Noo Yauk," she said cheerfully, "and heah I is. Ain't nothin' more to tell." She paused, ruminating. "Onct I mahied a real white niggah, but I reckon he wuz too white. He wuz always hittin' me. Anyways, he was trash. I ain't seen him in yeahs. I'm goin' to mahy a dark one sometime, but I don't get around to it on account of my chillun takin' so much time. I got six, and the youngest ain't a yeah yit."

The Belgian marble, of course, Susan was thinking, not hearing her. She sat silent, feeling this tremendous presence. Those great curves, those massive shoulders and breasts, the mountainous hips! "If I pay you twice what you get cleaning, will you let me make some drawings of you?" she asked.

"You mean just sit?"

"Yes."

"I ain't dressed fit to be seen. These is my workin' rags."

"I don't want you dressed at all."

286

"You mean—take off my cloes?"

"If you don't mind," said Susan.

Delia rose, shaking her head. "No'm, I ain't nevah took off my cloes before a lady." She paused, longingly, "Cudn't I keep on a little somethin'?"

"Yes, of course," said Susan.

"Kin you bar de do'?"

Susan turned the key.

"Well," said Delia, and sighed. "I sho' do need money. Turn yo haid away, honey."

Susan turned her head.

"Now," said Delia, "I sho' do feel funny."

She was sitting on a block of the white Paros marble, her hands on her great bare black knees, her head hanging, her shoulders hunched. "Sho' do feel ridiklus," she muttered.

Susan did not hear the woman. She was drawing upon the big sheets of white paper she had tacked upon the wall yesterday. She had chosen pencils and then she threw them down and took soft black charcoal. Delia stared at her.

"Do I look like dat, honey?" she wailed. "I sho' have lost my figger!"

"You're beautiful," Susan whispered. "Beautiful—beautiful—" She was panting a little. Let her learn this body quickly that she might begin the marble! She drew for hours.

"I'se gettin' mighty hongry," she heard Delia say out of the distance. "I usually eats somepin' befo' dis."

Susan looked at her watch. It was long after noon.

"Oh, I am sorry!" she cried. She found her purse and took out a bill. "There," she said, "put your clothes on and go and have a good dinner."

"Will I come to clean, Ma'am?"

"Yes," said Susan. "Tomorrow. There'll be a great mess on the floor by then."

She looked at the drawings for a long time. Then she took

them and tore them up. Her avid hands had already learned the curves of that black body and she did not want the drawings. They would only bind her with their boundaries. They were Delia. And she saw more than Delia. She would work direct in the marble, feeling not for simple Delia, but for that great dark female creature who, summoned from Africa to serve, poured the stain of her black blood into the white veins of a new America.

It was on this day she began her enormous black statue, one day to become so famous, of a sitting Negress, her legs apart, her hands holding up her full and aching breasts. She called it, from the first blow of the mallet upon the chisel into the marble, American Woman, Black.

. . . She looked up impatiently. She could no longer see. It was night. The room was darkening, and the darkness was drawing out of her hands this darker solid body. She could not see the outlines of the marble. She could only feel it with her hands. If only the night would not come to break this lifting rising surge of intense certainty of sight! She stood a moment in the dimness, feeling, feeling the creature she now possessed. Then she took off her smock and put on her coat and hat, and went half dazed out into the street and home. Her heart was singing light, though her arms ached. This strange secret lightness—it was sweeter than anything in the world, sweeter than love. It was fulfilment.

Here was a strange thing, she thought. She could do nothing under Blake's eyes, or under old Mr. Kinnaird's filmy gaze, but she did not mind in the least when these others came in to see what she was doing. Strange children stared in her window one morning, and going to see, she found they had walked along a narrow ledge and were clinging by their fingertips to the sill.

"Come in, if you like," she called.

288

They had come to the door then, shuffling and pushing, breathing hard over each other's shoulders.

"I'll go on with my work," she said. They stood staring. The head of the Negress was free now of the marble and she was beginning the outline of the thick shoulders.

"Chee," said a hoarse voice, "it's a dinge."

"It's for a grave," said another. "I seen a cemetery once and they was lots of angels all made out of rock."

"A dinge can't be an angel!" a voice whispered scornfully. "Angels is white. I seen 'em at a Christmas show in Radio City!"

They stayed a few panting moments. "Come on, let's go," they whispered, "there ain't nothin' here." In a body they were gone, having seen everything. She did not in the least mind them, she thought. Their eyes, so alive, so uncritical, had not disconcerted her at all. She began to sing under her breath, "Oh, that will be—glory for me!" The old deep satisfaction was creeping into every part of her being, like slow rain to the uttermost roots of a thirsting tree. She did not understand it or wonder at its quality. It was enough that it was so. She did not question her being.

She would like to have run to Blake eagerly with her joy. When two people love each other, the joy of one must be the other's. But Blake was angry these days because his first exhibit of moderns was being ridiculed by one of the directors of the museum.

"But, darling," she said, astonished at his rage, "so many critics have liked them." He had sat surrounded with newspapers the morning after the exhibit opened, reading aloud to her at breakfast all that they had said. He read without embarrassment the bright neat phrases, "extraordinary, sharp facility," "complete grasp of the abstract," "easily the leading of our moderns." And then old Joseph Hart had written to the

Times. She came home, full of her elation, to find him furious. "I could sue him," he kept saying. "How dare he call my things shallow? Smart—of course they're smart! They're meant to be. He's an old fool. He wants us to keep on doing copies of Michael Angelo and the Greeks. He doesn't realize that they were modern in their time and that's why they lived. You've got to interpret your own age—it's all you can know."

"Darling, one old man!"

"There oughtn't to be even one so stupid as that! Besides, he has influence. The *Times* shouldn't have paid any attention to him." Blake's mouth was a hard line, his eyebrows twitching. He could not sit still. He kept pacing the long length of the drawing room. "I believe I'll sue him for libel," he said again.

"Blake, don't be so foolish!" she exclaimed. "Why do you care?"

"Because I know I am right!" he shouted.

She thought he would never forget it. He was sullen for a week and with no appetite for food or work. Then one day when her patience was nearly gone, she had a letter from Paris. The Kneeling Woman had been rejected by the Salon.

"Damn them, how dare they?" Blake said without rancor. He smiled at her.

"I suppose it wasn't good enough," she said quietly, folding the letter. She had abandoned The Kneeling Woman, the woman she had made when she was first falling in love with Blake.

"Don't you care?" he asked, curiously.

"Of course I care," she said, "but nothing can stop me." "Anyway," she added, "I feel finished with The Kneeling Woman."

"Oh, well," he said, "it's probably politics there, too. You are a foreigner—the French are so close— Besides, you're a woman, Susanne. You can't expect—"

"What?" she inquired calmly.

290

"Quite as much as a man," he finished, and for the first time in days he laughed. "Don't you mind, Susanne," he said with unusual gentleness, and she perceived with wonder and without caring to understand why that he was somehow comforted.

Spring came and she felt she had not known what spring was before. In the country spring came with a hundred first signs. Snow thawed into whirling streams, willow twigs greened, and under dead leaves pale shoots stirred upward and the changing winds blew winter back and forth. But here in New York it was winter and then one morning it was spring. She walked every day to her studio and now she knew many names to call. The dirty-faced janitor was Dinny King, and Mrs. King had come downstairs to see her one day, a twin on each arm. She had sat staring blankly while Susan worked and when she rose to go away she said, "Well, it's good you've got the time for it, I says to Dinny. I cudn't, mesilf, with all I have to do."

She knew Larry and Pietro and Slavga, and Smikey talked to her sometimes and told her the names of others, pointing with a small filthy finger.

"Them's Connigans and their dad's dead. Name's Minty and Jim. Jim's been to reform, he has— That there's Izzy—we don't play wid him ever day—only when we wants to, see?"

"Doesn't he mind?" Susan asked.

"He's gotta take it," Smikey said scornfully. Smikey alone was always very bold.

She learned fragments of stories from voices crying out of windows, from heavy thuds and weepings, from doctors and priests coming in and out. One morning a splayed creature lay on the sidewalk, and a policeman was roaring back the crowd.

"It's ould Miz Brookes, on the top floor," young Micky King told her. "She was always a-sayin' she'd jump one foine day, and now's she done it. Chee, but my dad's sore at her, but he can't do anything to her when she's dead."

It was a very fine day, a day so full of spring that it must have been too much for this white-haired twisted shape.

"Is there anything I can do?" she asked the policeman.

"No, Ma'am, unless ye can call off these young devils. Ye'd think it was a show put on fer 'em."

"Come on, everybody," she said, "let's go down to the corner for ice cream."

She led the way and, counting their heads, paid the soda clerk for an ice cream for each. When she went back the sidewalk was clean. The policeman was on his beat and people were tramping back and forth over where old Mrs. Brookes had lain.

Hidden in the midst of all this life, she went on working steadily, without haste, without delay, in long absorbed hours. She walked through spring sunshine in the morning and when she laid down her tools, she went out into the bright spring evening. Sometimes a sudden rain blown against the window made her lift her head a moment, and the noises of the street died in the clatter of rain until the sun shone and the children swarmed out to make excited search into gutters and momentary pools.

Steadily day by day she hewed and carved, now driving off great flakes and chips, now cutting as delicately as she might have painted with a brush the curves of lip and lid, the pointing of a breast, the turn of knee and ankle. In the earliest days of summer she finished American Woman, Black.

Delia, pausing to look at it as she finished her cleaning, laughed high laughter.

"Sho' would worry me if I looked like dat!" she declared. "It was mighty relievin' when you tole me you was makin' it out of yo' own haid!" She paused, grave and enormous. "I wouldn' like anybody to think I wasn't a lady, honey!"

"Nobody would think this was you, Delia," Susan agreed.

"Naw'm," Delia said, "dey sho'ly wouldn' and is I relieved!"

She now knew that this great figure was only the first of many to come, how many she did not know. But around her were all these faces, these figures in procession. Every day she saw one which belonged in marble. She chose, from among them, a Swedish woman who, with her husband, ran a restaurant. They had no other help, and together they cooked and washed dishes and served the small tables covered with red and white oilcloth. In an earlier age they would have been plunging across the western deserts behind oxen. She went in one day and behind their spread of home-made smörgasbord, she asked, "Will you and your husband let me sit here and draw you as you work?"

"Sure," the woman cried heartily, "it don't do no hurt I guess, hay, Gus?"

"Naw," he grunted, his arms heaped with dishes.

She went every day for two weeks, watching, drawing, hearing them talk to each other. At the end of that time she tore up her drawings and began to hew out of the marble from Paros her figures which she called, America North. They were clothed figures in early Swedish costume, and with them they were carrying all they could of the chattels of their civilization. Their bodies were tall and lean and their steady faces were set in the bitterness of the north wind.

Smikey, coming in alone one day because it was getting hot in the street, sat down in the chair and stared at the head she was blocking out.

"That's Gus, ain't it? It looks sort of like him, only bigger."

She nodded, and went on driving off the hard white flakes.

Blake was charming to her all the time. They were perhaps not quite so close as they had been, and yet in one way they were closer. When they were away from each other all day, they talked eagerly at night as they had not when they were together all day. Then, living every moment together, there

293

had not been much to talk about. Each knew the other and they communicated with each other by touch and caress rather than by words. But words were a clearer means. There was no loss, or at least, very little. She must perhaps take a little more care not to be late.

She came back one night, her feet sore with standing and her arms aching, but she did not regard weariness. She had her splendid body. She had been too thin, but now she was growing into the strong fullness of her old shape. She ran upstairs, bathed and dressed quickly and put on a soft old rust-colored gown. Then she went to find Blake. Blake was perhaps a little changed to her, but she would not notice it. He did not, as he once had, come instantly to her room to find her. He did not draw her tub and brush her hair and choose her gown. He waited, formally, in the drawing room until she came down to him. Now when she bent to kiss him, he kissed her lightly, quickly. But she would not notice any of this. Besides, he was reading a book on Yugo-Slavian sculpture. She sank down beside him and slipped her hand into his and they sat quietly until Crowne announced dinner. She would not wonder about him, knowing that if she gave herself up to him, she would be consumed by him, by his wilfulness and emotion, his incessant demands on her attention. They were growing a little apart, but it was that or she would be lost.

They dined alone, and she sat quietly and listened to him talk of his day and afterwards they went upstairs together and she looked carefully at his work, seeing instantly what he meant and what he had done. He was working very hard. It was not her way of work, but she could see the beauty in the long lean lines, in the slant eyes and sloping brows, in the formalized shapes he loved and made so superlatively.

"It's the beauty of mathematics expressed in human shape," she said to him, and he was pleased. "You have caught something essentially great," she added warmly, not only because she loved Blake but because she believed what she said.

It was that next winter, the same winter he made his plaster of Marcia, that he made the statue of Sonia Pravaloff, the Russian dancer who was sending everyone mad. He was working very fast. In a month he had finished Marcia, tall and slim, her head drooping, her straight boxed hair falling over her narrow face, her thin hands clasped. It was Marcia, all feeling and excitement, her body as thin as a cat's body.

Marcia was already beginning to want to study nothing but dancing, and after she met Sonia at Christmas she begged Susan every day, "Don't make me go to school any more. Let me learn to dance, Mother, really dance, like Sonia!"

"Sonia's ignorant," said John calmly. "She can't read much, even—at least I never see her read a book."

"I don't like books, either," Marcia said quickly, biting her finger. "They're like dead people. Oh, Mother, let me dance, please, please!"

"The child should dance," Sonia told her. She came often to dinner, for she would not dance more than three times a week. Besides, Blake was doing her portrait in his famous terra cotta that was like none other, and she was excited by the sight of herself emerging from under his hands. She could not stay away from his studio.

When it was finished, for the first time Susan did not like what he had done. She stood before the flying figure and was silent. Blake waited, sure of her praise.

"Am I lovely? I think so!" Sonia cried ardently.

She sat on Blake's big couch, her knees under her chin, her muscular strong fleshless body folded together under her scant white satin dress.

"Oh, Blake, you are a genius! I so love myself you have made!"

295

But Susan said anxiously, "There is something wrong with it."

"What do you mean?" Blake asked.

She forgot that they were husband and wife, that they were in love with each other still. She forgot she was a woman speaking to a man. She saw only the plastic figure that was not Sonia. Blake had stamped his own style on Sonia. He had not come out of himself to see her as she was. For the first time his instinct had failed him in his material. She perceived, in this instant, that Blake would always be limited by himself. Whatever he chose to make must be like him or his gift could not encompass it. It was a narrow gift, though exceedingly fine.

"I don't think she's plastic material, Blake," Susan said. She looked at Sonia. "You see the shape of her head and her body —clay isn't the medium—nor anything plastic. She's glyptic. I've often thought so. Her dancing is glyptic—I mean, you could do a whole series of her postures in marble or stone—in quite hard stone, like Heptonwood, even. She's not delicate as you have made her—she's solid, and the strength of her dancing is its solidity. You have attenuated her, so that the clay will hold her, but still it is not strong enough for her. She has escaped you."

She saw instantly that he was fiercely angry.

"You are so hipped on carving, you can't understand anything else," he said. "Besides, no one escapes me."

"But I like your work, Blake!" she protested.

"This is the best thing I have done," he said.

"Marcia is better," Susan answered.

She could coax and yield and cajole—but not about work. About work there must be nothing but honesty. Sonia was looking at them strangely, her pale slant eyes full of light in her square-cheeked dark face.

"You don't see that is Sonia?" she asked Susan sharply.

"No," said Susan. "It doesn't speak with your voice. I always seem to hear a statue when it has caught life. But this seems only a statue. It is silent."

"Nevertheless I shall submit it to the Academy," Blake said.

"Blake, why are you angry with me?" she demanded of him.

"I am not angry," he replied. He smiled at Sonia. "I am only amused."

She saw his gaze on Sonia, still warm with anger, and suddenly she, too, was angry.

"Sonia, will you pose for me?" she asked clearly. "I will do you in marble and show Blake what I mean."

"You, too!" cried Sonia, and she laughed her loud Russian laughter. "Yes, why not? It will be funny."

"Let's go out somewhere," Blake said abruptly. "I'm sick of this house."

They went to a night club, as Blake often wanted to do, and she watched Blake dancing with Sonia so beautifully that she sat lost, her chin in her hands, admiring and enjoying their beauty. When he came back and lifted his eyebrows at her coolly, she shook her head and smiled. "I'd much rather watch you and Sonia dance again," she said to him.

"You are not honest!" Sonia cried, opening her eyes.

"Yes, she is," Blake said. "I'll say that for Susanne—she's too simple to lie. You are not in the least clever. you know, Susanne darling."

He was not angry any more, and she was glad. Besides, it was quite true that she was not clever. She did not think out of her brain cleverly and quickly and facilely as Blake did and as his friends did. She thought mysteriously out of the depths of herself, out of her heart and her bowels. She felt thought stirring in her womb. Only at last did her blood carry what she already knew to her brain and only at final last, if it were necessary, did she speak what she had first felt. She smiled at Blake.

"Dance again," she begged him, "you are both so beautiful."

He rose, laughing. "Oh, Susanne," he cried. "My perfect wife!—Come, Sonia!"

They were dancing and from somewhere a circle of white light shot down upon them, seeking them out from all the others. People were recognizing Sonia, and Blake was delighted to be recognized with her. His face was set in coldness and gravity. He seemed to see no one, to feel nothing, but Susan, knowing him, knew that because he saw everything he made his handsome face blank and his eyelids drooped. The band fell into low swinging music, playing for them. Everybody was looking at them. And Susan was drawing upon the back of a menu, with a pencil she begged from a waiter, the swift strong lines of Sonia to be made in marble. This was the beginning of The Dancing Russian, in her American Procession.

That night when they came home she went first into the long drawing room and at the door she turned, surprised, because they delayed so long behind her. There in the shadow of the hall she saw Blake draw Sonia against him and kiss her swiftly and hard. She looked away and went quickly to the fire, and an instant later they were there, in the room, laughing.

"Ring for something to drink, will you?" Blake was asking her. She did not feel the fire hot at all, though Crowne had piled it blazing high with dry logs. . . . Blake and Sonia! They were not disturbed no, not by that kiss. If not, then it could not be the first.

"Yes, of course," she said, dazed, and rang because Blake had commanded it. She sat down on the end of a couch and stretched out her hands to the fire. She was cold and she wanted to be warm. Crowne brought in whiskey and soda and because she never drank he did not pour a third glass.

"Crowne!" she said sharply, "I'll have one, please."

"Yes, Madame," he said, surprised, and she said to them all quickly, "It's very cold, isn't it!"

"Not for me!" Sonia laughed. "I am always so hot. Ah, I

am sleepy!" Sonia yawned behind a brown hand. "Take me home, Blake—when I have had one more drink. Susan, I come to you tomorrow morning at ten, yes? I have a fancy—a wish— to be made in marble. Marble will last forever, will it not? When I am dust and Blake's portrait of me is in bits like an old earthen pot, the marble will be there."

"Yes," Susan said.

No, they were not disturbed. It was not their first kiss.

In her bed, in her room, she lay waiting for Blake to come back from Sonia's hotel. He came very soon, without delay, and he was there sitting beside her on the bed. He was so natural, so charming, he was always so charming at three o'clock in the morning, that she could not say to him, "Why do you and Sonia need to kiss each other?"

If she said that, he would shrug his shoulders and laugh and tease her. "You are not jealous, are you? A kiss is nothing, Susanne. I will let you kiss anyone you like."

And if she said honestly, "I don't want to kiss anyone but you, Blake," he would only laugh again and say, "Kiss me, then," and bend to take her kiss.

No, she would say nothing. She did not want to kiss him.

"Blake is right, you know, Susan," Sonia said. She was danc- ing and flinging out fragments of her incessant talk as she moved from one sharp static pose to another. "You are very simple."

"Am I?" Susan said. "I have had no time to think of it." She was drawing rapidly one figure after another.

"Blake is like this," Sonia said. She began to dance in short nervous abbreviated steps. Her body took on the meaning of Blake. She was somehow Blake, without looking in the least like him. Susan stopped drawing and waited. It was impossible to draw now. She did not know how to catch this thing Sonia was doing. Watching her, she had not, she told herself, ever thought of wanting to do Blake's portrait. She could not imagine Blake in marble. There was an evanescence in him which could not be caught and held. Sonia was dancing quickly in evanescent staccato poses.

"And this is you—" Sonia stopped, shook herself, and stepped into slow, deep, elemental movements, a little stiff. "So simple, so like a child—no vanity, no coquetry—Blake has coquetry, but not Susan. Susan is sad, but she does not know it. She is not sad for herself, but because she knows life is secretly sad, and gayety is only for the moment. Sadness is the long reality—sorrow is the foundation, and to know that is to know peace."

But Susan was not listening. She was drawing as fast as her charcoal pencil could move, in the bold thick black strokes that were her peculiar way of picturing. She never sketched. She drew, tridimensional and solid, the figure she saw always in marble even while she was drawing upon paper.

"There," she said, "it is enough. I have what I want."

Sonia stopped, and came to her and took up the score and more of sheets.

"How differently you see me!" she cried. "And which is Sonia? Shall I believe Susan or Blake? What am I, then?"

Susan did not answer or hear. She was moving among her marbles toward a certain circular piece. She had not once remembered all morning that Blake had kissed this Sonia the night before. Or at least the dim ache in some far part of her being could scarcely today be called a memory.

But Mary discovered it again, ruthlessly, one May morning. Susan was finishing the first of the three figures of Sonia, carved in a solid circular group. Each was Sonia in part, and the three would make her entire, Sonia flung into a stiff beautiful pose of daring grace, Sonia static, her arms folded, her feet stamping, Sonia drooping like a willow tree. It was the most difficult thing she had done, for space was part of the whole. The bodies did not touch, but out of the pillar-like matrix one's motion flowed into the next and the next, so that by continuing motion all were related. She had shaped the lines into a block-like simplicity, making of Sonia not a woman but a dance.

Mary came in one noon.

"I'm on my way to lunch," she said. "Besides, I'm sailing for Paris next week. Parsdale and Poore are sending me over for designs. Miss Blume always goes and she has appendicitis—luck for me!"

She was thinner than ever, and very smart. She drew out her handkerchief, dusted the chair and sat down.

"Are you going to lunch with Michael? I haven't seen either of you for so long," Susan said. She was working on the arch of Sonia's lifted foot and she did not pause.

"Oh, Michael!" Mary said. "He's angry with me."

"You mean you've parted?" Susan looked up from Sonia's foot.

"I don't know what you mean," Mary said. She was looking at her narrow brown hands, and at her wine-red fingernails. "How parted, when we've never been together?"

Susan hesitated. "I don't know how," she said, "because I've never known anything about you two. You don't marry each other, and you don't marry anyone else."

"Marriage—marriage!" Mary exclaimed. Her old secret restraint was gone these days, at least upon her surface. She talked a great deal in a sharp jagged nervous fashion. "You've always been obsessed with marriage, Susan. You think women can't live without it."

"It's one of the things," Susan said gently.

"If I marry," Mary went on abruptly, "it will be a business. I may marry. I'll have decided by the time I am back. It depends."

"Michael's been very patient." Susan traced a muscle in the marble so lightly she seemed not to have made a line, except that one saw a strain appear in the stone as though it were flesh.

"Michael has nothing to do with this." Mary's voice was clear and depthless, brittle with clarity. "I shall never marry him. If I marry, it will be Bennyfield Rhodes."

Susan paused and looked at her sister. "I've never heard of him," she said.

"He's somebody in spite of that," Mary replied. Her sharp pretty nails were tapping like little woodpeckers at the arms of the chair. "He's the chief stockholder in the company."

Susan put down her tools. She was kneeling on the floor and now she looked at Mary sternly.

"Is that why you are marrying him?" she asked. She saw for the first time that though Mary's dark handsome eyes met her gaze with such seeming directness, there was no penetrating through them. They were so dark that the pupils were lost in the darkness.

"Why I marry, if I do, is my own affair," Mary said.

"How did you meet him?"

"He comes into the store a good deal."

"How old is he?"

"Not sixty—looks younger."

"Michael must be very angry," she said. She felt a little sick. There was no honor left any more in what people did. Some old health and sweetness was gone out of people's hearts. For a flitting second she missed Mark.

"I've been perfectly frank with Michael." Mary's voice was bright and hard. "I've never pretended anything. I've given him all I could. He knows I never could marry him."

"But why, Mary?"

Mary lifted off her hat, smoothed back her short closely cut hair, and put her hat on again, a little more to the left. She opened her bag and took out her vanity case and she powdered her straight nose. Then she put everything back in the bag and shut it hard. "Susan, anybody who marries Michael has got to give up everything. He'd never give up. I'd have to become part of him. Well, I won't. I won't be part of anybody."

"Not though you love him?"

"No, not however much I might love him. I couldn't stand it. You don't think, Susan. You just feel. You go along your life, feeling your way from one day to the next. Your eyes aren't open and never will be. But I plan and I use my head. Feelings are just nothing when it comes to practical everyday living. If I married Michael I'd never know where I was or how much money we had. If his mother ever dies I suppose he'll have something, but she looks headed for a hundred. He'll never make anything at painting the sort of things he does."

"You could keep on working, couldn't you?" Susan asked. She was thinking of the boy Michael who had come into her attic so long ago and drawn the picture of himself, riding headlong into the dark wood.

"I could but I won't," Mary said. "When I marry I want to stop work. If I can't, I'll stay as I am."

Susan picked up her chisel and mallet. She wanted to work, to work hard. She was suddenly very angry.

"Women like you," she said slowly, "—women like you set us all back for centuries. There's no hope for us except as we learn to take everything in life." She was pounding the marble furiously. She had left the delicately arched foot and was hewing at the mass of the base. The studio echoed to her blows. But underneath all the anger she knew what she was doing. Her hands were flying, alive with instinct. . . . "I hate women who think of nothing except how they can get the most out of some man. Look at Lucile and poor Hal! She thinks she's a respectable woman. She doesn't see she's sucked Hal dry until he's nothing. He's done nothing all his life except support

303

Lucile. He works all day to feed and clothe her and comes home at night and helps her wash the dishes and put the children to bed because she's tired. That's his life. Nobody knows what Hal is, really. He's never had time to find out himself. No, Mary, don't marry Michael! It's kind of you not to marry him. Perhaps if he's sure you won't, he'll forget you and be what he is, a great painter. It would be a pity to spoil him so that you could stop work and do nothing at all!"

She was pouring this out, between the blows of her mallet.

And Mary said, her voice like a cold quiet stream, "Your theories don't work, Susan. Nobody has everything, not even you." She paused, and then she said calmly, "You haven't Blake —Sonia has him."

She stood up. "There—I hadn't meant to tell you. It's none of my business. I've known it all winter. Everybody knows it except you. I'm only telling you to show you you're wrong. You've lost him. You can't have everything, though you've always thought you could."

There was nothing to say. Mary had cut away the earth on which she stood. She had not strength to lift her mallet, to strike the chisel, to break the stone. She put her tools down and suddenly, in the silenced room, she felt her mouth dry.

"You have always hated me—why?" she asked. Her tongue clacked in her dry mouth.

"No, I don't, Susan," Mary said. There was a shred of pity in her brittle voice. "I feel sorry for you. Everybody knows Blake Kinnaird better than you do. That's why I was so surprised—at that, you've done awfully well—you've been married nearly three years, haven't you? Sonia's the first I have heard of—"

"Three years in June—" Susan's voice was a whisper. On a bright June day she and Blake had gone into that little office in Paris and been married. She had felt she must marry him and she had gone straight away and done it.

"Michael said just the other day he hadn't expected it to last so long. It isn't as if you were Blake's type—you're really very simple, Susan. You're not like all these people."

She was still on her knees, looking up at Mary. Perhaps Mary was right. She was simple, too simple for Blake—for everyone. Sonia had called her simple. Only Mark had not found her too simple. But then he was a child, who had died young. And she was not able to comprehend this cleverness or to cope with it. She was too deep in reality—or perhaps in dreams.

"Well, goodbye." Mary bent and laid her cool dark cheek an instant against Susan's. "Don't worry, whatever you do. That's a wonderful Negro thing, over there—I must say you're improving, Susan."

She could feel Mary trying to be a little kind, but it was too late. She rose to her feet.

"Goodbye, Mary," she said. "I'm sorry I said what I did—you know best, of course, for yourself."

Mary went out, smiling and sure, her small red lips compressed. "Yes, I do," she said.

When Mary was gone, she sat down in the chair and painfully drew back into her mind the moment of Blake's kiss to Sonia. What had that kiss meant, and how had it been given, and why? She did not know. Why indeed should Blake want to kiss Sonia if he did not love her? She did not know. So he must love her.

"I shall have to ask him," she thought, simply.

She could think of nothing else to do. Even if she knew how, she could not spy upon him. If she could, she had not time to follow him where he went in the day. She had her work to do.

She looked at her watch. She wanted to go home at once and find Blake. But at this hour, one o'clock, he would be away. He seldom lunched at home if he were not working, and just now he was arranging for another exhibition. He was hoping, she knew, and expecting that after the exhibit some at least of the

305

figures would be sold for the museum. She sighed and took out of the pocket of her coat a package of sandwiches which every morning Crowne brought as she left the house and handed to her with dignity.

"Oh, thank you, Crowne," she always said and stuffed them in her pocket. Once he said, "Wouldn't you like your luncheon brought to you, Madame?" And she, frightened at the thought of servants and trays intruding upon her work, had answered quickly, "Oh no, I like sandwiches very much."

She ate them, and going to the faucet, bent and drank as at a fountain. Then she stood a moment wondering what to do, and because she still did not know, she went back to her work. Once she stopped to think, "This is Sonia's body I am making—how can I?" She waited a moment, and then went on. Deeper than Sonia was the desire to go on, to finish the thing she had begun. It was not Sonia. It was her work.

In the dining room at dinner Blake was telling her the vexation of trying to persuade old Joseph Hart that what he was doing was not "mere playing about in mud." When he paused, Susan asked, "Is that all, Blake?"

"It's quite enough for one day, I think, Susanne," he answered amiably, now that it was all told. He was not in the least different from himself as he had been. She had sat watching him as he talked and pondering whether indeed he were changed within. For surely new love must leave some small mark. But he looked at her with his clear cool gray eyes, and his hand, flecking the ash from his cigarette, never trembled, nor indeed did she notice any lesser quality in the kiss he gave her when she came in. She had had an impulse before dinner in her own room to put on the red and gold dress he had made for her. It hung in her closet, glimmering and glowing. But she was ashamed to do anything that might be coquetry, though at least she need not wear blue which he disliked. She put on at last a plain white chiffon and brushed back her long hair and knotted it as she always did. He had not noticed, eager to pour out his vexation.

"Because I have a question to ask you," she said. They were alone for a moment. The salad had just been served. It would be a few minutes before Crowne came back.

"Yes?" Blake lifted his delicate black eyebrows at her. But his voice held no alarm.

"Mary came in today," she said. "And she told me you and Sonia are in love. Is it true, Blake?"

But now she had taken him by surprise. He put down his fork and wiped his mouth with his napkin.

"Why should Mary say that?" he demanded.

And in the same quiet voice she said, "It came out because of other things I had said. She was not tale-bearing. She had not meant to tell me, I am sure. But she was annoyed with me."

She thought she would be angry with him, but she was not angry. She felt only still as death while Blake looked at her.

"Are you going to be angry with me?" he demanded.

"No," she said, "no, not angry—only I must know. Just tell me simply, Blake."

But he could not tell her simply. He was crumbling his bread on the plate. "Sonia—of course Sonia has loved a great many people—it is part of her nature—I suppose part of her art."

"If you would just tell me simply, Blake," she said again.

"It is not quite simple, Susanne," he answered. "Sonia has no relation to the way I feel toward you, for instance. That she appeals to a part of my—thought—I do not deny. Why should I? I might complain that I found you working in David Barnes' studio, but I do not. People like us—we do what we do because we must. Our nature demands much."

She stared at him. "Did you think David Barnes and I—" she began.

He shook his head and put out his hand. "No, no, Susanne!

I tell you I did not think! I took you as you were—I keep you as you are—whatever you do, you are Susanne."

There was such calmness in his voice and look that she was bewildered. She clutched at a phrase he had spoken. There must be truth somewhere, an absolute truth.

"You mean you must—love Sonia?"

"Susanne, you simple darling—forget about Sonia. What I think about Sonia has nothing to do with us."

"Yes, it has, Blake—anything you think and feel has something to do with me." That was clear, at least. But she felt as though she were trying to find Blake in a fog. She could hear his voice but she could not see his face.

"Susanne!" Blake's voice was impatient. "Will you please never speak of this again?"

"You mean you will not tell me, Blake?"

"I do not consider that it concerns you," he said with dry coldness. He suddenly looked like his father, pale and cold and not really unkind, only unable to feel beyond himself. . . . "You will not speak of this again, my dear," old Mr. Kinnaird's dry voice said to Blake's mother. And she said meekly, "Very well, Arthur. I am sorry." "It's quite all right," he replied. And he had told his son, "I was always very happy with your mother, my son." But she had died years upon years ago, though she had been so much younger than her husband. She had died when Blake was so little that he could not remember her. But perhaps she had already come to see that her little boy was only old Mr. Kinnaird over again, and so nothing seemed worth while. It was not as if she had anything else. . . . Inside of her Susan was crying passionately, "Oh, how lucky I am to have more than Blake—to have more than love—if I had had only love—"

She looked at Blake steadily. She said, not in the least expecting to say it, "I do not have to obey you, Blake." She felt

308

as if a voice were coming out of one of her own statues. "I am quite independent of you, you know," the voice said.

"Susanne—"

"No, wait, please. I have not finished. By all means do as you wish about Sonia. But until you can come to some decision about her which you can make plain to me, you will please let me alone."

"Susanne!" he cried. "You are absurd!"

"I could ask Sonia, but I won't," she went on, not taking her eyes from his face. "You will tell me."

"I can't tell you—I don't know."

"I will wait," she replied.

"Childish, silly jealousy!" he muttered. "Susanne, you are too simple to be alive!"

"I am simple," she agreed. "I have to have things plain and clear. My life must be comprehensible to me. I must understand my foundations. I am married to you and to me that means I have no room for anyone else. I am as simple as that."

"You are a woman," he broke in.

"I am more," she replied. "I am a working woman."

And while she spoke there was her work before her, and it became freedom to her and safety and refuge and expansion and then she was not afraid. When Mark had died she had not died. Even though Blake loved Sonia, she would not die.

"Mary is a fool," she said aloud.

"She is, indeed," Blake agreed.

"I don't mean it in that way," Susan said sturdily.

She saw Blake's eyes inquire. Crowne came in with fresh plates and she did not speak. She was thinking, "Mary is a fool to give up her work." But she went on eating her dinner. Food and sleep and a quiet mind—these were the necessities for work. She had loved Blake intensely and for a while he had destroyed her through love. Now he should not destroy her through sorrow. She would hold off sorrow from her real being, out of which alone came strength for her work.

Crowne had set the coffee out on the terrace and Blake followed her there. Before he sat down, he lifted her chin and kissed her sharply. She did not repulse him or turn her head away. She poured the coffee and handed him his cup and then she saw a look in his eyes, quizzical, a little laughing, and now triumphant.

"You still let me kiss you, at least," he said.

She turned her head. "Isn't the river lovely!" she murmured. It was lovely indeed. There was a faint mist upon the water still too cold for the warm night air and this mist was beginning to rise in long wavering lines of cloud, so that soon the stars were caught in a net of mist. It was so lovely that her heart suddenly broke into anguish and the tears rushed to her eyes. She began to tremble a little with inner weeping. She cared very much indeed. She loved him still. She waited a moment, gazing into the mist.

"But I meant what I said, Blake," she said steadily.

David Barnes, in New York again, was staring at the seven statues she had made.

"These are entirely new," he said. "I don't see the slightest trace of France in them."

"They are American," she said.

"I doubt you know what they are," he answered. And after a while he said, "Blake's had no influence on you, anyway."

"Yes, he has," she said.

"I don't see it."

"He's made me more myself," she replied, and then because he waited, tumbling his tangled beard with both hands, she went on trying to say what she felt. "I can use mallet and chisel so much more easily than I can my tongue, David. I think when Blake and I first loved each other I threw my life into his and I was lost. I didn't do anything for a year. And then something my father said made me see I had to find myself again—or I'd die, you know, one day—unfulfilled. And nothing would seem to have been worth having if that happened. And I began to work. I had to work independently of Blake, and I defined myself more and more as I worked—not consciously, except determining to empty myself by thinking of no one."

"Well!" he exclaimed. "Now I can ask you—what the deuce made you marry him?"

"He gave me something I'd never had," she said. Then, remembering all the hours of Blake's passionate love, her mouth quivered and her cheeks grew hot under David Barnes' close gaze. But she knew she must not look away from him. "He made me a woman," she said.

David Barnes flung aside his beard. "Susan," he began very gently, "the first day you ever walked into my studio in that old house in the country, years ago, I knew you were a beautiful woman. Did you know that?"

She shook her head. "No, Dave. I never thought about it."

He sat down on the bare floor, crosslegged, before her. "I knew you didn't know it," he said, "and I wouldn't tell you. And when you were in Paris and I was helping you, and when you came to my studio I could have told you. I wanted over and over to tell you—but I didn't. I didn't feel any man had the right to—touch you, because you happened to be a woman."

"I never thought of it," she said. "I didn't dream—"

"I know it," he said, "but if I had put out my hand—"

She shook her head. "I don't think so, David," she said gently.

He got up and sat down on the windowsill. "It doesn't matter," he said harshly. "Credit me at least that I never put out my hand. Blake did—but he had no more right than I. He thought of himself—I thought of you."

"I trust you," she said.

He gave her a long look.

. . . But Blake had demanded and she had given and she did not regret it. No, if she had it to do again she would do exactly as she had done, for Blake had fulfilled her life, too. Without him she would not have had everything. She thought of him still with a great rush of passionate longing. She would always love him in the narrow deep way she loved him now. Her mind was separate from his, their beings could never fuse, but in the narrow deep way of body to body, in that sightless sharp agonizing way, her love for him would last as long as her blood beat in her heart. She sat silent thinking this, and David Barnes sat watching her face until he could not bear her look.

"Well, to get down to realities," he said brusquely, "you've got to exhibit these things, Susan. Seven—it's rather few—but we can get that thing you did in Paris. It's time you started. It won't be too easy, your being a woman—it's a great handicap. The critics expect you to do small pretty stuff. We've got to beat it into them that you don't do Christmas tree decorations and bookends." He stared at the figures of Sonia. "Gosh, what a workman you are!" he muttered. "Blake seen that thing of Sonia?" he demanded.

"He hasn't seen any of them," she said.

"Hasn't seen them!" David's hairy face went blank under his beard.

"No," she said, "he's been busy—there's been one thing after another. I suppose it is my fault because I don't know how to talk much. I haven't talked about my work to him at all."

"Hm!" His enormous craggy hands were tearing at his beard again. "It would have been interesting if you had exhibited together—only I'm not sure I'd want to be in your shoes. See here, Susan, I've got it—come in on my exhibit—my Titans! I have twenty-one done, and I'm showing them in November, and I'll give you a place to yourself. David Barnes and Susan Gaylord—I'll say humbly it may give you a boost."

She was so grateful for his warmth that she went to him and took his great hand. It was the first time she had ever touched it and it was like holding the knotty root of a tree. He fumbled at her hand a moment, greatly embarrassed, and then pulled his hand away.

"I don't say thank you, David," she said gently. "My heart moves at your kindness. But I must work alone, and my work must stand alone. I can't lean upon your name."

"You don't know anything about this game." He rubbed his big flat nose. "I've been through it over and over. I tell you it's bad enough for a man to go through with the racket—it's hopeless for a woman. They won't take you seriously. It's all bosh about there being any equality. And artists are the damnedest, rottenest, selfish lot—everyone trying to down everybody else. A woman hasn't a ghost of a show. If she's good she makes the men rage—they're jealous enough of each other, but for a woman to rival them—it's sheer impertinence. You're damned the day you're born a woman—that is, if you do anything to compete with men."

"In this land of chivalry?" she said, smiling a little.

"Chivalry," he said pompously, "is only for the ladies, Susan. And ladies don't present any serious competition to men, you know. You're no lady, damn you! Look at your hands!"

She looked at them. They were grimy and calloused and the fingernails were broken. The other day Blake had taken her hand and looked at it and put it down again with a grimace.

"Charwoman!" he had said, and she had smiled and not replied.

"Lucky your hair curls," said David Barnes grimly, "though it won't do you any good with the critics."

She looked at her seven statues, and they looked back at her. She was sure of their voices, having heard each clearly in its time. "I'm not afraid," she said. "It doesn't matter to me about being a woman."

313

He pulled his old cap out of his pocket with a jerk.

"I shan't worry about you," he said, beaming at her suddenly through his beard. "You're through the woods and on the other side again, I see. Get your own show going. I suppose it won't make you mad if I go and see it and say what I think in the papers."

He was through the door when he turned and stuck his head in and grinned at her from under his brows.

"Say, Susan," he called, "I'd make you one of my Titans, darned if I wouldn't, if you weren't a woman!" He roared out his huge laugh and banged the door. Suddenly she heard shrieks and going to the window she saw him rolling down the street, his beard flaring in the breeze, his cap over one ear. Out of his pockets he was dropping pennies and children were pouring out of alleys and doorways after him, and he was whistling and pretending not to see them.

It was because her life with Blake seemed suddenly to have fallen into nothing that she first spoke to him of her work. On what had their life been built, she asked herself, wondering and sad, that now because she closed her door at night, the day seemed strained to emptiness? But she could not open the door, not while he said nothing of Sonia, not while he would open no door for her into himself.

Once, when they parted at midnight at the head of the stairs, he smiled, and underneath the smile she saw his eyes grow angry though his voice when he spoke was light.

"Isn't this a sort of physical blackmail, Susanne?"

She shook her head and answered him directly and without heat. "No, Blake. It's very simple. The thought of your flesh makes me a little sick—nothing else."

He was silent, and she saw he was shocked. She was beginning to know now that simplicity and directness were what he did not know how to meet.

"Pleasant wifely remark!" he said at last, and this she did not answer at all. And then at her door he had demanded, "Do you want to divorce me, Susanne?"

"Oh no!" she said quietly. "Why do you ask me that?"

"You don't love me any more," he said.

"Yes, yes, I do!" she exclaimed. "I love you—I always love you. Only there is myself. It stands away from you, waiting. I can't force myself. That would be wicked for me to do."

He stared at her a long time, and then he took her head in his long slim hands and kissed her brows.

"Good night," he said, and went away and she shut her door. There was no need to lock it. She knew Blake.

But she did not know what he was thinking behind his sea-gray eyes. She did not want to separate from him. What she had told him was true, that his flesh repelled her now while she did not know what Sonia was to him. She could not give only her body to him when the door was shut between their minds—no, no. That was too vile. Once Trina, in the freedom of woman's talk, had said, "You've got to go on sometimes when you're as tired as an old cat. They turn sour on everything if you don't. It's the only way to keep peace." She reflected on this, her body lying cool and quiet under the moon as it caught the corner of the window. But she could not so violate her selfhood, and such peace was not peace when it was so bought. There was something precious in her, which she was, and that must be kept whole. It was not her mere body. It was the energy which, working without impediment of distress, guided her mind to vision and her hands to create what she saw. Not even Blake could be allowed to stay that energy, because it was the deep stream of her life and when it stopped, all stopped, and she was lost. And lying in her bed in the big quiet room, she pondered on some other door into herself which she could open to Blake, while passion waited.

Then it came to her that she had never opened to Blake that

315

part of her. Perhaps now, if she did, they might find a new means of union. She decided at dawn that she would tell him of her seven statues, and ask his advice about exhibiting them. It would please him, perhaps. She would keep nothing back from him any more of that deepest part of her life. She had hidden herself, and now she would hide nothing more from him. So, deciding, she felt happier and released and she slept at last.

It was easy enough in the morning to say to him, "Blake, will you come and see some things I have made?"

He looked handsome and cool in his light gray suit. The dining room was shaded for their breakfast, and Crowne was bringing in iced fruits and coffee. She had put on a silver-white housecoat which he liked. By her napkin there was a letter from John at camp. She felt cheerful and full of hope, and so she spoke, at once.

He had come in a little earlier than she, and he rose while she sat down, and then seated himself again. He looked up as she spoke.

"Of course I will," he said, and after a moment he said, "I have wanted very often to ask you about your work, Susanne, but you are such an independent young woman!"

He smiled, but she discerned, or thought she did, annoyance in his voice.

"I didn't know you thought of it," she exclaimed. "I was waiting for you to speak."

"But why? I show you everything I do!"

She looked at him. She had, perhaps, been very wrong about Blake. "I don't know," she said at last. "I felt that part of me quite separate from you because, perhaps, I knew you wouldn't like it. Or perhaps because I am a woman," she mused, "perhaps I felt I had to prove myself—do something before I talked about it. I honestly don't know, Blake. I don't think why I do things. I feel I must and I do, that's all."

316

"Ah," he said quietly, "that is the reason you are so formidable."

"Am I?"

"Yes. One never quite has you, you know."

"I don't think I know what you mean," she said.

"I mean, because you don't think as other people do, you're always a little away from everybody. It's not easy to get close to you, Susanne. Do you know, nearly all of my friends are afraid of you?"

"Are they?" She was astonished. "Why, Blake?"

"They think you feel yourself, rather—criticize them, you know, the way you sit watching them."

"But I don't—it's not that." She was wanting to cry, very nearly. "It's just that I can't keep from watching people. I do it without knowing it."

They were talking back and forth like strangers and she could not bear it. The tears, held back, suddenly rushed into her eyes.

"Don't say you can't understand me," she whispered.

And he, not looking up, not seeing her tears, went on, bantering, "Don't women like to be mysterious and difficult to understand?"

She felt very far away from him, far, indeed, from everyone, as he said she was. While she had been working day after day people had been escaping her. She had had no time to make friends, no time to spend with anyone. Even the children had been glimpses and fragments at the beginning, at the end, of her days. And now she had shut the night against Blake, too. He sat at the end of the table, dim to her sight in the sunshine, and distant.

"Blake, say something real to me!" she begged. "Speak to me!"

If he had spoken to her she would have gone to him and knelt beside him and put her arms around him and cried to him,

317

"It doesn't matter about Sonia—nothing matters if you will only keep me close to you. I must be close to someone."

But he looked up and said in the same gay voice, "What shall I say, Susanne? That you are beautiful this morning? But you are always beautiful, and I tell you that so often— Come, eat your breakfast, and then we will go and see these wonderful things of yours."

He dipped his fingers in the bowl of water where a few red rose leaves floated and wiped them on the crisp linen napkin. Crowne came in with kidneys and bacon and he began to eat with his invariable relish. He ate heartily always and still maintained the tall thinness to which his body was born.

"Someone," he said, "actually broils kidneys with good taste!" His voice was earnest with feeling .

"I am so glad," she said. For she had spent valuable hours looking for a new cook because the kidneys he liked for breakfast were not done as he liked them, and then yesterday Jane had said in her grim fashion, "I'd as lief go, Mum, in the mornings and do them kidneys of his he's always rowin' about, if you'll make it plain to all of them downstairs that I'm sent special."

"Jane, thank you—you're always a help to me," she had said, and Jane had answered cryptically, "You'll be really needin' me again one of these days. . . ."

"Shall we go?" Blake was asking her.

She rose at once, and felt her knees tremble a little. "I'm not afraid of him," she told herself, and aloud she said, "I'll just get into my street things, Blake."

They stepped into the car and Bantie with solemnity drove them the four blocks to the studio and they got out. To this place where she had hidden from him, she was now bringing him.

"Susanne!" Blake exclaimed. "In such noise and filth!"

318

"It's really very nice," she said hurriedly. "There is so much room inside."

She ran up the steps ahead of him and unlocked the door. But when he had come in, while he was looking, she began to tremble again. She begged him, "Sit down, Blake darling, and I'll sit here on the arm of the chair."

So he sat down and she sat beside him, waiting, her heart pounding. When David Barnes looked at them she was so sure of them, but now under Blake's narrow gaze she did not know. They looked suddenly reserved, block-like, heavy, huge. Beside the exquisite sharp finish of his work they seemed crude.

"I am quite—overcome," he said at last. "Susanne, they are enormous. How have you done all this?"

"I have been working every day, nearly," she answered.

"I didn't expect such large things," Blake replied. He rose and walked among them. She felt them aware of his step and coming, but they did not shrink.

"There is a certain simplicity about them of course," he began, and did not finish. Outside a fire engine shrieked and tore by and children's voices yelled and the old room shook and settled again. Only the massive figures did not tremble.

"I see your idea," Blake began again, studying the inscriptions. "Sort of elemental America—roots, soil, first things and all that."

"Something like that," she said. "It is a feeling more than an idea."

He stood a long time before the triad of Sonia.

"Ah," he said in a very quiet voice, "you see her like that—a sort of peasant. I see her as something very different."

"She really is a peasant," Susan said. "Her father was a Croatian farmer—they lived among the Tartars."

And then he said, "Has she seen it?"

And she said, "Not since I finished it. She came here only to pose."

319

And he said, "So she told me."

Sonia had not been at the house since the night they had talked of her. But of course Susan knew they met, and Blake spoke of her carelessly now, as though with nothing to hide.

"You've done everything in marble?" he was asking.

"Yes," she answered, and then she said, "you don't like stone, but it's my material." He was still looking at Sonia's strong nude body and then she could not endure it.

"Do you like my black woman?" she asked, and he turned.

"Yes," he said, "it's good," and then he said with a sort of wonder, "It's really very good, Susanne."

She wanted to cry out, "Why should you wonder?" but she only said, "Yes, I like it, too."

Then he grew very kind. He told her how to go about preparing for her exhibition, and he gave her addresses and names, and he said, "Shall I do it for you, Susanne? Shall I prepare the way for you?"

But she shook her head.

"It will be fun for me. I want to do everything. You don't mind if I only use my own name?"

"Why should I?" he replied.

At the door he kissed her gently and said, "It is all astonishingly good in its own way. They are not modern, though, Susanne."

"They are only what I see," she said. "I don't know what they are."

"No," he said, staring at them. "I can see you don't. You haven't worked with your head, but with something else—I don't know what. It's instinctive work—in a way, it's incomplete. Do you sketch first?"

"Yes, but I tear it all up and work directly."

"Ah," he said, "only a few people can do that." She was not sure if he meant she was not one of the few. Then he bent and kissed her. "Goodbye, Susanne."

320

He was gone—no, at the door he stayed and a look of wilfulness came into his face. "I want you to lunch with me today," he said suddenly.

They had not lunched together in many months. It had come to be taken for granted that they took their separate ways until nightfall. She hesitated, looking at him. She had planned to spend this day with her figures, studying them for their final perfection. If she had been sure that he wanted her for love she would not have hesitated at all. But the glints of his wilfulness, which shone in his eyes and sharpened his smile, made her doubtful. She put her doubt away. In caprice she could not match him nor comprehend him.

"Yes, I will," she said quietly. "Where? At home?"

"No—at the Femme d'Or," he said, and then he added quickly, "Do you mind if Sonia comes?"

They looked at each other. Now plainly he was mischievous.

"I do—rather," she said.

"Ah, well, for once," he coaxed her, and then he said, "You must come. It will be the last time. She goes back to Russia next week, and next winter she will stay in Moscow." He came back and gave her shoulder a sudden sharp pressure and was gone.

And when he was gone her figures, which had been so quiescent in his quick presence, took on their being, and she put Blake and Sonia away from her and gave herself to them. She had learned how to do this. Long ago when Mark died she had first learned how to do this. But she could not do it then so well as she did today. The power of her will was very nearly perfected. Blake worked in such spasms of moods. He would have days of swift terrible work and then days when he could not summon his mood.

"God, I'll never work again!" he would groan, despairing. He could not make himself do what he did not feel like doing.

But her will was always there to summon the mood of work.

It was like touching a button which swung a lever to release an energy into a vast generating machine. But to put out the hand to touch off the will—that first moment was pure will. It was like the forcing of one's will to anaesthesia. That first moment—then her being, propelled by her will, was swept along into its fulfilment and every other consciousness was laid aside, but for energy, not for sleep. . . . She polished and smoothed, but not too finely, for the essence of her work was in roughness and not in smoothness. Her figures rose out of masses of rough rock, or they sprang straining out of high columns of rock. She forgot, and when she remembered, it was far too late for lunch.

"I need not see Sonia now," was her first thought, and she looked gratefully toward her people, who had made her forget everything. She went on working, glad and remorseful together. Would Blake mind? He would not mind. Perhaps he had planned some moment of melodrama between them. She knew there was melodrama in him. He could weep as a child does when he was too tired or when something upon which he worked went askew from what he had planned. She who so seldom wept, had been terrified at first, because she had not often seen a man weep. Then she perceived that Blake did not mind weeping at all—it was as meaningless as a child who cries because he is not given something which for the moment he wants. There was no ruggedness in him. So when he wept she allowed him to weep, without protest, and at last without pity.

"You don't care, Susanne!" he cried once.

"Weeping eases you," she replied, and instantly he had stopped weeping to cry at her, "How hard you are!"

And she had answered sturdily, "No, but I will not be torn to pieces." She was learning how to preserve herself, knowing that Blake's storms passed over him like a summer rain over a landscape. But she was not like him. Storm tore at her roots and she guarded herself, lest she be destroyed. . . . She was thinking, "And if he is angry when I come home tonight, I will tell him the simple truth, that I was working and I forgot. If he is angry, I will let his anger pass over my head."

Then suddenly the door opened. She turned, and Sonia stood there in a white dress of heavy silk. She stood, smiling, her pale eyes a deepening green under her white hat.

"Shall I come in?" she asked.

"Yes," said Susan. "I was just thinking that I had no apology to offer for not coming to lunch today except the truth—that I forgot Blake had invited me."

Sonia came toward her slowly. "You forgot! Let me see your eyes! No, you are honest. I see you did forget. Susan, there is not another such woman in this world, who forgets when her husband is lunching with me!"

She looked at Sonia, feeling her. She could not blame Blake, not wholly. One must be completely possessed not to see Sonia's gay mouth, her wide sweet face, the exact and flowing grace of her compact body. And Blake, too, perhaps was not one to be completely possessed.

"I didn't want to go away without seeing you, Susan," Sonia's deep golden-edged voice was saying. "I know you have been thinking many things of Blake and me. I have wanted to come to you, and I have not come."

What was in this woman's lovely eyes? She searched them painfully. But now Sonia had walked to her portrait and stood looking at it. She put out her square mobile hand and caressed her own marble cheek.

"You made me three. It is not enough. There are many more. One said, 'Go and tell Susan—' and another said, 'You and Blake give each other something necessary,' and to another Blake said, 'I do not rob Susan, Sonia. Susan understands.' And so—"

She shrugged, smiled, and put out her hands to the three.

"You and Blake still love each other?" Susan asked.

"What does Blake say?" Sonia asked, not looking at her.

323

"Not yes or no," Susan answered.

"I say yes and no," Sonia said. She looked at Susan fully and quickly and laughed her loud Russian laughter. "But you are not to be disturbed. It is over, what Blake and I have done. I am going home for a year, for two years. When I come back I shall be another creature. I never stay the same. Every year I am another. See, I promise you! I will dye my hair another color, even."

"You can't change your eyes," Susan said.

There was some quality in this creature which was like Blake, something not childish, but wild and elfin in its essence. It was a temperament. But it was not hers. She could not create in these flashes and angers and gayeties and perversities. Her people she made out of her deep steady rock-like foundations. Everything in her life had gone into that foundation of her being, out of which came, an eternal spring, the energy to create. She did not want wine to stimulate that energy, nor love to feed it, as Blake perpetually did, Blake and Sonia and all their kind. She did not want anything any more except the plainest needs of every day, food and sleep, the simplest intercourse with human beings and time in which to ponder and to work. She perceived all this and now it was no longer necessary to know anything about Blake and Sonia. She had forgotten, and forgetting had been the symbol.

"Ah, don't mind!" Sonia coaxed her. "Go your own way, Susan!"

"Yes, I will—I do," Susan said.

Sonia's eyes grew bright with laughter. "Ah, Susan!" she cried. "Goodbye, dear Susan! Remember, this Sonia will never come back." She kissed Susan on both cheeks, her red lips warm and soft. "There is nobody like you, just," she said. "You will always be a little alone because there is nobody like you—but you are not lonely." She waved her hand at the door.

"I haven't hurt you," she said. "I am not sorry for you!"

324

She was gone. And Susan stood listening to the old words that had followed her all her life— "Nobody like you—" the walls echoed. She did not fight against them now. They could frighten her no more. They were true. She sat down a little while and rested and then she put on her hat and went out into the street.

"H'lo, Miss Gaylord!" the children shouted. It was the first very hot day, and the street hydrant was turned on and in the gush of water a dozen thin small bodies pranced. Big Bill, the policeman, stood near and touched his cap.

"They'll be clean for wanct," he said and grinned.

"I'd like to be one of them," she said, and smiled. They were all her friends. She had many friends, but no being was entwined with hers. There were certain trees whose roots fed far and wide in the fields where they stood, trees whose arms were spread for shelter but who stood alone under the sky.

She went home and in the hall she called, "Blake?" But there was no answer.

There was no need at night to tell him she had forgotten, for he did not speak of it. He was silent all evening, reading a little, and then idle. And seeing him restless, she said gently, "Shall you miss Sonia too much, Blake?"

He looked at her sidewise. "I? I wasn't thinking of her."

"Then why are you so sad?" she asked.

"I don't know," he answered, "only I have felt melancholy as the deuce all day. I feel as if I'd never work again."

"But you will," she said. "You have felt so before, but you begin again."

"I've never felt like this," he insisted, "so—empty."

He threw himself back on the couch and closed his eyes. His face was sharp with sadness, tense with sadness. She studied it, struck by its beauty, but no longer moved. Marble could not be carved into its likeness—ivory, perhaps. He opened his eyes.

"Come over here," he commanded her. She went to him and

he laid his head on her knees and held her with his arms. She put her arms about him, and then she felt him begin to weep soundlessly against her.

"There, my dear, my darling, there," she said without distress. What his need was she did not know, nor perhaps did he, or he would not have held it back from her. He wept, carried upon some deep stream of sourceless melancholy, and she held him close, waiting in patience for him to return to himself and even perhaps to her. She did not need him any more but he was dear to her. If he could return to her, another love than that of need might grow between them.

Surely he would return to her. She went on steadily all summer, planning her exhibition, preparing for its opening at the beginning of the autumn, waiting for him.

"November is the best month for a beginner," Joseph Hart said to her. She had gone to see him one day in his old brown-stone house because David Barnes told her to go.

"I've told the old chap about you," he said. "He wants to see you. You'd better go—it's not often he wants to see anybody."

But when she went into Joseph Hart's drawing room he pretended he had forgotten about her.

"Never heard of you," he said shortly when she came in. His rooms were a museum of painting and statuary.

At first she could see nothing clearly. Rich dark Flemish faces looked out of old gilt frames beside pale American landscapes, arid and new. Then suddenly at the end of the room she saw Michael's wild horses. It was a long horizontal canvas, and the light fell well upon it. Nine silver white horses fled through the moonlight across the night-dark desert, and there was one, the fleetest of them all, a small black horse, who was their leader.

326

"Don't know your stuff," Joseph Hart was saying.

"I know you don't," she answered, "but you will."

"I won't if it's these hop-skip-jump modern things you do. I don't look at them," he retorted. Everywhere dealers and managers of galleries had said to her, "If you can get old Joseph Hart—"

"You're looking at those horses," he said.

"Yes," she answered.

"A Michael Barry," he said. "Most uneven young painter in the world, he is. Sometimes he does a thing like that—pure color, pure form, pure beauty. Then he'll go off and do a whole string of fanciful stuff—naked women stretched out on rocks—vicious stuff."

She did not answer. She kept looking at the horses, galloping wild and free across the desert.

"What's your medium?" he inquired. "Not mud, I hope."

"Marble," she said, and added, "I did one bronze."

"Where?" he demanded.

"The Halfred Memorial Hospital."

"You do that?"

"Yes. It was my first real work."

He took up a glass of wine he had set down when she came in and sipped it in silence.

"Pity you're a woman," he said at last.

"No, it isn't," she said. "It doesn't matter any more."

"You'll find it does," he insisted. "You won't get first places unless you're really better than anybody."

"I don't work for that," she said.

He did not answer. But after he had poured another glass of wine from a slender red bottle, he fumbled in his pocket for a card and wrote something on it.

"You take that to a man named Gelwicks at that address," he ordered her, "and tell him I sent you."

"Thank you," she said, but he had already turned his back on her.

She stood a long moment alone, looking at Michael's picture, and then she went away.

"I must tell Michael I saw it," she thought. "I must tell him how perfect it is."

She had forgotten Joseph Hart.

It was a small, very plain gallery. She had all her things moved, and at the last moment The Kneeling Woman had come in from Paris.

She and Blake had unpacked her. "The Rejected!" Blake had cried, stripping the shreds of stuff from her. Susan looked at her with critical eyes.

"Of course they didn't want her," she said. "I can see why. She isn't nearly good enough. I don't think I did anything good in Paris. I didn't really know what I wanted to do."

"Shall we throw her out?" Blake asked.

"No, let her stay," Susan said. "After all, I made her."

She and Blake were regaining a sort of comradeship. But he had not once demanded more of her. Sometimes it was very hard to talk to him, and then she drove her tongue to chatter, because silence was not to be borne between them, though she longed for silence, full and tranquil. But if they did not talk, an edgy silence surged up between them, not full, not tranquil.

"I think I'll have an old statue of Jane I once did sent up from the country," she said suddenly. "I think it was good."

"That old hag!" Blake said amiably. He was studying the black woman. "Shift her an inch to the right," he commanded the sweating draymen, and they heaved.

"No, Blake," she said, "that's too dramatic for her. The light must fall plain and straight, not slantwise, on my things."

"Marbles to you, my dear," he said gaily.

When it was all ready she and Blake walked slowly about.

"You mustn't mind if the critics pan you, Susanne," he said complacently.

"I won't," she said, surprised. It had not occurred to her to think of what the critics would say. What she had done was finished, beyond praise or blame.

The statue of Jane came the last day and that day she was alone and she unpacked it. It was crude and young in its touch, but still it was Jane, looking up startled from her work, wiping her hands on her apron. She had it set behind the door, a little away from the others, in a quiet corner, where Jane would be.

Then when she had paid off the last man she looked at everything quite alone, from Jane to the last thing she had done, which was a figure of a Welsh miner from West Virginia. She had found him quite by chance. He had come to New York, a delegate to a labor meeting, and she had drifted in at the meeting, as she did so many places, not knowing what she came to see, except people, and he had been making a speech. After the meeting she went up and asked him to pose for her, and he had come to the studio and sat talking, his shoulders hunched and his enormous hands outspread on his bent knees.

"I can't straighten now, Miss," he said. "I've walked bent underground too long for that."

In a way his was the best figure she had done. She had felt him creeping along under the earth. His eyes looked blind and robbed of the sun and she had made them so. His hands were great claws like a mole's claws, powerful out of all proportion to his hunched body, and she had made them so. Yes, every figure was better than the last. She had gone straight ahead. And these were only the beginning.

The day before the opening she brought John and Marcia to see her things. They were home for an autumn holiday. She said nothing, feeling shy before them of seeming to have done anything. But she walked between them, sensitive to every sign

329

and word, longing for their approval, feeling for it as she explained.

"This one I call American Woman, Black. And this one is America North—it is Sweden's part. And this is an Italian girl whom I call American Venus. And this—"

She could feel John's passionate attention. He was nearly as tall as she was now, and he was wearing his first suit with long trousers. He said nothing, but he stood absorbed before each figure, listening, gazing, his hands in his pockets. If he had ever looked like Mark, she thought, he had outgrown it.

"I see exactly what you mean," he said, and he drew in his breath. "They're swell, Mother," he said, and her heart leaped up in her breast.

Marcia said impatiently, "But why are they all so big and ugly, Mother? Why, you've even made Sonia ugly!"

"Oh, shut up, Marcia!" John cried out for Susan. "You don't know anything."

"I do," Marcia pouted. "I don't like such thick heavy people." She pirouetted on one toe as she spoke and whirled into a little dance, her arms uplifted, her fingers drooping. Among the solid, pillar-like figures she looked like a little moth, fluttering and unstable, a thing to touch and crush.

"All Marcia's brains are in her legs," John muttered.

"I know they are," Marcia's voice sang freely. "I think, I feel, with my legs! When I'm dancing I'm happy!"

She was quite happy now that they were not looking at Susan's statues, but at her.

"Why do you want that ugly old Jane?" she sang impudently, dancing to the door. "She looks awful. Jane's so ugly!"

"She's swell, and you know it," John cried. And on the way home in the car he told Susan shyly, "I'm doing a thing of Jane myself—in wood. I don't know why I like to work in wood. I guess because Granddad and I have always whittled together. Jane's been sitting for me every day since I came back home from school."

"May I see it?" Susan asked.

"I've seen it—it's ugly, too, because Jane's ugly," Marcia cried.

John cast her aside with a look. "You know how Jane's face is, Mother. I don't think it's ugly."

"Only Sonia is pretty," Marcia cried wilfully. "Sonia and Mary are pretty, and Blake is beautiful. Oh, I hope—I hope I'll be pretty, Mother, when I'm big?" She turned dark begging eyes toward Susan. "I'll die if I am not pretty!"

"I think you will be," Susan said.

"I don't," said John ruthlessly. "Your face makes me sick. You're always thinking about yourself, Marcia."

"John!" Susan said. She turned to comfort Marcia.

But Marcia was sitting very straight and cool, and needed no comfort from anyone. "I don't care what John thinks," she said brightly. "Blake likes me." They were home, the doors opened. "I don't want to see old wooden Jane," she said, and she skipped away.

In John's room Susan said, "I wish, John, you wouldn't speak so to Marcia."

She was surprised by the age and gravity of his answering look at her. "Mother, I must," he said. "You can't hurt her. You've got to knock her or she gets you crazy. And when she knows she's got you crazy, she's happy."

Now he was lifting somthing out of his closet and unwrapping it. It was a piece of wood about a foot high. "It's a root," he said. "I found it at camp, and it looked like Jane. See, I've only had to suggest her face. The curves are there. Of course it's not finished."

She forgot Marcia completely. It was like Jane indeed. He had carved away bark and surface wood, and out of the twisted root Jane's bent figure was emerging.

331

"It's wonderfully good," she said simply.

She was proud, proud of her son. She had made him, she had given him some of her own being. His young hands, caressing the smooth wood, were appealing in their thinness, in their size, a man's hands in shape but so childish in their bony youthfulness. Her flesh stirred at the sight and she wanted to lean forward and kiss them. But she did not.

She said, "Ought you to have lessons, I wonder?"

He shook his head. "No, I don't want them, Mother." He paused. "I shan't carve for a living. I just carve things. I'll probably go into some sort of science."

He wrapped the old silk handkerchief carefully about the little wooden statue. "I feel I can't bear to make money by it," he added, "even if I could." And then, his back to her, putting it away, he said casually, very adult, "You know, Marcia really has the outlook on life of a cat, Mother. She only thinks of herself. It worries me."

"She's very young," Susan said, smiling. John was born to be responsible. Yes, there was a little of the look of Mark in his shoulders and about the back of his head, though when he turned, the look was gone. It was not in his face, but hidden somehow in his being.

"She'll never change," John said. "It's the stuff she's made of. I always feel she's terra cotta, you know—not wood or marble—nothing lasting."

She stood, drinking him in, enjoying his nearness, amazed at his wisdom.

"You and I," she said shyly, "we ought to do more things together."

He blushed sharply, his fair skin scarlet.

"I'd like it," he said, "only you're very busy, aren't you?"

"Not too busy," she said. "I've always had time for what I wanted."

The moment was too sweet to bear. She broke it off suddenly. "We'll plan," she said, "after my exhibition is over."

She said so many times, "After my exhibition is over," that she felt a premonition of break and change. She felt it so strongly and so strangely that on the day of the opening she went very early to her studio and planned her next work. She had put down notes of ideas for her complete American Procession, of which the seven pieces in exhibition were the first part. But when she went over them now they seemed too slight. None of them seized her as inevitably to be made. Besides, her marbles were gone. She was not sure that she wanted more from Fane Hill. Yesterday, late in the day, Blake's father had come in at her invitation, to see the exhibition alone with her.

"Come and see your marbles," she said gaily, opening the door to him in the afternoon. The last cleaning had been done, and everything was ready.

He had come in, his smooth black derby and his gray gloves in his hand. Together they had moved from piece to piece, and with his increasing silence she had talked more and more quickly. "You remember this? It is one of the blocks from Paros. These people work in a restaurant nearby. Aren't they splendid? The man serves out soup as though he were a god feeding humanity."

"Ah," said Mr. Kinnaird, doubtfully.

"And this is the Belgian black." She laid her hand on the thick black knee.

Mr. Kinnaird averted his eyes. "It is very overpowering," he murmured.

When he had seen everything, he sat down and gazed at them all again.

"I can't tell you how I feel," he said, his face agitated. He passed his free hand across his forehead. "It's—they're so huge.

The room is a little small, perhaps. Each of them needs a great deal of space—they seem to bear down on one."

She waited a moment. Then she said, "I hope you aren't sorry you gave me the marbles."

"No, oh no," he said quickly, "only I had not perhaps—expected such large things from a—a—lady. It wants getting used to, that's all. I had thought, perhaps, of a lighter touch—something more classical."

"They aren't pretty, I know," she said.

And then he made quick amends. "They are very strong, my dear. They are really quite masculine in their technique."

"I don't think men and women create so differently," she said.

"I shall be very interested to see what the critics say," Mr. Kinnaird said without answering her.

In her studio now, remembering his bewildered eyes, she thought, "Poor old man! He doesn't like them. I mustn't take any more of his marbles."

But then it had been a curious varying day. For Michael had come in a little while, and looking about had whistled and cried, "Susan, they're enormous, they're splendid! They ought to be set out in the harbor somewhere, to show what's marched into America!" And then he looked at her haggardly and said with trembling lips, "Susan, Mary is married!"

"Oh, Michael!" She sat down suddenly, struck down with his catastrophe.

He nodded. "She wouldn't marry me—but she married that old chap Rhodes—a decent old chap—but Mary!"

He was swallowing hard, but he gave way. He sat beside her on a bench and put his head on her shoulder and she put her arms about him.

"Oh, dear, oh, dear," she murmured in deepest distress.

"I'm just a fool," he whispered, "it's ridiculous. I couldn't sleep all night. She called me up yesterday when she got in.

334

He'd followed her to Paris. That's all. Only I didn't think she really would."

She felt his shaking body. The quality of this weeping was terrifying and destructive.

"If I were you, Michael," she said gently, "I would—"

"I can't forget her," he said sharply. "Don't say that."

"I wasn't going to say that," she answered. "I was going to say, accept it as your life. Everything that is in your life goes into you—you can't forget, you mustn't forget. You need it all—everything—love and loss—all of it." She paused, distilling something from herself. "Deprivation—that's positive, too—that also is a sort of life."

She held him, waiting for him to grow quiet. What she had told him she told herself also. What Blake gave her was part of her life, but what he did not was her life too. What she had and what she had not, it was all the everything which she needed.

"I'm going north somewhere to paint." Michael moved away from her. He turned his back to her and cleared his throat.

She rose, picked up a cloth and dusted the foot of the stone Sonia.

"I always feel that you haven't really found what you want to paint." She longed for easily flowing words with which to help him, but she did not have them, so she went on as she could. "There is a sort of final material, native to you—when you find it you will paint from the inside out. All those pictures of Mary—none of them are painted from the inside of her—or of you. One works like that with what one has for the moment. But nothing comes clearly through until you find your own stuff."

He was listening, but he did not answer.

"I'm glad Mary has married someone else," she went on,

335

doggedly. "If she had married you, you would have stopped forever where you are."

"I wouldn't have cared." Michael's voice was thick. "Who cares whether I paint a few pictures or not?"

"Nobody," Susan answered. "A few pictures or statues, a little more music, a little more or less of anything—it doesn't matter. But it matters whether you are happy in your life. And you can only be happy if you find what you want to make, and if you can make it." She paused, trying to tell him what she meant. "Some people are pools and some are rivers—flowing to the sea. You are a river—you must flow on—you cannot be caught in a pool. You would be bound and angry and overflow at last in all sorts of wildness and misery. You must keep your channel clear."

All this she was saying to herself, too, as she polished the marble and made it dustless—only it did not matter about her. She must say something more to Michael, something real for comfort. She remembered suddenly, and she looked up at him, bright with joy.

"Michael, I saw your horses!"

"Horses?" He did not know what she was talking about.

"Your wild horses—the picture Joseph Hart bought!"

Now he knew what she said.

"Susan! What did you think of them?"

"Perfect," she whispered, "perfect, that's all. I felt when I looked at them—I felt—"

"Yes?" His eyes were eagerly upon her. She must tell him exactly how she felt so that he might forget Mary, so that he might be comforted.

"I felt that you were free at last," she said. "The endless desert, the endless sky, that pure cold moonlight on the water, those flying lovely shapes, whom no one had ever tamed, whom no one can ever tame—" They were looking into each other's

336

eyes, and an ecstasy of comprehension passed between them which had nothing to do with themselves.

"I know," he said.

Michael came over to her where she knelt. He touched her cheek with his hand and went away without a word.

And when he was gone, she knelt a moment more, motionless. Then she went to the telephone and called Mary's apartment. A brisk voice answered that Mary Gaylord's number was changed and gave a new number, and she dialed and heard a man's pleasant, rumbling voice, drawling a little into her ear.

"I want to speak to Mary Gaylord, please," she said, and heard the voice call, "Mary, honey, here's somebody for you!" And then Mary's crisp, very clear voice inquired of her, "Yes?"

"This is Susan," she answered.

The quality of Mary's voice did not change. "I was just about to call you, Susan, and tell you—"

"Michael has told me," she said.

"Has he? We only got back yesterday. I decided rather quickly." Her clear voice admitted no fault.

"Have you told Dad and Mother?" Susan asked.

"No, I am going to write today," Mary answered.

She heard the pleasant rumble and Mary said, "Benny wants to talk to you a minute. He saw the announcement of your exhibition this morning."

And there at her ear was the kind rumbling again. "Well, well, Susan! I was all excited. Mary didn't tell me you were going to have an exhibition. I just happened to see the name and I asked her if it was a relative."

This was Mary's husband, she thought, listening, answering a word or two—a kindly, good voice, a little dull, a little commonplace. Of course nothing was his fault. Mary would never tell him that Michael even lived.

"Yes, of course," she was answering now. "No, I am not

busy. Tomorrow I'll probably be much busier. I hope so, at least. Do come over now. I am quite alone." She threw the phrases into the receiver, between his questions. Then Mary was there again.

"Benny wants to come over, so we'll be there as soon as we get the car."

"I am here all day," Susan answered.

Waiting, she remembered Mary, a little girl at the piano, playing doggedly over and over, wrongly, a fragment of music, and growing sullen when she was told she was wrong.

"This is Benny," Mary said. Her face and voice were composed as ever and she was very smart in a new suit of brown velvet. Susan looked away from her into kind very blue eyes, small in a round red face under thin, carefully brushed white hair, through which the scalp showed scarlet. She felt her hand taken warmly into a plump, impulsive, dampish grasp.

"Well, well!" the rumbling voice was saying, "I can't tell you how proud I am!"

Mr. Rhodes pulled out his silk handkerchief and wiped his face and laughed. "It's cold enough outside," he said, "but I always perspire a little when I'm excited, and meeting you has certainly got me excited, hasn't it, honey?" He turned to Mary and she smiled a little smile. He glanced at the statues. "Is this— My goodness, Mary, you never told me your sister was a real sculptor!"

"I haven't had time to tell you all about my family yet," Mary replied.

"That's right," said Mr. Rhodes with heartiness. "Well, I'm going to start right in. I'm anxious to meet them all, Susan, especially your children. I'm fond of children. I've been married before—lost my first wife by typhoid when we were taking a world tour, and I never thought I'd marry again until I saw Mary here one day in the store." He laughed again.

338

She saw what he was, anyone could see what he was, a kind and good man, no longer young, and born in innocence. She looked at Mary reproachfully, and Mary met her eyes fully and arrogantly. There was still that sullen, stubborn child she had once been.

"Don't Mary look splendid?" Mr. Rhodes was demanding of Susan. He gazed at Mary lovingly and took her hand and patted it. She had drawn off her gloves and Susan saw the shining new wedding ring and another ring of diamonds and emeralds. "Marriage agrees with her," said Mr. Rhodes.

"She looks as if you treated her with the greatest kindness," said Susan with energy. She liked this friendly, childlike man, and she wanted to cry out to Mary that she must be kind to him, because it was wicked to be cruel to the old and innocent.

"I can't be too kind to her, that's what I think." Mr. Rhodes' face was grave. He was playing with the thick gold watch chain that was drawn a little tightly across his rounding waistcoat. "A man can't be too kind to a woman anyway, is what I think, and when a lovely young girl like Mary trusts herself to an old fellow like me—" he broke off. There were tears in his blue innocent eyes— "Well, I can't do too much for her. What she sees in me, I don't know. It can't be much." He paused, and went on shyly. "I don't mind telling you I feel awful humble when I think of myself. This morning when I was shaving I looked at myself and thought, 'You old son-of-a-gun, what makes you think she can love that?' I had to remind myself that if she didn't love me for some reason of her own sweet nature, she wouldn't have married me. I've often wondered, looking at some of the men I know, why their wives, sweet women, could marry 'em. Whyever it is, it comes out of their own good womanly natures—" his voice was trembling—"so I don't ask why—I only thankfully take what she gives me. She's a wonderful girl."

And he looked at Mary and adored her, and she stood smiling her small smile, cold and unmoved, in her strange secret beauty. She put out her hand and touched his hand lightly. "Nice Benny," she murmured, and then she said quickly to Susan, "We're going to buy a house in town, Susan, isn't it exciting? And one at Palm Beach! Benny spends months in the South every winter."

"You must bring the children and your husband and come to see us," he said. "Now, honey, we must stop chattering and look at all this—"

Behind his broad back Susan looked at Mary with grave eyes, but Mary's eyes were still blank, bright, impenetrable. "I will tell you," Susan thought with anger, gazing into the hard darkness of those eyes, "you must not hurt this kind old man. You can hurt him more than you hurt Michael even, because he is so defenseless. You must be good to him if you cannot be tender." But he would, she knew, want tenderness. He would beg Mary humbly for her tenderness and not understand why she withheld it, nor ever understand that it was not in her. And he was not like Michael who could go away. He would cling to her the more she hurt him, having nowhere to go away from her, because he was what he was, because he was old and had no refuge. Susan ached for him, her imagination running ahead into the years. She went to him and began explaining warmly and fully, though she knew he could not understand.

"I'll tell you the story of each of them, may I? I'd like you to understand all about them." And as she talked, she was thinking, "I'm going to be kind to him. I'm going to let the children see him often and grow fond of him. He's got to have something out of marrying Mary."

"Yes, I see," he was saying earnestly. "Why, I think that's just wonderful. My, but I'm proud of you." He turned to Mary. "We're awfully proud of her, aren't we, Mary?"

Mary smiled. "Yes, of course," she said. And bending her head, she adjusted a little the sables that she wore.

"How do you think it is going?" she asked Blake.

"Not bad," he replied.

They had stayed in the gallery most of the day, and now it was evening. All day small groups of people, single people, a few couples, had drifted in. There had been no crowds but she did not expect them. But she was pleased because people who came in casually to see the work of a new artist, unknown, stayed to look and to talk in low voices. She heard fragments of their talk, critical, praiseful, puzzled.

"It's big," she heard a young man say to an older one.

"Yes," the older man admitted doubtfully, "too big to be realized, perhaps. When an artist tries for too much it may escape him entirely."

"I shouldn't say anything had escaped here," the young man answered.

"Perhaps not," the elder said, and paused and said again, "It's as though the ruggedness with which she has worked implies more than is actually there—"

"That, I suppose, is art," said the young man with fierceness.

"Perhaps—perhaps—" the older man said equably. "I belong to a school that postulates less, reaches the grasp and completes it."

"Neatly," said the young man, scornfully, and they passed by.

Again and again people said, "It's not like a woman's work, is it?" And some shrugged their shoulders. "I don't see why artists want to do such ugly people—look at that big fat Negro! So coarse!"

At home after dinner, alone, she and Blake looked at each other and smiled.

341

It had been a strange and happy day, filled with a happiness she could not understand. For she would have said that she valued most her work in the doing, and that when it was finished her fulfilment in it was complete. But this was not true. Her work was not complete even for herself, she now perceived, thinking the day over, until she had given it to be seen, to be understood or not, to other human beings. It was like speech, meaningless unless it became communication. She heard Blake's voice.

"None of the important critics have come in yet," he was saying. "If they don't come in tomorrow, I'll ring up Lee and Sibert and one or two others I know."

"You're not to say I'm your wife," Susan said and smiled.

"It wouldn't do you any harm," he answered, bantering, his eyes glinting at her.

"No, no, Blake!" she begged him.

"All right, you independent woman!" He laughed at her, but he was a little annoyed. When she saw this she suddenly could not bear it at the end of such a day, and she went to him where he sat upon the couch and leaned against him, not thinking beyond her impulse to keep him happy for today.

But at the touch of her body he started. Then he put out his arms and lifted her into his embrace. And she felt him near as he had not been near in many months and she let herself be in his embrace. Her work for the moment was done. There was completion in her deepest being. She was content. Suddenly some part of her turned, still unfulfilled, toward him.

"Sonia?" her mind inquired of itself. But Sonia was gone. Blake had told her nothing and she knew now he would never tell her anything. Perhaps indeed it was best. Her thoughts were racing along as she felt his tightening, hot embrace. They would never meet everywhere. It was not possible, perhaps. Perhaps the comradeship she dreamed of in love and work was never possible for women like her. She must take what she had, and what she had not—that too was life—the not having. So she had told Michael. It was all part of the everything. If she and Blake could only meet like this, was it not better so to meet than never?

She seemed to see Sonia afar off, watching them with her pale passionate eyes, but she drove the picture away. Somewhere between herself and Blake there must be a bond to hold them fast together. His lips were pressing now upon hers, silent and hot and strong, and in a sad new passion once more she responded.

But in the morning, remembering, she looked, and seeing her body white in the dawn, she thought of marble and how it was made by the slow hardening of centuries until it was fit and ready for the hand, and how when the transient hand had left its mark and done its work, the marble stood shaped for centuries more. And her hands were only flesh, her body no more than a moment made to use that energy in her which she least of all could understand, because she only knew the power of its working, and not why it must work if she was to live. And thinking thus of her most perishable body she thought sorrowfully, "How can it be enough to hold together Blake and me?" When she thought of Blake this morning he was no nearer to her. No, for all the night had brought, he was no nearer to her still. She was tender to him, but very far away.

When she went downstairs late for breakfast he was reading the Sunday paper, a frown between his eyes.

"Well, Susanne," he said when she came in, "I see your old friend has come forward." His voice was brisk.

She went over to him, her tenderness, an echo from the night, still in her, and put her arms about his shoulders. But for Blake the night was gone. He struck the paper with his fingers.

343

"Barnes," he said. "It's very decent of him, of course, in a way."

She glanced down the columns. "David Barnes Praises New Woman Sculptor," Blake read aloud. "He's just a little extreme—I mean, for your own good. It sounds too much like personal praise, as though you needed backing up."

She went to her place.

"This will start the critics," he said. "Still, I might call up one or two of the more influential ones."

"Whatever you think, Blake," she said.

"I'll see," he replied. She did not ask for the paper. When she was alone she would read it. She put out of her mind the thought of it and looked at Blake. He was quite cool, even a little debonair. He had accepted the night, she perceived, not as renewal but as a matter of course, for which he had merely to wait a little while. She looked away from him, somehow ashamed.

"It will be amusing to see what happens," he said. "Anything Barnes says will bring attention." And then he said, "Barnes never has understood my work, of course."

His voice was nonchalant, but she heard bitterness behind it, and when she looked up, astonished, she saw in his eyes he was hurt.

"Blake!" she cried. "Oh, darling! It's only because David Barnes thinks I need a little help and you don't—"

"Of course I don't need help so far as my work goes," said Blake, "but it would be friendly of him."

"I think it's only because he thinks as a woman I'll have a hard time."

She was cajoling him again, she was coaxing him into good humor, and she stopped abruptly. If there was something in her which could stoop to peace, she would refuse to follow it, and she said, "Not that I want help. I stand on what I am. There ought not to be man or woman in work." She smiled a little. "Work is a sort of heaven, where there is neither male nor female."

"You'll find there's no such heaven, Susanne," Blake said. "Whether you're man or woman sets you, whatever you do."

"I refuse to accept it," she said.

"But women are under suspicion," Blake began. "The great artists, the great musicians, even the great cooks, are men, and—"

"Now, Blake, please—that old, old stuff!" she cried. "From you, of all men!"

"It's difficult for me to take women seriously, perhaps," he said and smiled a little self-consciously.

She was so angry at him, so angry at herself for anger in so silly and so old a discussion, that she would not speak to him. She ate rapidly and little, and then rose. "I think I'll just go down and see how things are opening this morning," she said.

"I'll be along soon," he replied.

It was impossible to believe that last night had ever been. And yet it had been, and was still, and she must lay hold of it again. She went over to Blake and passed her hand over his smooth cheek. He did not move to her, but she bent and kissed him and went away.

Joseph Hart was talking to her, pushing his pince-nez on his high old Roman nose, a broad black ribbon fluttering against his cheek. "A shade more and they might have been modern," he was saying. "If our conceited young artists only knew it, the difference between the extreme classic and the extreme modern is very slight, but very important. As it is, you've somehow struck a tempo of your own. Very original stuff—a bit too massive, perhaps. But you'll fine down as you grow."

Old Mr. Kinnaird had come in again today. He had been

in yesterday and gone away again without a word. Now he was sitting on a bench gazing palely at the figures. People were coming in, and since Joseph Hart had singled her out with his talk, they were staring at her. And then she saw Blake. He came in, spoke to his father, and came to her side. She smiled at him faintly and did not speak. Joseph Hart was lecturing as he spoke to her, and a few people gathered near to listen, and he was aware of them and continued a little more pontifically.

"It is not, however, enough to be merely original. Almost anyone can be original. The insane mind, the childish mind, these are original, too. But they convey nothing by their expression. The test of any work of art is what it conveys. If nothing is conveyed, there is no worth in it."

Blake spoke. "Something perhaps depends on the mind of the person who receives the communication. It may be he is able to receive only what is simple and obvious. Art can scarcely be judged entirely by the receiving mind."

"The two do not go together," Joseph Hart said. "I should call these statues simple in a certain massive fashion, but not obvious."

Blake looked at him furiously. "They are a little obvious," he said savagely, "to the sophisticated mind, at least."

Then this was what Blake thought! In his anger—yes, in his jealousy, he had spoken to Joseph Hart what he had kept hidden from her. For she knew nothing could make him so angry as this except jealousy of his work. She had seen him jealous of many others. If he felt this toward her, nothing could heal the wound between them. For she knew in Blake, too, there was that which was deeper than love. He was never really savage unless that in him was pricked and injured. And this she had done unwittingly, because what she had made pleased a wealthy, wilful, aesthetic old man who had too much influence. For this Blake would not forgive her.

346

She looked about the gallery desolately. It was becoming more crowded as the day went on. That was because of what David Barnes had said. But people were staying, talking earnestly, grouped about one figure and another.

. . . What use was it if Blake would not forgive her? For this moment that woman who had been Blake's beloved cried out, "What use is it?"

And Susan answered, "You're not everything, you know. You're only part. Besides, there's a right and wrong to it. If my work's good, Blake is wrong. There's justice, too, to be thought of beyond you."

She slipped away and went and sat by old Mr. Kinnaird. She would not be hurt by what Blake had said. He had a right to say what he thought. But she knew he had said it not to Joseph Hart, but to her. Now he had said it and he could never draw the words back. They were still arguing. Blake was standing very straight, his back to her. Joseph Hart was gesturing, the broad black ribbon waving with his hand. Mr. Kinnaird's gentle pallid voice was at her ear.

"I keep coming back to see your things, my dear," he said. "They grow on me."

"I am glad," she said. She saw Joseph Hart give Blake a stiff bow and turn away from him. She waited for Blake to come to her, but he did not. He walked to the end of the gallery and stood for a moment by the door, and then went out.

"I can't quite place you," Mr. Kinnaird was saying. "It troubles me. I don't recognize the technique. Blake now, I can place. He is definitely modern. But you are not. Nor are you classic, nor can I see any trace of the French in your art. Just what, my dear, had you in mind?"

"I don't know," she said. "I don't know. I don't place myself. I work as I breathe—unconsciously. I feel, from moment to moment."

"Ah," he said gently, "that is perhaps because you are a woman."

"Perhaps," she said, and did not care.

She was not listening.

"You are wanted at the telephone, Miss Gaylord," somebody said. The day was nearly over. She did not want to go home and she had stayed, waiting until she could think of seeing Blake. When she went to the telephone Crowne's voice said, "Madame, there is a telegram for you. Shall I read it?"

"Please," she said, wondering, and he read slowly, " 'Dad very ill. Come at once. Mother.' Is there a reply, Madame?"

"Yes," she said. "Telegraph to the same address, 'Coming at once. Susan.' And tell Jane to pack my bag and hers, and telegraph my sister at Palm Beach at the Hotel Regina—Mrs. Bennyfield Rhodes, you know."

"Very well, Madame."

"Is Mr. Kinnaird there?" she asked.

"No, Madame," he said.

She hung up the receiver. People were coming in now more thickly than ever. She saw a thin dark man with an ill-tempered face making rapid notes on a small pad as he stood before each figure. Old Mr. Kinnaird had come back again and was staring painfully at the statue of a boy from Italy. He had forgotten her, and she went away without speaking to him.

Less than an hour later, leaving Blake's house, she wrote a note to him.

"My dearest, Dad is ill and I am hurrying straight away, not knowing where to find you."—She had told Crowne to call his club, but he was not there.—"I go away remembering last night. Come to me if you can. I may be needing you badly. I don't know what is ahead. I am your Susanne."

She folded it and sealed it and gave it to Crowne. "Give it to Mr. Kinnaird the moment he comes in," she said.

He bowed and shut the door of the car as she and Jane stepped in, and then as Bantie started the engine he went in and shut the door of the house. With the picture of that door in her mind, shut, she went away.

"If I believed in premonitions—" she thought, troubled, "but I don't." She thought of Blake with sudden immense longing. This morning's anger was nothing. In this reality he would come after her quickly when he found her gone, and there, perhaps, in the shabby comfortable plain old house they would find each other as they had not before. Jane's voice interrupted her.

"I thought he looked poorly the last time we was home," she said, and sighed. "Well, we all have our mortal course."

"Hush, Jane!" Susan cried at her. "You always think the worst has happened."

"It always does, sometime," said Jane. "Not, Mum, that I don't hope for the best."

She would not answer. She could only realize Blake still—no one else. Blake must not stay angry with her for any cause. She was still thinking of Blake when she reached her father's house and Hal Palmer opened the door.

"Why, Hal," she cried, "where's Mother?"

"Lucile's with her," he said. His plain round face was sober and his little blue eyes were full of tears. "I guess you're too late, Sue," he said. "It was a stroke. It took him just like that."

She turned to Jane. "Telegraph Blake," she said, and throwing off her coat, she went in to her mother.

Hour after hour she sat listening to her mother's talk.

Lucile had risen when she came in.

"My, I'm glad you're here, Susan. We've done all we can, but it's not like the family. Where's Mary?"

"I've telegraphed," Susan replied. It was strange how Lucile and Hal should touch her life at these crises of death. For a moment she remembered, more vividly than she remembered last night, the moment of Mark's death.

"So long as you're here," Lucile was saying in a loud whisper, "I'll go on. Hal has arranged—you know—for everything. The minister's just been and gone, but maybe he'll come again now you're here. Will any other members of the family be here?"

"I am going to send for the children," Susan said. "And of course my husband will be here."

"Oh, do send for the children," her mother sobbed. "They'll do me good. I just haven't a thing left to live for!"

"Now, Mrs. Gaylord," said Lucile in her strong fresh voice, "you mustn't talk that way. You have your two dear girls and your wonderful grandchildren and there's lots of us here in the town who love you. And you must remember you've been a wonderful wife and mother. You haven't a thing to reproach yourself for."

"I've done the best I could, I know," her mother said, wiping her eyes.

"Not one thing you haven't done for your family," Lucile said cheerfully. "And now you must be brave. I expect Susan will want to wash and clean up a little from her trip and then go in and see her father." She turned to Susan. "He looks so natural. As soon as he stopped breathing all the terrible dark red went out of his face, and all the strain—"

"Did he suffer?" Susan asked quickly.

"We don't know how much," Lucile replied, "because we don't know how much he was conscious of. He didn't say a word."

"He'd just had a little argument with me," her mother broke in, her eyes reddening, "over just nothing at all. You know the way he would argue, Susan. Well, it grew worse on him as he got older. I couldn't hardly open my mouth but what he'd contradict me."

"The patience you've had!" Lucile sighed.

Her mother went on, her swollen lips trembling, "This morning he would go out in the yard and I told him he hadn't ought to because he'd had a real bad cold. Besides, I said if he felt well enough to go out, he ought to feel well enough to go down cellar and shake the furnace for me. I'd been doing it a day or two because he said the ashes made him cough. And he just turned on me and said he'd be—well, you know how he'd talk—and he wouldn't ever touch that furnace again. And I said it wasn't woman's work. And suddenly his face got red and his veins swelled the way they do—did—when he got mad— and then he fell—" She began to weep.

And Susan, listening, saw him fall. In a small futile quarrel he had died. But no, it was not the small single moment which had killed him. It was the anger of all his life here in this house which he himself had built and lived in and hated all his years.

"I'll be going." Lucile bent and kissed Mrs. Gaylord's cheek. "Send for me if you need me."

She was gone, and Susan was alone with her mother. She ought to comfort her but she could not. She was weeping too much to speak, not for her father's death but for his life, and seeing her tears, her mother began to weep again.

"Come," said Susan at last, "come, we must not. We'll send Jane for the children tomorrow. And I must go in and see him. And you must rest and let me do everything. Lie down on your bed and let me cover you, and I will bring your supper on a tray."

She helped her mother undress and put on her old-fashioned nightgown. It was impossible now to imagine that this thick unlovely body had once been the slender pretty shape which had seized and held and imprisoned all the years of her father's life. But it was—it was! How easily the flesh changed and how easily lost was that bond which she had forged again between herself and Blake!

A few minutes later she stood in the guest room, where her father had been put. He lay on the bed, dressed in his best dark suit, and his black shoes were shining and polished and his white hair smooth. His face and hands were marble and when she put her hand upon his shoulder it felt cold and firm under his coat. It was as though they had clothed a statue. She was not able to bear the intolerable sadness of his face, and she sat down beside him, weeping again. Still it was not death for which she grieved, but life, life which had carved his mouth into such sorrow and had set hollows underneath his eyes, which had given him dreams of love in his youth and then had robbed him, had given him dreams in his age of free islands in a blue and tropic sea and had held him locked in a drab house in a little town. And as cruel as anything was death, which revealed him like this, when he was helpless any longer to hide that which alive he had hidden.

She went away crying most passionately to her heart, "We ought all to be free. Everybody ought to be free for himself, somehow. No one ought to come to death and never have known what freedom is."

When she took the tray with supper into her mother's room she found her asleep. She woke at the sound of footsteps and cried out with a little start. "Susan, why— Oh, I forgot. Every time I go to sleep, I forget what's happened!" She began to cry, and Susan, setting down the tray, put her arms around her. "Anyway," her mother sobbed, "I always did the best I could!"

"Of course you did," said Susan. To herself she thought, "It's true she has, and that is what breaks the heart."

"Nobody could do more than that," her mother said, wiping her eyes.

"No one," said Susan quietly, and fetched the tray.

She longed unutterably for her own. For now this house of her childhood seemed no longer hers. Her part in it had died with her father. In that night, waiting, half expecting Blake, she remembered into the years past, and saw that however her mother had fed and tended them, it was he who had opened the doors of their lives. He said over and over again in the years, whenever a new thing came, "Try it—try it—why not?" It was he who had first put a pencil in her hand, who had bought her the first clay with which to model. And she had had the first desire to model because he whittled from wood little beasts and birds for the amusement of his children. Her mother had cried that day, "Such a mess, all over her hands and her apron!" And he had thrown her one of his looks. "I'll wash up after her," he had said, and when she had modeled a little figure he had praised it, and then they had gone into the bathroom and he had washed her hands carefully. And then he said, "There's no use washing that apron yet. We'll keep it for the clay. You'll want to use it lots of times." He had taken her little blue apron upstairs and hung it in his attic, saying, "There it is when you want it." He had put a board across the chairs by a window and set the clay there, with a jar of water for mixing it. "You can come up here and you won't bother your mother," he had said. "I don't mind a mess if there's something to show for it." All the years of her small girlhood she had sat happily at that board.

All the innumerable small things he had done rose in the night and she remembered him, and the sense of her loss grew intolerably. And yet, she thought, musing, Mary had been repelled by that very largeness in him. When he said, "Try it— try it—" she had shrunk back. "I don't want to," she instinctively replied. "All right," he said, the eagerness flying out of his face. And when Mary was gone he had given Susan a great hug. "You're my girl, aren't you, Sue?" he cried. . . . Mary had sent a telegram tonight. "Brokenhearted. Will come if you think best. Love, Mary." She had not replied. When everything was over, she would write and tell Mary.

Near midnight the telephone rang, and when she went, there was Blake's voice.

"Susanne?"

"Blake, darling!" she cried. "Oh, how I've wanted you."

"I've only just got your note," his voice said. It sounded small and far away. "I wasn't home all day, and didn't think to call up. Susanne, I'm awfully sorry. How are you, my dear?"

"I'm—Blake, he went so quickly. When I got here it was all over."

"Oh, my dear—I am sorry!" He was silent a moment. She heard the empty singing of the wires and she waited, half sobbing. He would say that he was coming to her. His voice began again. "Susanne, it's much better so. I hope my father dies like that."

"But I shan't see him any more! The house is so empty!"

"I know." She could hear him cough a little. "After all, Susanne, he was old. He'd had his life."

She wanted to cry into the telephone, "Oh no, that was it— he didn't have his life!" But she did not. A sort of dreariness was seeping into her as she listened to Blake's voice.

"I won't ask you to come, Blake, unless you want to."

"Susanne, darling," his voice said, a little defiant, a little apologetic, "I never go to funerals. I doubt if I shall go to Dad's. My own I suppose I must attend. But I hope no one else will—not even you. It is barbarous to go to funerals. No, Susanne, you go if you must. Then I beg you to take the next train home. It is so foolish to mope about on these occasions." She did not answer, and he called again, "Susanne, are you there?"

"Yes," she answered, "I am here."

"Do you hear me?" he asked.

"Yes, I hear you."

"You understand how I feel, don't you?" he begged.

354

"Yes, of course," she said.

"Then—is there anything else I can do?" he asked. "I will, you know, Susanne, short of—"

"No," she replied, "no, thank you, Blake. I'm going to bed. Good night."

"That's best," he agreed. "Good night, Susanne." His voice died into distance, and she put down the receiver.

Why had she thought last night—was it only last night?—that flesh could be a bond?

She suddenly began to weep as she climbed the stairs and she could not stop. She undressed and bathed and went to bed, her body trembling with weeping she could not stop. She did not know why she was weeping so ceaselessly, but she knew it was for more than death.

She opened the door next day to John and Marcia, ravenous for their coming. The thought of this moment had quieted her weeping at last in the night. She had remembered, "John and Marcia are coming tomorrow!" A great beam of comfort shot like light into her desolation. She dwelt upon them with passionate love. They were her children, whom she had made, whom she loved. In the morning she said to herself, "I mustn't cling to them or think of myself. I must remember that this is the first time they have seen death." And so when she opened the door, she would not let her heart out to enfold them. Instead, though she kissed them warmly for her secret comfort, she said cheerfully, "Come in, my darlings. Are you cold? Jane, could you make some chocolate for all of us?"

They were shy with her, not knowing how she would be changed. So she tried to be as she always was for them. And all the time her heart revelled in them, in their health and good looks, in their fresh cheeks and clear eyes. She forgot that Marcia had any fault, and saw only her slight dark graceful prettiness, and John was strong and beautiful, fair-haired and blue-eyed as Mark had been, but handsome and alive, quick to move and his mouth delicate.

"Jane told us, Mother," he said gravely. "She said the funeral would be today."

"Are we going?" Marcia asked quickly.

"Yes," said Susan calmly. "Grandmother would be hurt if we did not. And there is no reason why we should not, since we love Grandfather so much. Let's go in now and see Grandmother. She's in her room in bed."

They went in shyly and stood beside the bed. Mrs. Gaylord reached for their hands and burst into tears.

"You're all I've got," she sobbed, and they turned distressed eyes to Susan. Susan sat down on the bed, and John sat down and began to stroke his grandmother's hand.

"I'm awfully sorry," he said, his voice breaking. "I'm just terribly sorry."

But Marcia stood staring at the old woman's distorted face.

"Of course," said Susan gently, "we have all of us a lot to live for—each other, and lots more. Now, Mother, you're going to have something hot to drink, and then suppose you get up and let's all take a walk."

"Oh, I couldn't!" Mrs. Gaylord sobbed. "It certainly wouldn't look right, Susan!"

"We needn't walk through the town," said Susan. "But let's get outdoors, into the sunshine. Marcia, you go and tell Jane to serve the chocolate here."

Her practical voice calmed them, as she meant it should, and Marcia ran out.

"Are they going in to see him—before—before—" Mrs. Gaylord whispered.

Susan turned to John. "Would you like to see Grandfather as he is now, darling?"

356

He looked at her, his eyes widening. He turned a little pale. "Could I tell you after while?" he asked.

"Yes, of course," she said.

"What?" asked Marcia, coming back.

"I was just asking John if he wanted to see Grandfather," Susan said, her voice usual.

Marcia stopped halfway across the room.

"I do," she said eagerly, "I haven't ever seen a dead person."

"The child has no idea—" Mrs. Gaylord moaned and closed her eyes.

"Very well," said Susan.

"Let's go now," cried Marcia, wriggling her thin little hand into Susan's. Susan rose and they went out. She saw John watch them, doubtful, wavering, but he did not follow.

She led Marcia into the guest room without a word, and with her stood beside the bed. She looked at Marcia's face, watchful for fear..

But Marcia was not in the least afraid.

"He looks awfully still," she said, after a moment.

"Yes," Susan said, "I suppose that is what death is—complete stillness."

Marcia was silent an instant.

"Grandmother can't say I haven't any idea now," she said. Susan did not answer. They stood a little longer. "I want to go away now," said Marcia.

So they went away. Outside the door was John.

"I don't want to see him," he whispered. His lips were white, and he was trembling.

"Then he wouldn't want you to," Susan said.

"The last time he—I saw him—he was making my boat—my three-master—he was laughing, and when he said goodbye, he said he'd send it to me in three or four days—and he did. You don't think he'll mind if I don't go in?"

357

"It's the best way to remember him, as you do," Susan said. "He'd much rather."

She put her hand in his arm and led him away.

In the end her own comfort came to her out of herself. In the cold clear sunshine of the November day, it came to her. He was dead, but out of his death a life would come, a life which she would create. She would make and dedicate to him the finest work she had yet done, a work which should spring out of her memory of him. Out of her knowledge of loss came darting upward a clear flame, that strong familiar ecstasy of desire. It upheld her as she stood beside the open grave that afternoon, her mother clinging to her arm, her own hand in John's young arm. She gazed into a sky lit with early sunset, seeing no one of the crowd that was gathered, hearing no music and no speech. She stood apart in a silence of her own, fashioning out of the clay of her father's dead body his enduring image. Her ears caught the dull sounds of clods upon the wood.

"Dust unto dust—" The words were an echo from afar off. She did not see or hear.

"I shall make him in veinless marble," she was thinking in solemn exaltation. And seeing with her inner eye his image, she saw it finished and she heard it speak, and forgetful of the heaping earth she smiled and lifted up her head.

Blake had said, "Take the next train," but she could not. Back in the empty house the children looked at each other, not knowing what to do next. And out of this pause she said, feeling her wish as it shaped out of the emptiness, "What would you say if we all went to the farm for a few days?"

Jane said briskly, "It's a terrible good thought, Mum, if you ask me. It can't be so bad. I cleaned up good in the summer like I always do."

"Yes," said John. "Yes, Mother."

358

"I can't remember how it is any more," Marcia said.

"I don't care where I am for a while," Mrs. Gaylord sighed.

So they had piled bedding into the car and food and had gone at once.

At the last moment Lucile had telephoned, "We'll be over tonight—the first night's so hard. I know how it was when Mother went. You feel it the first night the body's gone."

"We're all going away to the farm," Susan told her, and she put up the receiver without waiting, and then she locked the door quickly and ran out to the car where they were waiting for her. It would be well to be busy making beds and cleaning and cooking—there was healing in such common necessity. Tomorrow she would persuade her mother to be busy and the children would be running everywhere. She'd let them miss school for a while. She needed them with her. She drove the car through the night to the end of the town, down the road she had last walked to find Mark ill, and up the lawn. The branches twined above them, bare against the dark night sky. There was no moon and the stars were glittering. And then they were at the familiar porch, and Jane took the big iron key from her bag.

"I thought I might just get down, so I brung it," she said. Susan went first into the house.

"Wait," said Jane, "I know exactly. I left the lamp here on the hall table and matches—safety—you can't trust mice with any others."

The lamp flared and they stood in the hall, looking about them.

"I remember now," said John. His voice was full of wonder.

"I don't, still," said Marcia. "It seems funny to me here."

But Susan did not hear them. She was thinking, "I shall have to tell Blake. I shall tell him I have a piece of work to do which I must do here." In an instant it was clear to her that she could not possibly make the statue of her father in that crowded noisy street. He had never been there with her, and he would escape her if she took him there now. But here she could work, here in this silence, in this space. She stood upon her own ground, as though indeed she was at last come home.

VI

SHE wrote to Blake every day. For it was only just that she make known to him each day what she discovered in herself. She wrote at first, "I shall be here awhile until I see what I want to make. You will understand that one is able to see a certain person more clearly in one place than another. I see him here."

Blake had replied, "Of course I understand that." And then he had gone on to say the thing he was really thinking about. "I have clipped the criticisms of your exhibition. All the critics had something to say, as I thought they would after what Barnes wrote. On the whole you've come out pretty well—of course they all said there was considerable merit in your work, since there is a peculiar handicap, especially in sculpture, for women."

She did not care what they said and told him so. For now the block of marble—she had telegraphed for it—had come, and she was beginning her new work. What was past was gone. She accepted without understanding it this forgetting and this fresh pressing on to new creation.

In the house Jane was cleaning and cooking, and her mother was polishing silver and mending curtains, weeping a little now and then, pausing when anyone was near, to tell something she had said and thought and what he said. . . .

John said to Susan, "I think I'll carve Granddaddy's head out of wood, maybe, Mother. I sort of would like to have it myself. Would you use cherry? I found a good dry piece in the barn. Could you help me a little with the drawing?"

Only Marcia was restless. "There's nothing to do here," she

said many times a day. "If we aren't going back to school till after Christmas, Mother, what'll I do all day?"

For day by day Susan pushed away their leaving this place. She went from room to room, gazing out of the windows at fields and hills and sky, thinking, pondering. She had wondered if Mark would come back to her here in this house, but he did not. He was gone, except as his life would always be a part of her life, as everything was a part of her life. Old friends came to see her, to ask her, "How long will you stay, Sue?", to hear her say, "I don't know," to tell her bits of gossip—"You remember Trina, Sue? Her husband was always fooling around—well, she finally committed suicide a couple of years ago, and he's married to another girl who is livelier than he is and he's doing the worrying now—serves him right, we all say."

She had gone her way which had not been theirs, and yet at meeting they took their old places in her life. Everything she had ever had she had still.

Once David Barnes wrote to her. "I'm going to have my exhibition in New York in January and then I'm going back to France to stay. I have finished my Titans. There won't be any more in my lifetime. I feel as though I were thrust out of Olympus. I have been living with gods so long I can't see as small as humans any more. You've got a grand start now. The critics don't know whether they like you or not, and so you aren't going to be forgotten. You've only got to go on doing your own stuff. You don't need anybody. Let me know if you come back to town."

She folded his letter and put it away. She would perhaps never see him again but it did not matter. They had given to each other all they had to give. One gave as he was able, and as the other could receive. Nothing was lost.

Blake wrote, "I begin to think you are not coming back to me."

362

And she wrote, "I don't know what I am going to do. Somehow I see only a day ahead."

It was then he telegraphed to her that he was coming at once.

She had not allowed herself to discover whether or not she wanted to see Blake. She would be completely guided by what he was to her. For now she knew she no longer saw Blake as she once had. He was a new person, to be newly seen. And she would not think only of how she saw him, but also of how he saw her. If he needed her she must consider it. But she knew she no longer needed him.

She said casually in the morning, "Blake is coming today."

Marcia's face lit and she cried out, "Oh, how spiffy! I *have* missed Blake, Mother!"

Jane said, "I'll have to get another piece of meat, Mum. He'll never eat Irish stew."

"To think your father never saw him," her mother sighed.

But John said nothing. He was drawing at the table and he went on with it.

He would be there at three o'clock, Blake had wired, Bantie driving him down. She dressed herself carefully, and waited for him in the living room. A few minutes after three she saw him, wrapped in his fur coat, stepping out of his car, his stick in his hand, mounting the steps. She went and opened the door.

"Come in, Blake," she said.

"Well, Susanne," he said, and bending, kissed her cheek.

He was so strange to her here in this house that his kiss on her cheek was a surprise. She stood waiting while he took off his coat.

"It's a hard place to find," he said. "Almost no one knew it. Beastly cold day, as well."

The tip of his handsome nose was a little red and he rubbed his hands together and there was the dry sound of dead leaves that his father's hands made when he rubbed them.

"Come in to the fire," Susan said.

John had brought in logs and built up a huge fire in the old chimney place. The room, sparely furnished, looked warm and cheerful and spacious. Jane had set tea on a small table by the fire, and her mother was seated by it, waiting.

"This is Blake, Mother," Susan said, and Blake bent over her mother's hand, and she looked up at him, a little frightened.

"I was just telling Susan before you came—" she began, and suddenly Marcia flew into the room.

"Blake, Blake!" she cried. "Oh, at last you've come!"

She had put on her best frock of crimson taffeta and tied a crimson ribbon about her short black hair, and her cheeks and lips were too bright.

"Marcia!" Susan cried. "Come here to me!"

Marcia looked at her with suddenly sullen eyes and came toward her slowly.

"What is it?" she muttered.

But Susan had seized her and was rubbing her cheeks and lips with her handkerchief.

"For shame, Marcia!" she cried, and Blake burst into his high intense laughter. They were all staring at the stains of rouge on the white handkerchief, and Marcia's black eyes were furious.

"I don't see what business it is of yours!" she cried.

"My soul and body!" murmured Mrs. Gaylord.

John came in. "I told her you wouldn't like it, Mother," he was saying. "How do you do, Blake?" He put out his hand and Blake took it, his eyes still teasing bright with laughter.

"I appreciate it, Marcia," he protested. "Indeed—"

"Go and wash your face, Marcia," Susan begged. She was secretly grateful to Marcia for being absurd, and she called after her, "And hurry back, darling! Jane has little raisin cakes for tea!"

But all the time she was conscious of Blake, and of Blake

364

only. For she saw with every movement that there was no longer any bond of flesh between them. His flesh was strange to her. There was no magic in it any more. She did not want to touch his hand, and that he should kiss her filled her with disgust.

She sat in growing dismay while she poured tea, while Marcia came back to sit chattering on Blake's knee, pretending nothing had happened. Once she buried her face in his neck and whispered, suffocating, "I love you best!"

And Blake had laughed at her again.

And all the time Susan knew the moment was approaching, was here, when she and Blake must meet or part. Before night fell it had to come. She rose suddenly.

"Now all of you run away," she commanded them. "Blake and I must talk."

Some power in her voice compelled even Marcia, and she and Blake were left alone at last.

She was waiting for Blake to begin that she might know whether or not he wanted her. For if he wanted her or needed her, there was her promise to him to remember, made that day in the little office in Paris. She waited, half afraid, and it seemed he must speak to demand of her with passion, "When are you coming back to me, Susanne?"

But when he spoke he said, "I came down partly on business, Susanne. Joseph Hart, the old eccentric—" he paused, half laughing— "you must feel very flattered now, Susanne—he wants to put two of your things in the museum."

She was so stunned, so turned aside, that it was hard to check her expectation and force her mind to his words. What he had said was at this moment of no importance to her. She could not answer at once. Blake lit a cigarette.

"He said he wanted your consent, or whatever the form is." He drew hard, and blew out smoke. "I suppose I could act for you," he added.

365

She forced herself to think.

"I don't want that series broken," she said at last. "It's incomplete. I have at least eight more figures to add. If ever it is to go into a museum, it must go in entire."

His eyebrows lifted. "I say, Susanne!" he murmured. "You don't expect anything, do you?" His voice was ironical, and her heart flew up.

"I expect everything," she said proudly.

"Well," he rejoined, "I hope you get it."

She did not answer.

"Am I to tell the old fellow?" he asked her after a moment.

"No, I will tell him myself," she replied. And then she leaned forward impulsively. "It doesn't matter," she said. "Blake, what of you and me?"

She had put it to him. He looked at her, and she met his gaze fully, her own eyes questioning.

"What do you mean?" he asked.

"Are you happy without me?" she asked.

"Are you without me?" he replied.

"I can't just—go on with you," she said. "It must mean something to us both."

"Of course," he agreed amiably. She waited, but he did not speak. A log slipped in the fireplace and when she moved he was ahead of her.

"Let me," he begged. And when he sat down again, he said, "You could make something rather decent out of this old house, Susanne. It has lines." He was looking about the room.

"Yes," she said.

Then she saw he would never speak to her from within himself. He had so long evaded himself, so long hidden from any truth whatsoever, that face to face with it he would not meet it. And she was born to truth and must have it. If they lived together, now that the bond of flesh was broken, she would in her intolerant necessity drive him again and again to a finality

366

which he as often would evade, until at last he would hate her, as even now she could not longer love him. No, she no longer loved him, but she would never forget that once she had loved him with completest passion. She was silent a long time, thinking, and he sat smoking and gazing into the fire.

"Blake," she said at last, very gently, "would you mind very much if—if I asked you to let me stay here?"

"Divorce?" He spoke the word out quickly and sharply.

"If you'd rather have it so," she answered. "I don't care—only let me live here and do my work."

"Haven't met somebody?"

She shook her head.

"No," she said, "no, of course not."

He smiled. "I'd understand," he said.

But she did not answer. It was still impossible to know how he really felt.

"I have been quite happy with you, Susanne," he went on in his even, pleasant voice. "At first I used to wonder sometimes if I would be. You aren't the type I've—you were challenging, though, because you were impregnable. At first I wanted to break down your pride, and then I fell in love with you."

"My pride is not broken," she said quietly.

"It's a damned instinctive sort of thing in you."

It was the nearest moment to truth in him, and now she understood him and she said with instant sympathy, "I know I am not a comfortable woman for a wife."

"You're only half there," he said, smiling. "A man likes to possess his wife."

"I know," she said, a little drearily, "and I am not to be possessed." She waited and then she said firmly, "And I was born so."

He did not answer, but he sat looking at her.

"I always wanted everything," she said to him, half pleadingly, to explain herself a little if she could. "I wanted to be everything—to be a good wife and the sort of mother the children would want, and do my work, too. And when you came, I wanted to be—your love, as well."

"I suppose," he said, half grudgingly, "you were all those things."

"I don't know why we talk as though I were dead," she said. "I am more alive than I have ever been—more aware of everything."

And indeed this was true. In this awareness she saw, in a great intuitive light and with a sad humility, that her grave fault lay in her very being, which differed too far from the average human, and so was not to be borne by them. Women were not her close friends because she did what they did and too much besides. Why else had Mary never loved her, and why now did Marcia draw back so often when she put out her arms, except that Marcia's own slight warmth was not enough to bear her mother's too rich loving? She had been too much for David Barnes, for whom his Titans were enough. She had been too much for Mark, and she was too much now for Blake. He would perhaps have forgiven her if Joseph Hart had not liked what she had made. Each had wanted something from her that the other had not. But she had given too fully to their need, and each had felt the weight of all else that she was besides, and each had known that he alone was not enough for her and the knowledge was too bitter and there must be escape from it. She was too much for everyone, and none could fill her and each knew it and went away.

There was no one left her, except John. She must be very careful of John. She must let him carve his figures small, in wood, and not let him feel the hugeness of her marbles. She would hide away her largeness from him until she died.

"You have told me so often I am simple—I think you said once, stupid—" she said to Blake. "You were so right. It has taken me so long to see what was wrong with me."

He did not ask her what she saw. "I meant," he said, "that you are naïve, expecting people to take you as you are. You go to them directly, as a child does. But you aren't a child and they don't know what to do with you."

"Yes," she said, "I know. People only take others as they themselves are—as they themselves are able. I should have understood that long ago, shouldn't I?"

They talked with long pauses, hers longing and doubtful, his half wary, and the afternoon was nearly gone. The sun was beginning to slant across the room. It fell upon the worn blue carpet, the carpet she and Mark had bought when they began their life. That life had been and passed, but it had taken its place in the whole. And now, by the very scantiness of the words she and Blake could speak to each other, she felt this life passing from her, too.

"I don't know," he answered. "Don't ask me, my dear, to probe into psychology. The plain truth is—" He paused a moment and turned his head away, and then he said, "Whatever we had, it seems to have escaped us."

"If I had not been what I am—" she began.

"I wouldn't have fallen in love with you at all," Blake finished. He was on his feet, belting in his overcoat. His face looked a little white, his lips dry. She was suddenly seized with a shadowy, enormous pain.

"Oh, Blake," she cried, "you've given me very much!"

"So have you given much to me, Susanne." But when she put out her hand, he shook his head. "No, don't mind," he said, "don't try to catch what's gone. I grieve that it's gone. I wish it might have stayed, but nothing stays. I know—I have that sense of end about everything. I always have had. Before I begin, I feel the end."

"Did you feel so about me, too?" she asked.

"I think I did," he said slowly. "I think I must have, because all this doesn't seem strange to me. I feel as though I'd lived it before."

He took her hand and kissed it and she saw his eyes were wintry. "He will look like that when he is old," she thought.

"We will see each other, perhaps, often," she said.

"Why not?" he asked. He was going toward the door and he bent and took up his hat and gloves. His stick fell, and he stooped to pick it up.

"I'll write you," he said, "we can settle the details easily enough. Strange!" He paused and looked about the hall. "I had the sense of this end even when I came into this room today."

It was impossible to tell whether or not he grieved.

"If I thought you were grieved," she said earnestly, putting her hand on his arm, "it would shake me very much."

"Are you grieving?" he asked her.

"I think I could, Blake—I feel somehow that I shall."

"Ah," he said, "you'll grieve because nothing lasts—that's all. It is the final grief we spend our lives trying to escape. Goodbye, Susanne, and thank you."

He had gone so suddenly that it seemed a vanishment. She saw him step into his car and the car darted away into the twilight gathering black under the trees.

She went back, dazed, into the room. The sun had left it, but the fire was burning with a steady richness of fallen coals, and the room was as full of warmth and light as ever. She sat down, still dazed. He had made the time pass half lightly, yet with such terrible finality. It was over. Did she grieve? She did not know. It was as though under some powerful anaesthesia he had given her a blow, and she had taken it.

"You will grieve because nothing lasts, that's all," he had said.

Ah, but in her everything lasted. She had all she ever had. Everything she had, the home she and Mark had made, his death, Blake's sharp and passionate love to make her know herself a woman, the children—she had all of it forever, to be the rich experience from which she drew her life, her life which was so much more than her mortal body was.

Yes, she would grieve sometimes, at night perhaps, but in the morning she would get up and go to work, and then she would not grieve. She would forget to grieve.

THE END